94

"Have you got a lap

She reached into _____ er Powerbook, booted up. Wexler gave her the Web site address for the Elixir of Youth Foundation. She input it. They waited a few seconds. Elixir of Youth's Web page opened up with a flourish of New Agey music, some jazzy light tricks and bold graphics depicting a youthful, athletic, male-female couple striding into a glorious dawn. Then the caption: ELIXIR OF YOUTH FOUNDATION—WELCOME TO LIFE EVERLASTING. In the background, a serene forest scene, and in the forest scene stood a bull elk. A Roosevelt. She stared. "That's Bogachiel."

Wexler smiled. "I was almost certain. I wanted you to verify that."

———————— ★ ————————

"Skye Moody writes with a rare combination of wit and style..."

—Janet Evanovich, author of *Four To Score*

"...vivid outdoor landscapes, rich background on Northwest Indians and wild medicine...the environmental mystery will draw fans of Nevada Barr, Beverly Connor and Dana Stabenow."

—*Booklist*

SKYE KATHLEEN MOODY

WILDCRAFTERS

WORLDWIDE.

TORONTO • NEW YORK • LONDON
AMSTERDAM • PARIS • SYDNEY • HAMBURG
STOCKHOLM • ATHENS • TOKYO • MILAN
MADRID • WARSAW • BUDAPEST • AUCKLAND

For my son, Simon Peter Kahn, with love

WILDCRAFTERS

A Worldwide Mystery/December 1999

First published by St. Martin's Press, Incorporated.

ISBN 0-373-26332-5

Visit us at www.worldwidemystery.com

Printed in U.S.A.

Acknowledgments

The author is grateful for the expertise, generous assistance and keen insights provided by editor Kelley Ragland, researcher Michelle Speten, brother/confidant Robert Moody, and agent Pam Ahearn. For research materials, the author thanks the United States Department of the Interior Fish and Wildlife Service, the World Wildlife Fund and David Jansen, M.D. Special thanks to writer/naturalist Daniel Mathews for his excellent "Cascade-Olympic Natural History, A Trailside Reference" (Raven Editions, 1994, Portland, Oregon), to Sarah Soffer and Peter Liberman for their friendship, Gregory Browning Smith for grace and gentility, and Tony Outhwaite for encouragement.

Any inaccuracy or factual errors inadvertently contained in the manuscript are entirely the author's responsibility.

Note: The Roosevelt elk is an officially designated species. At present, the Roosevelt is not listed as endangered, but the shy elk's habitat is rapidly falling prey to land developers, logging and epidemic human intrusion.

Who all my bones in pieces found;
Them in a handkerchief she bound
And laid them under the juniper tree
Kywitt, kywitt, kywitt, I cry,
Oh what a beautiful bird am I!

—the Brothers Grimm
The Juniper Tree

PROLOGUE

GELID BREATH FIRST, he emerged from the dense thicket, stood poised on the pond's edge. The still waters reflected his eyes, and a slice of the new moon, hovering above a canopy of tree silhouettes. He bent his head to the pond's surface, nuzzled it, drank slowly, deliberately, and when finally he stopped, his warm sigh crystallized, clouding the air. But his sharp vision pierced the sweet miasma and the night darkness, and he slipped sure-footed down the steep bank into the pond and swam facilely across, his condensed breath obscuring his head so that it seemed as if a stray remnant of mist drifted across the black water. When he reached the opposite bank, he clambered up into the shadows, shook violently, then took off suddenly in a fevered, thrashing run through the forest. The muddy earth squished beneath him, and before him tree boughs groaned, breaking when he passed. Faster, faster he ran, his breath growing hard, gleaming when it caught moonbeams in its nebulous web. Every creature in his path scurried to hide, shivering and cowering at the sound of his coming.

He ran as fast as his legs would go, stretching, leaping over great fallen timbers. In the distance, a crashing, thunderous breaker slammed the ocean beach. He ran toward the sound and it grew louder in his ears, and his breath strained harder, until, panting, he slowed to a brisk stride. When he had gone a little farther through the thicket, he slowed a bit. An owl hooted, flapped its wings, and the thrashing diverted his attention. He slowed to a walk. He didn't see the vole shaking with fright as it backed into a hollow stump. He watched the owl preen itself high on a cedar branch, as if mocking wingless, earthbound life, but then something more compelling attracted his attention.

His nostrils quivered. He turned halfway around, walked straight ahead toward a woodland clearing, and a dim, square moon. He moved softly, stealthily, the way he knew to move. When at last he reached the face of the square moon, he peered inside it and saw two creatures entwined, undulating, and he heard their sharp breath, their sighs. A thrill passed through him and he exhaled softly into the night air.

He sensed danger too late, only after the singing bullet struck his shoulder, pierced the skin and bone, seared into his heart. He felt his legs give out, and before the next bullet grazed his flank, he collapsed on the cold damp earth. Gasping breaths mixed with the blood gorging into his throat, suffocating him. The last thing he saw in this once idyllic existence was the jagged blade of a hacksaw bearing down on his hoof, and the last thing he felt was the hacksaw driving into his skin and bones, his hoof falling away.

PART ONE

ONE

PARIS AND MILAN

MAYBE IT WAS that her name was so common, or maybe it was because Theresa married a man named Winnipeg, or it might just have been a wanderlust—whatever inspired Theresa Nighteagle, when she delivered twins at the Bogachiel Indian Clinic on Valentine's Day, she named them Paris and Milan.

Theresa and Winnipeg brought the twins home the day they were born because the clinic turned them out. For lack of bed space, so they claimed. The Nighteagles' neighbors in Cedar Grove Trailer Park peered discreetly through their windows, surprised to see not one, but two infants, one blue bundle cradled in Winn's solid arms and a pink bundle held in Theresa's mindful embrace. Within minutes, telephones rang off the walls all across the trailer park and soon the men gathered down on the beach, in spite of a drizzling rain and a dank chill weeping off the breakers, to smoke and to gossip about Winn Nighteagle's mid-life potency.

In her third week of nursing, Theresa developed a breast infection and Winn drove all the way to Grays Harbor for her medication, and a breast pump. That was just like Winn, macho as he acted most of the time: driving such a long way for Theresa, for the babies. Winn adored the twins, maybe even more than he adored Theresa, or maybe you shouldn't compare the two forms of love. At Grays Harbor, Winn parked his pickup in Bartell's lot, got out, hitched his jeans higher up on his narrow hips, and went inside Bartell's. Without hesitation, he walked over to the "feminine products" aisle and began searching for the brand of breast pump Theresa had mentioned.

Pump-eze.

Winn wasn't the only male working his way along the feminine products aisle. The other was a white dude, fortyish, with ragged blond hair and a stubby beard, unkempt, wearing logger's boots and a plaid flannel shirt over shabby jeans. Winn thought the dude's green eyes looked glazed over, and they put him in mind of a female praying mantis he'd seen last summer in the woods behind the trailer park. Winn had never seen him before, not around Grays Harbor or anywhere else. He didn't look rural, even in those clothes. Winn guessed he might be another aging urban yuppie grunger over from Seattle, a dude with money but no sense of personal hygiene. The part that bothered Winn the most was the way the dude just lurked there in the aisle, not really searching for a product, more like loitering, although he pretended to study the ladies' douching supplies. So when Winn located the Pump-eze model Theresa wanted, he got out of the aisle and headed for the pharmacy counter to pick up Theresa's prescription and pay cash for everything, all the while feeling a cold chill at his back and a sourness in his gut. The stranger spooked Winn, like any feral-eyed stranger would.

The twins thrived on Theresa's milk flow. At three months, Paris resembled the Pillsbury Doughboy, except that his hair was thick and coal black, his skin the burnished shade of agates on Ruby Beach. Paris resembled Theresa through the forehead and eyes, but both twins had Winn's rosebud lips. And too, Paris had Winn's small ears, and he had a port-wine birthmark on his left foot, a lot like the one Winn had on his right hand, a flat pigmentation, copper-penny size, just a big freckle, nothing to worry over. In fact, Winn's mother used to say that's how she identified Winn in the hospital nursery among all the other little Indian babies. One look at that copper penny on baby Winnipeg's right hand and his mother knew she had taken the right baby home from the hospital.

Milan, who weighed more than Paris at birth, acquired less fat than her brother, but her hair grew in thick and straight and dark as midnight. Both babies slept peacefully through most nights, although once or twice, Milan awoke in the wee hours to practice singing. Milan, more than Paris, was gregarious, full of spark and guile, and Winn felt sure the girl had a future in show business. Whenever Winn and Theresa took the babies out in public, people gathered around and made a fuss. The parents soon tired of the commotion, but Paris, and especially Milan, thrived on attention, even from perfect strangers, and Winn wasn't altogether pleased about this development.

On the twins' nine-month anniversary, Paris, sitting in his mother's lap, plucked a cup of diet Coke off the kitchen table and started guzzling. He didn't spill a drop. Milan, on Winn's lap, soon mimicked her brother, and within days, the babies had weaned themselves from

Theresa's milk and graduated to carton milk, the regular type with high fat content. At first, Theresa felt hurt about the weaning, the twins rejecting her own milk, but Winn compensated by paying more attention to Theresa's breasts when they made love. Winn didn't mind that one bit.

Theresa was young compared to Winn, twenty years younger. Still, Theresa wasn't exactly wet behind the ears at thirty. Winn could see age lines forming on his wife's lovely face, but they didn't matter because in Winn's eyes, Theresa remained the doe-eyed schoolgirl he had married twelve years ago. Winn dearly hoped that Milan would grow up as pretty as her mom, or even half as pretty. Even after nine months, Winn still cursed the clinic for turning Theresa and the twins out on the very day of birth. He'd never forget that insult, and he thanked good gene pools and Divine Intervention for his family's quick recovery and excellent health. Not the midwife, not the techs. Not the federal government, or the state. Gene pools and the Powers That Be had brought Theresa safely through the ordeal and delivered him a pair of healthy babies. That's just how it was for poor folks. You had to depend on the invisible powers for your survival.

As some fathers will, Winn paid particular attention to his son. At nine months, Paris weighed twenty pounds and when he pulled himself up from a crawling position to a standing position, he was twenty-one inches tall. He had two teeth front and center on his lower gum and the top front teeth were already pushing through. His hair swept across his forehead like Raven's wing, his eyes were as wide and grand as Thunderbird's. He was a serene, watchful, curious boy, whose favorite activity was playing on the beach, along the rocky tideline. But Paris often suffered a reaction to the harsh winds that blew humid fogs in off the ocean. The frigid moisture pierced his chest, inevitably sparking fevers that led to chills and runny noses. Yet Paris loved the tideline and the driftwood and the great boulders strewn across the beach, the big gray sky and the sea stacks that reminded him of the Cat in the Hat. He loved the slimy seaweed-coated rocks with barnacles that stuck out their tongues at you, and the middens and clams and the briny scent of the air and the roar of the surf. He had a bucket and a yellow shovel and he knew how to dig for hermit crabs because Winn had shown him, and he knew how to catch a clam after it spat at him, betraying its hiding place. He loved the curious creatures and curly kelp on the tideline, but most of all, Paris loved the scents and sounds and the feel of spindrift coming off the ocean. Winn would tweak the boy's nose and call him "Little Raven," but Paris knew that his real name was "Ocean Boy," and pretty soon, he'd announce it to the world.

Winn loved taking the twins back up behind the trailer park into Bogachiel National Wildlife Preserve's rain forest, where moss-draped old-growth cedar and spruce trees soared to a heavenly canopy of branches and boughs that protected the vine maples and the fragile, fern-carpeted woodlands. Winn carried the twins, and Theresa used a disposable camera to capture these precious memories of the happy Nighteagles among thousand-year-old trees and the fronds of giant ferns, the four of them among the ancient whispering spirits of their ancestors. It might be trespassing on federal land, but the Nighteagles never harmed anything. Besides, this was their ancestors' home and they loved to be in the magical place. Paris especially loved the Hall of Mosses, where a velvety green raiment thrived on dripwater off the canopy, where heavy patches of lichen and clubmoss clung to the porous, alkaline trunks of the vine maples, where Great Elk hid among the lushness, foraging, feasting on maple leaves, where throughfall remnants of fog and rain inspired enormous underground fungi to sprout unsavory toadstools, and the maidenhair fern and the bracken offered thick cover to four-footed creatures and soothed the bellies of the crawling, slithering underlife. To their ancestors, no place was more sacred than the rain forest. Winn knew he didn't respect the rain forest the way his father and grandfathers had before him. Winn had little time to commune with the rain forest's powerful spirits. A man has to support his family, and that comes first.

One brisk November afternoon, a Sunday football day, Winn was chopping firewood on the north side of the trailer when he thought he heard a sound coming from the woods. His ears perked up, but after that first little rustling noise, he heard nothing. Winn finished chopping the wood, hoping to have it loaded on his pickup's bed in time to watch the football game on TV. He had another cord to chop, then had to bundle and bind the wood and stack it before the game started. The next morning, if the roads had dried out from all the recent rain, Winn would head down to Grays Harbor to sell the fire-wood.

Alder wood.

Winn was bundling the last cord when Theresa came to the trailer door and called to him, her voice barely penetrating the whistling wind. "Winn, honey, what have you done with Paris?"

Winn looked up, peered around the trailer. Theresa had on that pink angora sweater he'd given her last week for her thirty-first birthday, and her tight blue jeans. She had big woolen socks on but no shoes. Her hair was pulled back into a ponytail. He liked how she looked, how she filled out her clothes with more bone than flesh, how straight she stood in the doorway.

"I put him down to nap," Winn called back. He had to raise his voice because the wind was so high. "That was an hour ago, maybe more."

Theresa pressed her lips together. "Cut it out, honey. Have you got him in the pickup again? I hope you bundled him up good and warm."

Winn squinted at Theresa. She'd come off the trailer steps, was walking across the wood planks he'd set down over the mud between the trailer and the pickup. She wasn't smiling, just muttering under her breath the way she often did when Winn played jokes on her. Winn set down the bundling wire and went over to the pickup. Theresa was leaning inside the cab and all he saw of her was her shapely rear end and nice legs.

"He isn't in there, Tee. Like I said, I put him in bed."

"Well, Milan's in her bed, but Paris is missing. Where'd you put him to nap?"

Winn frowned. Deep lines folded his forehead into ridges that reminded Theresa of furrowed ground. He said, "I put his bassinet out in the backyard. He was fussing, Tee. It's too hot in that trailer."

"Maybe you put him in our bed." Theresa sounded desperate.

Winn sighed, tugged at his belt. "I put him out back. In his bed. That's where I put him down."

Theresa blinked. Her lips pressed tighter and she shook her head. With one slender hand, she touched her husband's arm. "Well then, Winn, Paris is missing."

Winn and Theresa dashed around the trailer to the backyard where the bassinet stood in a small clearing on the edge of the forest. Sunlight pierced Winn's cloudy breath as he reached into the bassinet, rumpled the blankets. Paris was gone.

"I told you, Winn. I looked out from the window. I saw his crib empty."

At nine months, Paris had just taken his first steps, and too, he loved to crawl. But he'd never climbed out of his bassinet before. Could Paris have climbed out of his bed, crawled or toddled into the woods behind the trailer park? Winn supposed he could have, but he had to stretch his mind to believe it. Had someone—or something—carried Paris off? Winn checked around, and that was when he saw the hoofprints on the ground in a helter-skelter pattern, coming out of the forest, ending at the bassinet, and then going back into the forest. Cloven hooves. Elk.

No man is ever prepared for the moment his world goes dark and fear creeps over him. Winn ran down to the beach where some neighbor kids were playing on the boulders and driftwood logs. Through the whistling wind and roaring breakers, Winn shouted to the kids. Had they seen Paris? The kids insisted they hadn't seen Paris, and they hadn't seen anything unusual. Winn ran back to where Theresa stood frozen to the ground. He grabbed her clenched fist and all but dragged her toward the woods behind the trailer park. Over his shoulder, Winn shouted to his neighbor, Bob Brightman, "Call 911. Paris is missing. Have Carolee stay with Milan." Winn and Theresa pounded through the woods, two reckless humans thrashing into bear country, up into the rain forest, along the path of Big Elk, and up the mountainside, where bighorn sheep stood hoof-to-ledge on perilous ground. All at once, Winn understood the nature of humanity, how a single human soul is both rare and insignificant. Now he understood that the world was larger than his little trailer park, larger than Iron County. When Raven flies in off the ocean and demands your infant child, when Elk steals into your camp and drags off your loved one, when the creatures of the forest and the beach and the ocean and sky conspire against you and your little family, then the duality of love and despair stab you in the heart, in the soul, and you are marked forever and will never be the same.

TWO

BLISS

FINALLY, the rain stopped. Rain had poured since dawn this Sunday morning, and now, finally, the rain paused. A tease, a trick. A native never trusts Seattle's sky. Rain would fall again, any minute now, ya sure, you betcha. Take it from a native.

A small woman with piercing green eyes and disobedient topaz hair peered out the Olympic Hotel's dining room window into a formal garden where Pan pissed into a koi pond, an obese robin flapping in the shallows. As if raindrops weren't good enough for a bird's bath. Across the table sat a genteel, dark-haired man who couldn't take his eyes off his companion. From the woman's lap, a white linen napkin absconded in a waiter's frisky wake. She caught it midair, spread it once again over svelte, muscular legs, anchored it with a tiny hand. Her other hand, the decorated one, raised a tepid double shooter to her lips. She sipped the rich, citric mud, swallowed. Euphoric waves crashed her brain gates.

Her companion reached across the breakfast table, caressed her decorated hand. When he smiled, she felt her pulse quicken. He loosened his grip, studied her hand, especially the ring finger, where his grandmother's fabled Alhambra diamond ring caught chandelier light, fractured it. She followed his gaze, watched the dazzling, dancing reflections, admired the stone's perfect facets, silently blessed its symbolism. Then she noticed the thin platinum band below the diamond ring.

"Gad," she said, "I think we're married."

Richard Winters raised a mimosa. "Here's to us."

He was tall for a husband, meaning he had a solid twelve inches on her. His thick black hair, trimmed short at the ears, looked even better, she thought, than when he'd worn it long. In the old days. Before they were married. Yesterday. He might be a demiurge, or he might just be an impossibly gorgeous human. One thing for sure, as

of nine o'clock last evening, he was her husband, and she was now
Venus Grace Winsome-Diamond Winters. A mouthful. Anyway,
Richard's wife. She hadn't decided if she'd adopt his surname.

Until six months ago, the idea of marriage had appalled her. She
had her work, her exotic, adventurous career, no tongue-in-cheek intended. Definite independence. Autonomy. She was a self-contained
individual. Make that an intensely private, oversensitive, terrified of
commitment, self-contained individual with a few emotional bullets
lodged in her heart. Certainly she wasn't seeking romance when this
god-man appeared in her life. Back then, six long months ago, Richard Winters didn't need another wife. He already had one, a doozy
of a dame, along with a broken heart and some nasty divorce papers.
Then this surprise collision of two unsuspecting souls. They'd clung
together—literally—while oddball events ebbed egregiously. Nothing
gooshy, nothing sentimental. White-hot, intense. A swift courtship,
maybe too swift, and now—"Mrs. Winters?"

Venus blinked. Across the table, Richard tilted his head. "You are
Mrs. Winters, aren't you? Or have I made some dreadful mistake and
taken the wrong woman on my honeymoon?"

She set down her coffee cup, leaned forward across the table, studied him in an exaggerated way. "My God," she exclaimed, "was
that you in my bed last night?"

Before she met Richard, he was Macho Man. Hunted bear and elk,
and as a reckless timber executive, cooperated in the decimation of
precious old-growth forests. Richard's metamorphosis to a greener,
environmentally friendly creature was complete by the time their
worlds collided in a remote southwest-Washington oceanside resort.
(Ozone Beach might be on the planet, but was not of the planet, and
from the start, their relationship possessed an otherwordly aspect.)
Now, Richard ran a multimillion-dollar forest conservation fund, trav-
eled the world espousing the benefits of saving what forests remained
on Earth. It was high-powered, stressful work that he passionately
embraced, a secret source of amusement for her. He'd make one heck
of a fire-and-brimstone preacher.

A thunderbolt seared the sooty sky, as the stray thunderbolt will
between sun breaks. Porcine clouds, steel-wool gray, rumbled omi-
nously. In a sedate corner of the dining room, a grandfather clock
struck nine times, and before it finished, the heavens erupted, releasing another pluvial flout, the rant of Seattle realized for the second
time since dawn. Abandoning their barely touched breakfast, the view

of the koi pond, and the robin drowning in the downpour, the new-lyweds strolled to the elevator, rode the cage up six floors, stepped out. Halfway down the hall, Richard said, "So, wife, what shall we do with the remains of the day?"

She smiled, an expression so reminiscent of how she looked last night, that he wanted to rearrange her right there in the hall, and the spark in his eyes betrayed him.

She said, "What time does our flight leave?"

He slid the key card in the door. "Eight o'clock. We arrive in Maui at nine p.m. Time travels backward going west. I guess you already know that."

"Hmm." She decided to skip the technicalities of international date lines and instead went over to the four-poster bed, sat on the edge. Through the windows and the downpour, she caught glimpses of Puget Sound and the Olympic Mountains beyond. Earlier, at dawn, a pink haze had floated over the Olympics' frigid peaks, announcing a sorbet sunrise. Then the brawny buffalo clouds rode in off the Pacific Ocean. Then rain. They had awakened to the sound of rain. She said, "Let's go scuba diving at Alki."

"We did that last week." He came over, pulled off his shirt, sat beside her.

"I want to go again." She kissed his chest.

"In this rain?"

"What does rain matter when you're under water?"

"Miss something the first time?" He drew her close, placed her head against his chest. She could feel his heart beat, hear it.

She said, "The treasure. I missed the sunken treasure."

He laughed. "If there's sunken treasure off Alki Point, I'm Captain Hook."

She broke away from him, studied him. "You'd never pass for Captain Hook. Your pirate's psyche got chopped off with all your hair."

"Anyway, what do we want with sunken treasure? I've got your dowry and you've got my inheritance, and we just scored a king's ransom in wedding gifts."

She sniffed. "Including a sterling-silver ice bucket shaped like a five-breasted woman. Do you realize that horrid bucket will actually outlive us?"

He smiled wryly. She leaned over, kissed him. A long, lingering kiss. She said, "Why don't we leave on an earlier flight? I'll bet we can get seats...."

He touched a finger to her lips. "Shhh." His other hand worked the buttons on her dress and when it dropped to her waist, she felt the cool air against her skin. He reached down, removed her shoes, her stockings, and said, "Hold still, Mrs. Winters."

THE DEPARTMENT of the Interior's Regional Director of Fish and Wildlife Service, Oly Olson, stared out his office window on the thirty-eighth floor of the Bumbershoot Building. For the second time today, the rain had abated, playing havoc with his perennially dark mood. Another sun break. A perfect day, after all, for a round of golf. He should be out on the course. Nobody should be working on a Sunday afternoon. It's not natural. Something about the Sabbath. Something about a day of rest. It was in the Bible; people aren't supposed to work on Sundays. It's sinning against the Creator. He should get the hell out of the office right now, before it was too late.

Olson swung around, so that his broad back faced the excellent view, so that his gaze fell to the fax on his desk. He'd already read it, he didn't need to read it again. He could crumple it up, trash it, pretend he hadn't seen it, leave the office and come in tomorrow morning acting innocent, like he hadn't seen the APB. What all points bulletin? I didn't find any APB on my desk. What APB? Who put it there? Dottie? Hell, you know how ditzy Dottie's been lately. She probably forgot to print it off the computer, so of course, he wouldn't have seen it. And too, Dottie probably erased all the voice mail by accident, so definitely he wouldn't have received the Iron County Sheriff's personal voice message.

Olson screwed up his mouth. He had a habit of pursing his lips, but this was no purse, this was a tighter seal, tight enough to keep the word on the tip of his tongue from escaping. He'd been trying to quit cursing, but the word pushed hard against the screwed-up lips. He put a fleshy hand to his mouth, spit the word into its palm, crushed it. He sighed and picked up the telephone receiver, punched in some numbers, heard a ring. While he waited for someone—or some voice-mail device—to answer the ringing phone, Olson reread the APB.

FROM: Jerome Wexler, Acting Secretary, U.S. Department of the Interior, Washington, D.C.

TO: Oly Olson, Regional Director, U.S. Fish and Wildlife Service, Pacific Northwest Region

SUBJECT: Bogachiel National Wildlife Preserve; Missing Child, Possible Abduction

MESSAGE: At 14:04 today, Iron County, Washington, Sheriff Tom Tobin issued an all points bulletin stating a nine-month-old infant has been reported missing in or near Bogachiel National Wildlife Preserve. (Sparse details included here.) Be advised, the event occurred in Department of the Interior jurisdiction. Tobin requesting DOI's immediate intervention. Send Diamond, then contact my office for further instructions.

Wexler had added a postscript:

Give Diamond the backup team. Report back this p.m. No excuses, no delays. Find the kid.

Olson snickered to himself. What did Wexler want? A miracle? You don't send your agents into a missing-persons investigation and expect results in two or three hours. It's unreasonable. He scratched the bald dome above his eyebrows. What a dilemma. When your agent is honeymooning, you don't just interrupt that.

A man's voice answered. "Honeymoon Suite, Groom here."

In the background, muffled laughter. Hers. Olson said, "Is that you, Winters?"

"Just a minute, I'll ask my wife."

More muffled laughter, and her voice went, "Woo-woo."

Olson spoke into the phone. "Venus, pick up."

Nothing. He tried another tack. "I know you're there. Packing for Hawaii. Well, unpack, then call me." He set the phone receiver down gently in its cradle.

On his desk, beside the memo, sat a mug of java. Kenya au lait. His personal trainer had forbade caffeine, but the Seattle's Best Coffee cart on Sixth Avenue had a Kenya AA roast on special today. He lifted the mug to his lips, sucked brown caffeine-laced acid through his teeth. The heat conduction hurt his bad bicuspid and he scowled. The phone rang. He picked it up and heard her voice.

Olson grinned sadistically. "Mrs. Winters, I presume."

"THIS CAN'T be good news." She was packing her suitcase, the phone receiver cradled between her chin and shoulder. Across the room, Richard leaned against the tall window, studying the darkening, fickle sky. A perfect day for winging to Maui. Get the hell out of Rain City.

Olson growled, "I don't like this any more than you do. Do you think it's fun calling off somebody's honeymoon?"

Venus groaned. "I shouldn't have rung you back."

"We need you up in Bogachiel this afternoon. A child, actually, a nine-month-old boy, is missing, maybe lost on the preserve. The boy was reported missing less than an hour ago. I'll put the team together. The chopper should be there within three hours. But I want you to head up there right now."

"Hey, chief. I got married last night. Remember?"

Olson suddenly felt tired. "This is an emergency." Hoarsely, he told her about the Nighteagle boy, what little he knew. It wasn't much. A Native American family. Poor. Living on the edge of the preserve. The baby left in its crib, outside in the cold. Maybe snatched by a bear, but no signs of one. Just some elk hoofprints near the baby's bassinet. That's about all he knew so far.

When he finished, she said, "So put Song in charge up there. Or Sparks." She shut her suitcase, latched it.

"No can do."

"Why not? They're not on their honeymoons."

Richard turned from the window, studied the scowl on his bride's face. She saw him look inquiringly at her, shook her head. Annoyed, Richard squinted. What did that mean, her head shaking?

Olson said, "That's your territory up there. No one knows it like you do. This is your case, Venus."

Exasperated, she said, "It's also my honeymoon." She sat down beside her suitcase. Richard came over, put his hand at her neck and rubbed. She reached up, felt his hand, gripped it. Moral support. She said, "I say it isn't serious. I say it's all a mistake. Maybe the kid's with the grandparents or something, and the parents just forgot. Maybe..."

Olson sighed. He hated arguing with her. She was stubborn. Nobody should be this stubborn. In his ear, Venus said desperately, "Can't you put Song in charge, just until we get back from Hawaii?"

"Wexler wants you taking charge."

"He knows I'm on my honeymoon," she protested again, whining, a mewling sound she despised in anyone's voice.

"We've already been through that. Now, tell Richard I'm awfully sorry. You can have as much time off as you want once we've wrapped this thing up."

Near the door, on a luggage rack, Richard's suitcase lay shut. On top of his suitcase lay the plane tickets to Maui. He could hear Olson's voice over the receiver, but couldn't hear what he said. Still, he could figure it out. He went over to the suitcase, picked up the plane tickets. He tucked one ticket in his jacket pocket. He placed the other on top of Venus's suitcase. Venus watched him, Olson barking in her ear. When she finally spoke, her voice sounded different, alert.

"Do you think this could be connected to the elk poachings on Bogachiel?"

"What suggests a relationship?"

She said, "The elk hoofprints. Since the last three carcasses we've found on Bogachiel have been found with the hooves sawed off, I'm just wondering..."

Silence. Olson could hear her breathing. He felt sick to his stomach. He shouldn't have to tell her. Wexler should have told her. He said, "I think that's stretching it." In a softer voice, he added, "Take Richard with you."

"I'm sure he'd love that."

"Get going. I want you to leave right now, by car. We'll have the team assembled in a couple hours. Three at most."

"You, too?" she said glumly.

Olson swung around, glanced at the sky. Gloomy clouds had again blotted out the sun. Rain might drench the golf course. Still, there was always a chance. "I need to stay here until the cougar report is tied up. So call me from up there tonight. Definitely no later than eight o'clock. Wexler wants a report sometime tonight." A pause. "Then, too, it might have been a bear. But it wasn't bearprints they found. It was elk. Maybe you're right. Maybe this is somehow related to the elk poachings we've had up there. Like, maybe some elk kidnapped the baby in retribution." Olson snickered.

"I'm not laughing, sir. And I haven't any warm clothes. Neither does Richard."

"For chrissake, get moving. Go home, get your clothes, but get the hell up there, do you hear me?"

"Ya sure, chief. You betcha. Don't get struck by lightning on the golf course." Sourly, and hung up.

Richard stood at the window, his shoulders hunched, hands in his trouser pockets. She went over to him, placed an arm through his, said, "I hate this."

No response. He might as well have petrified. She slipped around in front of him, between him and the window. He stood tall enough to see over her head, and he kept his eyes focused on a ferry crossing Puget Sound, bound for the mainland, its lights twinkling in the dismal pall. She put a hand against his cheek. He flinched, but otherwise didn't respond. She turned, faced the gloomy overcast sky, the little ferry plowing toward the landing pier, and felt the wind abandon her sails, her joie de vivre deflate, her mood blacken.

Richard said, "Why don't you just resign? You don't have to work."

She swallowed. Her throat felt dry. "This isn't about career."

He turned her around to face him. Disappointment had snuffed the light from his eyes. He said, "We're married now. Now *we* come first."

She folded her arms, pressed them against her small chest. "This is such a cliché..."

"What? Our marriage is a clich?"

"Not the marriage. I was thinking about the baby. How, say, if he were our child..." Her voice drifted off.

He folded his arms, sighed. "Well, he's not."

She nodded.

They stood silently, not touching, avoiding eye contact. She could hear his wristwatch click from one digit to another, and another. Time passing. A baby in danger, every second counts. Finally, she said, "This time of year, the storms on the ocean are incredibly romantic...."

Richard shivered. Californians never adjust to Washington's savage, lunatic coastal beaches. Lahaina Beach, now there's a swimming hole. Wives shouldn't call off honeymoons. He should be firm, insist. He said, "It's soaking hell up there." He left her standing at the window, went over to his suitcase.

She watched him double check the latches. Quietly, she said, "Where are you going?"

"You damn well know where I'm going." He reached in his jacket pocket, took out the plane ticket, glanced at it, put it back in the pocket. She could hear her heart pounding. He went over to the closet, checked to see that they hadn't forgotten something. Over his shoulder, he said, "Hurry up, Mrs. Winters. The Bogachiel Special leaves in three minutes."

She went over, embraced him. He felt stiff, and one of his graceful hands was clenched tight.

THREE

TOW-LEE-ACK

CALIGINOUS CLOUDS ruptured over Grays Harbor, dumping wind-whipped horizontal rain that slammed the Land Rover's windshield. No sane man would drive this fast in this weather except an angry man. Switching the headlights to low beam, Richard gripped the steering wheel, struggling to keep the Rover on the right side of Highway 12. Beside him, Venus squinted at her mental road map. "Aberdeen, then Hoquiam. Turn right on Highway 101 northbound. Then about thirty-eight miles to Humptulips. That's halfway to Lake Quinault. Maybe we should just go as far as Lake Quinault. Just until the rain stops."

"I can't listen to you and drive." Irritation.

Venus winced, folded the mental map, worked her lips silently. She trusted how he drove. They didn't speak again until, two miles north of Humptulips, the wind lost power and the rain slowed to a drizzle. Richard reached over, found her hand, squeezed. "Sorry."

He'd never spoken a sharp word, never exhibited anger of any kind toward her until today, this first day of their wedded bliss. Matter-of-factly, she said, "Who wouldn't be ticked off about spending his honeymoon in Hell's bathtub?"

"I don't call this a honeymoon."

Half an hour later, the spent clouds passed over, and a pale sun lit up the high prairies and silhouettes of ancient cedar forests. Venus said, "We're at the northeastern edge of the Quinault Reservation."

He gunned the engine, swung west. The Rover hugged the pavement, sailed across the Quinault's high prairies, then swooped downhill to sea level, where at the northwest edge of the reservation, the squalid fishing village of Queets met the Pacific Ocean. The heavy rains hadn't hit this section of the coastline; just a drizzly mist had fallen on the forested beaches where cloud tapers hung in suspended animation. Now the narrow highway ran parallel to the ocean, separated only by cobbled beach and a thin veil of ancient cedars. The trees flashed by, repeating themselves hypnotically. Once or twice, Venus caught a glimpse of the pounding ocean surf and the cliffs and the sea stacks shooting upwards from the ocean floor, breakers glancing off their age-worn walls.

The Quillayute tribe named this beach with its skinny stone sea stacks Toleak, meaning, "hole-in-the-wall rock." Or, if you believed the Clallam tribe's version, the beach was named for their word describing mussels, which is why the locals often called Toleak Beach "Mussel Beach." The cedar forests that reached down to Toleak Beach had, once upon a time, provided superb hunting, lush vegetation, herbs, and berries, and the fine cedars gave their bark for the native people's clothing, for baskets, their trunks for dugout canoes. In the dugout canoes, the natives fished the ocean, taking salmon, seal, and whale. The abounding beach provided seaweed, clams, rock oysters, succulent Dungeness crabs, driftwood logs for firewood, sparkling agates to delight a child's eye. A land of riches, of plenty, of enchantment. Toleak, a good place to anchor, had never met the modern world, and probably never would.

Five-fifteen. Dusk. Beyond Toleak, on a long stretch of 101, on the righthand side, they saw the sign to Bogachiel National Wildlife Preserve. Twenty feet beyond that, a forest clearing swung inward into a trailer park. "This is it." Venus zipped up her leather jacket, switched frames of mind. Honeymoon wife to Department of the Interior special agent. It was an easy segue, perhaps too comfortable.

Sheriff Tobin, his deputies, and a dozen locals had been searching since the Nighteagles' neighbor phoned in three hours ago. Now Tobin and a couple of deputies stood beside a rusted pink house-trailer. When Tobin brought Winn and Theresa Nighteagle out of the woods, Venus felt a coldness from them, as though they dreaded the arrival of a federal law-enforcement officer, as though her arrival signaled the gravity of the situation, the reality. Before her arrival, the parents could pretend the baby had just crawled away somewhere, was temporarily lost in the underbrush near the trailer. They could imagine a lot of harmless scenarios, until a federal agent came on the scene. Now, suddenly, the parents recognized stark reality, and things took a morbid, frightening turn for the worse.

INSIDE THE Nighteagle trailer, Winn and Theresa sat side by side on a beat-up rayon chenille sofa, holding hands. Winn Nighteagle stared straight ahead, his face bereft of expression, his eyes flat, unreflective, cardboard. Theresa trembled, shivered, and fought against panic. Venus sent Tobin and his deputies away. Richard went along, into the woods, to search. When she was alone with Winn and Theresa Nighteagle, she gently asked them to tell their story, including as much small detail as they could recall.

Theresa spoke in a soft, clear voice. Earlier this morning, a bone-chilling damp rode the ocean breeze. Inside the trailer, about eleven o'clock, Theresa fed the twins a lunch of strained meat and squash. In her infant seat, Milan, dressed in a pink woolen smock and matching woolen booties with a dishtowel tied around her neck, spit up a little of her lunch. Theresa wiped it up with a wet rag. Milan wasn't actually ill, she just didn't like strained squash. Beside Milan in his own infant seat, Paris ate voraciously. He wore a long-sleeved, cotton knit shirt of navy blue and denim overalls with real buckles. On his feet were miniature hiking boots that Frances Creed, Theresa's mother, had bought him at the Kmart down in Grays Harbor. Dressed like this, he reminded Theresa of Winn in miniature.

When the twins were fed, Theresa carried them one at a time into their bedroom, and placed them in bassinets standing side by side near the window. Winn had built two identical bassinets for the twins out of cedar strips woven together. Each bassinet stood on a pine wood frame, and the two pieces could be moved separately, for easy transport. Inside the bassinets were new baby mattresses, donated by the St. Jude Mission Church, made up with flannel sheets and woven blankets of the sort that "breathe." Theresa closed the shades and began crooning a lullaby. Milan especially loved her mother's lullabies, and she chirped along with her. Theresa leaned over Milan's crib, kissed her forehead. Bending over Paris's crib, she placed her hand gently on his head and smoothed his straight jet black hair. Paris smiled, his eyes sparkling in the semi-darkness. Theresa stroked his head and Paris reached up with one chubby fist, grabbed her fingers. Then she noticed Paris's little hiking boots. Removing them, she placed red woolen booties on his bare feet. More comfortable for sleeping. As she closed the door to their room, she heard Milan crooning softly. Paris made no sound. That was about noon.

Walking down the hall, Theresa felt a chill pass through the trailer. When she reached the thermostat on the wall near the living room, she saw that it was only sixty-four degrees inside the trailer. She pushed the temperature up to seventy-five. With the babies napping in their cribs, she lay down on the living room couch. From outside came the dull, rhythmic thud of Winn's ax against logs. In one corner of the living room, the television, its volume on low, was tuned to Channel Seven, KIRO from Seattle, and a sportscaster was interviewing football coaches. The football game wouldn't start for another hour or so. The monotonous buzzing of the refrigerator helped lull her to sleep, and as the temperature in the trailer rose, Theresa fell into a cozy slumber.

An hour and a half later, Theresa stirred, gradually aware that she was sweating, that she felt slightly ill. The heat was too high. She didn't want to get up, she wanted to go back to sleep and sleep all afternoon, that's how drained she felt, but Milan was fussing, so naptime was over. Theresa sat up, pushed her hair off her face, wiped her hands on her thighs and stood up. Now Milan was crying. Milan rarely cried, unless she was sick. Theresa went into the twins' bedroom. In the dim light leaking from the window shade, she saw Milan sitting upright in her bassinet, her face glistening with tears. But where was Paris? His bassinet was gone. Not the pinewood stand, just the bassinet part. And Paris in it. Theresa smiled ironically. Obviously, Winn had Paris outdoors with him again. She gathered up Milan, carried her into the living room and changed her diapers. Milan stopped crying and gurgled,

"Da-da-da-da-da," which Theresa took to mean "Daddy."

On the way into the kitchen, Theresa paused to turn down the thermostat. When she strapped Milan into her infant seat, the baby fussed again, but Theresa gave her some graham crackers and she chewed contentedly. Teething, that was Milan's problem, Theresa told herself as she peered outdoors and saw Paris's bassinet empty in the back yard. Now where had Winn put Paris? Theresa stepped outside. Walking over to where Winn stood chopping firewood, Theresa felt a sharp, unfamiliar pang of nostalgia that reminded her of how she felt a few days after the twins were born. Postpartum blues, Frances told her. Nothing to fret over. Every mother experiences loss when their babies are delivered from the womb into the world. It felt like nostalgia, Theresa thought as she approached Winn, but more than nostalgia, it felt sickening.

WINN SAT RIGIDLY beside Theresa, still holding her hand. Venus leaned forward, said, "Thank you, Mrs. Nighteagle. I know this is very painful."

Theresa, wild-eyed, nodded.

Venus said, "Do you mind if I have a look around the trailer?"

"They've done that already," said Winn. "You won't find anything here. Why don't you go out there in the woods like the others?"

Delicately, Venus said, "Just in case they missed something, Mr. Nighteagle."

Winn took his first potshot then. "You're looking for something to blame us. We didn't do anything wrong. We'd never harm our babies."

Venus stood up, walked down the narrow corridor and stepped inside the twins' bedroom. Theresa came up behind her. "There's nothing to see in there," she said. "I've been over this place a hundred times."

"We'll need an item of clothing. Something with his scent on it."

Winn appeared at the bedroom door. "You're sending out dogs?"

Venus nodded. "Soon as the chopper arrives. We'll send out search parties on foot, and we'll take out the scent hounds. The chopper has a heat sensor, and we'll also conduct an aerial search. If we're lucky, we'll find your little boy before dark."

Winn said, "The dogs won't hurt my boy?"

"No, Mr. Nighteagle. But they might find him."

Winn said, "Animals got him," as if testing the sound of that horrifying statement.

Theresa cried, "Don't say that, Winn. He just crawled away somewhere."

Winn almost yelled, "Then what about the footprints?"

"That was an elk, honey. An elk wouldn't snatch him up—at least, I don't think so." She turned pleadingly to Venus. "Do you think animals got him?"

"We'll proceed under the supposition that your son crawled or walked into the woods," Venus said carefully. "We'll hope that's what happened. But, Mr. and Mrs. Nighteagle, you shouldn't jump to any conclusions. We'll check out every possible explanation."

"Including parental abuse." Winn, rudely.

She nodded. It was true.

Theresa went to the plastic hamper where she dumped the twins' soiled clothing. Not their diapers. She used Pampers on them, because the washing machine was broken. In the hamper, she found a white undershirt that Paris had worn yesterday morning. She handed it to Venus. "That's all I have. That, and the blanket in his crib."

FOUR

DODGE MAN

WITH DARKNESS, the Pineapple Express roared in over Toleak Beach. Hawaiian air streams mutate over the Pacific, transfigure tropical energy to menacing storms that unleash howling winds and frigid, driving rain. The storm hit Toleak dead-on. Ancient trees that had survived monsoons stooped over and snapped like toothpicks in a titan's fingers. The ocean roared, merciless breakers smashed the cliffs at Toleak Beach. In its final rise, the evening tide mauled the cobbled ground, clawed the driftwood line, clambered into the cedar groves, then sucked its stolen treasures back into the churning sea. The Bell Jet Ranger, its blades whirring, rocked and swayed perilously as it inched up the coastline. Fish and Wildlife Agent Eric Sweetwater set the chopper down on the beach directly across the highway from Cedar Grove Trailer Park, a dicey landing that broke a sweat on his brow. Sweetwater struggled out onto the beach, followed by the rest of DOI's regional forensics team. Securing the chopper, they gathered their equipment and marched up the beach toward the highway.

Claudia Paganelli, a physician who performed more autopsies than healings, would examine the missing child's twin for signs of molestation or abuse. It was standard procedure in the case of a family with more than one child, when one of the children is kidnapped or otherwise abused. Al Yamada, an evidence expert, would comb the family's living quarters, record the general conditions of the home, pore over every millimeter of the scene. Again, standard procedure. Eric Sweetwater and Marla Mason, witness experts, would take statements from anyone willing to talk. Lean, limp, laconic Sparks came up from Ozone Beach with his woodsman's expertise. Last out of the chopper came four frisky bloodhounds in the tight rein of Special Agent Louie Song. Muscle-man, Lady-killer—they called him "Heartbreak Louie"—would join the forest search from behind the team of hounds and a new pair of Ray Bans which Venus dearly hoped he would lose before he tripped and fell on his face.

Yamada groused over the paucity of physical evidence, and made plaster casts of the cloven-hooved prints that led out of the woods to the baby's crib then back into the woods again where they disappeared in the thick underbrush and the shadowy dusk. It wasn't much to go on. Sweetwater and Mason combed the trailer park, including inside every trailer, around prolific junk piles, and inside every working vehicle and rusting steel carcass on the grounds. In spite of the bitter winds and rain, the Nighteagles' trailer-park neighbors all came out to search the wilderness. Bob Brightman, the next-door neighbor who had called 911, took off from his night-shift job at the county transportation barn and joined the search party. Bob's wife, Carolee, a self-proclaimed New Age healer and professional wildcrafter, danced around the Nighteagle trailer spreading a purple iridescent powder until Eric Sweetwater pulled her off the scene. Fuming, Carolee Brightman refused to join the more conventional search efforts, choosing instead to spew vitriol at Sweetwater until he finally grew weary of her sarcasm and marched her back to her own trailer. The Brightman's teenage daughter, Becca, was standing on the trailer's stoop, huffing and puffing, feeding a key into the front door keyhole. Carolee transferred her anger to the daughter.

"Just where have you been, Becca Brightman?" Harsh, accusatory.

Sweetwater heard Becca answer her mother. "Over at the Deans, Mom. Doing homework with Misty."

Carolee growled, "Don't you lie to me, Becca. Misty's out there with the rest of them." She grabbed the daughter by one ear, shoved her inside the trailer. Sweetwater heard the girl scream in pain, then Carolee slammed the door shut and Sweetwater went away, leaving the family feud to play out in private. As he returned to his post outside the Nighteagle trailer, Sweetwater noticed a sleek, black Porsche Boxster pull into the trailer park. The driver parked, got out, a nice-looking man who joined the search. Sweetwater marveled to himself that anyone who owned such extravagant wheels would volunteer to help search for an indigent Native American boy lost in the woods. Especially in this foul weather. You shouldn't too hastily judge the rich.

Teenaged Misty Cravus had joined the search, as had her older sister, eighteen-year-old Cindy Dean, and Cindy's husband, Daniel, a hell-bent stock-car racer, who took time out from bonging pot to volunteer. At first, Daniel resisted a search of his trailer, but Cindy drew him aside, whispered something to him, and he came back agreeing to let the federal agents invade his private domain. Eric Sweetwater and Marla Mason swept the filthy, trash-heaped abode. Marla found a small cache of pot and the bong, confiscated them, reported her find to Venus. Venus turned the contraband over to Al Yamada. They'd have to file charges, but Venus wasn't ready to do that. Not yet. Misdemeanors take a back seat to a baby's disappearance on the edge of the deep forest, apparently at the jaws of a beast.

Even the geriatric Polks, Lee and his osteoarthritic wife, Irene, hobbled off their trailer stoop, sloshing through the rain and muddy ground to join in the search. Irene Polk had a nose for trouble. Her husband bragged that Irene always managed to ferret out lost items and speculated on how that talent might work on babies, too. Mrs. Polk presented difficulties for the search crews, interjecting her disconnected ideas and advice at the most inappropriate moments, as if intentionally creating a diversion. Some people no matter how well-intentioned just don't belong near crime scenes.

From all ends of Iron County came volunteers of every age and description. So many came to search the woods that Venus decided to organize a double-flank formation in which, once formed, they plowed the wilderness like human minesweepers, slogging through mud and muck and falling tree branches, risking their own lives and limbs for this one lost child, this one little Indian boy.

Winn was flanked on one side by a man he recognized but couldn't say from where. The man was clean-shaven and smelled of expensive cologne. Immediately behind Winn, Richard took his place between a deputy and the neighbor, Bob Brightman. In the darkness, all the searchers had to guide them was the baying of the hounds and the dim beams from puny flashlights until Sweetwater took the chopper back up, searched the woods from the air, aiming a heat sensor and searchlight full beam through the forest canopy. The human rake slogged on. Richard felt movement at his side and glanced down through the inky shadows as Venus took his hand.

More people came, strangers, and some of them even walked side by side with Winn through the woods, just as if Winn was their brother, or as if it had been their own kid who disappeared. But Winn soon lost patience with the combing formation, broke free, and ran wildly into the darkness and the rain, shouting Paris's name.

On the beach, tribal fishermen from the Hoh reservation launched their small craft and scoured the shoreline until the Coast Guard arrived with a cruiser that hugged the rugged coastline, its searchlights probed the dark, boulder-strewn beaches, where animals often carried their prey, to gorge on it at the water's edge. In Olympic National Park, rangers ran foot patrols on trails as far up as timberline and searched all the park facilities. Claudia Paganelli, her examination of the missing boy's twin completed, sat vigil with Theresa as the rains pounded the trailer's metal roof. Paganelli hadn't observed a single sign of trauma on the baby girl. Milan Nighteagle seemed healthy, contented, well nourished. No indication of parental abuse or neglect.

By nine o'clock, with no sign of the boy, the search was suspended. Kind strangers returned home to dry off and revisit the event on the ten o'clock news. At the Fish and Wildlife Service's annex office in Forks, Venus set up an operations room. Richard and Sweetwater remained at the trailer park, in case, by some miracle, the baby crawled out of the forest or someone brought him home. Sheriff Tobin ordered roadblocks across Highway 101 and across every arterial road leading into and out of Iron County.

Time's cadence, time's swift march pressed on. Every minute counts when a baby is lost to the reckless whims of nature, or the ravenous impulses of a wild animal. Or a kidnapper. On the computer system, Venus called up a map of the preserve and surrounding roads, superimposed that map onto a county map, and over that the national park map, creating a nearly complete system of roads, trails, and coastal access paths. Enlarged, printed, the map was posted in the operations room and fed through the APB communications system. Yamada, concentrating on the kidnapping angle, went on-line and searched for data on criminal activity in the Toleak-Bogachiel area over a seven-year period, including where on this map any crimes had occurred. To his APB, Yamada attached a scanned snapshot of Paris Nighteagle, instantly transmitting the baby's image to every law enforcement agency in the region, including Canadian border patrols and airport security at Vancouver, British Columbia, and Seattle-Tacoma International Airport. You can't be too thorough. For the APB's scanned photograph and the standard Missing Child poster, the Nighteagles had chosen a recent picture Theresa had snapped of Winn holding Paris and Milan in Bogachiel's rain forest. In this shot, Winn's and Milan's backs were to the camera, but Paris stared straight into the camera's lens, as if transfixed by its magic eye. Ocean

Boy was grinning, showing two new teeth for a total of four, front and center.

That first night, neighbors poured into the Nighteagle trailer, bearing food and solace, creating confusion. Theresa sat on the couch, trembling from fear, blaming herself for everything. "It was so cold, Winn."

"I know, Tee. Don't think I blame you, because I don't. I blame myself."

"But, if only I hadn't turned the heat up."

Winn pinched his eyes. "If-onlys won't get us anywhere. Now, I want you to go lie down."

Theresa shook her head. "I can't do that. I can't lie down. I can't think about sleep."

Winn wrapped an arm around her. He just wished it wasn't so hard on Theresa. He'd take the pain for both of them, if he could, but you can't ever bear the load of a mother's pain, a mother's grief, not when you've got your own sick heart to tend.

At 2:00 a.m. the rain stopped. Louie Song came out of the woods a frustrated man. He'd run the hounds into the ground. Now they lay panting on the soaked earth. The downpour had completely dissolved any chance of a scent. In the darkness, Song listened to the hounds gasping, to the voices drifting out of the pathetic rusted pink trailer that the Nighteagles called home. Song sat on his haunches, lit a cigarette. Across the trailer park, he saw Venus at the spot where the empty bassinet was discovered. She was alone, walking around inside the yellow taped-off area, shining a broad-beamed Maglite on the ground.

She'd heard Song and the hounds come out of the woods. She knew they'd come up empty, like everyone else. The hoofprint pattern bothered her, the helter-skelter pattern as if the creature were crazed. She was examining the prints closely when a black shadow shot out of the woods about twenty feet from where she stood. She drew her .38 Smith and Wesson, aimed.

"Stop right there." The black shadow froze. Venus said, "Identify yourself."

A man's voice, calm, detached. "Dr. Bradford Kellogg. I was in the search party. I got turned around. I'm okay now, though."

If the man had the scent of the child on him, the hounds, resting nearby, would know it by now. They ignored him completely. Pistol first, she approached the dark shadow. He stepped forward into the thin light, hands raised absurdly high over his head, a rave dancer in the hinterlands.

"I'm not armed," he said nervously. "I swear to God, I'm harmless."

He was about forty, sleek, clean-cut, and manicured, with a physique any man other than maybe Song would envy. She said, "You got I.D.?"

He reached carefully for his wallet, handed it over to Venus. He had a California driver's license. Bradford Kellogg, M.D. L.A. address. Mulholland Drive. Hair: blond. Eyes: green. Height: 6' 0". Weight: 185 lbs.

She said, "What are you doing up here on the Peninsula?"

"Visiting my brother. Clint Kellogg. You know who he is, don't you?"

"Why should I know him?"

"He's a well-known author. He's on television a lot. He lives down at Grays Harbor. We heard about the missing boy on the news, came up here to help search."

She handed the wallet back. "You say you got lost out there?"

Kellogg slid the wallet back in his pocket. "Just a little disoriented. The search party got away from me. But I saw the lights of the trailer park and found my way back. I'm okay, really I am."

You can't arrest a man for the flicker in his eyes. She put her gun away, said, "Have a nice day," and walked over to where Song smoked and the hounds lay panting. From there she watched Kellogg saunter into the trailer park lot, climb into a snazzy black Boxster that she hadn't noticed earlier in the evening. It was parked beside a Jeep. In the Jeep, a man sat behind the wheel. The Boxster glided onto the highway, heading south. The Jeep followed close behind.

Song gazed at her through blue smoke, said, "For once, I'm a page ahead of you."

"Meaning?" She was cold, wet, exhausted. She wanted to find Richard and then go find a place to sleep.

Song said, "I've heard of Clint Kellogg, the writer. He was on 'The Jean Stanislaus Show' couple weeks ago. Talking about fables and metaphor. That was him driving the Jeep. He's a pretentious egghead."

"More brains than brawn?"

Song puckered his lips, made an exaggerated kissing sound.

She said, "What's that for?"

Song shrugged. He didn't know. He stood, stretched. He was medium height, built like a wrestler, very strong. He said, "Some psychopath has the kid. That's what I think."

"Not an animal?"

Song reconsidered. "I mean, if he wasn't snatched by beasts."

THREE A.M. Five miles north of Cedar Grove Trailer Park, Richard steered the Land Rover sharply westward onto the narrow strip of rugged cliffs and beach that separated Highway 101 from the Pacific. The Rover swerved off the highway into a clearing, its headlights aimed at a two-story, weather-beaten, cedar shingle beach house that roosted on a high bluff facing the ocean. A sign on the porch said TOLEAK LODGE. At one end of the porch another sign read GENERAL STORE. Near the store was a single gas pump, rusted, bent leeward.

The lodge door was unlocked. Inside was a small lobby, no visible sign of a registration desk. A gift shop crammed with native handicrafts, miniature carved totem poles, fetishes, and touristy crapola was closed for the season. Off the foyer, a cocktail lounge and a restaurant were all dark, all deserted. All lonely. Winter was setting in, and in Toleak, Washington, winter is a dank, still, deeply melancholy time.

A narrow cedar staircase led upward to darkness. The staircase creaked and down came a rumpled, sleepy creature calling himself the manager. He wore a thick parka over pajamas and long underwear, and Mukluks on his feet. He had auburn hair, and his bleary eyes were flecked hazel. He had long bony hands and a waterproof watch strapped to one wrist. All the bells and whistles. Maybe he wore it to bed. He rummaged through a small bureau, located a registration book and a credit card embosser.

"You should have made reservations." Gruffly.

"We didn't know we'd be coming..." Venus gestured futilely.

"You two must be Californians." With disdain.

"He is," Venus indicated Richard. "I'm a native."

"Well then, you definitely should know better. You don't just show up at a lodge way out on the edge of nowhere without reservations and wake everybody up at all hours. It's not how we do things out here."

Richard signed the registration card while Venus proffered the agency's credit card. The grumpy sleepwalker snatched it, studied it, embossed it, handed it back. "Oh, now I get it," he said. "You're the Fish and Wildlife folks. Sheriff Tobin called about you earlier this evening. You find the boy?"

"Not yet." Venus, taciturn.

Lodge Man wanted to shake hands now. "Bill Dravus. Don't be fooled by the auburn fringe. I'm half Quinault. Room or cottage?"

"Cottage. With an ocean view." Richard, tired.

"All our cottages have ocean views. For that matter, all our units have ocean views, unless you count mine. The manager's quarters face the highway." He studied a list. "There's Cottage Five. I have Cottage Five available."

"What about Cottage Three?"

Richard glanced at her, frowned. Venus might be giving Dravus a hard time for no other reason than she was exhausted. Dravus said, "There isn't any difference between Cottage Three and Cottage Five. Why would you want Cottage Three?"

"Better view."

Dravus squinted suspiciously. "You've visited us before?"

Venus answered, "Once, back years ago. I was nine or ten."

"And you remember the cottage number?" Incredulous.

They took the keys to Cottage Three, watched Dravus climb the cedar staircase, and once he was out of hearing range, she said, "It's not like I have amnesia."

Richard took her arm, steered her outside. "Let's get this unpacking business over with."

"What's the hurry?"

"I'm sleepy." He pinched her.

"Nature's cure-all," she quipped.

Cottage Three was perched suspiciously close to the cliff's edge, and if you weren't cautious walking in the dark, you could easily tumble a hundred feet over the cliff onto the rock-strewn beach. Safely inside the cottage, they groped for a light switch, in vain. In the pale moonlight leaking through a window, Richard grabbed her, embraced her, devoured her. Eventually, they found the bed.

Sleep didn't come easily. Who could sleep fearing a baby was captive in some beast's clutches? Was it feral, or human? A savage, a kidnapper, a killer? Some psychopath, some sicko? In the darkness leading to dawn, she fell off into restless slumber, imagining, in spite of her pragmatic intuition, a horrifying, four-footed beast stealing into its lair in the forest, clutching Paris Nighteagle in a bone-breaking grip.

FIVE

THE GECKO

AT 6:00 A.M., Venus awoke to Richard's gentle kiss. "Going jogging," he said. "See you later." After he left, she got up, dressed, and was searching barren cupboards for signs of a tea bag or coffee, any caffeinated beverage, when someone knocked on the door.

Song. She let him in. Before he tucked into a chair at the dining table, Song handed her a sheet of paper. "This just came off the fax." She joined him at the table, read the fax.

United States Department of the Interior, Fish and Wildlife Service. WANTED. (A scanned image of a white male, approximately fifty years old, gray buzz cut, deep-set green eyes, sunken cheeks, a razor-thin mouth that stretched across bad teeth.) Name: Earl Branson; Current Address: None. Details: Branson is wanted for the alleged kidnapping and molestation of a nine-year-old female. Branson allegedly grabbed the victim from a public rest room in Olympic National Park. He was seen driving away with the girl in the passenger seat at approximately 2:00 p.m. on November 1. According to the victim's statement, Branson took the victim to Bogachiel National Wildlife Preserve, into the rain forest, where he allegedly molested and then abandoned her. Victim, who lives in Iron County with her mother, found her way out of the preserve, and eventually went home. Victim did not report incident immediately, but waited two weeks to come forward with the allegations and a description of the suspect. Branson has a history of pedophile convictions, and is wanted in King County for stalking preschool children. Branson has one distinguishing feature, a tattoo of a gecko on his left forearm. If you see anyone resembling the suspect, contact the U.S. Fish and Wildlife Service: 1–800–555–4234. BRANSON IS CONSIDERED ARMED AND DANGEROUS.

Venus set the paper on the table, studied the man's face. Song lit a Gauloise, blew out smoke, watched her. He said, "Olson shot this up to us this morning. We're posting them around the state."

"Gecko."

Song said, "He's mine. I've got dibs."

"First, you'll get those hounds back out on the preserve. The Gecko will have to wait."

"I think he's our guy."

"Maybe, but the baby's our first priority. We want to find him alive, soon."

"If we track down the Gecko, we may find the baby."

Venus said, "Let's see what comes from the 'Wanted' posters. Meanwhile, you need to get back over there and run the hounds up in the rain forest."

"The hounds are tired out. I'm letting them rest."

"Well, get some more hounds. I want you out there with hounds right now, Louie. Can you grasp that, or do I have to walk you through the exercise?"

Song grimaced. "You sound just like Olson."

"Sorry. It's the stress. A missing child, a baby. Time is everything. We don't have much of it left before the next downpour." She showed him an empty hand, void of solutions. "I didn't get much sleep."

"I thought you didn't like humans. I thought you only cared about animals."

"Will you shut the hell up, Louie?"

Song gummed his lips.

Outside the cottage, Richard came jogging along the footpath. In the thin mist, he saw Dravus, the lodge manager, on the path, one hand clutching a clam bucket. Dravus had on the same parka he'd worn in the wee hours over his pajamas, only this time he wore hiking boots and heavy canvas trousers. When he saw Richard, Dravus grinned slyly.

"You two lovebirds having a good time?"

Richard said, "When does the store open?"

Lodge Man came back up the path to where Richard stood, set down his clam bucket. "My guy's off sick today. What'd you need?"

"Breakfast stuff." Richard inhaled the salt air, felt his lungs and esophagus turn stone cold. He rubbed his hands together. "And some logs for the fireplace."

Lodge Man grinned wide. "You like that fireplace, do you?"

"I like heat."

Lodge Man nodded. He shoved a bony finger at Richard. "Oh, that's right. You're from California. Northern or Southern?"

"Southern."

Dravus smirked, said, "I figured that."

Richard said, "So, if we want heat and breakfast supplies before noon, where would I go?"

Dravus pointed north on the highway, toward Forks. "Takes twenty minutes if you drive any speed at all. Or you can drive back down to Queets," he said.

"Keets, they've got a Stop 'N' Go, but it's a ripoff."

Richard headed for the cottage.

Dravus called after him, "Any news on the boy?"

Richard shook his head.

Dravus said, "You know what they say about no news."

Richard smiled saccharinely, nodded. Dravus opened his mouth. The words formed on his lips, and he stood there, reciting the bromide, but Richard didn't hear Dravus's tired axiom because he was distracted by a familiar Harley Davidson parked beside the cottage door.

Venus's old bike, he'd recognize it anywhere. No wife of his was going to be peeled off the pavement dead meat. He'd implored her to give it up and Venus reluctantly agreed, exchanging the bike for a sleek Alfa Romeo and a life with Richard. Now here sat the same old bike beside the honeymoon cabin door, and that meant she wasn't alone inside. The bike's new owner, Heartbreak Louie, was with her. Richard knocked lightly before turning the knob.

They were seated at the kitchen table, Venus in her black leather, Song in his. Song sat opposite her, sprawled across a chair, his jacket slung over the chair back. He had on a black T-shirt that Richard knew carried a pack of Gauloises in the rolled-up sleeve. A Gauloise clung to Song's lower lip, its smoke trail half concealing his beautiful eyes. Half Chinese, half Anglo, Song had smoky, sexy eyes. From the look on Song's face, Richard decided he'd interrupted one of Heartbreak Louie's legendary monologues. Rudely, he said, "What brings you into our honeymoon, Song?"

Venus stood, walked over to Richard, embraced him, said, "Song hated barging in so early."

Richard leaned against the kitchen counter. "Song can speak for himself."

Venus flushed crimson. She could sense Richard's emotions, could feel the depth of anger in his sarcastic tone of voice. Something was wrong with this honeymoon picture, things had swung off course. Right now, they should be on a Maui beach, constructing a sugar sand model of their shared architectural visions, their toes wiggling in turquoise waters. But the honeymoon was apparently over, even before it began. So this was marriage. Day Two of wedded bliss.

Song squinted through hot, wispy, cigarette smoke. He should apologize for the intrusion, but wouldn't. This was about work, and Song was just following Olson's orders. A long, uncomfortable silence ensued, during which Song smoked the Gauloise. Then Richard gently poked Venus's back and said, "Go into the bedroom and wait for me."

She protested, "Song just got here. We have a possible suspect."

Richard raised his arms to the futility of the moment. "Fine. Just fine," he retorted, and left the cottage, shutting the door harder than necessary.

Song screwed up his mouth.

Her pulse quickened, her mouth felt dry and she felt a seratonin rush. She inhaled some of Song's secondhand smoke, went back to the table, sat down. She stared at the cottage door, acutely aware that some cold, heavy object, maybe her heart, constricted her breathing, a knotted stone where lungs should be.

"You were saying...?" Song, being helpful.

Tersely, she said, "If you had attended the last two staff meetings, you'd know that we've found three elk carcasses on Bogachiel over the past couple months. In each case, they were shot with a .300 Winchester Magnum, loaded with one-eighty grain bullets. In each case, the individual was hit twice, in roughly the same spot. The first bullet penetrated the hide at the shoulder blade, shot straight into the heart. The second was a security measure. The hunter didn't need that second bullet. In each case, the individual's hooves were sawed off with a True Value Hardware hacksaw."

Song smoked, watched her. She'd seemed healthy enough lately. The malaria fevers she'd brought back from Asia had eased up, unless she wasn't telling him something. Still, Song thought she looked piqued this morning, too pale, and her eyes reminded him of green traffic lights. Maybe it was his presence in the honeymoon cottage that had bollixed up her common sense. He said, "Help me out here, Venus. I don't follow your train of thought."

She shrugged. "Maybe I'm wrong, but I feel a connection between those poachings and this incident."

Song's lips formed an O, but nothing came out, until finally he leaned forward and blurted, "Why?"

"The hoofprints. It's the hoofprints."

Song nodded slowly. "Ah, I see." But he didn't.

She changed the subject. "All that rain might have created an impossible situation for the hounds. Still, if you can get up the muddy slopes, up into the rain forest, with the heavy canopy up there, I doubt that ground took in much throughwater. I know it's a long hike up there, but we need to check it out. I've heard tales about an old sweat lodge that some Quinault warriors built back in the eighteenth century. According to some reports, it was constructed on or near that rain forest, and it may still be standing. It might make a handy hideout. It's just a thought."

Song snorted, said, "Don't count on it."

She ignored his obvious disdain, read her Swatch. Time was passing too quickly. She added, "Take Sparks along. He's got that feral sense you'll need up there. And for God's sake, take a telephone. It's easy to get lost in that Tolkienian landscape."

"That what?" Song mocked her.

"Never mind." He probably didn't get it.

Song said, "What about the Hoh reservation? Did you pull that search team together?"

"We don't have jurisdiction. The tribal chief put out the word. They sent their own search party around the reservation. Some even went out on horseback. So far, they haven't found anything."

Song lit another cigarette, blew out some smoke, watched her play with her platinum wedding band. He said, "We still best buds?"

"We're still friends, Louie. We'll always be friends."

Song flicked ashes into his boot cuff. Ever since she'd known him, nearly ten years, he'd flicked ashes into his boot cuff, and so far, hadn't immolated himself. Song purred, "Maybe that's not good enough."

Venus stared.

Song stood up, stretched. "Anyway, you shouldn't be married to anyone."

She studied her wedding band. She'd taken off the diamond engagement ring, placed it in its little jeweler's case. She rose from the table, went into the bedroom, and returned a moment later with the case. "Would you take this to Seattle, ask my mother to baby-sit it for me?"

Song popped open the little case. His eyebrows jumped. "I could retire on this."

"On second thought, keep it at your house, if you don't mind. My mother doesn't need to know about the aborted honeymoon."

Song said, "Your mother has too much control over your life. You should be your own person. Stop knee-jerking to Lady Bella's every whim and attitude. She'll respect you more."

She felt her face burn, but all she said was, "Get those hounds out, then rest this afternoon. This is going to be a very long day."

On the way out, Song said, "Tell Richard I'm not sorry about the intrusion."

She watched him straddle the Harley, rev it up. She watched until he disappeared up the little path and heard him pause at the highway, then rev the Harley again and spin out onto 101. The bike purred like a kitten and its purr brought back a thousand memories.

RICHARD WAS SITTING on a driftwood log watching the gulls maneuver around the lanky sea stacks, fighting one another for the crow's nest. Through the hazy mist, she walked up the beach toward him. When she reached him, she saw his hands were folded, his shoulders hunched. He looked cold, and she wanted to embrace him, warm him from inside out, but when she sat down beside him, he stiffened. She scooted closer, placed her hand gently on his back.

He said, "Maybe I should go back to Seattle."

"No, Richard. Don't leave me here without you."

"I'm not part of the process here."

She leaned over, kissed him. "I'd like to recruit you."

Richard laughed. "You can't just recruit someone."

"You're not just someone. You're Richard Winters. I hereby recruit you, Richard Winters, as my co-conspirator on the Nighteagle case. There. It's official. Besides, you aren't expected back at your office for three weeks. You've got time to kill."

"That's funny," he said ironically. "I thought you were going to say 'You're not just someone. You're my husband.'" He stood up. "It's cold out here. I'm going back."

"Me too," she said. "There's a certain ritual we need to perform, to make this all perfectly kosher." She tried sounding lighthearted, but it didn't come off.

"Give me a couple hours," he said. "Then maybe we'll talk about it."

He left her standing on the beach, listening to the wind whistle around the ancient sea stacks and the sea birds squawking, squabbling, beating wing against wing.

IN THE bedroom doorway, she cradled her digital phone between her head and shoulder. No wonder she complained of neck pain. Since she kept calling the person on the other end of the line, "chief," she obviously was speaking to Olson. Richard disliked the term. Chief. He caught her eye, motioned her over, and when she stood beside him, he pressed against her. When she finished on the phone, she broke away from him, reached for her sweater, and shrugging into it, said, "This has just got to be related to the poachings. I can feel it in my bones. Something about those hoofprints." Strapping her boots, she continued her monologue. "It's going to be one rough day. We'll take the hounds out again, but after all that rain... We've got all these local volunteers to watch. You never know when a helper is a perpetrator in disguise. The Nighteagles' backgrounds have to be scrutinized, their personal lives, all their secrets. I hate that, digging up people's darkest secrets. Gad, just imagine if someone did that to you."

"God forbid." His voice felt thick coming from his throat. He showered, shaved, and when he came out of the bathroom she was gone. Apparently forgot about saying good-bye. He dressed and went out too, locking the door behind him.

SIX

Oplopanax horridum ("horrid, heavily armed cure-all") member of the Ginseng family. Common name, devil's club.

DEVIL'S CLUB

BOB BRIGHTMAN, a big man, leaned down and kissed his wife good-bye because she insisted on this daily gesture, however insincere. Bob wore a grim expression, not surprising since he was on his way to the sheriff's office again to volunteer more time in the search for Paris. Carolee watched her husband maneuver his Pontiac out of the trailer-park lot, straighten it, put on the left-hand blinker. Did the sheriff suspect Bob and her? Carolee wondered. Just because they lived next door? Would Sheriff Tobin turn them over to the feds because he knew Carolee, and sometimes Bob, too, flagrantly violated the law by harvesting wild plants on the federal preserve? Next thing you know, they'd be incarcerating Carolee, just like a common criminal, just for some puny little offense that didn't harm anything, really.

Wildcrafting.

Carolee saw Bob's eyes reflected in the rearview mirror. She waved until the big boat-car drifted left on Highway 101 and disappeared, then she went back inside and reheated her coffee in the microwave. Two minutes. And stand aside, because you're still fertile.

"Hi, Mom." Becca Brightman, chubby, fifteen, and too bright for her own good, appeared at the kitchen door, all disheveled, in a dumpy bathrobe.

At the microwave, Carolee said, "Becca Brightman, march back there to the bathroom and wash your face and brush your hair. I won't have a daughter of mine appearing at the breakfast table looking like something the tide washed in."

Becca muttered under her breath, shrugged sullenly, and moved to the back of the trailer. When she returned a few minutes later, Becca's hair was neatly brushed and pulled back into a ponytail, and her face shone from a good scrubbing. She had on clean blue jeans and a T-shirt that said, "k.d. lang is my mother." She'd had the T-shirt cus-tom-made. When Carolee saw the message emblazoned on her daughter's pubescent breasts, she slammed down the plate of micro-waved waffles she'd zapped for Becca, and said, "Just what is this all about?"

Becca shrugged.

"Answer me."

Becca reached into the fridge, teased out a can of Diet Pepsi, popped it open, swallowed a mouthful and, on the rebound, said, "I'm questioning my sexual identity."

Carolee gaped. "What's that mean?"

The girl shrugged sullenly. "I'm just identifying my feelings, that's all."

"About what? Be specific, Becca. Your feelings about what?"

Becca reached for a glass to pour the cola into, but Carolee jerked the glass out of her hand. Carolee said, "Answer me, Becca Bright-man."

Becca sighed. "I sort of, like, don't know, like, if boys or girls turn me on the most. I'm a little confused, Mom, but don't worry. I'm not a confirmed lesbian."

Carolee pursed her lips hard. "You're running with that Cravus girl again, after I told you not to. I won't permit that Misty Cravus in my home again, and you're to stay away from the Deans' trailer. Those people are no good."

Carolee handed the glass to Becca. Becca poured, answering her mother insolently. "Misty doesn't have anything to do with this, Mom. Don't blame everything on Misty and the Deans. You always blame things on other people. I'm sick of it."

Carolee sat down beside Becca. "That Daniel Dean is crazy as a loon in heat. I'll bet he's the one who took Paris. I won't have you going over to their trailer again, do you understand me?"

Becca shrugged, buttered a waffle, slathered jam on top of the butter, bit into it. "Anyway, everyone knows Paris got eaten by the Unknown."

Carolee made a face. "The 'Unknown'? What is that supposed to mean? The 'Unknown'?"

"That's what we call him."

"Who?"

"That's what Daniel Dean calls it. The creature who snatched the Nighteagle baby."

Carolee stood up. "Finish your waffles. You're already late." Carolee went back over to the microwave, slid her coffee mug in, heated it up again. Stood aside.

"Mom?"

"What, now?"

"I saw that thing that ate Paris. Out back behind the house. Last night."

Carolee fished her cup out of the microwave, came back to the table, sat down. "That was just a wild animal. Your father has been out there checking. He saw scat."

"What kind of scat?"

"He said it was elk."

Becca hugged her chest. "It looked sort of like an elk, but it was part man, too. What I saw out the window last night was half-man, half-elk, Mom. A beast."

Carolee set her coffee mug down hard. "Becca, you are to stop imagining things. It's not amusing. You just saw someone from the search party, that's all it was. Now, go and change your T-shirt before the bus gets here. I don't want to see that shirt on you ever again." Becca scraped her chair back, got up and skulked away.

Carolee carried her coffee out to the back yard. The forest and the whole grove surrounding the trailer park was crawling with Fish and Wildlife agents, forest rangers, sheriff's deputies, civilians, everyone frantically searching for a scrap of clothing, anything. Carolee sipped, staring into the woods behind the house. She saw Agent Diamond, that strangely androgynous creature, dressed all in black leather, small, pantherlike person with yellow hair. Definitely not a local. Bob said she was the agent in charge.

Carolee couldn't tell if Agent Diamond was watching her or just standing near the spot where Paris had disappeared and meditating. She decided Agent Diamond was watching her, so she turned, walked around the corner of her trailer where the blond panther couldn't see her, couldn't stare. Ever since Agent Diamond had taken Carolee's statement last night, Carolee hadn't liked her one bit. Definitely not the sort of person Carolee would confide in. Carolee wasn't stupid.

That afternoon, yesterday, she'd been harvesting *Oplopanax horridum,* devil's club, out along a creek bed behind the trailer park, up in the rain forest, where the boughs of giant conifers formed canopies above the fragrant forest floor, where even the least experienced wild-crafter could harvest a multitude of organically rich and nutritious fungi, healing lichens, roots, and tubers. As remote as the rain forest was, Carolee never worried about getting lost. She felt confident she knew every inch of the rain forest, as any wildcrafter working there must.

She'd gone a few hundred yards along an old mule trail to the soggy creek bed where the lucrative devil's club crop grew in rich, black mud. The plant's huge umbrella leaves had withered, its prickly thorns exposed. You don't harvest devil's club in summer when you can't see the thorns. They prick, and too, the plant's spines are toxic.

Devil's club bark was used by Northwest tribes for healing and cosmetic purposes. Puget Sound shamans used devil's club in their magic ceremonies, and some Coastal tribes made fishing lures from the plant's thorns. The Lummi burnt the bark, mixed it with bear grease to make black face paint. Like a prick from its spines, the plant's berries were toxic. Native tribes stripped off the thorns and spines and applied the plant's bark to various ailments, from common colds to breast-feeding maladies to unpleasant odors. In recent times, some herbologists had claimed devil's club was nature's most reliable cure-all. Other herbal healers wouldn't go near the stuff. It just depended on whom you believed. A panacea is impotent without faith.

Now the plant's thorns and bark lay exposed and Carolee began harvesting the crop. While she worked, the wind must have been blowing due easterly off the ocean, because she could hear Winn Nighteagle's ax in the distance, as it crashed against alder logs, splitting them. Then suddenly, between ax falls, she had heard a baby cry. She could tell the difference between babies' cries. She could tell it was one of the Nighteagle twins: She wouldn't swear to it, but was fairly certain. It wasn't Milan's high-pitched howl. It was Paris. Paris had an insistent cry, stronger than Milan's. This was definitely Paris's cry, but it wasn't coming from the trailer park. It came out of the forest, from a deeper place than where Carolee stooped over the devil's club. She heard branches breaking, and the baby crying. She hadn't known what to think, except that her sense of direction must have been all turned around. Then the baby's cry had faded into the distance, and Carolee had turned her concentration back to her work. About an hour later, when Carolee had moved out of the rain forest, back down the path nearer the trailer park, she noticed the ax had stopped chopping. Then she heard Winn's voice roaring over the stillness, sounding an alarm in her, chilling her bones, and the next thing she knew, Winn and Theresa came running up the path, breathing hard, frantic.

"Have you seen Paris?" Winn had shouted at her.

"No, Winn. But I heard him. Him crying."

Theresa said, "Where? Where did you hear him?"

Carolee thought a minute, then pointed deep into the forest, toward the north, toward Mount Hoh. "Up that way, I think. But maybe my sense of direction is off."

Winn and Theresa had plunged into the forest, leaving Carolee to stand and wonder what was going on. When Carolee returned to her trailer, Bob told her an elk had snatched Paris out of his crib in the yard behind the Nighteagle trailer. Some said it was a horrible beast who had carried Paris off. Some even claimed to have seen it running into the forest with Paris in its mouth. But Carolee had more intelligence than to believe that, and she made sure Agent Diamond knew how bright she was, that she had a degree in Natural Healing from the Franey Institute of Herbal Medicine in Kettle Falls, Washington.

Carolee exhaled and her breath came out in a cloud. She wouldn't be surprised if they had an early snowfall. That would put a kink in the search for Paris Nighteagle. Anyway, you had any sense at all, you'd know that baby was dead. Satan had come for that baby. That's what Carolee figured out. She was good at figuring things out, and she knew how to read the signs. The sign of the cloven hoof meant Satan had come round. That child was dead, sure as she was standing here today.

Somewhere in the trailer park, a telephone rang. Carolee focused on the sound until she could pinpoint where it came from. Her own kitchen. The telephone rang two more loud rings before she got there. It was Dr. Kellogg, her favorite client, calling long distance from Los Angeles.

"Oh, hi, Doc. You got back already?"

DR. BRADFORD KELLOGG gazed out his office window on Rodeo Drive. A couple of nice legs swished by, and his eyes tracked them. Morning eye exercises, he called it, ogling through his slanted Levolors. Into the phone, he said, "Yes, I took the red-eye flight last night. Carolee, I wonder if you could mix me up a fresh batch of

Formula Number Twenty-one. I've suddenly come up short, and I have a patient coming in next week who desperately needs it."

Carolee said, "Don't you worry about a thing, Doc. I can mix that up for you and send it at the post office." A pause, then, "Well, all right, if you want me to give it to your brother, I suppose I can, but Clint doesn't like doing business with me. Like I told you, he's competitive. Even though he is a rank amateur."

Dr. Kellogg laughed. "Don't worry, I'll make sure he pays you a fair price. Say, have they found the boy yet?"

"No, they haven't found the Nighteagle baby. And they won't. But it sure was nice of you to join in the search last night, being as busy a man as you are."

A few minutes later, Carolee visited Becca's bedroom. In a shabby pile on the floor, she found the k.d. lang shirt. Pinching it with two fingertips, she carried the shirt back into the kitchen and dropped it in the garbage can. k.d. lang. A mother figure, for cripe's sake.

THE AUTUMN SUN imparted thin light through a damp haze rolling off the ocean. A warm day by a native's standards, a dry, gentle day in the wake of the Pineapple Express. An ideal day to clean up after the storm, or to search for a missing child. By 9:00 a.m., most of the Nighteagles' trailer-park neighbors had come to volunteer again, and others, too, complete strangers. Agents Sweetwater and Mason tried in vain to interview each person who joined the search, but the word had spread like wildfire across the county, and everywhere people were searching for Paris Nighteagle. Rumors spread that a beast, half man, half elk, had carried off the child. "The Unknown," locals called it. Television and radio spots hyped the story of the Unknown and called for more volunteers. By noon, the countryside teemed with gun-toting posses calling out the baby's name, an eerie rondo that the autumn winds diminished.

Winn and Theresa returned to search the preserve, but Venus soon spotted the couple thrashing aimlessly at some vacant underbrush, recognized exhaustion, and ordered them off the search. "You'll just make it harder for us all, Mr. and Mrs. Nighteagle. I want you to go home and wait there. You've both been awake now for over twenty-four hours. Try to get some sleep."

Winn would've protested, but he saw how tired, how distressed Theresa was, and he led her back to the trailer and made her lie down. Theresa wouldn't go into the bedroom, so Winn made her lie on the couch, covered her over with an afghan, and gave her a pillow from their bed. Theresa thrashed around on the couch, her eyes wild, her voice quivering as she rattled off bizarre, unlikely scenarios that all featured Paris in a safe place, waiting for her to come for him. The grandmother, Frances Creed, came and took Milan to her house on the Hoh reservation, where Milan could get some attention and not be overwhelmed by her parents' distress. Just for a few hours. Winn hated Frances Creed.

Early in the afternoon, Theresa entered panic mode. Winn tried holding her down on the couch, but Theresa fought and struggled to her feet. "Goddamn it, somebody's got my baby," she shouted, "and nobody's goddamn doing a goddamn thing about it." She screamed and beat her fists against Winn's chest, and when finally exhausted, she looked at Winn's face. She saw him crying, and she, too, dissolved into a tearful, helpless state. They cried together for the first time in their married life, because this was the first time the Nighteagles had ever had reason to cry. Several times, one or the other of them would start out the door, intent on searching in all the same places, all over again, but each time, a federal agent helped the desperate parent back into the trailer, and ordered them to stay indoors and rest.

Winn wanted a drink. He'd been off whiskey and beer now for twelve years, since the day he married Theresa at St. Jude Mission up in Forks. As part of their personally composed marriage vows, Winn had promised to stay sober the rest of his life. But that didn't take into account the recent course of events. When your baby is missing and all you can think about is that some wild animal is chewing him to pieces, or some pervert is molesting him, then alcohol comes to mind. Each time the urge came, he thought of Paris and how Paris probably didn't have anything to drink, or eat. Everyone said that Winn in his middle age had developed a strong, forthright character. So Winn resisted.

In the afternoon, Gordon Toolong and some other men from the Hoh reservation drove into the trailer park, got out of Toolong's pickup truck, went inside the rusted pink trailer. Winn covered his face in his hands as Gordon Toolong reported that the men had scoured every inch of the reservation by vehicle and on foot, and had found nothing, no sign of Paris. Toolong promised that the men would go out again on horseback, after the ground had dried up, and search again. Winn thanked the men from the bottom of his heart, and so did Theresa. Toolong put a hand on Winn's shoulder, but no comforting words came to him.

SEVEN

FISH

The Bogachiel Indian Clinic outside Forks served hundreds of unemployed, underemployed, and destitute Native Americans each week. A decrepit, concrete-block, one-story building, the clinic housed twelve beds, a birthing center, and a surgery. The entrance was lit by two wall sconces, bare incandescent bulbs, each one hundred watts, each fading fast. Venus went inside, found a woman wearing white clogs and a nurse's uniform, and asked to speak to the physician on duty.

"There's only one physician at our clinic," she sniped. "That's Dr. Fish."

"Is he here now?"

"Dr. Fish is always here. Except between midnight and six a.m., when he goes out back to his cottage to sleep." She waved an arm. "Follow me."

Fish, a family practice physician, had recently completed a residency at Children's Orthopedic Hospital in Seattle. Now, Fish told Venus, he was repaying his federal government medical school loan by serving four years with the Bureau of Indian Affairs, assigned to Bogachiel clinic. In the second year of his tenure, Theresa Nighteagle, a twenty-nine-year-old female of Native American ancestry, was seen in the clinic for possible complications of her first pregnancy.

Fish recalled the prenatal examination, which indicated that the Nighteagle woman was pregnant with twins. Two distinct heartbeats. Amniocentesis wasn't performed, nor was a sonogram, since these procedures were not available at this federally financed clinic for impoverished indigent populations. The records indicated Dr. Fish examined Mrs. Nighteagle twice before the births, the second time being a brief visit when the patient was in labor. Dr. Fish had been interrupted to perform an emergency appendectomy on another patient, so a midwife and a couple of licensed practical nurses had actually delivered the twins.

The midwife reported no complications after normal deliveries. Both infants had had normal vital signs, as did the mother. At the parents' request, the male infant was circumcised. The mother and both infants, by all indications healthy and normal, were sent home that same afternoon. On their departure, the Nighteagle twins were presented with a case of Similac, a handy gift in the event the mother's milk failed.

The twins' birth certificates listed times of birth as 7:16 a.m. (Paris) and 7:23 a.m. (Milan).

Dr. Fish saw Mrs. Nighteagle on one occasion after the twins' birth, and on that last recorded visit, removed the patient's sutures and pronounced her milk adequate for the two sucklings. Some weeks later, according to Dr. Fish's meticulous notes, he received a telephone call from the mother, who described severe pain and swelling, and several large lumps that had formed in her breasts. He had called in a prescription to the Bartell's Pharmacy in Grays Harbor and, over the telephone, instructed the patient in the use of a breast pump. He recommended the Pump-eze brand.

Fish made Venus photocopies of the twins' medical records. The female infant weighed five pounds, two ounces at birth, was seventeen inches long, and bore no distinguishing birthmarks. Her vital signs were still normal at her postnatal examination, and she appeared to have perfect health with no signs of malformation or other defect.

The male infant, the firstborn, weighed four pounds twelve ounces at birth, was eighteen inches long, with normal vital signs and no evidence of malformation or other defect, although a small, round port-wine birthmark was evident on the outer side of the left foot just above the arch. The midwife, in her notes, had described the mark as a "beauty spot." During the male infant's postnatal examination, a slight arrhythmia was detected in his heartbeat, and Fish had made a note that this minor abnormality should be monitored. Arrhythmia was not unusual in infants, and most "grew out of it," nevertheless, in all cases, it should be monitored; the doctor had explained this carefully to Mr. and Mrs. Nighteagle on that postnatal visit to the clinic.

Fish's records indicated the infants had, at their six week checkups, received all the appropriate inoculations and vaccinations against diseases, had been given blood tests, producing normal results. The male infant, Paris, continued to manifest the faintest arrhythmia, but Fish wrote in the medical record that the child would most likely grow out of it. Beyond the curt details and orderly medical records, Dr. Fish believed he and his staff had little to offer the investigation.

Venus watched Fish struggle with an overstuffed file-cabinet drawer. When finally he managed to shove the medical records in and close the drawer, Fish said, "They keep promising us a new computer. We've only got one, and that's used by all of us. I can't keep all my records in there." He went over to the window and stared out from a shabby, cluttered, understocked concrete box into a verdant Sitka grove on the edge of Bogachiel preserve, where a brook slinked over its rock bed, potable mountain spring water lilting to the sea. He said, "I wish I could be more help."

She joined him at the window. He opened it slightly, moved over, shared the therapeutic view and the fresh air. The brook's gurgling melody sounded inappropriately joyful. Something anomalous about rocks and water and gravity. So capricious, yet so predictable. The little bridge crossing the brook was constructed from wood, curved like a Chinese bridge. Altogether a Zen experience. Every office should have such a tranquil view. She said, "Can you describe a normal nine-month-old child's physical and psychological state?"

Fish grimaced. "I could, but my personal opinion is that the boy is dead. Killed by a bear or cougar, or another carnivore native to the region. Cougar attacks are definitely on the rise. I treated two tourists last summer for cougar-related injuries. One broke her leg climbing a tree, and the other was in shock after being mauled by a stray cub." Fish shook his head thoughtfully. "At the very least, a baby alone in the forest during last night's storm would surely have suffered serious exposure trauma, if he wasn't killed by a falling branch."

"Why do you think that?"

Fish sighed wearily, an old man though he couldn't be over thirty-five, forty at most. "I'm not a native, obviously. I'm very much an outsider. I don't see and hear a lot of what goes on, and I'm not privy to gossip. But from my outsider's perspective, I'd say that a nine-month-old baby who disappears around here wasn't kidnapped. These people aren't that type. These are basically gentle, good-hearted, economically strapped folks. Not kidnappers. Their culture around children is very gentle, unless there's alcohol involved. And I seriously doubt any outsider would want to come all the way out here to the ends of the Earth to kidnap an Indian child." Fish shook his head. "Besides, there were the hoofprints, and I still say that by now the baby has succumbed to exposure or been eaten by animals. The mother's milk on his breath could have attracted wild animals."

"He was weaned. Both the twins were weaned."

Fish made a face. "Still, he could have crawled out of his crib and wandered into the woods. And I hate to say this, but I doubt you'll find even a trace of him. Of course, I'm no forensics expert."

Venus's eyes followed the snaking line of the brook. She said, "Could he really have crawled out of his crib?"

Fish shrugged. "It's likely. I can't say it definitely happened. But it's likely, unless the crib had very high bars that he couldn't climb over. I heard it was a bassinet."

Venus went to Fish's desk, laid her notebook down, drew a sketch of the boy's bassinet. Fish studied the drawing. "Definitely," said Fish. "I'm sure he could have crawled out by himself." He folded his arms across his chest. "Is this part of my official statement?"

Venus shook her head. "Your professional opinion about the incident, your conjecture on what took place, are entirely off the record. As a physician treating the native population, you may possess certain knowledge that law-enforcement folks like myself don't. I know this territory, Dr. Fish, but I don't live here seven days a week. What I know about is the flora and fauna, the marine life, the forest. You're in constant contact with the people. Anything you can tell me that might be related is off the record, but most welcome."

Fish nodded and went on. "Like I said before, this is a destitute population up here. Ironically, the people out here, the Native American population especially, are generally in better physical condition than the majority of Americans. Not much obesity. People live hard and live long, unless they get shot or stabbed to death in a fight. And there's a high suicide rate, especially among teenage males. Everybody out here has to work hard just to survive. Even the kids, even the infants. I'm not speaking of the tribe that owns the casino up at Whaler's Landing, but the natives out here along the Northwest coast. Over fifty percent of the population is either out of work or woefully underemployed. Decent jobs don't exist. They fish and shell for a living, or do odd jobs. They just eke out their lives from one day to the next.

"The Nighteagle couple are typical," he continued. "He's a woodsman, I gather, and she's an at-home mom. Their income level is probably just slightly below the average for this area. We're talking extreme poverty here. The worst disease? Alcohol and drugs. Whatever numbs the stark realities of life on a reservation, or in a remote trailer park for that matter, in this god-awful dismal climate. The natives who live off the reservation, like the Nighteagles, are probably worse off economically because they aren't subsidized by federal funds. The Nighteagles would be better off moving back onto the reservation. Still, they'd be dirt poor."

Venus said, "Why do they live off the reservation?"

Fish shrugged. "Could be any number of reasons. I think Winn Nighteagle is a Muckleshoot, from over by Puget Sound." He said it correctly, like a native Pacific Northwester. "Puget Sound," without the outsider's telltale misplaced article.

"Maybe a Muckleshoot can't live on Hoh land," ventured Fish. "Or maybe Nighteagle got thrown off the reservation for violating tribal laws. Or maybe they just wanted to live on the highway. There are any number of reasons for living off the reservation."

"Back to the child. What about curiosity? Could the baby have seen something, or just been intrigued by the forest and crawled out of his crib and into the woods?"

Fish considered. "Like I said, a nine-month-old Indian baby has to be strong to survive these living conditions. He could've crawled around looking for his parents, he might have gone searching for them and ended up in the woods. But that doesn't explain the elk prints. There are two or three scenarios I can think of, but they all lead to the same fate, I'm afraid. And don't forget that bad storm last night."

At the window, she watched as dusk fell over the forest scene. It seemed to happen all at once. Now, the brook water flashed black across its rock bed, the spruce trees receded into shadow. Now the sun slipped out of the forest, sank westward, over the ocean. Now the forest and all its creatures prepared for night.

"If he's out there, in the forest, is there any chance he's still alive?"

"It's been…what, over twenty-four hours since Paris was reported missing?" Fish shook his head. "Maybe he's alive, but not for much longer. Ninety percent says he's dead."

"That ten percent. Talk to me about that."

Fish folded his arms across his chest. "That's reserved for the unlikely event that he was snatched by someone and is being cared for. Even then, baby-snatchers aren't usually the greatest caregivers. I expect he'd become ill almost immediately."

Venus said, "His chart mentions a slight arrhythmia. Does he have a heart problem?"

Fish shook his head. "Nothing to worry about. The faintest irregularity. He'll grow out of it, I mean, he would, if he were still alive."

"I'm going to ask you one more question Dr. Fish, and then I'll leave you to your work."

Fish blinked, nodded, stuck a hand out inviting the inquiry.

Venus said, "Imagine for a moment that the hoofprints were faked by someone, and that Paris Nighteagle was kidnapped and is being held somewhere. Say his kidnapper isn't harming him, but is actually caring for his needs. What's going through the boy's mind right now?"

Fish checked his watch, said, "He's probably hungry for dinner."

"He's not terrified?"

"What's to terrify? If his captor is being gentle with him, he's probably doing just fine. A scenario I doubt, but in your hypothetical case, he's probably okay. Now, if the hypothetical captor is, say, a pedophile, and is molesting the child or harming him in any way, then you have a more serious situation. In that case, the boy is likely traumatized to the point of numbness. His system would shut down, beginning with his emotional state. His brain is still very vulnerable. Even if he weren't otherwise physically harmed, he could suffer serious brain damage, irreversible trauma. Let's hope that's not the case. He'd be better off dead."

She followed Fish down a cold, concrete-block corridor, past examination rooms out of which came the moans and cries of his suffering patients. She felt guilty for taking so much of his time. Over his shoulder, Fish said, "By the way, you should just call me Lawrence. Everybody does."

"All right, Lawrence. I'd like to continue our conversation later, when you're not so busy. When will you be off duty?"

"In one year, one hundred and thirty-eight days. But I'm taking appointments now."

"I'll phone you," she said. "Maybe I'll get lucky and sneak in before the crowds. How about tomorrow evening?"

Fish said, "The later the better."

THAT NIGHT, the honeymooners dined in silence. When she left Richard at the cabin, to rejoin the search, he was reading a book of poetry. Edna St. Vincent Millay, his favorite romantic poet. When she returned five hours later in the early hours of morning, Richard was fast asleep on the couch, Edna's poems resting on his chest.

EIGHT

THE CRAFT

ON TUESDAY MORNING, Clint Kellogg, best-selling author and wild-crafter extraordinaire, awoke in the dark confines of the luxurious bedroom in his tony bachelor pad overlooking the Pacific Ocean at Grays Harbor Beach. A dedicated wildcrafter, Clint always kept his clothes near his bed so that when the alarm clock went off one hour before dawn, he could dress under the covers where it was warm. Clint dressed, struggled into a pair of tall rubber boots, zipped up his goose down jacket, reached across the bed and the Abyssinian cat slumbering there, and plucked a woolen watch cap off the bedside table. Somehow the watch cap usually ended up on Luxor's side of the bed every morning. Clint tugged the cap over his sorrel curls and down around his ears, covering his forehead completely. With the heels of his palms, he rubbed his eyes until sleep fled and he could focus. When he shut the beach-house door behind him, the irritating sound stirred Luxor. The cat mewed. On the mantel, an antique French carriage clock struck five times. Not all men of leisure sleep late.

Crossing the dark deserted highway, Clint entered Bogachiel Wild-life Preserve. Moving quickly up an overgrown mule trail, his flash-light illuminating the way, he ascertained that no one had seen him enter the preserve, no one followed him. Already, a crimson lip marked the horizon and any minute dawn would break. The *Prunella vulgaris* had to be harvested before daylight fully arrived, before the buds closed up, which occurred at the crack of dawn. Clint could hear the crack of dawn, a unique talent possessed by few. He had never met another person who could hear the actual sound of dawn breaking, and he doubted he ever would. Not many humans were as sensitive to nature as he was, or as poetic.

This morning, even before the sun popped into the crevice between the two Brothers peaks, Clint felt the air's mysterious, invigorating embrace, what he called winter vapors. Winter was setting in early this year. Leaving the familiar mule trail, he plunged into an ever-green thicket, gloved hands first, protecting his face, and stepped gingerly to avoid disturbing the underbrush, the monkshood and win-ter fairy bells carpeting the rich black earth. Some wildcrafters tram-pled indiscriminately over precious seed beds, priceless plants. Locals, with no sense of the fragility of the environment. Being a progressive Californian, Clint knew better. Emerging on the other side of the thicket, he entered Goat's Meadow just as the cold sun rose between the peaks, washing the frigid slopes in golden splendor. He had to move fast now, before the sun completely emerged from behind the Olympic range, before the hedge-nettle and crazyweed saw sunlight, before the self-heal bent to dawn.

Prunella vulgaris. The market called it by its common name, self-heal. Their deep violet blossoms smudged a quivering purple blanket across the evergreen meadow, a lake of late-blooming flowers rippling in the morning breeze. The harvest would be rich this winter, thanks, Clint conjectured, to El Niño. Harvesting self-heal requires nimble fingers. Clint pulled off his gloves, rubbed his hands together, warm-ing them for action. Surveying the field of self-heal, he estimated the widely scattered blossoms covered almost an acre. The job would be tedious, and he'd have to work quickly, but if he concentrated and didn't pause to rest, he could harvest most of the crop before the sun popped whole over the mountain range. He reached into his pocket, fished out his mesh gathering bag, and waded into the gentle amethyst sea.

While he picked, Clint watched for federal agents. They'd been all over the preserve since yesterday, searching for the Nighteagle baby. Of course, they'd never find Paris Nighteagle, not in a million years. Anyone who knew this forest like Clint Kellogg did knew how easy it was to conceal a secret, no matter how many searchers flooded the woods. Bogachiel preserve's deep hollows, overgrown with giant ferns and underbrush, produced ideal conditions for hiding. You could even build a camp, live beneath the forest's voluminous vegetation, and never be discovered. There were caves and hollowed-out stumps where you could hide something. Or bury something, for instance, a human body. There was Elk Pond, where, if you weighted down a human body, you could submerge it in three hundred feet of still black glacier water. There was the moss-draped, labyrinthine rain forest, where arcane secrets of evolution had escaped humankind's grasp for thousands of years. They were wasting their time.

When the federal agent in charge of the case, Agent Diamond, had interviewed Clint yesterday morning, he'd lied through his teeth. He'd told her that he was at home watching football at the time of the child's disappearance, when actually he'd been on the preserve, back in the woods on the north edge of Elk Pond. Harvesting amanita mushrooms. You can't just blurt out certain incriminating details to law officers. In the report he signed for Agent Diamond, Clint stated he'd been home with his friend Marilyn, cooking Sunday dinner and watching Huskies football on the tube. No one would bother to check with Marilyn to verify this statement. Marilyn was a local who oozed insignificance, and people ignored her. And on that day, Marilyn had in fact been cooking their Sunday dinner, and Clint did come home at some point during the second half of the football game, so if someone did ask Marilyn to verify Clint's whereabouts, she'd probably say yes, he was at home with her, with insignificant Marilyn, when Paris Nighteagle got snatched from his crib. Clint had a credible story, a mostly truthful story, and besides, no one had ever suspected him of doing anything illegal. And today, nothing tied Clint to the Nighteagle kidnapping. Not a shred of evidence.

Clint worked the meadow, concentrating on the harvest, pushing these other thoughts from his mind. If he really focused on the harvest, he might complete it before the sun rose too high, before the blossoms pinched up against daylight. The owner of an herbal apothecary in Seattle had promised Clint a case of Chateau Petrus, 1982 vintage, in exchange for this rare bumper crop of *Prunella vulgaris*.

Not that prolific Clint couldn't buy his own French merlot. He could buy all the merlot in Provence on his book royalties alone. His recent book on eco-friendly stock market investments had made *The New York Times* best-seller list, and his agent believed his new book of fables was a sleeper, destined for glory. Clint didn't need anyone to buy him a case of French merlot, and he didn't practice the wildcraft for profit. Clint wildcrafted for the sheer love of nature, unlike Carolee Brightman and these other locals who practiced the craft out of financial need. Poor, uneducated, primitive folk.

The wind burned Clint's neck. He put a palm against the prickling flesh, skin like an armadillo's coat, and rotated his neck. Wildcrafter's neck.

What's that? He heard a thin, melodic sound. A high, light quiver, a siren's voice, like Debussy. Then he saw Theresa Nighteagle.

When she saw him, Theresa stopped singing Paris's favorite lullaby and moved down the steep slope, through the meadow toward him. The unromantic Clint Kellogg felt his blood pump, his senses heighten. What about her suddenly clutched his heart? Maybe compassion. Maybe the song. Theresa tripped over something and fell to the ground. Clint leaped to help her.

"Are you hurt?" Clint put his arms around her waist, hefted her up. She was light as snow. Her eyes met his, and he thought then that even in fear and grief, she was beautiful.

"I'm okay," she said. "That was clumsy of me." She stood on her own, brushed off her clothes, reached down and rubbed a slim ankle. On her feet, she wore soft brown leather boots. "I turned my ankle, but it's all right now." Theresa pointed across the meadow, up the slopes, toward the mountains and the sunrise. "I came over that slope," she explained. "I told those searchers to come up here to the higher meadows, but they won't listen to me." She studied Clint's face. "Why aren't you helping us look for Paris?"

Clint removed his cap, rubbed his forehead. "I'm sorry. It's this harvest…" Immediately, he realized the absurdity of this excuse. Prodded by a pang of guilt, he said, "Can I help you look for him?"

Theresa gazed at Kellogg, trying to decide if she could trust him. Finally, she said, "All right. Then we'll go up to the high prairies and look up there." Abandoning his harvest, Clint took Theresa Nighteagle's arm. As they headed up the slope, she said, "The doctor put me on pills. I'm a little spacey, Clint."

Hiking northeast along the trail, Clint followed Theresa's lead, wading through a field of sawgrass, pawing through every clump, every burrow. Overhead, the search helicopter churned into view. Below them, search parties scoured the forest edges. Theresa said, "I want to check the old Perkins barn."

The roof had caved in and the barn cramped sideways. They didn't go inside right away, but stood still and listened to a trilling sound. Suddenly, a pigeon flapped its wings and flew out of the barn, nearly colliding with Theresa. Her hand flew up in defense. The pigeon veered off, flapping something awful, circling her. Clint batted at it, but the bird kept circling. Theresa ducked inside the barn. Thin autumn sunlight streamed through the broken roof, washed the barn floor. Maybe in here, she'd find a scrap of clothing, or a bootie. Two days ago, when he disappeared, Paris had been wearing those red booties that Theresa herself had knitted from new wool. Red booties with little red pom-poms.

The pigeon followed her inside the barn, and she watched it fly into the eaves, where, no doubt, it had a nest. There was more trilling, louder now, as several pigeons beat wings against the eaves. Theresa stepped out of the sunbeam into a dark corner of the barn. Reaching into her pocket, she pulled out a flashlight, shone it into the blackness. A startled rat stared back at her. She made a hissing sound and the rat scurried away. She stepped into the rat's nest and searched with her free hand through matted hay. The hay tickled her nose. She sneezed into her sleeve and pawed through the damp, gnarled grass. From the barn door, Clint was watching Theresa's graceful body, the way it moved, its intrinsic seductive language, when Carolee Brightman came up behind him and exclaimed, "My God, you guys scared the life out of me."

Clint had met Carolee in the woods, at the markets. She always horned in on his business. She'd even stolen a couple harvests right out from under him. Clint considered Carolee a stupid and superstitious person, unworthy of a greeting.

Carolee approached Theresa, placed a hand on her hunched shoulder, and said gently, "Honey, Paris isn't in here. I've already been up here and looked." She borrowed Theresa's flashlight, and aimed its beam at the rafters where a frilly gray-green fungus grew on the underside. "That variety's worth eighty dollars a dry pint." She handed the flashlight back to Theresa, clambered up a rickety ladder to scrape off the lichens and place them in a canvas gathering bag. When she came back down, Theresa was shining the flashlight at the pigeons' nests, sending the birds into a frenzy of wild flapping and shrieking.

"Now, why did you do that?"

Theresa said, "I hate pigeons."

Carolee tossed the bag of lichens over her shoulder. "I'll go down now, and help look for Paris. You better come down too, honey. They'll be looking for you."

Theresa nodded, but her heart wasn't in it. Clint sucked his teeth, made a face at Carolee. "You just go on, now, Carolee. I'll take care of Theresa."

The pale sun cast its thin shadow across the field. A cold wind came up and Theresa shivered. Clint placed an arm around her. Halfway down the mountainside, they paused on the rim of the high prairie, stared at the sky as two Stealth Bombers screamed overhead, scraping parallel white lines across the blue void. The jets shot southeast, growing smaller until they evaporated into the atmosphere. The solid white contrails lingered, and Theresa watched them break up and fade.

"Take my hand, Clint," she said. He obliged, and together they walked along the prairie's rim. Below, the squiggly highway ran parallel to Toleak Beach, the sea stacks, and the big sand bar where everyone dug for clams, where Paris loved to play in the putty sand, where the raging tide made Paris shriek with sheer delight. They didn't speak, just walked side by side, stopping every few yards to inspect a suspicious clump of bushes, prod a gopher hole, study a shard of something that glinted in the sunlight. Near the end of their downhill journey, she turned to him and he saw the tears coming and so reached out and pulled her to him. She wept, her tears staining his jacket. When she finished, he gave her his cotton handkerchief and she wiped her swollen eyes.

At Toleak, they headed down into the preserve and followed the old logging trails to the highway, entering the road a few yards from the trailer park, where searchers still combed the underbrush. Theresa looked at Clint and attempted a smile, but it fractured into anguished gratitude. Clint held her again, stroked her hair. "Don't give up," he whispered. "Don't ever give up. I'll always be here for you, Theresa." She broke away from him and ran to find Winn.

AT TOLEAK LODGE, people gossiped. In the restaurant, Clint could hear them talking about the beast that carried off the Nighteagle baby. Half man, half elk. A terrible, frightening creature. The Unknown. Somebody ought to hunt it down, kill it. Who would be brave enough? Clint was ordering breakfast when Carolee Brightman approached the table, materializing from nowhere like she often did. Clint looked up, said, "To what do I owe this distinctly unpleasant surprise?"

Carolee plunked a small package, wrapped in plain brown paper, on the table. "That's for your brother."

Clint sighed and slid the package across the table until it rested near his coffee mug. Carolee flicked her unruly hair over her shoulder and sat down. "Clint, honey, you need my vitamin cocktail. You look gaunt. Where's the waitperson, anyway?"

When breakfast came, Carolee speared a sausage link, bit it sideways, chewed it. Smacked her lips and said, "You can't be a wildcrafter. You're too urban. Don't have the instinct for it. Wildcrafters need a natural infinity for the forest."

"Affinity."

"That's what I said. And we need nimble hands for harvesting." She gestured with one bony hand. "Your fingers are too short."

"Shut up, Carolee."

They finished breakfast in silence, surrounded by the gossipy wagging tongues.

Outside, in the parking lot, Carolee said, "I talked to Brad this morning. He told me about your little problem. You guys need a spiritualist. You can't resolve this issue without a spiritualist."

"Well, Brad shouldn't have told you about that, Carolee. That's our business."

A smarmy grin crossed Carolee's face. "I'm discreet. How about you? Are you discreet?"

IN THE CHAOS, in her Valium haze, Theresa didn't notice Clint Kellogg turn up at the trailer park that afternoon. Carrying a backpack, he signed up for the search. Theresa sat inside her trailer, along with some federal agents. He could see them through the window. He saw Agent Diamond. Through the window, her eyes met his, and he felt another pang of conscience. He shouldn't have lied to her about where he was, what he'd been doing. Now it would be too embarrassing to admit he'd lied, to come out with the truth. Better just to let it go.

Clint walked along toward the Brightman trailer. As he passed the Brightman's kitchen windows, he saw the girl, Becca, seated at a table, maybe doing her homework. She glanced up. Clint motioned to her. Becca got up from the table and went outside to where Clint stood at the edge of the woods. He was holding a book in his hand. He held it out.

"It's fables," he said.

Becca studied the book's cover. "It has your name on it."

Clint smiled. "I'm a talented man."

Becca stared. "You wrote this book?"

Clint nodded.

"Get out. I thought you were just a wildcrafter like my mom. I didn't know you wrote books."

Clint smiled. "I play around at the craft. But my profession is writing." He nodded at the book she held. "This is my latest effort. And my favorite."

Becca read the title out loud. "*Fables of the Rain Forest*. Is this a children's book?"

"It's for all ages. You should always read fables out loud."

Becca hugged the book. "Thanks, Mr. Kellogg."

"Call me Clint. And Becca, don't tell anyone I gave you this. Don't tell your mom."

"Okay, Clint. Thanks for the book."

ON BOGACHIEL PRESERVE, Clint moved swiftly, sure-footed up a sloping bank, over the other side, down into a sunlit glade. A light mist lingered over the glade, filtering the sunlight. On the water's surface, gnats darted in and out of the jack-in-the-pulpits. Clint heard frogs and crickets, and the occasional red thrush, all competing for the gnats. At the edge of the water grew a cluster of wood's ear mushrooms. An unexpected bounty, but Clint was prepared. He pulled a plastic bag from his pocket, stepped gingerly through the marshy glade. Harvesting the mushrooms, he worked swiftly, beating off the gnats that surrounded his head. Once, he saw a red flash when the tongue of a glade frog snapped up a gnat. He paused, fumbled in his jacket, took out a piece of paper, a pen, and wrote something down. Maybe a romantic thought, maybe something profound. Then he went back to harvesting the fungi. When the last mushroom was in his bag, he stood up straight and looked around just in time to see a bull elk meander into the glade. A beauty. Seven points on the antlers. The huge elk bent down, lapped up water, sending the gnats into a tizzy. When it had enough to drink, it straightened up, gazed across the glade at Clint, who raised his hand, put two fingers in his mouth and whistled sharply. Startled, the elk dove into the woods. Clint waited a minute, smiled ironically to himself, then followed in the animal's hoofprints.

THE SIGN READ: GAS, FOOD, FISHING LURES, ESPRESSO. The place was called Rick's, a glorified all-night truck stop in downtown

Forks. When Venus had phoned Fish earlier, he'd suggested they meet at Rick's. Now Fish slid into the booth. "You just caught me," he said, "on my way out the door." He removed his jacket, hat, and gloves. He shivered. "This dank climate shoots right through my bones."

Venus said, "Do you treat anyone else from Cedar Grove Trailer Park? Besides Mrs. Nighteagle and the twins?"

"Most of them. Medicaid patients, welfare cases. I'm not at liberty to discuss anyone's medical history, though."

"I was wondering what else you might know about them, things you could talk about without breaching confidentiality."

Fish ordered a Beck's. When he sipped, he held one pinkie out. She couldn't read his mind, but guessed he was sorting out what to say. Finally, he set his glass down and said, "That's a peculiar community over there at Cedar Grove. The Nighteagles are probably the only really normal people there. The others are basically dysfunctional individuals whose battered old trailers will be their coffins."

"Does that include the Polk couple?"

"Lee and Irene?" Fish shrugged. "They're eccentric, if any rural person can really be termed eccentric. Irene's a wildcrafter, like a lot of them in that trailer park. They're people who harvest wild herbs and mushrooms and shoots and so forth, sell them to companies that manufacture herbal medicines and organic products for health-food nuts. She's one of them. She's fairly weird."

"Example?"

"Folks around here say Irene belongs to a wiccan. I don't know if that's true or not. And I guess these days, wiccans aren't all that esoteric. But don't let that stoop fool you. Irene Polk's a healthy old gal. She could prance around a bonfire with the best of them."

"What else?"

Fish shook his head. "That's really all I know about the Polks. Just, they're weird, in my opinion. Irene Polk is very primitive in her thinking. The Hippocratic oath prevents me from going any further than that."

"Osteoarthritis? Is that what causes her stoop?"

Fish nodded.

"What about the Brightmans, the family living next door to the Nighteagles?"

Fish's mouth pursed. "Your typical mixed-race couple. Brightman's a dull, macho white guy, his wife's part Anglo, part Quinault.

They've got a teenaged daughter who's very bright, but I'm afraid she doesn't stand a chance in hell of escaping this backwater. She'll most likely end up pregnant, unmarried, on welfare. Too bad. She's got a good brain.''

"In their statements, the parents said that he's a truck mechanic working night shifts, and she's a natural healer.''

Fish said, "Bob's a mechanic. Carolee would never tell you, for fear of being arrested, but she's a wildcrafter and she's harvesting on the wildlife preserve. Bob is too, but Carolee's the real expert. Probably the most successful wildcrafter on the peninsula. These little health-food companies are always seeking her out, buying from her.'' Fish shook his head. "If you guys don't put a stop to all that wildcrafting, before you know it, this whole peninsula will be stripped bare. I don't understand why they can't just cultivate their own farms, grow the stuff themselves, instead of stripping the parks and preserves.''

Venus said, "Some wildcrafters have their little farms. I saw a small herb garden out behind the Polk trailer. But you can't cultivate a lot of the species they harvest. They'll only grow in the wild, in a perfectly balanced ecosystem.''

"Well, they should be arrested.''

She said, "We do the best we can. In case you haven't noticed, the federal treasury isn't exactly overflowing with funds earmarked for environmental protection.''

Fish snorted. "Or for health programs for the indigent.''

She said, "What about the Deans, the couple who live next door to the Polks?''

"Now, there's a tragic case of bad seed. She's a wildcrafter. He's a louse. You met them?''

"Briefly. They volunteered in the search last night.''

Fish said, "How about Cindy Dean's little sister? Did you meet Misty Cravus?''

Venus said, "I didn't actually meet her. One of my agents took their statements.''

She thought she could trust Fish, the physician, the outsider. She said, "Something about Daniel Dean's statement didn't jive.''

Fish seemed to come alive. "Really?''

"Dean said he was away from home when the boy disappeared. Says he was doing some work for a man named Clint Kellogg.''

"The writer.'' Fish nodded. "Clint throws awesome parties.''

"There's a hole in Dean's story."

Fish raised an eyebrow.

"Dean says he was at Kellogg's home all afternoon the day before yesterday. Sunday. Only problem is, I personally took a statement from Clint Kellogg yesterday morning. He was one of dozens of volunteers in the search party. Kellogg's statement fails to mention Daniel Dean. Kellogg states he was at home with a lady friend, just the two of them, watching the football game, getting ready to sit down to dinner."

"Interesting. Have you confronted Dean with this?"

"I'm waiting for some more information."

Fish sat back, folded his arms across his chest. Venus said, "I wonder if you would help me assess a suspect's mental state."

"I'm not a psychiatrist."

"But you've had some training, in medical school?"

"Not that much. But if you just want another opinion, sure, I guess I can help you out."

"Thanks. First, I have to identify a suspect."

Venus stood, tossed some money on the table, got up. Fish followed her outside into the dark street. Forks, Washington, doesn't exactly jump at midnight on Tuesdays. A light mist fell, and the temperature had plunged. When she spoke, Fish could see her breath.

"By any chance, did you treat the Gecko's victim?"

"Gecko, gecko..." Fish searched his mind.

"A nine-year-old girl alleges she was molested on the preserve by a man named Branson, who had a gecko tattoo."

"Oh, that. Yes, I did examine her. She was definitely molested. Not raped in the clinical sense, but molested. She told me the man had a gecko tattooed on his arm. At the time, her mother wanted the incident kept confidential. Then on Sunday for some reason the mother filed a report over at your Port Angeles station. So then I sent a report of the medical examination I performed on the daughter. That's all up at Port Angeles, I guess."

"Actually, it's already made its way to our Seattle headquarters. Did you get DNA samples?"

Fish shook his head. "Nothing solid like that. Just the girl's statement, and a few scratches on her arms."

Venus said, "You think the Gecko's involved in the boy's disappearance?"

Fish considered. "Maybe. He could be, come to think of it. What he did to that girl was pretty sick. Could be."

"What ties him to a baby's kidnapping?"

Fish scratched his nose. "I don't have any plausible theories. I might be jumping to conclusions in my wish to help you out."

She said, "Do you have a fax number? In case I need to reach you with information?" He gave it to her. "By the way," she added casually, "what's a typical mixed-race couple like?"

Fish looked chagrined. "Oops. I think I just failed PC class."

She said, "I appreciate your time. I know you're very busy."

Fish stuck out his hand. "Don't mention it. I've rather enjoyed your company. It's like having a friend from the real world. I feel like an alien up here."

Venus shook the doctor's hand. "Me too, Lawrence."

EVEN BEFORE she opened the cottage door, she knew Richard was gone. Bag and baggage. An ugly, sinister pall had replaced him. The hearth was stone-cold, like her. She found his note on the kitchen table. Short and sweet. "Venus, I've headed back to Seattle. Caught the bus. Maybe it's best we don't talk until you're ready to come home. Keep safe. And dry. Love, Richard."

NINE

JACKPOT

THE DAYS dragged by with no sign of Paris, not even a baby's hand- or footprint to call a lead, except, on the ground near the baby's bassinet, the elk hoofprints, but that might be coincidental up here in Roosevelt elk country. Or, it might be a trick. Why would an elk snatch up a human infant?

Richard didn't call, and Venus refused to call him. How could he desert her under these circumstances, when she needed him? Or was she the selfish one?

ELK ARE OF the Order *Artiodactyla*, or cloven-hooved mammals, and are the second-largest member of the deer family, outsized only by the moose. Elk are socially gregarious, communicating via bugling sounds, whistles, squeals, and a sort of barking noise. If frightened or alarmed, elk communicate through body posture and scent. Bull elk measure about five feet tall from hoof to shoulder, can weigh as much as a thousand pounds, and can grow up to eight feet long. Each spring, bull elk grow antlers which they use to indicate dominance. Elk rarely use their antlers in a confrontational manner, although if charged or otherwise attacked, a bull elk can joust with the best of opponents, and might gore his attacker. The antlers on a bull elk can weigh as much as forty pounds. Old antlers are shed each spring and the new antlers begin to grow immediately.

Elk cows and calves form loose herds, except during calving season, when a female will go off by herself to drop the calf. About one in three hundred elk births are twins. Bulls travel in roaming bands, except during the rut. Humans are an elk's main enemy, followed by wolves and mountain lions, and occasionally, the grizzly. In defense posture, elk often flail their hooves.

Washington's Olympic Peninsula is home to a unique elk species: the Roosevelt Elk, named after Theodore Roosevelt, who, in 1909, decreed that a large portion of the Olympic Peninsula be set aside and preserved to protect the native species. The Roosevelt is the largest elk, a herd animal with precise social habits that change according to season and an individual's age. Roosevelts have migrated as far north as British Columbia and as far south as Northern California. They are shy creatures and rarely spotted. The best place to spot the Roosevelt during autumn is at timberline, although elk forage year round in the lower meadows and forests on the national park and surrounding wildlife preserves. The Roosevelt is vegetarian, surviving primarily on plants like sword fern, but, being more finicky than humans, it generally avoids fungi.

The temperate rain forests of the Olympic Peninsula have for centuries provided sustenance and lush cover for the Roosevelt, but since the nineteenth century's logging-boom era, the Roosevelt's natural habitat has shrunk drastically; now the Roosevelt is primarily limited to protected government preserves, and Olympic National Park.

Elk are ungulates, or hooved animals, with a "split" hoof of two equal-sized toenails. Elk hooves are composed of keratin, solidified hair, the identical substance that forms human fingernails. The hoof's outer rim is much harder than its central portion and, in winter, the softer central portion retracts and the hoof becomes concave in shape, all the better for traction on rough surfaces. Evolution didn't factor in paved highways, though, and on hard, smooth surfaces like paved roads, the contraction works against the elk, causing many a fatal road accident. From spring through autumn, the elk hoof is convex, and the outward bulge gives spring to the elk's stride. Like human fingernails and toenails, elk hooves grow continuously. The hooves are naturally manicured by abrading against rocky surfaces and hard ground.

Tracking elk is easy once you've learned to read their distinctive hoofprints. The cloven track is sharp-edged when fresh, rounded when laid before the last rain. As wind disturbs the soil or sand, the edges soften even more. If you spot an elk hoofprint containing bits of debris, you can be sure the elk passed before the last strong wind. Bulls' hooves, sometimes as wide as eight inches across, tend to leave drag marks in freshly fallen snow. Cows step higher. In snowfall exceeding one inch or so, all elk and deer leave drag marks.

Venus ducked under the yellow tape, bent over the distinctive tracks. The hoofprints were definitely those of a large bull elk. Still partially visible, they formed a disconcerting random pattern, as if an elk had danced around the bassinet, sometimes on two hind legs. Once again, she tracked them into the woods, under the heavy tree canopy, where the prints were sharper, deeper, where they hadn't been worn down by the storm, and followed the prints into the forest, along an old logging trail, where they eventually veered off into a thicket and faded away in the brambles. Who, or what, had made these prints? She stood still and listened. Magnificent silence, a quietude experienced only on Earth's few remaining sanctuaries, and, possibly, in outer space.

The heavily forested preserve, with its alpine meadows, its rain forest, woodland glades, and wind-battered ocean beaches, is native territory to more than three hundred species of birds and over seventy species of mammals, many of which are unique to the Olympic Peninsula. More than twelve hundred plant species dwell here among thousand-year-old conifers, their rich nutrients providing food and forage. On the peninsula's Pacific Ocean beaches, a national marine sanctuary protects habitat for seabirds, clams, salmon, octopus, crab, and the world's most diverse collection of whales and dolphins. From snowcapped peaks to wildly turbulent tides, the northwestern Olympic Peninsula is more suited to native species than to encroachers. But encroachers came, and they left their careless marks. Bogachiel itself, the entire forest and beach preserve, had at the hands of humans become an endangered ecosystem, heedless progress leaching from all sides.

Each day for five days, from dawn to dusk, Venus combed the preserve, and each evening at sunset, she emerged from the forest, equally amazed at its splendor and infuriated by its hushed, taciturn tranquility. At night, she labored in the operations room, poring over maps, planning the strategy for the next day's search. She sent the others out in groups, but she always went alone, because she preferred tracking in silence. In her formal training, she'd learned to track bear, deer, mountain lions, cougar, every species of every order. But her best training as a tracker had come from Olson, the irascible Humpty Dumpty, the chief. Olson knew tracks like most people knew televisions ad jingles; he could rattle off the fine details in his sleep. Olson had taught her to always track alone, and she remembered that lesson now whenever in the distance she heard sounds of a search party.

On the fifth day of the search, Al Yamada waited for her in the operations room. Dawn was just breaking over the preserve, and a light mist fell. Yamada said, "You better look at this."

Yamada had recreated the elk hooves' "dance" around the bassinet. This elk was no Arthur Murray. The hooves made impulsive twists and turns, as if the creature had been intoxicated, or gone mad. After she'd studied Yamada's sketch, he said, "I showed this to Olson. He says he wants you to start carrying your Magnum. He says someone reported that you're going out there armed only with your Wessie."

"That's all I need."

Yamada protested. "These prints were almost certainly made by a bull elk. And this bull is crazed. You need that thirty-ought Magnum out there."

Some bull elk antlers measure as wide as forty-seven inches. The rack, as hunters call antlers, is a hunter's pride, a measure of macho, and killing a bull elk is a big-game hunter's dream. Big-game hunters come in all genders, with women increasingly joining in the sport. It takes a big gun and powerful bullets to kill a bull elk. A .300 Winchester Magnum with a Swift A-Frame or Nosler Partition bullet is ideal for the job. Swift A-Frame bullets can pierce bone while retaining their lethal mushroom shape. On a broadside shot, any heavy-duty bullet can puncture an elk's rib. Most hunted elk are hit angularly and often struck at the shoulder bone. The bullet must penetrate the elk's thick hide, and several inches of rib and muscle. A big-game hunter knows that a wounded elk can attack, and that the bull's antlers are great for goring its enemy. Still, with the sophisticated weaponry on today's firearms market, an elk doesn't stand much chance against the big-game hunter, unless it's close enough to flail with its hooves. Then it leaves dancing hoofprints.

Yamada waited for her reply. All she said was, "I'm not hunting elk. I'm hunting something much more dangerous." She drove back to the preserve, to the dismal, dreary work of gathering sparse, elusive evidence. In the Land Rover, she took out her phone, made the call she'd been stubbornly avoiding. She heard her own recorded voice say, "You have reached the home of newlyweds Richard and Venus. Can't talk now, we're on our honeymoon."

She aborted the call without leaving a message.

ON THE SIXTH DAY of the search, all the sheriff could say was that this wasn't his jurisdiction, that this forest preserve was federal land

and he couldn't spare his deputies anymore. Same with the state troopers. So if they didn't find Paris before the week was out then it would be left up to the federal agents who managed all this land surrounding Cedar Grove Trailer Park. On Sunday evening, as dusk fell and the search parties disbanded, Winn felt a horrible sickness in his gut, and a violent fury seared his chest. He felt as if the entire world was deserting him, as if all the excitement of the event had worn off so people weren't interested anymore in searching for Paris. For days, Winn and Theresa had cried together, had grieved. Their sobs were heard all over the trailer park at night. Winn's despair had hung out for everyone to see, to hear. Winn wasn't ashamed but still he hated sharing it with everyone, especially total strangers. It didn't feel right. It felt womanish to cry so loud that other people heard you.

Most of all, Winn felt so alone he could no longer face Theresa. He resented Theresa's holding on to a fantasy that Paris would be found alive and safe. He hated the federal agents, especially the white woman in charge, who seemed too fragile for this work and too cerebral. He didn't trust her or any of the government agents. He felt completely alone in his despair, so it didn't surprise Winn, or anyone else, for that matter, when Sunday night, he showed up plastered at the casino on the highway up by Whaler's Landing. What did stun everyone though, including Winn himself, was that on this one-week anniversary of his son's disappearance, Winn Nighteagle hit the big jackpot on a one-armed bandit, making him instantly rich.

When they came with the champagne and his check, who should be standing there to congratulate him but Clint Kellogg, the white wildcrafter who people said wrote books. Kellogg wanted to buy Winn a drink, but Winn just cashed in his big jackpot and fled into the rainy night. He'd never live down the guilt of that big bonanza, coming on the heels of Paris's death. For that's what Winn now believed in his heart, that his only son Paris was dead.

ONCE THE RAIN STOPPED, the rich, black, insatiable earth swallowed its remnants and almost immediately sent up new shoots. In the darkness, Winn gazed out the trailer window. Beside him in bed, Theresa slept, clutching baby Milan. The baby had a habit of blowing bubbles, even in her sleep. Winn could hear the soft popping and when he turned to look at her face in the moonlight, he could see her little mouth working, blowing up little clusters of milky bubbles. Winn looked at Theresa. Even asleep she frowned and grief distorted her features. She looked old, Winn thought, old and haggard, and he wondered if that was a result of the drugs Dr. Fish had prescribed to help her sleep, or if Theresa had actually aged that much during the past week. He wondered if she would ever regain her youth, or if life was so unfair, it had robbed it forever.

What if he told her? Would his big jackpot thrill her, or would it turn her stomach, like it did his when all the lights and bells went off? Winn lit a cigarette. Lately he'd started smoking again. He inhaled. He picked up the check made out in his name for two hundred ten thousand thirty-three dollars. He'd never felt such smooth, velvety paper. He'd have to drive into Grays Harbor tomorrow, find a bank, open up an account. He'd have to deposit the check and order a checkbook. There'd be taxes to pay, then whatever was left was his to keep. To spend. From now on he'd pay for everything by check. Keep track of his spending. He knew what Theresa would want to do with the money. Spend it on the search. In Winn's mind, that would be futile. Money can't produce your kid if he's dead. Before he'd gone out and got drunk and rich, a forest ranger had called to tell Winn and Theresa that a scrap of clothing had been found in the woods. There was blood on the scrap, they were pretty sure it was a scrap of cloth diaper. They told Theresa over the phone that it looked like some wild animal had snatched the baby, eaten him alive. Theresa laughed bitterly and said it couldn't have been Paris's diaper. Paris didn't wear cloth diapers. Paris wore Pampers.

A POUNDING FIST crashed against the trailer door, rattled the walls, and shook Winn awake. He pulled on his jeans, brushed hair out of his face, went to the door. Carolee Brightman, still in her house robe, stood there in the rain.

"You better come now, Winn," she cried. "Bob 'n them's over at the Fish and Wildlife office. They found something up in the forest, way back by Elk Pond. They were hunting up there and they found it. They took it to that Agent Diamond."

Winn grabbed Carolee's shoulders and gripped hard. "What? What did they find?"

Carolee started crying. "Hurry, Winn, go over there to Fish and Wildlife. You gotta talk to them."

She broke free, ran back through the drizzling rain. Winn watched her run across the muddy ground toward her trailer. He yelled, "Goddamnit, what was it?"

Carolee stopped running. She turned around. Her house robe flapped in the wind. Her hair blew everywhere. She opened her mouth and in a tight, strained voice cried, "It was the remains. Bob 'n them found a baby's heart."

Winn heard a noise behind him. He turned around. Theresa lay crumpled on the floor.

Later, after Milan woke up, Winn fed her breakfast. Theresa sat at the table, holding the cordless phone. From across the table, Winn could hear a voice crackling through the receiver but couldn't make out the words. Theresa interrupted the voice.

"I don't give a good goddamn what you think, Agent Diamond," she barked into the phone. "Tell me exactly what Bob Brightman found up there at Elk Pond."

The voice crackled some more. Milan blew bubbles with her food and Winn shoveled some more mush into her mouth. Theresa said, "That's a goddamn lie and you know it. I don't care if you are from the government, I don't have to believe anything you say."

Winn looked at Theresa. She shook her head, curled her mouth into a sneer. He'd never seen her do that with her mouth. She said, "You are full of shit, all of you. My baby is not dead. He's out there somewhere, and you goddamn well better find him."

The voice crackled some more. Theresa wiped her face on her arm. Into the phone, she shouted, "What are you talking about? Just who the hell do you think you are?"

Winn kept feeding the baby, listening. The cereal globbed all over Milan's face and hands and now was getting in her hair. Her bib was spattered with mush and applesauce. The baby looked disgusting. Winn heard Theresa say, "Well, I don't know about that. My husband didn't say anything about that."

When Theresa hung up the phone, Winn said, "Bring me a wet rag."

Theresa brought the rag and wiped off Milan's sticky face and hands. In a quiet voice, she said, "That white woman says it's part of a human heart." She smoothed Milan's hair across the crown of her head. "They still have to test it to be sure."

Winn grimaced.

"Anyway," added Theresa, "it has nothing to do with Paris."

Even though he wanted to say something, Winn kept quiet. Theresa continued, "He's alive, and he's okay. We just have to find him, that's all."

The trailer's front door groaned open. Theresa's mother stepped inside. Frances Creed had on a rain parka and rubber boots. She came into the kitchen, plucked Milan out of her highchair, carried the baby into the front of the trailer. Theresa reached across the table and shook a cigarette out of Winn's pack. She lit it, inhaled. After a minute, she said, "Now, what's this about you winning over at the casino?"

Winn showed Theresa the check.

If you could read anything from the way she held her mouth a little sideways, you'd say she looked disbelieving, like somebody was playing a stupid joke on her. But gradually, the lines in her face smoothed out and for a brief moment, a glimmer of an idea sent her eyes dancing. She opened her mouth as if to say something, then the glimmer died out of her eyes. She curled her lip and said, "That's trash, Winn. Tear it up. That's evil money."

Winn put the check away. He wanted to protest that there was no such thing as evil money, but he stayed quiet. He wasn't about to tear up the check. Theresa might be angry now, and disgusted with him for going on that drunken binge last night and then winning all that money, all because Paris was missing. She might be mad now, but sooner or later, she'd see the bright side of the jackpot.

Theresa said, "And you're drinking again."

Winn's foot tapped against the floor. He looked at his wife and said, "Don't start now, Tee. Please."

Theresa shoved her chair back, stood up.

Winn looked up at her. "Where are you going?"

"To find Paris."

She left by the back door, disappearing into the woods and the drizzling rain.

TEN

LOOKOUT

BECCA BRIGHTMAN raised her hand in class. When the teacher asked what she wanted, Becca requested that she be excused to go to the rest room. Walking along the high school corridor, Becca looked around to be sure no one was watching, and ducked out the first exit door. On the highway, Becca hitched a ride with a nice woman going to the shopping mall in Grays Harbor. The woman dropped Becca at Cedar Grove Trailer Park. Becca looked around to see if anyone noticed her coming home early from school. Cutting class.

A small search crew stood conferring beside Agent Diamond's Land Rover, but no one seemed to notice her at all. Checking to be sure her father and mother weren't home, Becca went inside the trailer and changed her shoes, trading her Converse sneakers for a pair of rugged hiking boots. At the door, she checked to be sure no one was looking, and darted off into the woods behind her trailer. She walked about half a mile through sun-dappled forest and climbed a ridge, leaving distinct footprints in the soft earth. When she reached the Little Hoh River, she crossed over a primitive wood-plank bridge, stopped at the other side, looked around furtively, decided no one was following her, and moved up higher.

Near the Little Hoh River, deep in the forest, Venus heard Becca coming, stepped behind a cedar tree, and watched the teenager trudge up through the woods. When she had passed, Venus moved quietly behind her, keeping a distance and following in the tracks Becca's heavy-soled hiking boots made. Maybe Becca Brightman was a budding wildcrafter, stalking some lucrative wild garnish. Maybe she came out here to meet somebody. Whatever Becca was doing in the woods, she was doing it as a truant. Venus recalled that Fish had said the girl was bright. Bright students don't usually skip school.

In a few minutes, Becca arrived at the rain forest and entered the tree-canopied Hall of Mosses, disappearing into the darkness. Venus moved swiftly, quietly, the way she'd been trained to track wildlife. Here under the evergreen canopy, the sun rarely shone. The darkness and moisture nourished primitive mosses, lichens, and fungi that grew as big and wide as a house. On the forest floor, giant ferns waved monstrous emerald fronds. The ferns were nourished by decayed cedar stumps that stored throughwater and small nutrients, gnats and flies that dropped in with the runoff from the moss-draped canopy. Becca moved faster now, her tracks wider apart. She came to another stream that trickled through a gully: flowing, green, algae-enriched water. Becca was crossing the stream, hopping from stone to stone, when suddenly a voice cried, "Becca Brightman, what are you doing up here?"

Her father's angry voice triggered fear, and Becca froze. Venus heard Becca reply, "Oh, gosh, Dad, you scared me. What are you doing all the way up here?"

"Answer me, Becca. Don't turn my questions around like you always do."

"I...I hate school, Dad. I just came up here to be by myself."

Venus could see them now, Bob Brightman and his daughter. Brightman growled at the girl, "You could be arrested for cutting school. Hell, they'll arrest me, too, did you know that? How would you like it if I went to jail because you skipped school? How would you like that? Don't you ever do it again, do you hear me?"

"But, Dad..."

"Do you understand me, Becca?" An angry foghorn.

"Yes, Dad. What are you doing here?"

Brightman held up a canvas bag. "Valerian root."

"Should I help you?"

"No. You go home. Turn right around and go back home."

Becca came tripping back through the forest. As Venus watched from her hiding place, the girl passed less than ten feet from her. Should she follow Becca Brightman? Or stay here, keep an eye on the father? She decided to stay behind, keep Bob in her sights. He moved farther into the rain forest, and she moved in tandem, where she could see him, see what he was doing.

Valeriana sitchensis, Sitka valerian, grows in subalpine meadows, encouraged to life by snowmelt. The young red shoots change color as they mature, eventually producing delicate, hairy, white flowers. On the natural medicine market, where plants known to possess healing properties are called "phytomedicines," valerian is often referred to as "God's Valium" or "natural Halcion." Naturopathic physicians prescribe valerian for anxiety and for sleeping disorders. Naturopaths say valerian "tames the brain" and relaxes tense muscles, and they say valerian has no negative side effects, no sleeping-pill hangovers. The natural soporific quality of valerian reportedly can prevent panic attacks. The active ingredient in valerian that produces sedation hasn't yet been identified, although some scientists believe the plant's natural compounds act synergistically to induce a state of relaxation and serenity. In small doses, valerian may be safe enough, but large doses have triggered nausea, headache, restlessness and, like the synthetic prescription drug, Halcion, sometimes produce inertia and morning hangovers. Some patients taking valerian have experienced an anomalous reaction, becoming highly stressed and overexcited. The Food and Drug Administration lists valerian as a "Generally Recognized as Safe"—or "GRAS"—product. Valerian extract is more commonly used in Europe than America, but its popularity is growing throughout the world, and it's a lucrative crop for wildcrafters.

Venus watched Bob Brightman dig at the ground and yank up valerian root, disturbing the fragile ecosystem. When he dropped some root into the canvas bag, she moved in. He didn't seem startled when she appeared before him, just stood up straight and aimed his blank eyes at her.

She said, "I'll have to confiscate your crop."

Brightman handed over the canvas bag.

She said, "You'll be cited for illegal harvesting on a federal preserve, Mr. Brightman. You could receive a prison sentence."

Brightman said nothing, just stood there looking at her, or through her. When he realized she wasn't taking him into custody, he turned and headed down through the woods, following the tracks his daughter had made on the rich, yielding earth.

ON HIGHWAY 101, between Ruby Beach and Toleak, a lookout point allows tourists to pull their vehicles over and enjoy the raging ocean vistas and blazing sunsets over the Pacific Ocean: views that might inspire *Sunset* magazine, only wilder, more ruthless, Nature at her fiercest. Venus eased the Land Rover into the lookout area, parked, got out, and walked to the precipice overlooking the beach. She needed a break from the search, from the operations room, from all the people who weren't Richard. Out here, leggy renegade beach pines perched suicidally on overhanging bluffs. Bald eagles nested on sheer cliffs that plunged to the beach, where a bone-white driftwood necklace and ageworn stones took the full brunt of rollicking tides on the edge of nowhere.

Ten days had passed without a word from Richard. After the one aborted attempt to reach him by phone, she hadn't tried again. Each time she'd started to make that call, some dreadful stubbornness disguised as professional duty stopped her. Why hadn't he phoned her? His silence hurt more than any angry words he might have lobbed at her, were he the type to argue. They had never argued, never had reason to before now. Even if they disagreed strongly over this situation—whether she should stay on the job or return to Seattle to be with him, with her husband—she doubted they would exchange harsh words, and that scared her more than any potentially vitriolic scene might. Did his silence mean lack of interest? A diminution of his love for her? His silence hurt her profoundly, as her stubbornness must have hurt him.

SHE WAS FEELING the biting, tingling breeze against her face when Clint Kellogg's Jeep pulled up. Clint parked, got out, walked over to where she stood at the lookout's edge. When he spoke, his voice was soft, too close to her ear.

"Any news?"

She looked straight ahead at the breakers. "Nothing."

Clint sighed. "That's a shame. It breaks my heart to think about that baby."

He sounded sincere. She turned to face him. He had nicer eyes than his brother, a kinder expression. He had a wide forehead, a scruffy beard. Little metal glasses, so chic.

She said, "Imagine how the parents feel."

He shook his head. "Poor Theresa."

"Poor both of them," she corrected him.

Clint ignored that and said, "I saw you up here last summer, when old Aggie MacGregor was murdered. And I've seen you with the park rangers up at Forks. I've always wanted to meet you. You're elusive, though. You come and go."

Venus shrugged. "Maybe you're the elusive one."

Clint laughed. "Anyone who wants to can find me. I'm just your proverbial hermit writer, cooped up in my cabin most days and nights. Don't get out much. Don't care to.''

She said, ''After I interviewed you, I reread your statement. I didn't understand part of it.''

''What part was that?''

''You didn't mention that Daniel Dean was at your house that afternoon.''

Clint frowned. ''Who said that?''

''Daniel Dean.''

''He's never been to my place. I doubt he even knows where I live.''

She said, ''Something else didn't make sense to me. You said you were at home with a friend on the afternoon Paris disappeared, watching the Huskies football game.''

Silence, then, ''That's right.''

She said, ''The Huskies weren't playing. College teams don't play on Sundays. It was the Seahawks.''

He didn't respond right away. He turned to face the wind coming off the ocean, closed his eyes. After a while, he said, ''I'm not a very good liar. But I'm not a kid molester, either.''

She said, ''The other thing that bothers me is the part about moving up here to the boondocks. I didn't understand that part.''

Clint said, ''Back when I was in college, studying botany, I did field studies up here. I fell in love with the place. A couple years ago, I made a killing on a best seller, and invested in a beach house here. It had been a dream of mine for years, to have a place up here on the peninsula.''

''Does your brother visit you often?''

Clint said, ''Brad? Sure, he comes up now and then. Brad's a physician. He specializes in anti-aging treatments. He's got this clinic in L.A. called the Adonis Anti-Aging Spa. It's very famous. Ever heard of it?''

Venus said no, she hadn't.

Speaking about his brother, instead of about himself, Clint relaxed. He said, ''Adonis is all about cutting-edge anti-aging therapy. It's a medical clinic, but it's also a full-service spa: everything from simple massage and facials, to aromatherapy, naturopathic medicine, laser skin-resurfacing—even lunch lifts, and the age-reversal treatments. It's all available at Adonis. That's why it's such a radically popular place. You go in looking fifty-something and emerge a few hours later a young thirty-something. I've seen some miraculous work done there."

"Lunch lifts?"

He laughed. "Mini face-lift. Everyone's having them done. Guys, gals. Lots of men go for the lunch lifts. Keeps them looking young and fresh. But the anti-aging treatments my brother administers actually reverse the effects of age. Adonis is all about youth worship, longevity. Brad says that soon humans will routinely live to a hundred twenty-five, a hundred fifty years, and still look and feel like they're in their thirties. Brad's on the cutting edge of that industry, and he's making a fortune. Longevity's a hot business in Southern California."

She said, "Your brother's a plastic surgeon?"

Clint flicked a shock of hair out of his eyes. His face had never felt a scalpel, never needed it—at least, not yet. He said, "That's right, but Brad doesn't perform much surgery anymore, not since he got into the age-reversal business. In L.A. they call my brother 'Ponce de Len' because he's really discovered the Fountain of Youth."

"What about you?"

Clint touched his chest. "What about me?"

"Why'd you leave L.A.?"

"I got tired of it. Decided to follow the flocks northward. I'm one of those California influxers people up here despise so much. Invading pristine territory. It's a great place for a writer, and my pad's very cushy. Hot tub, sauna, great ocean view. A bachelor's dream pad. I throw some faboo parties."

"I thought you said you're a hermit."

"I go through stages."

She glanced down. His boots had spike moss stuck to the laces. She said, "Most bachelors don't live so far out of the gene pools."

He shrugged, rubbed his chest with two fingers. "I love it out here, especially up in the rain forest. It's my wild nature. My brother's the cosmopolite. Brad can't tolerate silence. Most of the time, I thrive on it."

"Which rain forest?"

Clint's eyes flickered. "The Hoh, of course. It's open to the public. I wouldn't trespass on Bogachiel."

Venus said, "You ever harvest on Bogachiel preserve?"

Clint smirked. "Oh, hey, I know what you're doing. You're interrogating."

"Right." She smiled politely. "And I'll need a new statement from you, too, so don't be surprised when one of our agents shows up at your place. Or, you might do yourself a favor by dropping by our office in Forks, giving a voluntary statement.''

He shifted his feet, tugged at his ear lobe. Behind him, in the clearing, they heard crows arguing. Clint said, ''I might want a lawyer to sit in on this.''

''Maybe you better look into that.'' Understated, a mild suggestion.

Clint exhaled deeply. ''So anyway, I get to L.A. once or twice a month. Rub shoulders with Brad's friends, his patients. The glitterati.''

''Lucky you.''

Clint leaned forward. She didn't flinch. His skin gave off a pungent melon odor, like fruited aftershave without the alcohol. He said, ''Now, what about you?''

Venus shrugged lightly. ''Nothing to tell.''

Clint sucked in his cheeks. ''Just a federal agent?''

''You might say that.''

The crows squawked bitterly. Clint said, ''Did your husband ever come back?''

After the pain subsided and she could speak, she said, ''You've got one heck of a rumor mill up here.''

On the highway, Daniel Dean's maroon pickup truck sped past, heading south toward Toleak and the trailer park. Clint said, ''Speaking of the local rumor mill, it's saying a Lovecraftian beast, half man, half elk, grabbed Paris Nighteagle. They're calling the beast 'the Unknown.' Makes a great horror tale. Another fast-moving rumor is that Daniel Dean killed the baby. Took its heart for bait. He's a big-game hunter. Elk, bear. Talk about your poachers. But then, that doesn't explain the hoofprints.''

''Rumor mills eventually implode on themselves.'' She watched the ocean, aching inside, wishing the man beside her now was Richard. Where was Richard when she needed him? Was he asking the same question about her?

Clint said, ''Rumor mills bore me.''

She said, ''So what do you think?''

Clint cocked his head sideways and his hair fell across his forehead, across his eyes. He brushed it back, a chronic nuisance. He said, ''If you pressed me? I'd have to say a wild animal got him. His father shouldn't have left him out there alone like that. That was stupid. You should press charges against the father.''

She didn't reply. She was still thinking about Richard, wondering what he was doing right now, trying to picture him in her mind, telepathically communicate.

Clint said, "So, how long you staying for?"

Venus shrugged. "As long as it takes."

Clint rolled his eyes. "Standard cop response."

She didn't reply.

He said, "That Daniel Dean's a dangerous fellow. You keep your cabin door locked. Never know what Daniel might try."

She watched him ease the Jeep onto the highway, head south, drive away. A few minutes later, she, too, headed south. Through the windshield she watched the forest fly by, the peek-a-boo spaces where midday sunlight encroached on the darkness. As she passed Cedar Grove Trailer Park, she saw Dean's pickup truck standing on the highway shoulder. She saw Dean jump out and run into the dense forest while the pickup idled. Exhaust poured from the tail pipe, soot-black and prolific.

THE COTTAGE FELT deadly without Richard. A mirror image of her heart. Avoiding the bedroom, she lingered in the kitchen but the sight of a single coffee mug, a single juice glass, only depressed her more. The living room felt vacuous, joyless. She went into the bedroom, collapsed on the bed. Hideous gloom washed over her, waves of misery. Clutching guilt, she wept hot tears, and finally fell into exhausted sleep. The sun set behind the ocean, and in the darkness the air grew frigid and a light drizzle fell softly over the forest and the beach. Inside the cabin, shadows expanded, overlapped. She dreamed the boy had been captured by wolves, taken to their den and raised as a wolf. Wolf Boy.

The telephone rang, startling her awake. Groping for the phone, she saw the numbers on the digital clock. Ten p.m. She'd slept three hours.

"It's Claudia, Venus. Did I wake you?"

"That's okay. What's up?"

Claudia said, "The tissue didn't belong to the Nighteagle baby. It's from an infant, though probably an infant who died at birth or shortly thereafter. We can't date it." Venus sat up, switched on the bedside lamp. Claudia continued, "It was a full-term baby. But the DNA doesn't match the Nighteagle DNA."

"And you can't pin down the age?"

Claudia said, "Not the age, not even how long ago death occurred. Could've been weeks ago, could've been years. We still have some more lab results to come in, but right now, we can't say much at all, except that the DNA doesn't match. Sorry."

"Anything else?"

Claudia sighed. "Wexler's coming in from D.C. tomorrow. He wants to meet with you."

"If he wants to see me, he'll have to come up here." She sat on the edge of the bed, pulled on her boots.

Patiently, Claudia said, "How are you holding up?"

"I haven't committed suicide yet, if that's what you're getting at."

"You don't sound good."

"I'll be okay." Unconvincingly muttered.

Claudia said, "Richard will come around eventually."

"Spoken like a stalwart Nord. I still can't believe you married an Italian."

"You've got to keep your mind on your work, Venus. This baby may still be alive. If you can't handle it without Richard, you better come back and let Louie take over."

"No way."

"All right then. This DNA evidence gives us hope that the Nighteagle baby could still be alive. Try to focus on that. Everyone's counting on you now."

"One more thing, Claudia."

"What's that?"

"Is there any way we can match the hoofprints from the Nighteagle case with the elk hoof castings from the poaching cases?"

"We have the hoof castings from the poaching incidents, and castings from the recent incident. Do you want me to see if they match up?"

In the living room, Venus switched on a lamp. "Yes. And tell Wexler to meet me up here in the morning."

She piled logs in the fireplace. Fragrant cedar logs, alder stick kindling. She lit the kindling. The fire crackled to life. Its warmth comforted the palms of her hands. She held them to her chest. Felt the warmth penetrate. Felt the cold stone beat.

Half an hour later, Claudia called back. "It's a match. The hoofprints from the Nighteagle case match exactly in size and shape with a set taken from one of last summer's poaching scenes."

Venus said, "Male?"

"Yes. His hoofprints were a good seven inches wide. He was a big bull."

Venus said, "I thought so. Thanks, Claud." She hung up to face another long night alone.

NIGHT WAS HARDEST, spent on the edge of sleep, yet not true sleep, only an abyss, a snake pit. On the edge of the snake pit, Theresa saw herself standing naked but for a thin red veil on her head, her face smeared with Whale's blood, her feet torn and bleeding from the snakes' teeth. On the other side of the abyss stood Paris, naked and crying, terrified. The snakes crawled out of the pit, attacking the child, and she tried to lift her feet off the hard ground, to leap across the abyss and save Paris, but her feet wouldn't come loose from the ground, her feet were part of the ground, one huge monument, she a carved statue smeared in Whale's blood, and the snakes dragged Paris down into the pit, and she heard his cries as they devoured him.

The edge of sleep does not discriminate between waking and falling off. The edge is always the same: full of beasts and guilt and despair, a delving into primal fear, a grim, horrifying epoch without hope of release, without deliverance. Prayer was meaningless—a clown's squeak, without power over the iniquity. Yet prayer was all she had, and so she dropped to her knees, begging the ancient spirits and the Holy Mother and all the saints to intercede for her, to flood the skies with their powerful intercessions. She prayed until every word in every language had passed her lips, and still, the child shrieked from deep in the abyss. Raving, fear-blind, soul-dead, Theresa stormed through her once-peaceful home, smashing ceramic memories, emptying kitchen drawers, breaking mirrors and cutting herself intentionally. When she came to the thermostat, she rammed her clenched fist into it, shearing the skin off her hand. The only room she left unscathed was the nursery. Though it was after two o'clock, and no moon lit the sky, she ran headlong into the forest, screaming, "Paris. Paris. Paris."

Winn stood beneath the light pole in the trailer park lot, watching Theresa running crazed into the dark woods, unable to move from where he stood, riveted by a heavy, despairing heart, heavier than ever since learning tonight that Gordon Toolong's sixteen-year-old son had slashed his own wrists and bled to death.

ELEVEN

ELIXIR

ACTING SECRETARY of the Interior Jerome Wexler drove up to the lookout point in a steel-gray government sedan with all the telltale antennae and plates. The sedan itself was ostentatious enough, but when Wexler stepped out, dressed in a cashmere jacket and Italian loafers, a brushed aluminum briefcase under his arm, he might as well have been a camel in the rain forest. He opened the passenger door of the Land Rover, got in. Venus pursed her lips against involuntary wisecracks. When he finally settled into the passenger seat, she looked at him, but not directly into his eyes. Not yet.

The Acting Secretary had recently taken a shine to the British film star, Lady Bella Winsome-Diamond, and for this honor, Wexler had set aside his normal requirements that his partner in ecstasy be at least two generations his junior. Suppleness was Wexler's measure of bedability. He particularly admired the youthful, gymnastic figures of the Dallas Cowboy cheerleaders. Lady Bella was none of the above—certainly not gymnastic, except supple in a soft sort of way—but she possessed such great beauty and vitality, not to mention the most breathtaking legs on the American film scene, that Wexler could not resist Bella's seductive charms. This was the Wexler version. Lady Bella's version of the ongoing mutual admiration society differed only in one regard. Lady Bella was the seducee, never the seducer, and would never overtly flirt. Who was seducing whom mattered little to Venus. The part that rankled was the bald fact that her mother and her boss shared the occasional, albeit discreet, tête-à-tête.

A bold seagull landed on the Rover's hood, stared the camel in the face. Wexler unlocked the sleek briefcase and opened it. Venus didn't look directly inside but her peripherals caught a glimpse of Antaeus cologne and a natural-bristle hairbrush. Also inside the briefcase were a few file folders and a large manila envelope, sealed. That was all she could see without actually turning her head and chancing a meeting of her eyes with his. Better avoid what might turn into a shouting match on the subject of bosses who canoodle with their underlings' mothers.

Wexler plucked out the large manila envelope, closed the briefcase, unsealed the envelope, reached inside, pulled out a document, thrust it at Venus. "Read this."

The document was over twenty pages long. She said, "Now?"

Wexler opened the passenger-side door. "I'll take a walk on the beach."

When he had disappeared over the driftwood bulkhead, she began reading the document. Stamped "Classified" in red ink across the top, the cover letter was printed on the official stationery of Lance Lanai, the pro-environment senator from Southern California.

Dear Acting Secretary Wexler (the letter began):
In the spring of last year, my office opened an investigation into what I loosely refer to as the "Fountain of Youth" industry, which manufactures and markets products they claim can reverse the aging process. These elixirs and tonics and vitamin cocktails supposedly return the human body to its formerly youthful state. This fast-growing industry operates throughout the United States and is monopolized by several mail-order concerns which, among them, gross in excess of five billion dollars annually in sales revenues.

My investigation was precipitated by complaints from certain of my constituents, who say some of these companies are marketing potentially deadly snake-oil placebos under false pretenses and claims. Some are manufacturing their own products, others are apparently importing product from Mexico and Eastern Europe, notably Russia. Some also are exporting their products through a circuitous route that, so far, we have been unable to penetrate. These mail-order companies, posing as medical authorities in the aging process, have posted statements on the Internet charging that "the FDA has entered a conspiracy with American pharmaceutical companies to mislead the American public about the so-called dangers of ingesting certain phytomedicines and other organic products."

Enclosed you will find a complete copy of the report resulting from my undercover investigation of three of these companies which I believe to be bogus operations. To be honest, the investigation has lagged far behind schedule because my office ran out of funding for such projects. I cannot, however, let this one slip through the cracks and loopholes. Be advised that this report is not to be reproduced in any fashion and does not now exist on disk or in hard copy except for the original document which is securely locked in my safe, and the enclosed copy entrusted to your safekeeping. This level of secrecy is necessary as my investigation has time and again been thwarted by cronies of the elusive individuals who operate these bogus companies. The three corporations are: SpaVida, Limited, the Life Eternal Institute, and the Elixir of Youth Foundation. Of the three, by far the most active and profitable is the Elixir of Youth Foundation, as you may see for yourself by calling up their Web site at www.YouthElixir.com.

My interest in involving the Department of the Interior stems from evidence I obtained in a rather embarrassing fashion. I inadvertently discovered that my wife, Lana Lanai, the Hollywood talent agent, has been for at least the past two years using products from the Elixir of Youth Foundation, which supplies her through an arrangement with Adonis Anti-Aging Clinic and Spa in Los Angeles, owned by the anti-aging guru, Dr. Bradford Kellogg, a popular Hollywood physician who serves stars and celebrities. Upon inspecting these products in my wife's possession, I realized that certain organic materials derived from endangered species of plants are being incorporated into these potions. Thus far, the worst offender is, again, Elixir, whose products reportedly contain numerous endangered plant species, including *Castilleja levisecta,* the Golden Paintbrush. I was able to discreetly borrow an Elixir age-reversal injection product from my wife's personal supply, and lab tests showed it indeed contained minute traces of Golden Paintbrush. A botanist with your California regional office verified that finding. While we can prove beyond a shadow of a doubt that Elixir is in violation of the Endangered Species Act, we believe that further investigation, indictments, and arrests should go forward under the jurisdiction of the Interior Department.

If Interior is willing to cooperate in this investigation, I will forthwith provide you with all relevant documents and the names and locations (in all cases, we have only post office box addresses) of persons we have been watching.

Any assistance you and the Department of the Interior may see fit to provide this investigation will be greatly appreciated.

> Very truly yours,
> (Signed) Lance Lanai
> Senator, State of California

Venus tucked the letter back in its envelope. The remainder of the document was divided into three sections, titled "SpaVida," "Life Eternal," and "Elixir"—the Elixir file being the heftiest. She leafed through the pages. Formulas for age-reversing tonics that sounded like so much gobbledygook, Web site advertisements, order forms, mission statements, testimonials from satisfied customers. All of it was intriguing, but two words in particular caught her eye. On the top page of the Elixir file, in Wexler's handwriting, appeared a name. Clint Kellogg.

Wexler's face was windburned, his nostrils glistened, and his eyes watered copiously. "It's freezing out there, and my loafers are shot to hell," he complained.

"You sound like my husband." She'd been wanting to test-run the word.

Wexler raised an eyebrow. "You're still married?"

On the rebound she said, "How do you see this tying into the boy's disappearance?"

Wexler shrugged. "Might be no connection at all. May be a separate case entirely. Two things bother me. First, the brother connection."

"Clint and Brad Kellogg."

Wexler nodded. "Senator Lanai states that Dr. Kellogg uses Elixir products at the Adonis Anti-Aging Clinic and Spa in Los Angeles. Kellogg's a plastic surgeon, but this is a fancy-dancy sort of spa place, where they do a lot of things."

She put up a hand. "I know. Clint Kellogg told me about the lunch lifts."

"You've met the brother?"

"Only briefly. Clint Kellogg may be actively harvesting on Bogachiel. When I saw him yesterday, he had spike moss stuck in his bootlaces. Spike moss is abundant on Bogachiel. But if he's looking for Golden Paintbrush, he's out of luck. It's been extirpated from Bogachiel for years."

Wexler said, "Senator Lanai told me that Clint Kellogg has bragged around Hollywood about his rain forest adventures. He's rumored to be providing certain plant species to his brother for use in his anti-aging therapies. If we can prove he's trespassing on the preserve and illegally harvesting anything, I don't care if it's dandelions, that alone is enough to send him to prison. The doc, too, if we could prove his spa is being supplied by the brother up here."

"How did you make the connection?"

Wexler shrugged. "I read your witness statements. You made reference to Brad Kellogg joining in the search. And somebody on the team had interviewed a Clint Kellogg."

"I did."

Wexler raised his eyebrows. Like he was impressed. "I found it intriguing that both brothers were on the scene shortly after the Nighteagle baby disappeared, and particularly intriguing that they both volunteered in the first night's search."

"Everyone volunteered in the first night's search. And by the way," she said, "I've already cited one wildcrafter for trespassing. The Nighteagles' next-door neighbor. But that might be totally unrelated."

"Maybe."

"Also, we had a report of a teenager's suicide. Slashed his wrists in the high school gym. We're checking it out."

Wexler grunted. "The world has gone to hell."

She said, "Who's working the other end?"

"L.A.? I'm in the process of recruiting an undercover agent. Lanai's people were less than discreet. They've all blown their covers. I need somebody from the outside. When I find that person, I'll have him or her report to you. I want you to handle this case."

"But, the Nighteagle case hasn't been closed...."

Wexler nodded. "At this point, I believe this should be our priority."

Now she stared straight into his lake-blue eyes. Pools of mystery. Retinal memory in peak form. For a flickering second she saw Bella reflected in his eyes. She said, "I can't wrap this case until we find the child."

Wexler waited until he saw the pulse in her neck slow down, then said, "I'm not saying we close the search. I'm saying, downgrade the search. Keep a presence, but allow enough space for someone to take a chance and maybe trip up. I think there's a connection between the baby's disappearance and the Kelloggs. I want you to stay up here, keep a low profile, but watch the Nighteagles and Clint Kellogg. Meanwhile, we'll have someone check out the brother, Brad Kellogg, in L.A. I think that's the best chance we stand of finding the baby.''

"Why do you say that?"

Wexler said, "Two reasons. I have a devious mind. That's what makes me a great investigator. I want you to develop a little of that. I want you to learn from me."

She watched him dubiously. He'd never been this personal with her. She wondered if he was sincere about the mentoring offer, or if he was just trying to mollify Bella's daughter.

She said, "Give me a hint. Something to grab onto."

Wexler locked the brushed-aluminum briefcase. "I did a little old-fashioned research into Theresa Nighteagle's background. Using her social security number, I was able to locate some old medical records, going back fourteen years. At age sixteen, Theresa Nighteagle was admitted to Providence Hospital in Seattle where she delivered a still-born baby."

Venus said, "Why did she go all the way to Seattle?"

"Because the pregnancy was a secret. No one up here was supposed to find out about it."

"Who was the father?"

Wexler said, "She didn't name a father on the hospital admission forms. But the name of the person who brought her to the hospital was listed."

"Who was it?"

"Clint Kellogg."

A long silence while she absorbed this. Then she said, "What's the second reason?"

"Have you got a laptop?"

She reached into the back seat, retrieved her Powerbook, booted up. Wexler gave her the Web site address for the Elixir of Youth Foundation. She input it. They waited a few seconds. Elixir of Youth's Web page opened with a flourish of New Agey music, some jazzy light-tricks, and bold graphics depicting a youthful, athletic, male-female couple striding into a glorious dawn. Then, the caption: ELIXIR OF YOUTH FOUNDATION-WELCOME TO LIFE EVERLASTING. In the background, a serene forest scene, and in the forest scene stood a bull elk. A Roosevelt. She stared. "That's Bogachiel."

Wexler smiled. "I was almost certain. I wanted you to verify that."

She tried scrolling through the Web site. Each time she tried, the screen blinked, froze. Wexler said, "Forget it. The Web site's been frozen for weeks. Probably Lanai's investigation got too close for comfort. But they'll be back on line eventually, when they think Lanai's backed off. Anyway, it's mostly gobbledygook, fake scientific reports and so forth."

She turned off the Powerbook. Wexler got out of the Land Rover. Before shutting the door, he said, "One of these days, I'm going to teach you the fine art of background research."

STEPHEN, Bella's personal assistant, answered the phone. "How's Hawaii?" he asked.

"Fine, Stephen, fine. Very pleasant. Is my mother home?"

"Lady Bella has just come in, not ten minutes ago, and you are fortunate to catch her because she'll be off to the set very shortly."

"She's making another film?"

"*Queen of Park Place*. It's about Monopoly. The board game."

"Sounds like a blockbuster. Would you please put Mother on?"

While she waited, Venus watched Heartbreak Louie tossing stones at the water's edge, as if they'd skip in the surf at Toleak Beach. Song had been spending too much time at the lodge, at her mythical honeymoon cottage. She'd have to speak to him about that.

Bella came chiming to the phone. "Venus, why are you ringing me up all the way from Maui in the midst of your honeymoon?"

"Just to chat."

"How is the beach, darling?"

Venus held the phone towards Toleak Beach. "Can you hear the surf?"

"It sounds marvelous. How is Richard enjoying the Lahaina Club?"

"Oh, he's in heaven. Listen, Mother, I have a personal question for you."

Bella scoffed. "I refuse to discuss subjects of an intimate nature, and you know very well, I never offer advice on personal relationships. If you must have questions, I am certain there are plenty of marriage counselors on Maui."

"It's not about intimacy. It's about the aging process."

Silence. Then, in Bella's firmest contralto, "I do not discuss age. I do not believe in age."

"What I meant is, part of your secret of eternal youth and beauty has to do with your faithful devotion to health maintenance."

"Venus, in the very first place, you are far too young to obsess about the aging process. In the second place, I never divulge my personal regime, not even to my most obsequious child. This is private territory. Such intimacies are simply not your business. And I might add, inherited genes play a huge role in my youthful appearance."

Pulling teeth from a cheetah. Venus tried another approach. "Don't you frequent a spa when you're in L.A.?"

"You mean Adonis Spa? Of course. Everybody frequents Adonis. Why?"

"Do you know the owner?"

"Brad Kellogg? I don't know him well, but certainly we've exchanged air kisses and so forth. Venus, why in the world have you rung me up all the way from Maui to interrogate me about utter nonsense? You should be out on the golf course with your husband."

"Actually, that's where we are." A tiny white lie for Bella's own good. "Here's the thing, Mother. Richard and I have this bet going, and I'm determined to win."

"You should never win against a man, darling. A lady always lets a gentleman hold the upper hand. Honestly, Venus, I wish you would finally grasp the subtleties of ladylike behavior."

"Right. I've got a little interference here on the line, Mother. Now, here's the bet. Richard says Adonis uses synthetic ingredients in its products. I say Adonis uses only all natural ingredients."

"Venus, are you two so bored with each other's company that you must reduce your conversations to such low levels?"

"It's what people my age do with their partners. I mean, we fall into these inane discussions. So, which of us is right about Adonis products?"

"First of all, Adonis does not manufacture products. The clinic discreetly carries a brand of products called 'Elixir of Youth,' which I understand aren't yet approved by the United States Food and Drug Administration, but you know how behind the times these bureaucrats are when it comes to natural remedies. At any rate, these products are only administered to Dr. Kellogg's patients. Dr. Kellogg is quite a remarkable plastic surgeon, but his specialty is the anti-aging business, and I understand he has a huge following. Back to your question: I do not know where Elixir is manufactured, but the fact is, they aren't Adonis products. Now, that may just be an insignificant technicality in your wager with Richard. However, Woofy Benson has gone down for treatments with the product line, and I can assure you, they use only the freshest natural ingredients in all of their products. That includes their vitamin supplements, their creams and lotions, and of course, the elixir itself."

"How can you be so certain?"

"Woofy told me. Honestly, Venus."

"Elixir of what?"

"Oh, really, I don't know, Venus. I don't use it. I find it ethically questionable to monkey with the natural aging process. If you really want to know about that subject, you'll just have to contact Adonis, ask them to help you. Don't call Woofy. She doesn't want anyone to know she's on the elixir, and she'd scalp me if she knew I mentioned it to you. Now, I have answered your original question, and I suppose this means you win the wager with Richard. I do hope you'll humor him, though. It's the smart thing."

"Sure, Mother. How's Timmy?" Timmy was Bella's adopted son. Eight or nine years old, no one knew for sure.

"How should I know? Timothy hasn't spoken to me for three days."

"Why's that?"

Bella sniffed. "He wants to appear in this film. I won't permit it."

"What's wrong with Timmy being in the film?"

"In case you have forgotten your own upbringing, Venus, I subscribe to the rule that children are not exploitable commodities. Timothy is not going to suffer the same fate as Macaulay Culkin. Now, I have to ring off. Everybody is waiting for me on the set."

"How's the filming coming along?"

"Dreadful. Seattle is not New York, no matter how desperately hard they try to fake it. The light just isn't the same, but can you tell that to these chintzy producers?"

"What's the budget?"

"I don't discuss money. Mine or anyone else's. Suffice to say, it is paltry."

"Under or over a hundred mil?"

"Over by far. Still, insufficient. They would have been far better off just renting two blocks of Park Avenue. But never mind. Now, give Richard my best regards, and you two enjoy the remainder of your honeymoon."

"Sure, Mother. And, thanks. By the way, have you seen Wexler lately?"

"Jerry?" A pregnant pause, then, "As a matter of fact, I understand Jerry is in Seattle on business, though actually, we are dining this evening. Shall I convey a message?"

"Yes. Tell Casanova I said to keep his paws off of you."

"I am hanging up now, Venus."

The phone line went dead. Venus turned and faced the beach, made a swinging motion. "Oh, look, Louie. I just shot a hole in one."

Song's pretty eyes followed the imaginary golf ball into the surf. "Just for that," he said, "I'm cooking you dinner tonight."

"You'll never cook like Richard cooks," she retorted ungratefully.

The next stone Song lobbed into the surf actually skipped twice.

WINN PUSHED the grocery cart hell-bent in fury. Milan grabbed onto the kiddy bar and shrieked with joy. The other shoppers in the Forks Thriftway paused long enough to wince at the screeching baby and wonder aloud about how some parents ought to have their kids taken away from them. At the beer cooler, Winn shoved aside all the sissified microbrews and landed a six-pack of Bud. He landed another, and another. Milan gurgled and tugged at Winn's plaid shirt sleeve. Winn ignored her. She tugged again about the time Winn reached the nachos, and once again he ignored the baby. Milan opened her mouth and let go.

She had horsepower but Winn didn't respond, his mind occupied with Paris and how he disappeared and where he might be now, whether or not he was still alive. Milan couldn't read her father's mind; all she knew was she wanted his attention, and she knew how to scream. Even the stocked dry-goods shelf wasn't enough to muffle the infant's awful tirade. People plugged their ears with their fingers and then someone whispered that it was Winn Nighteagle with the other twin, Paris Nighteagle's twin, the one who didn't get snatched and eaten by the cloven-hooved beast. How could a man whose baby son has so recently come to tragedy have the time to grocery shop? Something didn't set right in your gut, when you really thought about that. Why wasn't he out searching for his boy, or at least, for his remains? Well, okay, a body has to eat. And they did have the other kid to feed. That Nighteagle family was full of bad spirits, doomed by some mysterious evil—a family to pity, but pity doesn't carry over into supermarket aisles. Shopping is a sacred ritual. People need quiet to shop. The only useful noise for a shopper is the backbeat of canned music they pump to get your hands moving, to help you imagine you have more cash or credit than you really do. But this shrieking Nighteagle baby—this just stabbed your sensibilities. Someone better stop that baby's howling.

At the cereal section, Song turned around and saw Winn Nighteagle. He saw the missing baby's twin, the little girl, screaming for attention. He caught the wailing baby's drowning eyes in a riveting gaze, smiled a Song smile. Milan nearly choked on her own tears so suddenly did she jerk silent. Song winked. Irresistible. Milan coughed off a hiccup and fell silent, her ebony eyes riveted on Song's amandines.

Winn didn't notice all this because he had Paris on his mind and because he had to select a cereal Theresa would eat. She wasn't eating anything. Then, too, deep down, Winn Nighteagle might have needed to get away from the scene, the place where he left his baby out in the cold to get snatched. Stood to reason.

Song crossed the aisle to Milan. She held out her thin baby arm, reached out her slender pink baby fingers. Song offered her his thumb. Milan grasped it on the first try and when Song playfully drew his thumb back, Milan grasped harder, and like a Chinese finger puzzle, locked on.

Milan gurgled pleasantly, her devotion to Song's thumb measured by the decreasing distance between it and her teething gums. Song disengaged his germy thumb and instantly Milan's lower lip trembled and her eyes welled up. He wasn't sure what to do next, but he got some help from a powerful hand that shoved him back against the cereal shelves.

Winn growled, "Don't touch my baby."

"Just trying to calm her down," Song said smoothly.

Winn was taller than Song, had forty or fifty pounds' advantage, and his quads resembled footballs. Song held out a hand to shake but Winn wouldn't touch it. "You leave my little girl alone, understand?"

"Sure." Then, offhandedly, "How are you holding up, Mr. Nighteagle?"

Winn leaned into Song, sneered, "You sons-of-bitches aren't doing a damn thing to find my boy."

"We're all doing our best. We'll find him." Song turned, walked a little way down the grocery aisle before Winn's meaty hand yanked him by the collar and shoved him up against the dry-goods shelves.

"What gives you the goddamn right to touch my baby? You're some kind of molesting Chinaman? Don't you ever come near my kid again. You got that good and straight?"

Song, suddenly devoid of charm, felt his pulse race. Nighteagle's mouth was just a couple inches from his face. He could see the man's perfect molars, the uvula, the florid, angry tongue.

Nighteagle shouted, "Goddamnit, answer me you chink son-of-a-bitch."

Song's fist tucked up under Winn's chin, jerked hard. Winn's teeth clamped down hard on his tongue and he yowled, setting off Milan, who howled louder than ever. Song walked casually away and Winn let him go, thinking to himself that there's no better introduction between two men than a good skirmish. Right then, Winn decided to respect that dude, if they ever met again.

TWELVE

CARCASS

ON THE twelfth morning after Paris Nighteagle's disappearance, a Coast Guard vessel trolling the waters of Quillayute Needles National Wildlife Refuge off Ruby Beach netted an elk carcass. A male bull, with the antlers and hooves sawed off. Another trophy hunter, poaching on National Park land, must've scored the bull on Ruby Beach, left the carcass, and the tides then hauled it out to sea. But why the hooves? A Coast Guardsman made a note of this strange mutilation. The sailors dumped the bloated carcass back into the ocean. The carcass sank, then bobbed to the surface, and rode a strong ebb tide out toward Destruction Island. On Ruby Beach, Theresa lowered her binoculars and sat wearily down on a wet driftwood log, weathered cedar gone to bone. The Coast Guard boat disappeared behind a sea stack, where Theresa's eyes rested on the gulls. The sea birds were scrapping along the jagged stone monoliths, weaving in and out between them. Exhausted, emotionally drained, Theresa shivered from the piercing chill that seeped through her parka. Her ears burned from the cold, and the screeching gulls didn't help any.

In the first place, she shouldn't even be up here. There was the forest to search behind the trailer park, and the beach down there. Why would they search for Paris all the way up here at Ruby Beach? The trailer park where he was snatched was almost twenty miles south, on the opposite side of the highway. Trolling the ocean was a stupid waste of time. She could maybe understand another beach search down close to the preserve, closer to the trailer park. They didn't need her here, so why did they insist she stick around while they searched?

A thin, ringing sound startled her. Theresa reached deep inside the inadequate parka, fished out the cell phone the Fish and Wildlife Service had loaned her. It was Frances, with a choke in her voice. Theresa put a cold hand against her ear, blocking the ocean's roar.

"Milan's running a fever," she heard Frances say. "One hundred one." Frances usually sounded calm and in control of things, but now her voice was tinged with concern. "I need to take her to the clinic."

"Where's Winn?" Theresa heard her own voice shouting.

"Gone with that white woman to sign some papers."

"What papers?"

Frances barked, "I don't know what papers. You coming with me or not?"

"I'm coming right now."

The Coast Guard boat had turned around and was heading south, following the shoreline. Theresa called the number they'd given her and got a man's voice. "I'm leaving the beach," she shouted into the phone. "My other baby's sick. I need to go home right now."

The man put her on hold. She winced into the stinging breeze, waiting for something else to happen. Finally, another man's voice came over the line. "You can go home now, Mrs. Nighteagle," said the voice. "We've finished out here. We didn't find anything. Sorry, ma'am."

Trudging along the beach, Theresa's downcast eyes spied a blanket of ladybugs on the tide's edge. Blown in on the wind, or maybe washed in on the tide. From where? From Japan? Ladybugs lay thick at her feet, a treasure trove of drowned wishes. Theresa raised her foot, stomped down hard on the accidental immigrants, crushed them into the undulating sand. At the same moment, her eye fell upon a curious rock. She picked it up, licked its salty surface, revealing a green stone shaped like an eyeball with a bloodred pupil. Like those olives stuffed with red peppers, but in stone. She'd take it home, polish off the salt until it gleamed bright green, ruby red, then show it to Milan. And Paris. Soon as they found him and brought him home to her.

AT THE Fish and Wildlife annex, with Venus standing by, Winn signed the release forms permitting periodic searches of his trailer and his pickup truck. Just a precautionary measure, Venus explained, in case later on they think of something that might provide a lead. Winn felt it was more like they suspected him of killing his own son. Sheriff Tobin, who had come to lend Winn support, said, "It's okay, Winn. This is standard procedure. Nobody's accusing you of anything."

Burning inside, Winn said, "You're not finished. You haven't found his body."

Sheriff Tobin nodded somberly. "This here's a great team of agents. If Paris is out there, they'll find him." Winn looked at Venus. She reminded him of a child, so small, so tiny. What good was she, anyway?

Venus said, "Starting today, Mr. Nighteagle, we're downscaling the search effort, but we'll still be out there actively searching, we'll be around. Right now, I'd like to concentrate on giving the kidnapper, if one exists, enough room to make a mistake."

Winn stared. "You think my boy's still alive?"

"I'm not saying anything's for certain. I'm asking you to be patient for the next few days." Winn looked bewildered. Venus added, "We want a chance to bring your boy back alive. His abductor, too."

Sheriff Tobin placed a hand on Winn's shoulder. "You okay with that, Winn?"

Winn's mouth tightened. "For right now. For the next few days. But if you don't find my boy in the next few days, I swear to God..." Winn choked on an embarrassing sob. "Oh, this is just too much. Paris must be dead by now, for chrissake..." Tobin squeezed Winn's shoulder comfortingly.

Winn turned to Venus. "You really think he's still alive?"

"Maybe. Maybe he's somewhere safe."

OUTSIDE THE ANNEX, Carolee Brightman, Winn's helpful neighbor, waited in her Ford Fairlane. Winn slid into the passenger seat. He didn't speak, and she wouldn't press him, unless he wanted to talk. Carolee said, "You hungry?"

Winn shook his head.

"Then let's go home." Carolee swung out of the parking lot, drove cautiously through Forks. When they reached the 101 South turnoff, she gunned the Fairlane and soared along the highway. Winn slumped in the passenger seat. He hated being the passenger.

At the hairpin curve between the Hoh reservation and Toleak Beach, the Hoh mission cemetery rose on a small prairie set against the forest. Winn noticed a group of people standing in the cold wind, gathered around somebody's gravesite. He caught a glimpse of Gordon Toolong and his wife Minnie, and he saw Sandy Lightfoot and Simon Thundercloud. It must be Jeremy Toolong's memorial service.

Sixteen years old, and the kid slashed his own wrists. Winn swallowed back a rush of bitter gall.

Carolee shot home in a record twenty-eight minutes. When they pulled into the trailer-park lot, Winn saw his truck parked carelessly beside the trailer. When he went inside, he saw Frances's humpy back at Milan's crib. He heard Milan fussing. He said, "Where's Tee?"

Over her shoulder, Frances said, "Out there in the woods. Out there, looking for him. Now, Milan's sick. We just took her to the clinic. Doctor says it may be serious. She's got a bad fever, and I'm taking her back home with me. Theresa wants me to." The woman gathered up the baby and left the trailer. For the first time since Paris had disappeared, Winn was alone. He went over to the refrigerator, fished out a Bud, popped it, upended it, and swallowed. Milan had been cranky and Frances smelled like rotten doughnuts. He was glad they went away.

Winn went outdoors, walked around the side of the trailer to the grassy clearing on the edge of the forest. That yellow police tape, flagging in the wind, marking off the spot where he last saw Paris, where he'd set Paris down, here was the starting point of great heartache, ground zero of evil, as if the soil itself were malignant. As usual, Winn's eyes focused first on the ground, where the hoofprints led into the thickets, into the forest. The rains had almost obliterated the prints, though he could still make out the cloven part of the hooves. His eyes followed the searchers' beaten path into the forest, and he saw that the old logger's trail, too, had been beaten back by searchers. Then he saw Theresa, slashing a desperate, improbable path to a baby's hiding place. Theresa would never give up. He should go after her, comfort her. But the thought enraged him.

Over in the Brightman trailer, a female voice shouted. Maybe Carolee, or the girl, Becca. Some kind of family argument. That's what you get when a white man takes an Indian wife. Part Indian, anyway. Winn considered Carolee a half-breed. More female screaming, then Bob Brightman's foghorn voice, shouting back. Winn couldn't make out the words, didn't care to. He heard something—an object of some kind—crash against a wall in the Brightman trailer. Then female sobbing and Bob shouting loud enough to wake the rocks on the beach. The wind carried the sounds directly to Winn's ears. Just to escape from the awful racket, he plunged into the thickets and followed the trail Theresa had cut through the woods.

HEARTBREAK LOUIE nabbed the Gecko on a clear, brisk morning. The suspect had made a strategic error, as desperadoes will, when he stuck up the Queets Stop 'N' Go and got caught on video. Within three hours of the armed robbery, Song had the Gecko in custody. Some said it was luck and timing. If you knew Song, you'd say it was determination and expertise. Song found the fugitive holed up in a deserted house in Grays Harbor; kicked in the door himself. When the Gecko answered with gunfire, Song put a bullet in the fugitive's left thigh, just high enough to worry the man. He came along peacefully, denying everything. In the Grays Harbor jail, the Gecko refused to give a statement, except to insist he'd never molested any little girl and never stolen anybody's baby. The public defender immediately charged Song with excessive force and promised to see Song at the prison farm. This vow only amused Louis, and when Venus arrived at the jail, he said, "I've got your man."

"Maybe I've got other ideas." Venus brushed Song aside and entered the small room where the Gecko sat in a straight-back chair, watched over by a beefy cop. Venus pulled up a chair, put six inches between her knees and the Gecko's. "All right, Mr. Branson, let's have your story."

The Gecko sneered, pressed his lips together. Venus studied her fingernails, waited. The Gecko fidgeted, but made no sound. A war of wills ensued. Half an hour passed without a word between them. The Gecko cleared his throat a couple times, but made no other sound. Venus folded her arms and sat back, prepared for a long standoff. She studied the tattoo on his left forearm, a fine color-rendering of the lizard. Another half hour passed. The Gecko had to use the bathroom, so he spoke up, addressing the beefy cop. The cop escorted him to the bathroom, the Gecko limping badly, leaning on a crutch. In a few minutes, the guard brought him back, and they sat for another half hour before he got so bored with her company that he said, "Oh, the hell with it."

"So tell me, Mr. Branson, why did you molest that young girl?"

"Didn't do nothing to her. She come with me voluntarily. We went for berries."

"You didn't fondle her?"

"Like I told 'em all, I didn't touch that girl. Her mamma's a liar."

"The physician at Bogachiel clinic, who examined the girl, says you did."

"Then he's a liar, too."

"You know the girl's mother?"

The Gecko nodded. "She was my ladyfriend, before I caught her with a badass kid named Dean."

"Daniel Dean?"

"That's him."

Venus said, "How long have you known the family?"

The Gecko sighed. "Maybe six months. She's trying to frame me, the mother. She set me up with the girl, made it look bad. I didn't do it."

"What about the baby? You know anything about the baby?"

The Gecko sniffed, raised his handcuffed wrists, rubbed his nose. "I heard about it. Some animal run off with that little Indian boy. That's all I know about it."

"Did you know the Nighteagles?"

"The boy's family? Hell, no. I don't know nobody in this county. Except that girl and her mama. I'm tired. Let me go to my cell."

She watched him limp away, the guard at his side. She called to him. "Branson."

He turned slowly, laboring over the crutch.

She said, "You a hunter?"

"Naw."

"If you were a hunter, Branson, would you saw off the hooves of your prey?"

The Gecko spread his lips, let out a sickly braying quiver, turned and followed the guard into lockup.

Outside the jail, she met the public defender, a snarly, unkempt twenty-something, maybe six days out of law school. He whined, "I pressed charges on Song. You better tell your agents to ease up."

She said, "What are you, the ACLU?"

"I'm a member. What's that got to do with anything?"

"I don't know. You just look the type."

She was halfway across the parking lot when he yelled, "I know what I'm doing."

Song met her at the trailer park. "You got his confession?"

"You didn't have to shoot him, Louie."

Song sucked in his cheeks. "I did what anyone else would do. He fired first."

She sighed, shook her head. "I'm going to fix things up with the Grays Harbor sheriff, get that charge against you dropped. So go back to Seattle. I don't need any more fiascoes."

"Heard from Richard yet?" By the way.

She saw that defiance sharpened his features, electrified his smoky eyes. Something had ticked him off. She said, "That's none of your business."

After he'd gone, she glanced down at her wedding ring, wiggled the finger. The ring didn't budge, but a deep ache gripped her heart.

FRANCES CREED held a cold wet rag to Milan's forehead. Milan's soft brown eyes pooled tears and her limbs jerked around. Frances started singing.

> Sun wakes up
> Beach turns red
> Baby sleeps
> in soft fine bed
> Baby wakes
> to greet Great Sky
> Baby Raven
> learns to fly.

After a while, the high, rhythmic song put Milan to sleep. Frances sat on the couch and smoked. After two cigarettes, she picked up the telephone and called Father Brendan.

"I'm bringing Theresa over there tonight."

"Sure," said Father Brendan. "Bring Winn, too."

Frances scoffed. "Winn won't come near church. What time can I come?"

"On the early side, Frances. Does Theresa have a rosary?"

Frances scoffed again. "Not for too long now she hasn't had one."

Father Brendan had some difficulty sorting out this reply, so he just said, "Come on over around dinnertime. I have a fresh chicken from Gordon Toolong. It's cooking now."

THIRTEEN

GUARDIAN SPIRIT

FATHER BRENDAN'S RECTORY house in Forks was a small cottage on the road behind the Forks Timber Museum, in the shadow of the lumberjack statue. If Theresa looked out the dining-room window, she could see the lumberjack's ax, grasped the way a soldier holds a rifle. Theresa's brother worked as a tree marker for Roundtree, the big timber company in Forks. He didn't use an ax, he used a fat grease pen and sometimes the blade of his hunting knife to mark trees for cutting. John—her brother—didn't decide which trees to mark; a tree manager stationed at a computer terminal decided and told John which ones to mark. John liked his job and the benefits, and Theresa had often suggested to Winn that he apply at Roundtree. Winn refused, but never gave a reason why.

The whole baked chicken, stuffed and trussed, reminded Theresa of a dead infant. She didn't touch a bite. She politely ate potatoes—two or three forkfuls, but that was all—and drank some tepid coffee. "It's decaf," the priest explained. "So you won't lie awake all night."

Theresa shrugged. "I don't sleep. Not now."

The chicken disappeared, its remains whisked off to the kitchen by Pauline, Father Brendan's Hoh housekeeper. Pauline was seventy-five and felt close to God in the rectory where Father Brendan held Mass every morning at seven o'clock. Maybe one day they'd have a real church, but now they worshipped in the shadow of the rectory television screen and Father's favorite armchair. Frances Creed had bad knees, and sat in Father's armchair during Mass.

Frances said, "You need to come to church, Theresa," meaning she needed to attend Mass in Father Brendan's living room.

Father Brendan said, "Don't push Theresa, Frances. It has to be her own decision."

Frances muttered to herself.

"What, Mom? What are you mumbling?" Theresa sounded more irritated than curious.

"Those babies should've been baptized. Now Paris's soul is stuck in Limbo."

Father Brendan spoke sharply to Frances. "That's not necessarily true, Frances. Paris might still have a Guardian Angel, even though he wasn't baptized. He might not be in Limbo, but still alive, in a safe place."

Theresa studied her fingernails, bitten to the quick. To Father Brendan, she said, "Maybe I'll bring Milan up at Easter. Is that when you baptize?"

"Easter is the best time for baptism. But, well, in this case, I think we should baptize Milan right away. We could take care of it tomorrow."

"It's no big rush," said Theresa. "We could always do it after we get Paris back."

Afraid of sabotaging the baptism plan, Frances dared not argue with her daughter. Father Brendan said, "Bless his little soul. Surely God takes pity on the innocent babies."

Theresa snapped, "I don't want to discuss it. I'll send Milan up here in a few days with Mom, and you can baptize her. Then maybe Mom will quit pestering me. Anyhow, it's time to go. I know Winn's had enough of Milan by now." She stood up, and with a trembling hand, brushed off her jeans. Frances noticed how Theresa's jeans sagged, how her daughter's weight had drastically dropped to what Frances thought was an unhealthy level. Frances honestly wondered if Theresa would survive this tragedy.

At the door, Pauline slipped up behind Theresa, grasped her closed fist, opened it, dropped something in and closed it again. Theresa slipped it into her pocket and left without saying a word to Pauline. That night, undressing, Theresa reached into the pocket and pulled out the rosary. Amethyst crystals, with a silver cross. Winn was already in bed, apparently asleep. She took some of the sleeping medication Dr. Fish had prescribed for her, slipped under the bedcovers beside Winn, her fisted hand clutching the rosary, and lay awake listening to night sounds.

When Winn finally heard Theresa's soft, even breathing, he gently slid out of bed, grabbed his clothing and boots, and in the darkness, groped toward the living room. Feeling his way along the trailer's corridor, Winn passed Milan's room and listened. No sounds. Just to be sure that she was still there, Winn poked his head in. Moonlight poured through the window. Milan lay in her crib, wide awake.

Theresa stirred when Winn put Milan in bed beside her. The baby fussed and cried. Winn closed the bedroom's thin door, dressed in the living room and went out.

Light from the single pole shone across the trailer park's junk-strewn grounds. Winn picked his way in the shadows, steering clear of the light's dim path. Passing the Brightman trailer, he heard only silence and guessed the family argument had some way or other resolved itself. That was good, because Winn liked Bob Brightman. He liked Bob, and he liked the daughter, Becca. Becca was suffering, too, Winn reminded himself. She always baby-sat the twins; she was close to them. Then, too, today even Carolee showed real compassion, like she understood how Winn felt right now after losing his boy.

After the Brightman trailer came the Polks, the elderly couple. Lee Polk had served as a senior officer in the army, in Vietnam, and when he got out, retired here in the trailer park with Irene. Lee Polk had told Winn that he'd been in the Special Forces, and Winn believed it. Lee had that kind of personality: forthright, watchful. He drew an army pension, but it wasn't enough to live on, so Irene grew a big garden and became a wildcrafter like Carolee Brightman. But Irene Polk, unlike Carolee Brightman, never wildcrafted on the national parks and in the preserve. And Irene made fresh bread and shared it with her neighbors. She had that god-awful stoop that embarrassed Winn whenever he looked at her, and, in a way, he pitied the old woman. Still, she did belong to that wiccan, the one that danced up at Ruby Beach every equinox or whatever, their flaming bonfires and their bright torches flickering in a long yellow line as they danced their jive witch dance. But she sure baked great bread. Now the Polk's trailer stood dark and silent, and Winn guessed they were in there sleeping like a couple of old logs. Winn wished he could sleep, but sleep didn't come, as bad as he felt tonight.

Beside the Polks lived the Dean couple from Yakima, Daniel Dean, his teenaged wife, Cindy, and her little sister, Misty Cravus. White trash. Winn had never liked them. Daniel's pickup was gone, their trailer dark. Maybe they'd gone nighttime clamming, like they often did this time of night. Or said they did. Winn wouldn't be at all surprised if Cindy was one of those witches, too. He'd seen her over at the Polk trailer lately, hanging with Irene Polk. Cindy was learning the wildcraft from Irene Polk. He tried to steer clear of the Deans and that precocious little Misty. He felt they had a dark side about them, something they'd rather keep hidden, and he'd rather not know about.

Behind the Dean trailer, a smaller trailer—just a one-room aluminum shack on wheels—sat beneath an ancient cedar on the highway's edge. It had been vacant since Winn could remember. No one knew who owned it. Every few months, some wayward soul would move in, set up house. The occupancy usually lasted about a month. A month living next door to the Deans was all anyone could take. All that pot smoke leaking from their trailer was enough to make you puke. Not that Winn didn't toke a weed now and then, back before he had a family to look after. Back in his carefree days.

The highway made a straight-of-way in front of the trailer park for a few hundred feet, then turned sharply in both directions, north and south, twisting up to Forks, winding down to Grays Harbor. Winn stepped out onto the highway. Outside the shelter of the cedars, a nasty wind drove straight through his clothing. He walked to the center line, felt the full blast of the wind. He stood there, waiting for a speeding logging truck to strike him head-on, crush him beneath its wheels, lay him flat and dead. When nothing came from either direction, Winn crossed to the beach.

From the driftwood logs where Winn stood, he saw the clam diggers. Dozens of them, their lanterns flickering points of light that moved across the dark beach, between the rocky shore and the roaring breakers, on the sand flats of a low tide. Little fireflies bent over, digging clams. Once or twice, one clam digger would shout something and everybody would swarm around, and Winn thought it a pretty sight, though he personally hated clams unless they'd been deep-fried.

How could such appalling tragedy and such great fortune strike the same man within one week? Does it matter which comes first? When tragedy strikes before fortune, does it diminish the power of the good fortune? Is it better, or just different, when fortune strikes before tragedy? Winn had no one to ask, except, if he were brave enough, his guardian spirit.

Winn had never revealed his guardian spirit to anyone. Since the morning of his ninth birthday, when his parents left him alone in the forest down on the Muckleshoot reservation to meditate and to listen for its coming, Winn had never talked about his guardian spirit. For eight days and nights, young Winn had stayed alone in the forest with nothing but a campfire to keep him company and warm him, without food or shelter, without companionship, drinking only water from a clear stream, never speaking, just listening. Finally, on the eighth night, Elk came to Winn and announced that he was Winn's guardian spirit.

"You must never tell anyone who your guardian spirit is," said Elk. "If you reveal my identity, I will punish you. But if you keep it a secret, I will guide you safely through all your trials and travails."

Winn promised Elk never to reveal their spiritual connection. At first, Elk wasn't convinced Winn could keep their secret. "I want proof that you will never reveal your guardian spirit," said Elk.

"Please trust me, Elk," said Winn. "What can I do to prove my trustworthiness?"

Elk said, "Bring me fresh food every day for one year. If you do this, I will believe in your trustworthiness and I will always protect you."

For one year afterward, every day, Winn gathered fresh vine maple leaves and brambles and carried them to that same spot in the forest, set them beside the murmuring stream and waited for Elk to come. Elk always came and always ate the food that Winn brought. Through this time, a bond formed between Elk and Winn, and when the year had passed, Elk said, "Now I trust you, and I will always protect you from harm." Then Elk told Winn to lie down on the forest floor. Winn lay down. Elk placed a hoof on Winn's chest and Winn felt Elk enter his soul. Elk said, "Now I live in you, and I will live in you forever." After that, Winn never hunted elk, and as he grew into manhood, he felt Elk's life inside him and it made him feel strong and good.

Even through the struggles with alcohol, when Winn got so drunk he couldn't recognize his own family or his friends, Elk stayed inside him, and Winn knew that he would somehow conquer the disease. It must have been Elk who brought Theresa into Winn's life. Ever since then, Winn felt blessed and protected, connected to the spirit world, a whole person. Then this. Then some unknown evil force coming to claim his baby son, the heart of his heart, the light of his life, his flesh and blood. Where was Elk now? He couldn't feel Elk inside him, he felt only dead space where Elk should be. Guardian spirits should keep their promises.

The wind off the breakers blew the tears from Winn's eyes. He wiped his face on his shirt. He was standing on the driftwood, a tortured, vacant soul, when he heard a voice behind him. He turned around. Carolee Brightman put out her hand, and he helped her up onto the logs. Standing side by side, they watched the clam diggers for a few minutes before Carolee turned her face up to his and said, "You better accept it, Winn. Paris is dead."

FOURTEEN

FOOT LOOSE

AT TOLEAK HIGH SCHOOL, Becca Brightman avoided Misty Cravus like the plague, but everywhere Becca went, Misty popped up. One day in homeroom, she sat beside Becca in the twin rows of desks, so close that Becca could smell Misty's dog breath. Becca asked to be moved, but the teacher refused. Immediately after homeroom, Becca grabbed her books and got out of there. At her locker, Becca put on the makeup Carolee wouldn't allow her to wear at home. She had a mirror on the inside of the door, where she could watch herself. She outlined her lips with Mink Vixen Maybelline pencil, filled them in with Cherry Vanilla gloss, and was blotting them on a tissue when Misty's face appeared in the mirror.

"I'm not supposed to talk to you," said Becca.

Misty retorted, "Oh yeah? Well, too bad, because I know your secret, and I might even go to the police and report you."

Becca shut her locker door. "You're demented."

Misty grabbed Becca's hand. Becca tried jerking it away, but Misty was strong. She said, "Your lipstick looks real nice."

Becca felt her stomach turn sour. "Let go of my hand."

Misty pulled Becca close, kissed her lips.

Becca jerked away and this time Misty let her go. Misty said, "Did you like that?"

"No, I did not." Becca wiped her mouth and reapplied her lipstick.

Misty, hands on hips, hips cocked sideways, said, "I think you liked that."

"Well, I didn't." Becca blotted her freshly repaired lips. "It made me want to barf."

Misty laughed. "Be nice, or I'll tell the police."

Becca looked around to see if anyone was in hearing range. They were alone. Becca growled, "If you say a word to anybody, I'll kill you, Misty Cravus."

Misty threw her head back and howled. And kept howling all the way down the corridor.

After school, the bus dropped Becca and Misty off at the entrance to the trailer park. They watched the bus disappear down the highway, then Misty went home. When Becca reached her trailer, she saw that both her parents' cars were gone. Becca smiled to herself, went inside, changed her clothes. On her way out, Becca reached underneath her mattress and pulled out Clint Kellogg's book of fables. She left by the rear door, shutting it quietly, and stole off into the forest, checking over her shoulder to be sure Misty wasn't watching. In the rain forest, Becca followed a clear brook to where the brook branched off from the Little Hoh River. The sun was setting rapidly, and dusk would soon darken her path. She hurried faster. If she could just get to her destination before dark, everything would be perfect. Her mother thought she was staying late at school for an athletic event. Carolee was so naive. Becca had better things to do than sports.

She was hurrying down the path when she saw the elk. A cow. At first, Becca thought she might be just resting on the ground. As she drew closer, Becca saw the elk's eyes were wide open, and blood streamed from her mouth. Dead. Then Becca saw the legs. She wanted to scream, but nothing came out. She took off running as fast as she could. She had feet to carry her. The dead elk lay hoofless.

BEFORE COMING to the United States, Claudia Paganelli practiced forensic medicine as the Chief Coroner for the City of Oslo. In Oslo, Claudia only autopsied humans. When she arrived in the New World, Claudia married an Italian-American, a big-game veterinarian. Working with her husband, Claudia soon learned to dissect a wide variety of cadavers. When DOI hired Paganelli, they paid her three times her predecessor's salary because she was worth it.

"The weapon was a .300 Winchester Magnum," she told Venus over the phone. "The elk was struck by two 180-grain bullets. The first penetrated the hide, nicked the shoulder blade, and went straight into the heart. The second went through the rib cage, but it was just for security. The hunter didn't need that second bullet."

"Same weapon as the earlier killings?" Venus was on her digital, somewhere in the rain forest.

Claudia said, "Of course. And like the earlier incidents, the hooves were sawed off with a True Value Hardware saw blade."

"Definitely the same poacher. Have you heard of this happening anywhere else?"

Claudia said, "There is, come to think of it, a vaguely similar case that comes to mind involving moose in Canada. The hooves and, in the case of bulls, the antlers, were sawed off and as I recall, no other part was harvested. Again, the poachers used hacksaws."

"Keratin, is that what they're after?"

"Right. I read this in a Canadian journal. According to the article, there's a growing demand for big-game keratin. The author of the abstract didn't say why, didn't elaborate on that point, other than to cite these two instances that occurred near Banff. The moose were both full-grown bulls."

"Who's the author of the article?"

"A guy named Jim Clever. He's a wildlife biologist with British Columbia Fish and Game."

"C-l-e-v-e-r?"

"Correct. You want his phone number?"

Claudia went to her desk, checked her database, read off the number. "That's in Banff. They're an hour ahead of us, so he might already be in his office."

Venus said, "What about those lab results on the tissue the hunters found up here on Bogachiel?"

Claudia sighed. "Still not back. Something is wrong in the lab. They are making sloppy errors, and are as slow as mud lately."

"I think you mean molasses."

"Maybe. Speaking of slow, how is Dottie these days?"

"Behaving like an airhead," said Venus. "No one can figure out why. She won't talk to anyone. She just moons around all the time. Olson's threatening to can her."

Claudia said, "One of us better talk to her before that happens."

Clever answered on the first ring. Yes, he'd authored the paper on moose poaching in the Canadian Rockies. The practice had declined during the past two decades, but suddenly, last spring, the number of poaching incidents rose dramatically. Clever had hard evidence in a dozen cases in just a three-month period. No poachers had been arrested yet. Mainly racks were harvested, and some individuals had been killed for their meat and hides. But the two instances he cited in the abstract were different. He'd never seen anything like this before. In these poachings, the individuals' antlers and hooves were crudely sawed off. He hadn't gone so far as to check what brand of hacksaw was used, but in both cases, the bullets had been 180-grain, probably from a .300 Winchester. Clever had no idea of motive.

Venus said, "Any possible connection with the local Asian community?"

"You mean Asian medicinal practices?"

"Any chance of that?"

Clever said, "I doubt it. Although we have had bears poached up here for their gall bladders. But moose? I doubt this is related to Asian medicine. I might be wrong."

Venus said, "You must have a theory."

"No. No, other than the black market in keratin. To be honest, I don't understand what that's all about. But if you have evidence of a similar crime in the U.S., I'd like to hear about it."

"Right now, I have four solid cases, and one reported sighting of a carcass floating in the ocean. Its hooves were missing. That carcass wasn't recovered."

"Well, if this keeps up, call me, eh?"

"Sure, Clever. I'll do that."

THERESA WAS SITTING at the kitchen table, studying a map of the preserve, when Winn came out of the bedroom dressed to go out and reeking of Aramis. He walked down the corridor toward the living room. Theresa called out, "Where are you going?"

Winn paused. He was standing beside the new thermostat. Automatically, he checked the temperature. Seventy-two. She always kept it too hot. Winn said, "I need some fresh air."

From the kitchen, Theresa said, "I thought we were going to rearrange the furniture in the twins' room."

Winn winced. "The furniture's fine the way it is."

He heard Theresa's chair scrape against the kitchen floor. Theresa came padding down the corridor. She wore the pink angora sweater, her hair up in a ponytail. Winn thought he saw a glimmer of the old Tee, but mostly he saw a tired old woman.

Theresa said, "You said we'd do this tonight. That's why Milan went home with Mom. So we could fix up that room."

"I can't do it tonight."

A silence, then Theresa said, "Are you gambling with that money, Winn?"

"What I do is my business. It's not your business, Tee."

"Winn, you promised you wouldn't touch that money, except for absolute necessities. Until this is all over."

Winn, who had his back to her, turned suddenly and shouted, "What's 'this'? There is no 'this.' It's over now, Tee, and you better just face up to it and get on with your life."

Theresa pressed her lips together hard. Quietly, she said, "I need you to stay home, Winn."

"You can't tell me what to do."

Theresa felt a sickness in her heart. "I really need you to stay home with me tonight."

Winn strode to the door, opened it. "Stop telling me what to do with my life. You're always trying to control me. I won't have it, Tee. I won't be controlled."

Theresa came and stood beside him on the threshold. Any other time, she would have tossed her chin, too proud to beg. But now she said, "Winn, please stay home."

Winn shouted, "This is no home. It's a goddamn trailer, for chris-sake."

"It's our home, Winn. It's what we have."

Winn laughed sharply. "When are you ever home? Huh? When do you keep house and cook decent meals and do the laundry? Hell, this marriage is a goddamn joke. All we ever do together is cry and argue over whether or not he's still alive." He slammed a fist into the side of the trailer, denting the rusty corrugated skin.

"Winn, I'm asking you, as your wife, not to leave. I need you to stay with me tonight." Theresa's flat voice died in the wind.

The Polks had come outside to see what all the racket was about and Winn felt their stare on his back. Somewhere in the woods, an owl hooted. Theresa stood her ground on the front stoop, her arm outstretched, her hand open, entreating. From the highway came the sound of a vehicle. It turned into the trailer park, its wheels squealing, a knock in the engine. Bob Brightman's Pontiac. Never trust a me-chanic who doesn't service his own vehicle. Brightman pulled up between his trailer and the Nighteagles'. He got out, carrying a sack from the Stop 'N' Go down in Queets. He looked around. He saw Theresa standing on the stoop, and Winn halfway to his pickup, shoulders hunched, fists clenched. He saw the Polks on their front porch.

"What's going on?" Bob Brightman asked.

Winn turned to Bob and growled, "Stay the hell out of my business, Brightman."

Bob looked at Theresa. "You all right?"

Theresa nodded tiredly.

Bob went inside, and Winn saw him through the window, standing in the kitchen with Carolee. Carolee was unpacking the Stop 'N' Go bag, pretending to ignore the scene outside. Winn turned his back on all of them, walked to his pickup, got in. He left rubber on the highway, a double black line that faded gradually northward.

THE CASINO was jumping when Winn strolled in, looking pretty damn sharp for a guy who just lost his son to the jaws of the Unknown. When he pulled out his wallet it looked thicker than usual, and just as fast as they'd judged him, the gamblers made room at their tables for the man with the fat roll of bills. Winn Nighteagle might have sorry luck in his personal life, but he had big money and someone really should take some of that off his hands. Serve him right, if you want to get judgmental again, if the house won back all that money.

"Hey, Winn, over here, buddy. Pull up a chair, man, we got your drink covered."

"We got a fine hand of jack goin' here, Winn, maybe you want to cut in? We don't mind, hell no, buddy, come on in."

"You been feelin' okay, Winn? We're all thinking of you and your family, buddy."

"Hit me."

Winn played eight hands and won eight hands. What gave Winn Nighteagle such good luck? Every hand he played he won. Every hand they played, they lost. Maybe if they got him drunk.

"Hey, Winn, here's another G-and-T for you. Bottoms up, good buddy."

"Hit me."

The last time Winn came in the casino, that time, he won the house. And that time, he was drunk as a skunk. So maybe gin wasn't such a good idea, after all. Might bring him luck.

"Oo-wee, that's a tight hand he played there."

"Hit me one last time, then I'm finished. Winn's got it all locked up here anyhow."

"I don't see how you do it, buddy, how you can scrape the table, as drunk as you are. This is my la-a-a-s-s-t hand, and...ouch."

"Did it again, Winn. Robbed the house blind. Just kiddin', I know you won fair 'n' square. Well, see you boys tomorrow night, if the old lady doesn't kill me first."

Winn looked up and saw Carolee Brightman sitting at the bar. She was alone, sipping a glass of beer, and if he wasn't mistaken, her eyes were riveted on his table, on him. Winn winked clumsily. She laughed, picked up her drink and came over, sat down beside him. The other players didn't like that, and, anyway, they were tired of losing while Winn won every hand. Soon Winn and Carolee sat alone at the table.

Carolee laid her hand over Winn's. "They got a band upstairs, Winn. A dance band."

Winn watched Carolee over his gin and tonic. When he finished the drink, he set the empty glass on the table, pushed back his chair.

"Let's go on up, Carolee."

PART TWO

PART TWO

FIFTEEN

LANCE AND LANA

HERE ARE Senator and Mrs. Lanai in their fine home in Pacific Palisades, working out in their home gym. Lance has his personal training regime, Lana has hers. Lance's goal is dropping thirty pounds and gradually revisiting his physique of yesteryear, fifteen years ago, when Lana discovered him at an audition for a Spielberg film, and launched him on a film career that fizzled faster and louder than Alka-Seltzer. He'd quickly switched to politics, a performance art he understood, his father having been a notorious glad-handing senator from Missouri. Lance had inherited Dad's Machiavellian genes, and he excelled. Along the way, Lance had married Lana, probably the smartest move he ever made. Lana knew better than anybody how to manipulate public opinion, and she championed all the charitable causes that lent a tender cachet to the senator's revisionist aura. Leave it to Mrs. Lanai, that's what Lance said whenever his staff wavered under public scrutiny. Leave it to Lana.

Here's Lance at the bench, pressing, sweating like a pig. Lance doesn't know or even care if pigs really sweat. What matters is, Lance sweats. All Lance cares about is meeting his goal at the bench and winning a second term in the Senate. After that, maybe he'd pull a Ronald Reagan. Politics are half deception, half performance art. Lance understands this intimately, like he understands what oils Lana. Lance weighs one hundred ninety pounds. Lance can bench-press one-fifty, ten repetitions, and he can win elections. Popular Lance might even return to movies after he tires of politics.

Lithesome Lana's physical training is more complex than Lance's, for not only is Lana fanatical over the shape and silhouette of her body, she's also concerned with developments her personal trainer Jules Coco ascribes to the aging process. That is, gravity and cell degeneration. Lance, being male and forty-three, hasn't yet fretted over gravity's tug on his facial flesh, and, being born and raised in

Kansas City, Missouri, he's not so concerned with micro-managing his cells. Lance eats beef and pork and veal. Lana eats oranges, arugula, and tofu. Lance drinks a single-malt scotch whiskey and full-bodied ales. Lana nurses merlots and the occasional oreganotini.

Lana's routine, unlike Lance's, varies day to day. On this sunny autumn morning, Lana begins her workout on the mat near windows facing the Pacific Ocean. When you live in Pacific Palisades you enjoy this view. Lana begins stretching, goosed on by Jules Coco. Stretch, stretch, stretch. Next comes pliés. No one in L.A. sculpts over-forty bodies like Jules Coco. Lana thinks Jules doesn't know her actual age, but Jules reads the body like a preacher reads bibles and he recognizes the telltale signs of ladies who are ten years older than their mates. Here's Lana Lanai, at fifty-two and a half—Jules actually knows her exact birthdate—looking a smart forty-something from the collarbone down. Above the collarbone, Lana looks about thirty-two, thanks to Doc Kellogg's latest lunch lift.

There's something else about Lana that Jules Coco knows. Lana actually told Jules about the injections, actually took him into her confidence. Jules wouldn't personally try the injections, not yet. The secret formula hadn't been proven totally safe, without side effects, hadn't been approved by the Food and Drug Administration. So, no, Jules wasn't indulging, not yet, and anyway, he didn't need to, being a well-preserved thirty-four. He has to admit, though, that Lana's once-a-week injections of Elixir of Youth are working wonders on her. Two years into Elixir injection therapy, riding the cresting wave of anti-aging science, Lana's whole body has acquired a more youthful appearance. Firmer skin tone. Fewer fine lines. Leaner muscle-to-fat ratio. Smoother musculature. Increased energy. A miraculous reversal in her libido, formerly sluggish at best. Jules knows that Lance has to work twice as hard as he used to before the injections.

Lana's been through an alphabet soup of anti-aging therapies, always surfing the net for the latest trends. She's done Botox, DHEA, melatonin, grape seed and Pycnogenol, kava-kava QE3, and now, Elixir's secret hormone therapy formula. Lana told Jules that the stuff is all natural, all organic. Seems to Jules that everyone in Hollywood's on some form of anti-aging hormone therapy. Except Jules himself, and Senator Lanai. Maybe not everyone, but Jules guessed just about every major male star over forty and every leading lady, regardless of age, injected, drank, or otherwise ingested variations on the cutting edge age-reversal hormone therapies. This Elixir of Youth, now:

Lana says you have to get that from Internet sources, or from Doc Kellogg's secret stash. No one sold Elixir of Youth over the counter. The FDA would swoop down in a New York minute, Lana said. So no one dared.

Jules rolls Lana onto her stomach. Lana says, "Jules, honey, I've had enough of this for one day. Let me up."

"Give me thirty of your best, then you get up."

"Give me a break, honey. I'm not exactly awake yet."

"Three—four—five...late night?—seven—eight—nine..."

"Oof. Yes. Look, this is killing me, honey, honest it is."

"Eleven—twelve—thirteen—keep it up."

"Lance, what are you doing over there?"

Jules counts while Lance answers.

"I'm on the phone, Lana. Don't bother me now."

"Twenty-one—twenty-two—twenty-three—almost done—twenty-five..."

"Oof." Lana gasps and puffs.

"Twenty-eight—twenty-nine—thirty. Stop, aaannd...rest."

Lana rolls over on her back. A dark moat skims her jealous eyes, fishtails flicking in murk. Lana says, "He's talking to that little Tiffany bitch again."

Tiffany-bitch is Lance Lanai's Capitol Hill intern.

Jules's ears redden. He tries ignoring her comment, tries walking away.

"Come back here, Jules."

Jules goes back to Lana, his chief source of income.

Lana says, "How do I look, honey?"

"Great. Faboo."

"How old?"

"Do you look?" Lana nods. Jules hesitates a beat. Then Jules says, "Thirty-five. Definitely no more than thirty-five."

Lana glances over at Lance. He's sitting on the bench, his back to them, muttering into the phone. Lana snakes across the room, circles Lance and the bench. Lance doesn't notice his wife; apparently he's too engrossed in the telephone chat. Lana goes back over to Jules, who's standing stone-faced, not daring to move a muscle. Lana blows Jules an air kiss. "Thanks, honey. See you mañana."

Lana disappears inside the cavernous abode. Jules Coco exits next, lugging his gym bag and a sweatshirt. In front of the house, Jules slides behind the wheel of a red Mustang, ponies off the curb. Senator Lanai hangs out in the gym, purring into the phone.

Senator Lanai says, "Whatever you need, Agent Diamond. Don't hesitate."

SIXTEEN

ADONIS

MARY'S TRUE VALUE Hardware in Grays Harbor carried three models of manually operated saws: the slim-blade bottle-nosed compass saw for cutting through small wooden items, the regular wide-blade tool for sawing through thicker or wider lengths of wood, and the hacksaw for cutting metal pipe and other hard materials. The hacksaw has an arc over the blade and a handle on one end. Someone using a hacksaw, holding it by the handle, might need more leverage, more weight against the blade. This is accomplished by gripping the metal arc above the blade and pushing while bearing down hard on the object being sawed. Venus picked up a hacksaw, hefted it, carried it to the front of the store.

The clerk at the cash register was talking on the phone. When Venus placed the saw on the counter, he stared straight through her and said into the phone, "Cool." Two or three minutes passed while the clerk continued his telephone conversation, punctuated occasionally by his murmuring, "Cool." He could pick his teeth, slick back his pompadour, scratch his chest, and perform a few other tricks while conversing on the telephone. Waiting on customers was apparently one trick he could not execute while engaged on the horn. Venus swooped up the hacksaw and went in search of another clerk. She found one in the back of the store, hunched over a roll of plastic bubble wrap, his fingers lovingly caressing the bumpy surface.

Pop. Pop, pop. Pop, pop, pop, pop, pop, pop. Pop.

"Pardon me," Venus held out the hacksaw.

Pop, pop. The clerk glanced at the hacksaw, at her hand. His eyes traced her arm up to her neck, found her face, met her eyes, but his fingers never left the bubbles. Pop, pop, pop. "Yeah?"

Venus said, "Do you sell a lot of these hacksaws?"

He was about eighteen, shaped like a python, with shoulder-length hair and peach fuzz over acne. He uncoiled and when he stood up, he was about ten feet tall and she had to crane her neck to hear what he said. He said, "Yeah," and reluctantly, he parted with the bubble wrap.

Venus said, "Who buys them?"

The python said, "Guys who cut things."

"Plumbers?"

"Yeah. And pipe-bomb makers." He guffawed, and it came out in little rat-tat-tats.

"What about hunters? Do hunters ever buy them?"

He smiled crookedly. "What would a hunter do with a hacksaw?"

She shrugged. "Saw up his prey."

Rat-tat-tat. "Oh, like, you mean, hack up a deer so it fits in his freezer?"

"Something like that. And saw off the antlers."

The python grinned. "In that case, he wouldn't use a hacksaw. He'd use a rack saw." Rat-tat-tat.

She let that fade into obscurity and said, "Do you sell a lot of these hacksaws?"

The python shrugged. "Depends what you mean by 'a lot.'"

She said, "Is the manager around?"

The python nodded. "That's me. What can I do you for?"

From the front of the store, she heard the clerk, still speaking into the phone. "Cool." Caught between Mr. Cool and the python, she took a pragmatic detour. To the python, she said, "I'd like to buy this hacksaw, but only if it will saw through bone."

The python twitched. "Sure," he said, wary now. "Bone's cool."

She said, "Has anyone else asked you that?"

He rubbed the peach fuzz, thought it over. She heard the other clerk guffaw and then she heard him hang up the phone. The python said, "One guy did ask me that. But that was a long time ago."

"How long ago?"

"Like, months. Last summer, maybe, or last spring. I don't remember."

"Do you remember what he looked like?"

"Not much of a hunter type," he said. "More like a bone surgeon." Rat-tat-tat.

"What's a bone surgeon look like?"

The python scratched his greasy head. "This one had real soft hands. That's all I can remember about him, his soft pink hands. I don't remember what else he looked like."

"Did you catch his name?"

"Naw." Rat-tat-tat.

"Kellogg sound familiar?"

The python shrugged, reached out for the hacksaw. She handed it to him. He said, "Naw." He went over to a cash register, rang up the sale. He placed the hacksaw in a large plastic True Value bag, handed it to her, winked. "You're the first girl I ever sold a hacksaw to," he said. "Whatcha gonna do with it?"

She said, "I've got a problematic boyfriend."

The python nodded, impressed. "Well, be careful." Rat-tat-tat.

At the front counter she paused, said to the clerk, "Are there any other True Value stores on the peninsula?"

He said, "No," then added hostilely, "I could've helped you up here in front. You didn't have to go back there to the manager. Now you got me into trouble."

Over her shoulder, she said, "Cool."

In Cedar Grove Trailer Park, Carolee Brightman squinted at the buttons on her Princess phone. The double dose of eyebright she'd prescribed for herself wasn't up to the job, the numbers blurred something awful, so she just pressed away, hoping for the best, and when the receptionist answered, she said, "It's Carolee Brightman, Moira. Give me Doc Kellogg."

Perched behind Adonis's pink marble reception stand, Moira wore a clingy gown and satin ballerina slippers. She'd just had a Turkish massage, a glycolic face peel, and her makeup applied by Chandler. Before her on the marble desk stood a frosted glass half full of Miracle Enzyme Tonic. Moira sniffed discourteously and said, "Dr. Kellogg's on the other line, Mrs. Brightman. Can you hold?"

"I'm long distance, honey. Get your buns off that stool and go get the Doc."

Moira made a rude face at the phone, put Carolee Brightman on hold, and slipped off the high stool just as God's Gift to Actors swept up to the desk. Moira pointed down a long marble corridor. "You're down there this morning, Mrs. Lanai. With Velma."

"Thanks, sweetie." Lana clicked down the corridor, leaving Chanel air. Moira pinched her nose to avoid any stray Lana pheromones. Slinking across the spa's pink marble floors, Moira glided past the mud therapy baths and massage rooms, around a corner, past some more private treatment rooms, past the surgery, and finally reached her destination, the secluded and ever so serene offices of the spa's owner, Dr. Bradford (Adonis) Kellogg.

Kellogg sat at his desk, cradling a cordless on his shoulder and massaging a desktop keyboard. When Moira rapped on the glass door, Kellogg waved her inside, and once in hearing range, she soon surmised Brad was speaking to his brother, Clint, who lived in Washington state. Moira had dated Clint a time or two before he turned intellectual and started writing books. All Moira really heard of the conversation was Doc Kellogg saying, "That kind of carelessness isn't acceptable. And we'll need that ingredient by tomorrow because I'm bringing Mrs. Lanai up for her treatment tomorrow afternoon. Now, I have someone in my office, so I'll have to call you back."

Doc Kellogg swung around to greet Moira. "What's up?"

Moira shimmied up to the Doc's desk and purred, "That wildcrafter woman's on line four. I didn't know if you wanted to speak to her. She's holding."

Doc Kellogg's smoldering gaze devoured Moira's right-angle curves, causing a tingle she didn't dislike. Moira wasn't the only female employee who dug the doc, but, being his newly appointed personal assistant (plus, still the receptionist), she was the only staff member with unlimited access to the doc's private offices. That gave her a leg up in the race to capture Doc Kellogg's heart—well, bank account.

Doc Kellogg said, "Oh, hey, I need to speak to Mrs. Brightman," and reached for the phone. "What line did you say?"

"Four." Moira curled her lip, slinked to the couch, and eavesdropped. Savoring the tingle.

"Hey, Carolee, Doc Kellogg here." (Pause, listen.) "No, I've told you already, I don't like sending that product through the mail. I'll pick it up tomorrow when I visit my brother." (Pause, listen.) "What? Yes, Clint told me they've pretty much stopped searching for him." (Pause, listen.) "Well, it looks pretty grim, doesn't it?" (Pause, listen.) "Is that right? Poor kid, it must have scared her to death. You say the hooves were actually sawed off? Heavens, no, I'm sure Clint wasn't involved. Clint doesn't hunt, at least I don't think so. (Pause, listen.) No, I don't have any patients to refer to you at the moment. So, hey, Carolee, great speaking with you. Have a nice day. Bye-bye."

"Patients," Moira snickered. "I didn't know you had patients."

Doc Kellogg made a sour face. Even making a sour face, Moira thought Doc Kellogg was handsome as sin. "How long have you worked for me, Moira?"

Moira studied a tiny fish tattoo on her ankle, a souvenir from her Sedona Christian era. "Five months."

"After five months," admonished Doc Kellogg, scribbling on a notepad, "you should know that I am a licensed physician. Look up there on the wall. Is that a medical degree? If I didn't have medical training, how could I perform lunch lifts? Adonis has *clients*. I personally have *patients*." He tore a paper off the notepad, thrust it out.

Moira journeyed over. When she finally arrived, she snatched the note, leaned provocatively across Doc's lap, and said "Which am I?" His strong, slim hand caressed Moira's derriere. "Patient. Definitely patient."

To Moira's great disappointment, that was as far as Doc Kellogg ever went, patting her bum. Pouting, she glanced down at the note, frowned. "What's this all about?" He'd already forgotten she was there, and her voice startled him.

"Oh, that," he said. "It's about that Native American baby, the one who disappeared up near where Clint lives. My brother's organizing a fund-raising drive, to help out the family. I want you to make up some fliers that we can give out to clients."

Moira said, "What do they need money for? They've got one less mouth to feed."

Doc Kellogg said, "You're a cold-hearted bitch, Moira."

Moira rested a slim hand on her razorbone hip. "And what are you?"

He shrugged. "We might get some great publicity out of this, if we handle it right."

Over her gracile shoulder, Moira wisecracked, "That's what I thought, Ponce de Len," and undulated out.

Moira kept a large tilting mirror on the reception desk. Curving the magnifying mirror to her face, she leaned in close, studying a faint crosshatch forming at the jawline below her mouth. The birth of jowls. That Miracle Enzyme Tonic wasn't helping anymore. The glycolic peels no longer worked their magic. Maybe it was time to start using that black-market product line Doc Kellogg secretly administered to his clients—or was it patients? Elixir of Youth. God knows, it couldn't hurt. Leaving the desk unattended, Moira removed a set of keys from her pocket and slipped down the corridor. At the third door, she turned a key in the lock, and ducked inside.

Dr. Kellogg's private surgery contained a long operating table, a padded leather chair that tilted up and back at the push of a button, some elaborate computerized surgical equipment, stainless-steel tables draped with fresh white cloths holding sterilized medical instruments, and a lot of lights and Byzantine hanging things she didn't enjoy seeing. In the anteroom, there was a refrigerator and floor-to-ceiling shelves freshly stocked with the latest shipment of Elixir of Youth products. Moira moved down the line of products. Elixir of Youth facial creams and toners, Elixir of Youth vitamin supplements, hair products. She selected a small jar of the firming "Youth Regenerator" facial cream, scrutinized the label, which read, "All herbs and roots and other secret ingredients contained in Elixir products are ethically wildcrafted, harvested at peak potency and crafted with veneration to Nature and gratitude for Mother Earth's healing gifts."

Moira didn't know why, but she snickered.

Doc Kellogg had tacked a note up near the products that said, "Elixir products are NOT to be publicly displayed, nor are they to be used by any staff. They are strictly for the use of Dr. Kellogg."

In the refrigerator, Moira discovered bottles of vitamin tonics, packages of fresh herbs, gnarly roots, mud packs, seaweed wraps, and glycolic acid. There was a line of homeopathic cures. A bottle of valerian extract, a bottle of feverfew extract, and a few other organic wonder drugs. This garbage wasn't what she was searching for. Here it was, way in the back. Elixir of Youth's tonic preparations. Moira removed a jar of "Youth Restorative" capsules and a bottle of Elixir of Youth Restorative Injection Formula, adding these to her cache. She wrapped the goodies in paper towels, tucked them into a plastic trash bag, and returned to her desk.

LANA LANAI, swathed in green algae mud, snatched the phone from the Adonis attendant. If one thing annoyed her, it was being interrupted during her sessions. Any disturbance in the sequence of therapies put a damper on the whole process. Mud should be respected. Lance knew that better than anyone, but did he honor her wishes? Not Lance.

"Lance, I am in the midst of my mud. My mouth can't move or it will crack the shell. Now, what is it?"

Senator Lanai peered over his Ben Franklin reading glasses and studied the Washington Monument outside his office window. A drape of snowflakes billowed from an anemic sky. If he left early, he might make it to the airport before it closed on account of snow. If he used his congressman's privilege, he could score the four o'clock flight to Los Angeles. On the other hand, snow always provides a good excuse when you'd rather be in your office than up there in that turbulence. "You need to hear this, Lana."

Lana made a face and the dry shell of mud crenulated. "Can't it wait until tonight?"

"I might not make it home, tonight. Looks like a bad snowstorm here."

"Too bad, darling. It's Free Tibet night at the Getty."

Lance fidgeted with his bow tie. "Listen, Lana. Call me as soon as you leave the spa. I need to convey some information."

Convey some information. Congressman jargon. "Lance, I am too busy for euphemisms. Get to the point."

"It's about Adonis, Lana. I really shouldn't—"

"The point, Lance." Strident.

"The point is, my investigation is heating up in a big way. You need to sever ties with Doc Kellogg, Lana. That's all I can say right now, and I shouldn't even have said that much over the phone. But I needed to convey this information..."

"I know, darling. Now, I have to go. We'll chit-chat later."

Handing the phone back to the attendant, Lana intoned, "My mud's gone to hell."

LANA HAD SHOWERED and dressed and was sipping wheatgrass juice while Dana did her manicure and pedicure. When Dana got to her middle toe, the especially sensitive one, Lana grimaced.

"Am I hurting you, Mrs. Lanai?" asked Dana.

Lana smiled weakly. "That's all right, honey. I can handle a little nail torture. Think of what the Chinese did to the Tibetans."

Dana looked up, said, "And what the Japanese did at Nanjing."

"It's not only Asians. Look at the Albanians in Kosovo."

"Tsk."

After Dana went away, Doc Kellogg popped his head into the lounge. "Hey, gorgeous."

Lana made eyes at the doc. In her sweetest voice she crooned, "Isn't today special dose day, Brad, honey?"

Brad said, "There's been a small glitch. I thought I'd be bringing back the ingredients last night. Things didn't work out the way I'd planned. You'll have to go up there with me tomorrow."

Lana scowled. "Do I really have to go up there?"

"It's the safest way. Don't worry, I'll be there to hold your hand."

Lana sighed. Life is complicated. "I have the leukemia fund-raiser tomorrow. I'm co-chair. How would it look if I didn't show?"

Brad placed a hand on Lana's shoulder. "You do too much for other people, Lana. You need to take care of yourself first, then all these other causes. This is the millennium."

Lana leaned into the nearest mirror, raked a Lilliputian comb through her eyebrows. "Now, Brad, honey, I need my car and driver."

Bitter feelings about Lana Lanai had drained Brad of all defenses. Lana knew too much of Brad's private business, and their secret financial arrangement gave her too much power over him. Lana added, "So be a good boy, and go fetch."

Doc Kellogg trotted off, obedient as a trained pup. Lana whipped out her cell phone and speed-dialled her leukemia fund co-chair. She wouldn't be attending the event tomorrow night. Something urgent had come up.

SEVENTEEN

OVERDOSE

ON THE TUESDAY before Thanksgiving, exactly sixteen days after Paris Nighteagle disappeared on the edge of Bogachiel National Wildlife Preserve, Heartbreak Louie, unrepentant, announced the Gecko's escape from the Grays County prison.

"It's that old holding facility," he complained to Venus. "It wouldn't hold a glass of water. You can't keep prisoners unshackled in an understaffed facility without electric fences and expect them to stay put. He walked right through the service door alongside the UPS delivery person. Somehow he'd got hold of the deputy's gun, used the driver as a human shield. Now we start from scratch."

Venus read her Swatch. "How long ago?"

Song said, "An hour at most. Sheriff's got APBs out. They're combing the parks and beaches. He commandeered the UPS truck, got as far as Queets before bailing out, and disappeared in the woods at the southern edge of Bogachiel preserve."

"A UPS truck can't outrun patrol cars."

"The Gecko made his hostage drive while he held the gun at her temple for motivation. Sheriff says you wouldn't believe how fast this baby flew. Hold on, Olson wants to speak with you."

Song put Olson on. "You and Wexler rendezvoused?" Olson asked, a tinge of envy in his voice.

"Briefly." Cautious response. She knew Olson preferred that all communications between Washington, D.C., and the Pacific Northwest regional office filter through him. He had a point, being chief of regional operations. She didn't expect what came next.

"Did Wexler tell you that your status had changed?"

"Status. No, he didn't mention anything about status. Don't tell me I'm fired again?"

Olson snorted. "When have you ever been fired? I might have threatened a few times, but so far, you've escaped the full brunt of my wrath. Anyway, soon you'll no longer report directly to this office."

Her stomach churned, ground zero of psychic turmoil. First, her marriage flounders, now this. She said, "What's that supposed to mean?"

Olson sounded tired, defeated. "Once this case is wrapped up, Wexler's taking you out of Pacific Northwest. He wants you working directly for him."

"He can't do that."

"He's Secretary of the Interior now. He can do it."

"Acting Secretary. And what if I don't agree?"

Olson snorted louder this time. "Then Mama cuts off your allowance."

"That's not funny. Bella has nothing to do with my professional life."

Olson said, "Right. Other than having Wexler wrapped around her little finger, she's got absolutely no power over your professional life."

"Hey, chief, you're my boss."

"Not anymore."

She said, "I don't like this."

"Get used to it. Think of it as a promotion."

"I'm not going to Washington, D.C." Resolute. "Do you realize that if Wexler hadn't pulled me off the poaching case up here, we might have prevented the Nighteagle baby's kidnapping?"

"Nothing proves those poachings are connected to other current events."

"They're related."

"Show me." Olson wanted to hang up, but she wasn't finished.

She said, "Has Claudia got her lab results back yet?"

"What lab results?"

"On that human tissue the hunters found while trespassing on Bogachiel. Claudia said the lab's been slow with the findings."

Olson grumbled, "Nobody ever tells me anything."

CLINT KELLOGG had a lot on his mind. The eggplant casserole needed checking every five minutes. The CD player was on the fritz. The woman he planned to bed tonight had been lollygagging in his bathroom for half an hour, and God only knew what she was doing in there. She wasn't an intellectual, so she wasn't in there reading one of his books.

It was Lana Lanai, the famous Hollywood agent, one of Brad's patients. He'd met her a few times at Brad's parties in L.A. Now Brad had brought her up here for special treatment and disappeared somewhere, leaving Clint to baby-sit her for the evening. Not that he minded, really, it was just that Clint had been planning to spend the evening writing. He had a new story on the tip of his brain and didn't appreciate the intrusion. He'd just have to make the best of it. But what was she doing in there? She didn't wear that much makeup, so she wasn't just touching up. He could imagine a lot of things he'd rather not, so he concentrated on the eggplant. The babe still hadn't emerged when the telephone rang. It might be Brad. Clint went into the kitchen for privacy. It wasn't Brad, it was Theresa Nighteagle. He could barely understand her, her broken, mumbling voice over the phone. Something urgent, life or death urgent, Clint got that much out of her incoherent lament.

Clint shouted at the bathroom door, but Lana didn't answer. He turned off the casserole. Blew out the candles. He called to Lana again. He could hear her in there, in the shower. What the hell, he wasn't going in there.

Outside, the air was crisp and clear, the sky glittering with stars. He drove at breakneck speed up the highway, but by the time he reached Theresa, she'd already taken the rest of the pills.

IT WAS 8:00 P.M., and Lana's jowls had dropped. Lana was in the bathroom, preparing for an evening with Clint. Lana and her cosmetics case, arsenal against age. Lana's cosmetics case contained a virtual cornucopia of youth restorative products. Lana stood before the mirror and studied the area around her mouth, the faint suggestion of furrowing along the upper lip, on the chin, a hint of jowls, and the revisiting of sagging turkey wattle. Brad's lunch lift hadn't held up even six months. Lana would demand a full refund.

Lana trolled the depths, fished out a jar of Elixir of Youth Lift Contour, dipped her fingers into the plump pink cream, rotated the cream across her jowls, into the furrows, the neck, especially the décolletage. Concentric circles, pausing on the upswing. After the Lift Contour, Lana located a tube of Elixir of Youth Lip Wrinkle Eraser. She squeezed this on her fingertips, rubbed it gingerly across her upper lip, patted the leftover around her eyes. After that, Lana ministered to the rest of her fifty-two-and-a-half-year-old body. Elixir of Youth concocted a potion for every body segment, every part, and Lana covered them all until she'd plumped up everywhere. Then she plumbed the arsenal and drew out a tiny vial. Tonic of life. Fountain of Youth. Lana fished out her diabetic's paraphernalia, perfect for the job at hand, and filled a syringe with the stuff from the tiny vial. She'd been on the substance for two years now. She'd never felt better in her life. Tomorrow morning, she'd get an injection of the new, improved formula. All natural, all organic. There's nothing artificial about Lana Lanai, no.

In a few minutes, Lana was ready for an evening with Clint. She'd reapplied her makeup, changed into a particularly seductive outfit, and now felt confident she could meet all the expectations of a man seventeen years—or was it eighteen?—her junior. He'd never guess she was an older woman. Lana fluffed her hair around her fortified face and opened the door.

"Clint?"

No answer.

"Clint, my wine needs refreshing, honey."

Still no answer.

Lana looked around. She couldn't find Clint anywhere. Not in the kitchen. Not in the bedroom. Not in the living room by the fire, or on the deck. Not anywhere. Pretty soon, she spied the bottle of wine. She snatched it up, fuming. When Lana gets angry, better watch out.

DR. FISH wasn't at the clinic—at least, the nurse on duty couldn't locate him right away—but the nurse knew what to do. Theresa, though limp and drowsy, fought the whole time, but Clint managed to hold her down while the nurse shoved the thick plastic tube down her throat, down the esophagus, down into the stomach where the mixture of Halcion and Valium already lined her shrunken, malnourished stomach. Theresa lost consciousness. The monitor on the wall said her heartbeat had slowed to a crawl.

The tube sucked blood-streaked fulvous bile out of Theresa while Clint held her hand and watched her eyelids, hoping they'd pop open and she'd be back again. If she came back, Clint vowed to himself, he'd take care of her: nurse her to health, get her off the poisonous prescription drugs Fish threw at her, start her on Brad's new Elixir plan. He'd bring her back to the vibrant woman she had been before all this terror had stripped every bit of youth and joy from her body, leaving her like this—a moribund skeleton, haunting the forests and beaches, the tragic mantra streaming from her withering lips.

"Paris. Paris. Paris."

IN THE TRUCK CAB, Winn turned up the heater. Carolee could see her breath and was complaining about it. He didn't say anything, just turned up the heat. He was pretty sure no one had seen Carolee hop up into the cab in the casino parking lot. Carolee snuggled beside him, a little too close, but it was dark out, and nobody drove down this far on 101 at this hour.

The best place he could think to go was Toleak Lodge, except that someone might see them, recognize them. But if he rented one of those little cottages— He had almost decided on Toleak Lodge when he remembered the federal agent, the white woman, Venus. He'd heard she was staying at Toleak Lodge with her husband, and that her husband had walked out on her. Winn didn't know who her old man was and he didn't really care, but he cared that because she was shacked up at Toleak Lodge, he couldn't go there with Carolee tonight. He backed off the parking lot, peeled onto 101 again, heading north this time, settled in his mind.

The Pine Fresh Motel in Forks. He'd heard that nobody asked questions there. Sure, they'd recognize him up there. Most people in Iron County could pick Winn out of a crowd. Especially now, after all the publicity. But Carolee could stay in the cab until he got all checked in and, under the dark of night, no one would notice his truck at the Pine Fresh.

The Pine Fresh Motel turned out to have clean sheets and more soap bars than you could use in a month. The queen-size bed felt all right, especially after a glass of Wild Turkey straight up, double shot, and another, just for the hell of it. Carolee didn't drink whiskey, but she had some weed, and they smoked it until they both giggled, falling all over each other across the lumpy bed.

"Oh, Winn, honey, it's so good to hear you laugh again."

Winn reached up under Carolee's sweater, unhooked her bra. She had soft fleshy breasts, about ten times the size of Theresa's, and when he massaged the nipples, they tightened into hard balls. Winn kept massaging until he felt himself getting hard. Carolee pulled off her sweater and her jeans but left her panties on. A skimpy thong, like Winn had seen in the clubs down in Grays Harbor back in his wild days. Maybe his wild days were back.

Carolee took Winn's hand and guided it down where it felt good to her. The last thought of Theresa left Winn's mind instantly. A savage urge gripped him, and Winn gave Carolee everything she wanted from him, everything and double that. Carolee moaned and cried and begged for more. Winn gave it to her gladly, and he didn't stop until he'd satisfied himself, and then he rolled over on his back, sweat glistening across his smooth powerful chest.

"Good Jesus," he wheezed.

yCarolee giggled. Rolled against him. Placed her hand possessively across his chest. Winn removed it, turned over, put his back to her. Carolee said, "Winn, honey, did you like that?"

Winn grunted.

"What did you say, Winn?"

"I said, 'You're a good hump, Carolee.'"

He fell asleep instantly.

Carolee lay in bed smoking cigarettes until she had worked things out in her mind. Then she smiled sideways and switched off the bedside lamp.

WINN GOT HOME around 5:00 a.m. and saw his baby girl was missing from her crib. He went into the bedroom. His wife was gone. He went into the kitchen. All Milan's food was gone, her milk and cereal. Her highchair, and her feeding spoon. Her bib. At first he thought he was imagining things, or had drunk too much at the motel. Someone had been in his home, his private sanctuary. Someone had taken his wife. His baby. Winn roared through the trailer pummeling the walls, swearing, shouting, howling. Bob Brightman, just home early from work, heard all the racket. When Carolee and Bob broke down the door and went in, Winn was holding a butcher knife and he came at them in fury. Bob shoved Carolee outside and stood his ground with Winn.

"Settle down, Winn."

Winn didn't reply, just stood holding the butcher knife, his breath hard and fast, his heart pounding. Bob spoke to Winn in monotone, delivering the news the way he'd heard it from Clint Kellogg.

Outside, a roll of thunder played across the sky, clouds blotting out the waning moon. A cold mist fell and Carolee could see her breath and wondered if today would bring the first snow. The wind blew in the wrong direction and she couldn't hear what was going on inside, but she could imagine. Winn needed help bad and she hoped Bob could talk him out of that knife. She wondered if Bob had seen her drive into the lot just a few minutes before Winn. Did Bob have it figured out? Across the grove, Irene Polk opened her curtains and peered out through the misting rain and saw Carolee standing in front of the Nighteagle trailer. Curious-nosy—old Irene shuffled down her porch stairs, came bobbing across the grove. The two women watched in silence as mist turned to sleet and their breath froze. Carolee looked up at the white sky and saw the first snowflake drift down to rest on a cedar frond, followed by another and another and another. By the time Bob came out of the Nighteagle trailer, holding the butcher knife, the grove and all the rusty car carcasses and all the junk and trash lay hidden beneath a pristine white blanket.

OCEAN BOY gurgled when Becca entered the room. She knelt down, stroked his little head, offered him her finger to chew. "Don't worry, Paris," she said gently. "We won't let your daddy hurt you anymore. We'll keep you safe from your daddy." Ocean Boy pulled himself up off the blanket. Becca held him by one arm. "There now, Paris, see? You can walk."

She changed his diaper, walked Ocean Boy up and down the small room, and then fed him some warm cereal she'd made in the microwave. When she finished feeding him, she put him on the training pot and while she waited for him to figure out what to do, Becca said, "I'm going to read you a story today, Paris. Would you like that?" Ocean Boy looked up at Becca and grinned. "Mmm-mmm-ma," he said. Becca placed Ocean Boy in his bed, and began reading from Clint Kellogg's book of fables.

Once not so very long ago, an enchanted elk was born to the king and queen of the forest. They named the little prince "Wapiti" because he had a white tuft on his rump. All the creatures of the forest loved Wapiti. He was swift, surefooted, highly courageous and, best of all, he didn't eat meat. All the creatures, even Coyote and Bear and Raven, loved Wapiti and whenever they saw him coming, they scampered and flew toward him, not away, because being in Wapiti's presence gave them eternal youth.

No one knew why or how Wapiti worked his special magic. Even Wapiti himself didn't understand his powers. But he used his power generously and soon the forest was filled with vitality. Then one dark winter morning when fresh deep snow blanketed the forest floor, Wapiti was foraging for lichens and roots to eat when suddenly a terrible creature appeared from behind a cedar tree. The creature walked on two legs, and it had fire in its eyes, and it shot an arrow into Wapiti's side.

"What are you doing?" cried Wapiti.

The creature didn't care what Wapiti said and kept shooting arrows into Wapiti. The third arrow struck Wapiti in the lungs. Blood filled his lungs and soon there was no room left for air. Wapiti fell to the snow-covered earth.

The other creatures of the forest were all sleeping and they didn't hear Wapiti's cries for help. Even the forest sprites were sleeping and missed Wapiti's bugle cry. The creature on two legs stood over Wapiti's wounded body and made terrible grunting sounds. In one hand, he held a sharp, flashing object. He drove it into Wapiti's stomach and then he cut off Wapiti's hooves, all four of them, and blood spilled out of Wapiti, onto the fresh snow. Wapiti was very weak and he had just enough strength to say, "Why are you doing this to me?"

The creature answered, "I am taking your life to save my own. You possess the secret of eternal youth and I want it."

"But I will grant you eternal youth," said Wapiti. "You don't have to kill me. I'll give you eternal youth, if only you don't kill me."

The creature laughed. "You forest creatures are so ignorant. The only way to gain eternal youth is to make an elixir from your organs and your hooves. I am going to make the magic elixir and drink it and you will die and I will live forever as a handsome young man."

Wapiti said, "If you spare my life, I will grant you eternal youth, but if you kill me, all the secrets of eternal youth will die with me."

The creature ignored Wapiti's offer and stabbed him until Wapiti was dead. Grabbing up all of Wapiti's hooves and organs, he put them in a bag. He put Wapiti's blood in a bucket.

He went out of the forest, taking the parts of Wapiti with him. When he got to the village, the creature went to the market and bought fresh herbs and roots. He ground up Wapiti's hooves, then he mixed these with Wapiti's organs and blood and the herbs and roots, and drank down the sweet elixir. Right away, he became younger. When he went home, his old wife said, "How did you become young again?" He told her, and she said, "I want to be young again, too. Get me some of that elixir."

The young man said, "There isn't any left. I drank it all."

"Then go back to the forest and get some more," demanded the wife.

The young man said, "No. Now that I am young again, there are many things I want to do. I am leaving you, you old hag."

The wife went into the forest and looked for Wapiti, but she didn't find him, so she shot her arrows into Bear and took his paws, and his organs and made an elixir and drank it. When she looked in the mirror, she saw her young self again. The young-again woman cried for joy and went out to show off her re-claimed youth and beauty. Everyone in the village wanted to know how to get the elixir of youth, but the woman refused to tell them unless each person paid her a gold coin.

Becca closed the book and listened. She heard Ocean Boy's soft breathing. Reaching into the crib, she placed her hand on the baby's chest and began crooning. When she was certain he had fallen asleep, Becca went to the refrigerator and fished out a Diet Pepsi. Ocean Boy stirred in his crib and began fussing. Becca opened the book again, and finished reading the fairy tale.

One by one all the aging people in the village came to the beautiful young-again woman and paid her a gold coin for her secret, and each time, the woman went out into the forest and killed a creature and took its paws or hooves, and its organs and its blood and made an elixir. Everyone who drank her elixirs became young again and soon the woman's fame spread throughout the countryside and she became very rich. But soon people began following her into the forest, killing creatures themselves and making their own elixirs, which they sold for gold coins. Their arrows flew and the creatures fell to the snow-covered ground and howled with pain as their blood spilled over the earth. By springtime, the forest was depleted of Great Elk, Bear, Cougar, Deer, and all the other creatures, and the village was full of handsome young men and women.

Without the creatures, the forest fell still and silent. When the snow had melted away, the forest bloomed and new grasses shot up from the earth and new tips came on the ferns and the wildflowers opened their faces to the sun, but in the stillness, no creatures came to sniff the blossoms, to chew the ferns and munch the grass. The neglected bushes and grasses grew wild and unruly and finally choked the forest until the last tree died and fell with a disconsolate sigh. This is how the people of the village became eternally young, and ever since that time, people have hunted four-footed creatures in search of eternal youth.

Becca felt a chill, so she placed an extra blanket over Ocean Boy. She leaned over and whispered, "Happy dreams, baby Paris."

EIGHTEEN

MRS. LAPIDUS

CLINT BROUGHT Theresa home the next morning. It had snowed all night, and Clint kicked his Jeep Cherokee into four-wheel drive. The rain that had come before the snow had laid sheets of black ice on the highway, beneath six inches of sparkling snow. The sky was the color of smoke, and the crisp stillness and the landscape's white beauty brought a feeling of serenity to Clint but little peace of mind. Heading up the highway to the Forks Texaco, Clint slowed down at Cedar Grove Trailer Park and looked for Winn's pickup.

Not there. The bastard had probably never even come home. His wife could have died for all Winn cared about her. A man shouldn't take on responsibilities he can't handle. Clint wasn't Theresa's husband, and here he was saving her life and taking care of her. Maybe now it was time to do what he should've done years ago. Anyway, word was going around that Carolee Brightman had her sleazy eyes on Winn.

Maybe Bob Brightman didn't know, or maybe he didn't care. It was none of Clint's business. Or was it? Clint and Theresa had too much history just to ignore what Winn was doing to her. And here was Theresa, grief-stricken and void of common sense since her baby disappeared. Maybe what Theresa needed was a man who could take care of her. And this time, Clint wasn't in such a rush for the physical aspect.

Dr. Fish, who saw Theresa in the morning, said she could go home today if she promised never to abuse her prescription medicine again. They stopped at the reservation to pick up Milan, who had been rescued by Frances. Taking the right turn off the highway into the reservation, Clint slowed to avoid a snowdrift and when he had safely negotiated it, Theresa said, "Look there, Clint." Clint looked where Theresa pointed at the sign that said HOH RESERVATION. Someone had used red paint, or blood, to write on top of the sign. Now it read, HATEVILLE. The letters had dripped before they dried. Theresa said, "Who would do that, do you suppose?"

"Kids." Clint shifted into low gear for the steep downhill drop to the beach.

"Why would kids do a thing like that?"

"Hey, it's two hundred miles from nowhere out here on this reservation. Don't you remember what it was like living in there?"

Theresa said, "I had nothing to compare it with."

"Well, kids on the reservation today have televisions. Look at those satellite dishes. You think they don't know what's going on out there in the world? They know what's out there, and they know they'll never live like that. You'd be pissed off, too, if you were fifteen years old, stuck out here in the boonies with no way out."

"You think that's it? You don't think it's anything else?"

"No, I don't. And that's paint, not blood."

Theresa stared out the window. The snow made time stand still: froze it, belabored time until nothing forward seemed to matter, only that which had passed, or the present moment. He's indoors somewhere, dressed in warm wool, playing with a toy. He's happy, even though he's teething, and his new family loves the way he laughs and they scoop him up and hold him, rock him, hug him close, smother him with affection. He's indoors, he's indoors, he's indoors. His new family feeds him warm, nutritious food, and when he's had that, they might give him a treat, like peeled apple, or an orange section, or banana pudding. Someone loves him. Someone loves him.

Milan didn't want to come home with Theresa. Theresa stretched out her arms, pleaded, but Milan just bawled every time Theresa came close. It wasn't right, her own child rejecting her, just like Winn had done. Desperation overpowered common sense and Theresa grabbed Milan, struggled with her, carried her kicking and screaming to Clint's Jeep. Frances came after them, wiping her hands on a dishtowel, marveling at her daughter's unreasonable behavior. When they reached the Jeep, Milan started howling and the neighbors came out to watch the unpleasant domestic scene. Theresa got in the Jeep and fought to keep Milan on her lap. Clint revved up the engine, let out the emergency brake, but Frances came around to his side of the Jeep and rapped on the window. Clint lowered the window. Frances leaned in, her cloudy breath smoking up the inside windows, and said, "Where's Winn?"

"He never showed up. I stayed with her all night at the clinic. I just went to get some gas and then went back to get her after the doctor released her. Winn wasn't anywhere around, not even at home, far as I could tell driving by."

Frances said, "Get Milan from Theresa and bring her back inside."

Clint shook his head. The car's interior grew cold. Milan howled like a wounded coyote. Theresa couldn't control her and Milan scratched at her mother's face, bit her on the hand. Finally Theresa handed the girl over to the grandmother and Frances carried the snuffling baby back indoors where there was heat, and security.

On the drive home, Theresa sat stone-faced.

HERE'S LANA in her office, a bipedal panther pacing off the long, lonely trail from her desk to her door: the well-worn path known around Hollywood as the Calvary of the Stars, where waves of ineptitude swept in through Lana's door, beached at her desk, and—mortified under Lana's merciless scrutiny—crawled back along the carpeted ten-mile Valley of Tears to the door, fizzling out before aborning. Lana has no time in her packed calendar for the partially talented. Small, jejune talent infuriated her, all the more because it got your hopes up just a tiny bit then failed so bitterly to measure up. Failure should be branded into these individuals' foreheads, the better to see them coming.

Lana had a cordless grafted on her ear, and her pace picked up as her voice rose. "I won't be treated like that, Brad. Not by your brother or by anyone else's brother. I don't have time for the Clints of the world. Or the Brads, for that matter. Now, I want what you promised me, or I'll tell Lance everything. Do you understand?"

In his serene office suite, Brad was sweating bullets. "Clint's an infantile, narcissistic pedant, Lana. He doesn't deserve a night with you. Now, please, just give me another week. I'm sorry we didn't deliver this time. There were complications up there that we just couldn't foresee. I'll have the fresh material in a few days. In the meantime, I can inject you with a very good substitute."

"Let me tell you something, Brad," Lana spat into the phone. "I am a very, very busy woman. I spend more time and more money on charitable causes than anyone else in this town and I run a successful business besides. Not to mention my active role in keeping up Lance's reputation with his constituents. I mean, I may not have a bunch of brats at home, but other than that, I've got one hell of a jam-packed lifestyle, Brad. I don't have time to run up and down the Coast. Now, here's the way it's going to be, Brad, honey. That new product better be in my possession within forty-eight hours. And this time, you will be Mr. Fetch Boy. I refuse to go up there again. Do you understand, honey? Because if things don't fall into place pretty darn soon, I'll be highly motivated to tell Lance everything. And I know you don't want me to do that."

Brad cleared his throat, said, "You've been injecting the stuff for two years now, Lana. You're as implicated as I am."

"Don't even think about blackmailing me."

"Tit tat."

"Sorry, honey. It doesn't work that way. See, I'm married to Lancey Lance. I'm quite safe and secure. You are his target, and you better believe I'll tell him every single little thing, unless you get me that product."

Lana hung up, thoroughly disgusted with incompetence. She dialed another number, clicked her nails until it answered. "Tiffany, angel, let me speak to Lance." Lana added, "Oh, and Tiff, just so you and I are reading from the same page, I know what you're doing with my husband. What you two do on Capitol Hill is your business, but don't think you'll snatch him from this marriage, because the Senator will never leave me. Now, put him on."

MRS. IDA LAPIDUS, aged eighty-four, suffered daily from osteoporosis of the hips, liver dysfunction, hemorrhoids, occasional incontinence, water-on-the-knee, and golf ball sized bunions. In spite of chronic aches and pains, a limited retirement income, and Medicaid dependency, Mrs. Lapidus never complained about her physical condition, or, for that matter, anything else. Life for Ida Lapidus had always been a struggle, unlike the sheltered, pampered lives enjoyed by her two children, Lonnie and Lana. Baby boomers never struggled like Ida's generation to get ahead. Baby boomers had it all handed to them on a silver platter by hard-working, sacrificing parents whose own youth had been robbed of its rosy gilt under the shadow of World War II. Ida's generation knew from sacrifice. Her children, especially her daughter, Lana, only knew from privilege.

"What, I should complain of old age?" Mrs. Lapidus often remarked to her daughter, Lana Lapidus Lanai. "Aging is the natural course of events. If God had wanted us to live forever, He would have made us out of Teflon. But God didn't use Teflon, he used skin and bones and all these fragile materials. God doesn't know from Teflon.''

Lana watched her mother across the table at Perry's restaurant. Ida's gnarled, liver-spotted hands struggled with the Venetian herb bread, and when she finally managed to tear off a bite-size chunk and bring it up to her mouth, her upper bridge came loose. Lana, grimacing across the table, actually saw the gap between the roof of Ida's mouth and the upper set of dentures. Ida's upper dentures slipped halfway out of her mouth and nearly hit the table, but she clamped down just in time, catching the teeth and shoving the bread into her mouth all in one graceful swoop. Lana, relieved that her mother hadn't caused a scene in the middle of Perry's rarefied luncheon crowd, said to Ida, ''Mother, you really should see about those teeth.''

''My teeth are fine. Leave my teeth alone.'' Ida chewed obstinately. Children shouldn't criticize their parents' teeth.

Lana, thinking to herself how old and pitiful her mother looked, said, ''Have you been to see Dr. Gates lately, Mother?''

Ida managed to wrap an arthritic hand around her wineglass, brought it to her lips and drank, making odd sucking sounds that she couldn't hear, being partially deaf, but that grated on Lana's nerves. ''I saw him yesterday,'' said Ida.

''What did he say about your liver?'' Lana cut into a particularly plump arugula leaf.

Ida said, ''That my liver doesn't stand a chance in hell of surviving the millennium. What does he know anyway?''

Lana leaned forward. ''A transplant operation?''

Ida waved a hand. ''Nobody's damn liver's going inside my body. I won't have it.''

''But, Mother, if Dr. Gates says you need—''

''Shut up,'' snapped Ida. ''I won't have a liver transplant, I don't care what you and Lonnie and the Dr. Gateses of the world try to tell me. I'm happy with my own liver, thank you very much.''

Lana watched her mother struggle through a main course of lobster au gratin and young peas. Excruciating—that's what Lana thought. Simply too painful to endure, this curse of old age.

''I have to go to the bathroom,'' Ida said, interrupting Lana's meditation.

Lana helped Ida into her walker and pointed her toward the ladies' room. As they crossed the crowded dining room at a snail's pace, Ida's walker collided with a waiter, three tables, a movie star's funny bone, and a few other things. Tics and murmurs spread through the dining room, little hushed commentaries about the clumsy old woman and her daughter.

"Isn't that Lana Lanai, the talent agent?"

"Of course, darling. And that old lady is her mother."

"Really? So that's what Lana will look like in another twenty years. How unfortunate."

Lana brought up the rear, apologizing profusely, mortified at each collision of Ida's walker. Why did Mother insist on dining at Perry's where everyone who was anyone in Hollywood saw in Ida Lapidus the Lana Lanai of the future? The journey from the dining table to the door of the ladies' room seemed eons long, so slowly did Ida amble in her walker. When finally they reached the door, Lana held it open for her mother. Ida moseyed—yes, and probably on purpose, she moved so slowly—across the threshold while everyone watched.

Next thing you know, thought Lana to herself, Mother will be asking me to accompany her into the stall. Then it will be...well, you know how old people revert back to dependency. Maybe soon Ida would need diapers. And someone would have to change those diapers. It wouldn't be Lonnie, thought Lana darkly. And Ida didn't have enough money to hire a nurse. Lana, thank her lucky stars, had the wherewithal to hire a nurse for Ida, and would see to that immediately. The time had come.

Ida finished up her business, shuffled over to the washbasin, washed her disfigured hands, and stood stooped before the mirror. Peering into the glass, Ida said, "Hand me my purse, Lana."

Lana handed Ida her purse. Ida struggled with the clasp, refusing Lana's offer to help, and rummaged around in the purse until she located her tube of lipstick. It seemed to Lana that it took Ida twenty minutes just to remove the top off the lipstick and twist it up. Scarlet Sin. Ida's trembling hand drew the lipstick across her mouth, missing the mark. Lana exclaimed, "Mother, why don't you let me do that for you?"

"Don't be an ass," retorted Ida.

"But, Mother, you're making a mess of your face."

Ida pressed her lips together, smeared the mess around. "Well, it's my face, now, isn't it? You tend to your own face, Lana. Leave mine alone."

"Mother, I'm just trying to be helpful..."

"Well, you're a pain in the butt, Lana."

Ida shuffled over to her walker and, swallowing her pride only temporarily, allowed her daughter to hold open the door for her. Finally, Ida reached the dining room, and miraculously negotiated the return to her table without bumping into a single object. As she struggled into her chair, the dining room crowd stood and recognized her with a wild ovation. Ida bowed deferentially, acknowledging the applause.

Lana, burning with embarrassment, whispered, "Mother, these people are mocking you. Don't you see that?"

Ida settled back into her chair and through Coke-bottle lenses, studied the dessert menu. "Never mind," she said. "They'll all grow old one day."

"Not me," Lana told herself. "Not me."

BECCA CHECKED to be certain her mother wasn't home. Sometimes, lately, Carolee left her car up at the casino and rode back with Winn Nighteagle. Lately, Becca never knew whether or not her mom was home just from looking in the driveway. She went indoors, checked around. No sign of big, sexy mama. Great. Becca went into her bedroom, changed into comfortable clothing, put on her hiking boots. Reached under the mattress for Clint Kellogg's book of fables. Tucked it under her arm and went out, stepping into the woods when she thought no one saw her. Irene Polk saw her, and so did Cindy Dean. Irene and Cindy just happened to be seated at the Polk's kitchen table by a picture window, and they saw Becca Brightman, book and all, head into the woods. Irene and Cindy exchanged glances. Irene nodded and then Cindy did, too.

Irene and Cindy had just gathered a crop of peppermint from Irene's herb garden. The pungent leaves sat in a pile between them. The two women picked at the leaves, separating out foreign debris and rotted leaves.

Peppermint oil was recommended to the ancient Romans by Pliny the Elder, who suggested applying the volatile leaves to the forehead, for treatment of headaches, or as a tea, to soothe the stomach, discourage cramps, or calm a spastic colon. Menthol is the pharmacological element that makes peppermint a potent phytomedicine. Menthol in its pure form is toxic, although the FDA classifies peppermint

WILDCRAFTERS

oil as "generally recognized as safe." Knowledgeable health practitioners warn against allowing children to inhale peppermint oil, a fatal exercise if overdone. Too high a dose of peppermint can cause miscarriage in pregnant women. Pure menthol is never a good idea. Peppermint oil is safer, but in small doses.

Irene said to Cindy, "That Becca Brightman must have a boyfriend."

Cindy agreed. "That's where she goes when Carolee isn't home. Meets him in the woods. She better watch out, though, with Carolee and them always back in there."

Irene said, "That whole bunch oughta be brought up on charges. Harvesting on the preserve. It's not right."

Cindy sighed, bit into a peppermint leaf. "They've been harvesting on the preserve for years, Irene. Do you think anyone does anything about it?"

Irene stewed. "I've got a good mind to do something myself."

NINETEEN

POTLATCH

ON THANKSGIVING DAY, Winn and Theresa took Milan to the reservation. Frances and her father, old Simon Thundercloud, were giving a name-day potlatch for Milan, in spite of the tragic circumstances. Frances and Simon had scrimped and saved five years to have the honor of hosting a potlatch. Whoever holds a potlatch gives gifts to all who are invited. Frances had made three quilts a year for five years, and her eighty-year-old father had carved fifty perfect medallions on fishbone, each with the likeness of Thunderbird. Months earlier, Frances had gathered fresh berries and made preserves, tying festive colored ribbons around each jar. She had prepared salted fish, smoked salmon, and pickled corn. In the weeks preceding their potlatch, Frances had little time to prepare, what with the tragedy that overshadowed her life, and then too, taking care of Milan. But in the week before the potlatch, as Milan's fever seemed to abate, Frances really applied herself, baking four dozen loaves of her famous sourdough bread, twenty dozen chocolate chip cookies, and scrubbing fifty yams to perfection. Frances made camas cakes and chokeberry preserves, and old Simon caught ten plump Sockeye salmon to grill over cedar planks. At the last minute, Frances took the tribal boat up to La Push and there she purchased five Dungeness crabs and brought them home. She boiled them in her deep pot, cracked them, and chopped the rich white meat into squares. Concocting a tomato aspic with shrimp and green pepper, she added the crab. She made so much crab and shrimp aspic that she couldn't fit it all into her refrigerator, but the tribal center had space in their big fridge so she put it there, with a note on the door: "Frances Creed's potlatch aspic. DO NOT TAKE!"

The word "Hoh" is Quillayute for "fast-moving water," or "snow water." In Quinault, the word "Hoh" is a corruption of a word meaning "that place" or "boundary," and may mean "can speak the (Quinault) language in that place." In the eighteenth and nineteenth centuries, when European mariners scouted the Pacific Northwest Coast, explorers referred to a certain prodigious landing site as Queenhithe, but long before they came, it was the territory of the Hoh tribe. On September 11, 1893, in a backhanded compliment, Grover Cleveland, the president of the United States of America, declared the Queenhithe territory to be the Hoh Indian Reservation. Thus, the territory recovered its identity and lost its independence.

Frances Creed's ancestry was Hoh, with one exception on her mother's side. Frances's maternal grandmother was Makah from up at Shi-Shi Beach. Her Makah grandmother taught Frances how to make yellow dye from bracken spores and weave baskets from the shiny black stalks of maidenhair ferns, and it was her Makah grandmother who taught Frances how to find her guardian spirit. When she was just seven years old, Frances went up to visit her Makah grandmother for the summer. One day her granny took Frances to the beach at Spirit Point, and told Frances to build herself a campfire and stay beside it without saying a word until her guardian spirit arrived. Young Frances endured six nights and days on the rugged beach, in spite of wind and saltspray and the dark, lonesome nights. Finally, on the seventh morning, Bald Eagle came to announce he was her guardian spirit. If you revealed your guardian spirit, that was a sign you were approaching death. Frances never revealed her guardian spirit, and it protected her faithfully.

ON THANKSGIVING MORNING, the day of Frances and Simon's potlatch, a thick mist blanketed the Hoh reservation, obscuring the ocean and the rocky beach. The first thing Frances saw when she poked her head outside that morning at dawn was Bald Eagle sitting in the Douglas fir in her front yard. An omen. Frances paid four teenagers to go down on the beach and build a bonfire with driftwood and cedar logs. By the time the mist had cleared, the boys had built the bonfire and lit it, and Bald Eagle had flown away.

The bonfire's fragrant smoke rose against a pale green ocean, drifting upward into a crystalline blue sky. The boys went a little farther down the beach where a sand flat undulated beneath their feet, and there they dug up clams and dropped them into big buckets and carried them back to the bonfire. Some neighbor women who had offered to help Frances came down to the beach and washed the clams. Up at Frances's wood and tarpaper cabin, Father Brendan arrived hauling two buckets of vanilla ice cream, his housekeeper tripping along behind lugging cartons filled with homemade apple pies.

Frances counted thirty people gathered around the bonfire. Last year, when Gordon Toolong gave his potlatch, there had been twice as many, and Frances worried about tribal loyalty until she saw the four truckloads of neighbors from the upper reservation heading down the gravel road toward the beach, and behind them, Winn and Theresa, with little Milan all dressed up. Frances felt a shallow contentment. This would have been Paris's first potlatch, too, and Paris's naming day.

So colorful was the food, so gay the folk, that for a flickering moment they forgot their day-to-day struggles, and when they met down on the beach for the ceremonials, a quiet, contented aura embraced the potlatch. Even the ocean lay tame against the shore, the gulls soared silently, reverently, and the only sound came from the crackling cedar planks in the bonfire where Simon's salmon sputtered juice. A soft wind blew aromatic smoke off the grilling fish and camas cakes. The black smoke curled and rode an updraft. From the color of the smoke, Simon knew it was time to turn the fish. Several women came forward to help. Simon preferred doing it himself, but the women insisted. When the salmon were all turned and all the people silently gathered, a thin melodic sound announced the arrival of dancers. Frances and Simon had made a donation to the tribal fund and in turn, the tribal dancers came to perform at their potlatch, and in their dance, they told the story of the origin of the gift-giving ceremony.

One day, a peculiar bird appeared on the ocean. Young men of the Quillayute tribe spotted the bird and tried to kill it with their arrows. None of them could kill the bird, they kept missing with their arrows. Blue Jay, the slave of Golden Eagle, watched the young men as day after day, they shot their arrows at the strange bird. Then one day, Golden Eagle told Blue Jay, "My children could catch that peculiar bird."

"But your children are girls," Blue Jay protested. "They can't shoot arrows and kill the strange bird."

The daughters of Golden Eagle heard their father and Blue Jay. The next day, the two youngest sisters stole into the woods and there, in secret, they made arrows. When they brought the arrows back to the village, they saw that the men had gone out in their canoes and were trying to hit the queer bird with their arrows. The two sisters tied their hair around their faces to disguise themselves and paddled their canoe out into the water, making a zigzag line until they came near the strange bird. With her third arrow, the older sister killed the bird.

That night in the village, the girls told their father that they had caught the bird and hid it in the forest. "We want to make gifts of the bird's feathers, for they are very colorful," they said, and they asked their father to invite all of the birds to their lodge on the next day.

Golden Eagle's slave, Blue Jay, delivered the invitations, and when many birds had arrived at Golden Eagle's lodge, he said, "My two youngest daughters caught the many-colored bird, and they wish to give each of you a gift."

The two girls gave certain colors to the different birds. To Robin, they gave red and brown; to Wren, a very rich brown. They gave yellow and brown feathers to Meadowlark, and yellow and black to Finch. They gave each bird feathers until there were no more left.

Since that day, different birds have had certain colors, and also since that day, there have been potlatches, for this was the first potlatch, when gifts were first given from the people who host to those who are their guests.

FRANCES HAD NOT invited the Brightmans, or the Deans, or the Polks, or anyone else who lived in Cedar Grove Trailer Park. Frances had never liked Theresa and Winn's neighbors, never trusted them. Besides, Carolee Brightman was a wildcrafter who cared nothing about the sacredness of the earth and its gifts. There was no good reason to invite Carolee Brightman to her potlatch, so when she saw Carolee come down the beach with Cindy Dean, Frances turned away to avoid them. But Carolee wouldn't be snubbed. She came right up to Frances and said, "Where's Winn?"

Frances shrugged.

"I got to find Winn," Carolee insisted.

Frances said, "Go look."

Cindy Dean spoke up then. "It's the same beast that ate Paris. It's killed again."

Carolee slapped Cindy across the face. "Shut up." To Frances, she said, "Help me find him. There's a dead body up in the woods."

Frances deeply resented Carolee storming in like this and spoiling her potlatch. She pointed at the tideline. "There's Theresa. Go ask her."

Carolee hesitated, then walked down the rocky beach to where Theresa squatted at the water's edge, holding Milan, showing Milan some tiny hermit crabs. Carolee's shadow fell across Theresa. Carolee said, "Where's Winn?"

Theresa looked up. The sun reflected in her eyes. She squinted. Carolee wore brown lip pencil drawn like a cartoon mouth, a lot of black eye-makeup. Theresa said, "Why do you want him?"

"There's a dead body up in the woods. Back up by Elk Pond."

Theresa stood, shifting Milan to her other hip. "I'll tell Winn."

Theresa moved quickly across the beach, pausing to leave Milan with Frances, heading toward the tribal center. Carolee followed, Cindy in tow. At the tribal center, in the parking lot, Winn and some other men were drinking beer and watching football on a portable television resting on the hood of Winn's truck. Winn had bought the television with his casino money. Theresa went up to the men and said, "Carolee says there's a dead body up by Elk Pond."

Winn said, "Shit."

"I called the Fish and Wildlife." Carolee, matter-of-factly.

Cindy Dean wailed, "It's the beast that killed Paris."

Carolee grabbed Cindy's ear and pulled it hard. Cindy screamed. Winn stepped in and pried Carolee's fingers off Cindy's ear. Winn said, "Calm down, honey." Cindy trembled in his arms.

The men began dispersing. Nobody wanted to get involved. Winn let go of Cindy, put the television in the cab of his truck, told Theresa to get in. Backing out of the parking lot, he said to Carolee, "Did you see it?"

Carolee nodded. "Irene Polk found it and called me over. We were up there fishing. I mean, I was fishing and Irene was yelling at me for fishing on the preserve. Irene said it's a man's body, but I couldn't tell."

Winn paused a beat, then said, "What killed him?"

Carolee shook her head. "I didn't get a good look. It made me vomit. Irene said his head had been kicked open. He's all mangled. And there were those cloven hoofprints, Winn."

LAWRENCE FISH got the call from Venus just as he was sitting down to Thanksgiving lunch with his nurses and clinic staff. Instead of grabbing the turkey drumstick, Fish grabbed his black bag. When he arrived at Cedar Grove Trailer Park, Fish followed the growing crowd back behind the rusted pink trailer to the footpath leading into the forest and up high on a ridge, over the ridge to Elk Pond. When he saw Venus, with Winn and Theresa Nighteagle and Bob Brightman, Fish irritably shoved them aside and bent over the victim.

A savage, terrifying end. Hoofprints engraved into the face. The skull split open, the swollen brain, bruised and purple, extruding through the wide fissure. Hematoma disfiguring the facial features. The jaw hanging to one side, limp, fractured. Legs and arms broken. The feet, twisted at the ankles, wore hiking boots, but Fish could tell the ankles were crushed. He studied the corpse's vacant eyes, shut the swollen lids. If there was one thing Fish deplored, it was brutality.

He stood up, brushed pine needles off his trousers. "It's horrible," he said needlessly.

The mangled corpse with the cracked-open skull was airlifted to the Fish and Wildlife forensics lab in Ashland, Oregon. Claudia Paganelli worked on the cadaver straight through the night.

THAT EVENING, Theresa Nighteagle, raving hysterically, was admitted to Bogachiel clinic. Winn signed an admission form and Dr. Fish, noting that Mrs. Nighteagle was hallucinating, prescribed a sedative, which the nurse injected into Theresa's right flank. She slept a few hours, then awoke in the dark and broke out of the clinic. She ran screaming up Highway 101, where a logging truck almost hit her at the hairpin curve outside Bogachiel. An hour later, her bare feet bloodied, she flagged down a speeding pickup truck. The driver turned out to be Daniel Dean. Dean got out, gathered Theresa up in his arms and poured her into the passenger seat. When he brought her into the trailer park, he could see Winn's lights on. Dean went up to the door. Television noise came from inside. Dean shouted that he had Theresa out in the truck. A minute later, Winn Nighteagle came to the door, bleary-eyed, plastered. He lurched down the steps, stumbled against Daniel's shoulder, grabbed hold of Theresa and dragged her into the trailer. Dean trudged home, a disgusted sourness in his gut.

VENUS WAS ASLEEP on the couch, fully clothed, exhausted, when she heard the noise outside the cabin and woke with a start. She sat up and listened. A dull, scratching sound. She reached for her gun, moved over beside the door. She heard a soft thud, then, in semi-darkness, she saw the door knob turn. The door was locked. The knob turned again and again. She stood very still, cocked her pistol—ready. She heard another noise. Someone trying to jimmy the lock. She reached out, unlocked the door, pulled her arm back, waited. The door opened slowly, creaking, and she aimed her pistol at the intruder's head.

The intruder dropped his suitcase and a bouquet of roses, held up his two hands, one clutching a bottle of Dom Prignon, and said, "This is one hell of a welcome."

She set the gun down on the table, rushed to Richard, embraced him.

TWENTY

POSTMORTEM

SHORTLY BEFORE DAWN, Claudia bailed out of the autopsy room, went to a wall telephone, and called Venus. When Venus heard the phone ring, she slipped out of bed and took the call in the living room, so as not to disturb Richard. Claudia said, "This is the strangest cadaver I've ever seen. Human or animal. In the first place, just moments prior to his death, the man's pituitary gland was surgically excised. Neatly."

"Laser?"

"Endoscopy. He may have been dumped on the preserve, but he didn't die there. He died of anesthesia poisoning, in an operating room somewhere, during an endoscopy in which his pituitary gland was removed."

Venus felt her scalp crawl. "Harvested."

"It does sound awfully Robin Cook-ish, or like an incredibly macabre form of poaching. I've seen tumescent pituitaries and such taken from human cadavers, and normal pituitaries removed from cadavers for teaching purposes. Even though this pituitary gland was carefully removed by an experienced hand, I doubt it was tumescent, or done for teaching purposes. My colleagues agree."

"Go on."

"The victim had been dead for approximately twenty hours when discovered. The blows from the hooves occurred after death. The condition of the skull and brain mass indicates clearly that the endoscopy came first. The part that confuses me is, most surgeons don't have cloven hooves. They have human hands." She paused. "I think I'm too exhausted to be funny."

Autopsies have no nerve endings, no soul. They are merely data, an essential forensic tool for the police. Combined with Fish's curt report, only an inconclusive theory could be fashioned, and that wasn't good enough for the law.

Venus said, "What's your best guess?"

Claudia said, "I am not allowed to guess. That's your department."

"Come on, Claud. Give me your best shot."

Claudia sighed tiredly. "All right. The victim was probably under anesthesia when surgery was performed. He expired from an excessive dosage of sodium Pentothal. It's possible the person administering anesthesia made a mistake, that the death was accidental, unintended. Possibly the intent was to just remove a small portion of the pituitary gland, in which case he might have survived. But whatever the intent, the patient died from anesthesia poisoning. Then his body might have been taken to the preserve and dumped. I suppose an elk might have come across the body and for some reason or other trampled it. Although I can't say why an elk would do that. Then again, I know very little about elk behavior."

Dawn light cast a golden shimmer over the ocean. From the window, Venus watched a group of men carry a set net down to the beach. Set netting was illegal along this portion of the Northwest coast, where a marine life sanctuary protected ocean life along the fragile, ecologically threatened shores. One of the fishermen wore a fedora with a feather. The others trudged behind him hauling the hundreds of square feet of fishing net.

Venus said, "Claud, have you ever come across anything even vaguely similar to this?"

"We've all seen brains and other organs harvested from wildlife, in poaching cases. Not by endoscopy in operating theaters, but with hunting knives out in the woods. But a man? No, I haven't seen anything remotely like this."

"Okay. What else can you tell me?"

"Under a microscope, a section of the brain tissue appeared spongy, an indication he was developing a spongiform encephalopathy. In plain English, the dead man had contracted Creutzfeldt-Jakob disease. But he probably didn't even know it, it was in such an early stage."

"Mad cow disease?"

"The human version. We refer to it simply as 'CJD.'"

"What causes it?"

"CJD is a slow degenerative disease of the central nervous system which causes progressive dementia and brain degeneration. It can be contracted through infected bovine-derived materials, even from infected bone meal. It has also been reported in a few patients who received hormones from infected human pituitary glands.''

Venus said, ''Are the hormones taken from living subjects?''

''Heavens, no. From cadavers. Human growth hormones used to be harvested from the pituitary glands of cadavers and injected into children with arrested-growth problems, and into dwarves. But because of the instances of CJD, this method is no longer practiced. Now, a form of recombinant human growth hormone—a synthetic version—has been developed.'' Claudia sighed tiredly.

Venus said, ''Anything else? Anything that might identify him?''

''He was wearing a gold wedding band, looks like eighteen carat, with the initials 'JH' inscribed on it. And the wedding band was on his right-hand ring finger. From everything I've seen, I believe he is European, possibly Scandinavian, maybe Finnish. Oh, and there were numerous needle punctures in his left flank. He wasn't diabetic, though.''

''Could they be from the surgical procedure?''

''No, I can't imagine that. Too many of them, and they're shallow, made by very small needles. I really don't know what that's all about.''

''Anything else?''

''That's it for now. We have several lab results yet to come. Now, Venus, I haven't yet spoken to Olson, haven't even faxed a report. So when he contacts you, remember to act surprised. God forbid we violate the chain of command.''

''Wexler needs this information. Fax Wexler, too.''

''Where? At your mother's house?'' Claudia waited a beat, added, ''Just kidding. I really am overtired.''

''He's back in D.C. I'm going to call him in a few minutes, but I'd rather he receive the information first, so we can discuss it.''

Silence. Then, ''We have another chain of command problem here. How will Olson feel if I bypass him on the way to Wexler?''

''Just fax Wexler. I'll take the fall if Olson freaks. Meanwhile, I need a copy of your autopsy report faxed to me.''

''Fax number... Just a minute, I have to find a pen that writes.''

''Here's a thought. Send it to me in care of Dr. Lawrence Fish at this number.''

She gave Claudia Fish's fax number. Claudia said, ''Where does he receive his faxes?''

"At Bogachiel Indian Clinic. It's a small charity clinic operated by the Bureau of Indian Affairs."

"He's a physician?"

"Yes. Why?"

"Are you sure that's safe, to fax it there?"

"Why wouldn't it be safe?"

Claudia said, "Is it a surgical facility?"

"All right, fax it to me here, in care of Toleak Lodge."

"That sounds much better."

"I guess you know my next question."

Silence. Then, "The lab results on the tissue sample from off the preserve. The report is sitting on my desk. I'll call you back later, once I've had a chance to read it. First, I need to close my eyes for a little while."

CLEVER MISSED IT on the first ring, but answered the phone promptly on the second. Venus said, "We've got a case here that might interest you."

"Like the last one?"

"Similar," she said. "Only the victim wasn't an elk. And they didn't take the feet."

"What was it?"

"A human."

Clever sniffed. "Is this some kind of a joke?"

"Hardly." She told him about the body, about Claudia's autopsy. He listened intently, interrupting once or twice to ask specific questions about the endoscopy, how the pituitary gland was excised. When she finished, Clever said, "Ahhh, just how do you see this as related to my moose findings?"

She explained about the hoofprints found near the body, the hoof imprints on the head of the corpse. "It's thin ice, I know, but I just thought I'd pass it by you. Are there any other details you remember about the moose carcasses? Any other unusual finding?"

"Well, let's see. Oh, yes. About a month after the journal article was published, I got a phone call from a lady biologist in Vancouver who said someone's selling ground moose hooves in a medication. She bought some, sent it to me. Sure enough, it was liquified moose keratin."

"Where'd she purchase it?"

"She bought it over the Internet. From some natural pharmaceuticals company. Off the top of my head, I can't recall the name of the company."

"Elixir of Youth? Does that ring a bell?"

"Yeah, that does sound right. I tried calling up the Web site, to order some? But the site was frozen. Then I forgot about it, sorry to admit. And I don't remember the lady biologist's name, either. I'm not much of a record keeper."

She said, "We're one step closer to our perpetrator."

"God, I hate that word."

"What would you call him? Or her?"

Clever said, "Savage. I'd call him a savage. Or her."

IN THE BEDROOM, Richard slept soundly. She crawled under the covers, moved against him. Held him. He didn't budge, just breathed a little deeper, and his eyelids fluttered but he didn't awaken. She lay beside him, watching him sleep. Back home, without her, he'd distanced himself from her work, concentrated on writing an article for a conservation magazine, and now was nearly finished. He'd come back to her as a gesture of his love. Next time, she'd have to give, compromise. Meanwhile, would he be patient while she tried to make sense out of the strange events on Bogachiel preserve?

Were the brutal elk poachings related to Paris Nighteagle's disappearance? Had someone dismembered the elks and sold their hooves to the Elixir of Youth Foundation? Was this unidentified man's mutilated corpse related? What about the similarities? In the instances of the elk killings, the hooves were missing. In the two cases involving humans, the hoofprints were present, and the location of both people, one dead, one living, was Bogachiel preserve. Or, was Paris also dead, another of the killer's victims? Could she trust Fish? And, where did the Gecko fit in this ghastly picture? Rumors that a cloven-hooved beast, the "Unknown," had killed Paris Nighteagle pervaded local gossip. Was somebody creating mythic monsters to divert attention? Using chopped-off elk hooves to make prints and destroy evidence? Or, had an animal actually plucked Paris out of his bassinet and carried him off into the woods? Was Paris alive, hidden somewhere, being abused by a human captor?

Pituitary.

Richard rolled over, opened his eyes, smiled a Richard smile.

She said, "Tell me about the pituitary gland."

Instead, he reached over, touched her. His touch. His whispering. She loved that he talked to her when they made love.

Later, as they were dressing, she brought up the subject again.

"Why do you want to know about the pituitary gland?" Richard asked.

"Before I tell you, just off the cuff, tell me what you know about it."

"The human pituitary gland, or another species?"

"Start with human." She reached for her toothbrush.

Richard said, "The pituitary gland is one of the endocrine glands. Actually, the major endocrine gland. It's small, shaped like a bulb, located at the base of the brain."

"What's its purpose?" Through toothpaste, brushing.

"As I recall from a premed anatomy course, in the days when I fantasized about going to medical school, the pituitary gland controls the functioning of the body's other endocrine glands. Also, it's the gland that secretes growth hormones."

"I knew that."

"This has something to do with the dead man. Is that why you're so interested in pituitaries?"

She told him what she'd learned from Claudia. His immediate reaction was predictable. "This isn't just about finding a kidnapped baby. It's too bizarre, Venus, too dangerous. I want you to quit this case. Let Song have it. Let's go home today."

"I can't, Richard."

"If you want to, you can."

"Then I don't want to. I'm not a quitter, even in the worst of circumstances. You know that."

He went into the kitchen, put coffee on. She followed him, toothbrush in hand, held like a wand. "Please try to understand. I just can't walk away from this, as weird as this whole thing is, I can't defect now."

They carried their coffee outside and drank it while watching the fishermen set their illegal net across the rocky beach. The man with the feather in his hat was orchestrating the task. When the tide rolled in, the net would fill with salmon and mussels, and, too, with rare forms of sea life. Unless she went down there right now and cited them for violating federal law, ordered them to remove the net.

Richard watched her agonize. Should she make the effort? So

many more pressing issues than a set net and a few indigent fishermen just trying to survive. A baby missing, maybe dead, maybe still alive, and in danger. A mangled corpse. A fugitive loose nearby.

She sighed, handed him her coffee mug, and started down the narrow path to the beach. Behind her, he said, "That's my baby. Go sic 'em."

SONG SHOT UP from Grays Harbor, scent hounds in tow. More search parties scoured Bogachiel, this time only Fish and Wildlife agents and a few of Tobin's deputies. Couldn't trust anyone else as far as Venus was concerned. The hounds bayed and howled and made tracks through the woods but came up with nothing more interesting than a rawhide shoelace that could have belonged to anyone's shoe. Venus turned the shoelace over to Al Yamada, who scowled at the insult. "If we don't do any better than this," Yamada groused, "we might as well turn in our badges."

"Just check it out, Al. See what you find under the scope."

Yamada ran the shoelace under the microscope. Besides canine saliva, he plucked off four human hairs and a few that might have been off a hound—or possibly an elk. "They'll have to go to the lab." He put the shoelace and the hairs in a plastic bag, wrote on the bag's label, handed it to her. Venus sent it to Claudia via Sweetwater and the chopper. A costly airlift for a single shoelace, a few hairs.

Song said, "It's the Gecko's, five to ten."

Venus held out her hand. "Bet's on."

Song watched her walk away into the forest, fearless, as if nothing dangerous had ever lurked in there. She had forward motion, never backpedaled, never hesitated, never faltered. Except maybe, in love. He was thinking that her marriage to Richard wouldn't last more than six months. He felt it in his bones.

WEXLER'S VOICE sounded groggy, the tone irritable. "Venus, why in God's name are you phoning me at home? I have never given you permission to call me here. What time is it?"

"Nine a.m., your time. I take it you haven't made it to the office yet this morning?"

"No. No, I haven't."

"Then you haven't seen Paganelli's faxed autopsy report on the body we found on Bogachiel?"

"What are you talking about?" Slightly more alert, not exactly standing at attention.

"You haven't heard from Paganelli or Olson?"

"No, I have not." Impatiently.

She told him about the mangled body, about Claudia's autopsy on the dead man.

When she finished, Wexler said, "Hold on."

Muffled voices. Female chimes. Clear, glorious chimes, reminiscent of London church towers. Not Dallas Cowboy cheerleader chimes. More mature, more developed, more, shall we say, maternal. Wexler came back on. "Listen, Venus. I can't talk about this right now. I'm having my breakfast. Give me the number where you are. I'll ring you back in half an hour."

She gave him her digital phone number. For the hundredth time.

She said, "You might want to check your faxes before returning my call. Also, I have a recruit to work the L.A. connection."

"Oh? Who is that?"

"My husband. Only I haven't asked him yet. But I'm sure he'll be interested when I mention free massages."

"Okay, okay. I have to hang up now."

"One more thing, sir."

"Well, what is it?"

"Bella thinks I'm in Hawaii. On my honeymoon. Unless you've already blown my cover?"

"No, certainly not."

"So don't burst her bubble, if you get my drift."

"What? Oh, oh sure. Well, have a Maui Masher for me, Venus. That's coconut milk and some liqueur, I don't remember which. So, aloha, and all that."

"Sure. Aloha. And all that."

DRAVUS SLOUCHED BEHIND the bar, slaking his thirst with a diet Coke. Maybe a smidge of rum. Venus slid onto a bar stool. Dravus came over, wiped the counter around her folded hands. "My bartender's out sick today."

"Sorry to hear that."

Dravus sighed. "Some folks think running a resort lodge is an ideal existence. Paradise, all expenses paid. Every morning, you wake up to the enchanted rain forest, the fragrant air, snow-capped vistas, romantic ocean views, orcas romping in the waves. I don't have to tell you about the views from the cottages.'' He laughed privately. ''They see it all through a tourist's eyes. Hell, my life is all about soiled linen, chefs and bartenders, maids and clerks who don't show up for their shifts, and whiny tourists who supposedly worship Mother Nature, but they can't tolerate her wild side, y'know? They come up here for the natural experience and all they do is complain about the damp, the rain, the fog, the treacherous beaches where the barnacles gouge their dainty feet and the lack of modern conveniences just drives them mad. By the way, I have a fax for you.''

He went away, disappearing through a small door at one end of the bar. Venus slipped around the bar, shot ice and tonic water into a glass, added a section of fresh lime. In a few minutes, Dravus came back with the fax from Claudia.

Venus glanced at it, put it away, said, ''You ever get any celebrities up here? Like, say, movie stars, the Hollywood crowd?''

''Sure. What do you want to know about them? Other than they're all a bunch of spoiled, whiny brats.''

''I was hoping to have a look at your registration records for the past couple years.''

Dravus folded his arms. ''Off limits. I can let you see the guest book. But the celeb types never sign that. They value their own autographs too much.''

''How about just a quick peek at your guest registration list?''

''I told you, that's off limits. Unless you come in here with a search warrant.''

Venus sipped the tonic and lime. Tonic contains quinine, the traditional natural treatment for malaria. She had contracted malaria ten months earlier while tracking bear poachers in the Chiang Mai, and had thus far survived the recurrent fevers—just barely. The taste of quinine triggered bittersweet memories. Horrid hallucinations, romantic Asian nights. A whole Pandora's box of memories. She hadn't experienced the fevers for three months now. Maybe her liver had finally purged the conniving parasites that dwelt there. Maybe. Right now, she felt fine. So why this sudden thirst for quinine water?

Dravus said, ''Aw hell, I'm too nice a guy. Tell you what I'll do. I'll call the guest registration file up on the computer. It's back in my office, back there.'' He pointed at the small door. ''Then I'll forget to close the file, come back in here. When my back's turned, you go in there, make yourself a copy of what you need. But don't go any farther than the office. Don't even touch the other doors in there. Those are private. Private rooms. Got it?"

She nodded. Dravus went through the little door. Five minutes later, he came back, slid behind the bar. Several new customers had come in and were clamoring for service. She leaned over the counter, "Thanks," she said.

"Don't mention it. To anyone."

"By the way, who's the owner?"

"Of Toleak Lodge?" Dravus looked over his shoulder at her. "Quinault tribe owns us, lock, stock, and barrel."

She was halfway across the bar when Dravus called out, "That Dr. Paganelli seems real cultured. I'd like to meet her sometime."

The office was a small, cramped room with no windows, a lot of sophisticated computer hardware—too much for a small hotel office—and three doors besides the one by which she entered. All three doors were locked tight. Bolt locks. She put her ear to each door, listened. At the first door, nothing, no sound. Same with the second door. From the third room came a whirring sound, like the sound of a dentist's drill, and soft voices, murmuring words she couldn't understand through the heavy door. She felt eyes on her back, turned around. Dravus was watching her from the bar. He crooked his finger.

Two names jumped right off the guest registration at first glance. Johann Hintikka. "J.H." From Finland. No further address.

And, Lana Lanai. The famous Hollywood talent agent. Senator Lanai's wife.

OCEAN BOY was sleeping. Becca found a note that said, "He needs a bath." She waited until he woke up, then bathed him and dressed him in fresh clothing. She sat on the floor and let him toddle around the room, encouraging his precarious footsteps until gradually, Ocean Boy gained more confidence. Now he could walk. Really walk. Becca let him play a while then placed him in his playpen and settled herself in a chair. "I am going to read you a tale about a fox, today, Paris. There aren't really foxes in our forest, but Mr. Kellogg apparently didn't know that when he wrote this story. So here goes, Paris, are you listening?"

Once not so long ago, on a cold and gloomy day, Pacific Fox closed the door to her den, leaving her whole life behind. Her mate, Angry Totem, had lost all interest in her, never paid her even the slightest compliment, not even the occasional friendly nudge, and he told her that she had grown old and ugly. The relationship had lost its enchantment, so with a broken heart and much grieving, and feeling ever so doubtful about her charms, Pacific Fox set out to seek a new life. She hadn't gone far into the forest when she came upon a handsome young man. At first, the young man was startled to see the fox and thought she might harm him, but Pacific Fox calmed him by saying, "Don't be afraid. I'm quite harmless, really. And I need to talk to someone."

"You mean," asked the young man, "you are soliciting advice?"

Pacific Fox waved her paw. "No, no, no, no, no. Nothing like that. Just your sympathetic ear."

"All right," said the young man, "I'll give you a few minutes. But hurry up because I have to get to work."

"Oh? And where do you work, young man?"

"I am a stockbroker. And I am late for an appointment with a client."

Fox made a clicking sound with her tongue. "Busy, busy, busy. Why are people so busy all the time?"

"Because humans have very large brains that require constant stimulation. Otherwise, we might just as well be, well, foxes."

Pacific Fox laughed. "There are other things in life besides a big brain. Now, sit down and let me spill my troubles."

The young man sat on a hollow log. Pacific Fox pranced before him, moving remarkably like a Rockette from Radio City Music Hall. Then suddenly, she crouched to the ground and began weeping. "I tried. I tried. But you see, I'm no longer the youthful fox I was once upon a time. I'm so horribly sad."

The young man reached out and touched her fine silky coat. "Please don't be sad."

"How can I help it?" Standing on her hind legs, she shimmied around the trees, disappearing, then reappearing. "I am such a miserable creature," cried Pacific Fox. "Such an uninteresting, unattractive, incompetent, dull creature. Worst of all, I'm growing old."

The young man stared, not knowing what to say.

Pacific Fox blurted, "My mate was cold and bossy and very

stingy. If I asked him for the time of day, he charged me ten cents a minute. He was always making fun of my small cranial capacity, and when I'd spend all afternoon grooming for him, he'd come home at night and merely stare right through me, as if I didn't exist. He never appreciated me.''

The young man said, ''Maybe he was busy with more important things.''

''Preposterous. Nothing is more important than petting the fox. Everyone in the forest knows that.''

''Not being from the forest...'' ventured the young man.

Pacific Fox rolled her eyes. ''We already know that about you.''

The young man was growing tired of Pacific Fox's complaining. He said, ''What makes you so special, fox?''

''First of all, I am a Pacific fox, a very rare, endangered species. There are only five Pacific foxes left in all the world. And, too, I am a blond fox. Look at my tail. Have you ever seen such a delicious silky tail?''

''Once I saw a white bunny—''

''Get out! Bunnies are pure fluff. Don't talk to me about bunnies. You can't compare foxes to bunnies. They're not in the same class. Besides, no white bunnies dwell in this forest, and even if they did, I'd still be the softest, slinkiest creature of all. Now, what did you say you were doing here?''

The young man spoke through clenched teeth. ''I am trying to get to a meeting with my client. How many times do I have to tell you things? Don't you have any memory at all?''

Pacific Fox smiled uncomfortably. ''It's the first to go, the memory. But I hear that Wapiti, the Great Elk, possesses the secret to eternal youth. I am going to find him tonight and learn the secret from him. Then I shall be young again. I shall regain my beauty and brains and become desirable again.''

The young man had heard in the village that Wapiti, the Great Elk, had long ago been killed by a poacher, but he dared not disappoint Pacific Fox with this sad news. Instead, he said, ''But you are quite lovely just the way you are. And quite clever, too.''

Pacific Fox stared at the young man and exclaimed, ''Do you really mean that?''

''You're the foxiest fox I've ever seen. Honest.''

"No, really. Be candid. Do you really find me—attractive?"

The young man studied the fox. "I think you are the most beautiful fox in the forest. I would go so far as to venture that you are the most beautiful, most extraordinary fox in all the forests of all the world."

Pacific Fox purred. "You are such a sweet young man, really you are. Your kind words have reawakened my youthful spirit and rescued it from Angry Totem's curse. In return, I am going to give you a wonderful gift."

"Oh, good," said the young man, reading his watch. "What is it?"

"I am going to let you see the faeries dance. Come along, follow me."

Pacific Fox leaped over the hollow log and pranced into the forest. The young man followed. "I can't stay long," he warned the fox. "I must accomplish something today."

Pacific Fox hadn't heard him. She was dancing along, jabbering to herself. "Enchantment, ecstasy, that's what I'm all about. Joyful, joyful, joyful. Ebullient and dazzling. I'm beautiful, I'm beautiful, I'm beautiful."

Pacific Fox went a little way through the misty forest, finally stopping in a grove of giant ferns. The ferns grew so tall and wide that they formed a magnificent green canopy overhead. Pacific Fox skittered around, searching for something. "Not here, not here, not here, not here. Now, where did I see that witch's butter?"

"Is that it over there?" asked the young man.

"No, no. That is *amanita*, Death's Angel mushroom. Stay away from that. No, here's the witch's butter, over here. Come closer, take a look."

The young man drew close to the fox. She stood beside a tree trunk, and on the tree trunk grew a beautiful golden yellow fungus that indeed resembled the butter they served in the village, with crumpets and jam.

"This is where the faeries dance when they want the rain to stop," said Pacific Fox.

"They can make the rain stop?" exclaimed the young man.

"The faeries—they're really sprites, if you want to get technical—can make the rain stop and the wind stand still and the sun beam down and chase all the bad weather back out to sea.

Let's see if I can scare them up.'' Fox whistled. In a few moments, the young man heard a faint ringing sound. "Look," said Fox. "The bluebells are announcing the faeries. Here they come now." Out of the forest came the tiniest creatures the young man had ever seen, so tiny, in fact, that one of the faeries rode on the back of a dragonfly. The faeries were so exquisite that the young man could hardly believe his eyes. When they reached the witch's butter, the faeries spread their gossamer wings, flew up to the yellow fungus, and began dancing.

"You see," Fox exclaimed, "they dance divinely, more mesmerizing than a Sufi, if you ask me."

As the faeries danced, the sun came out and kissed the chill off the air. Every creature in the forest came to watch the grand performance. Pacific Fox leaned over and whispered in the young man's ear, "Now here are the three secrets of the forest. If you are very kind to the forest, the creatures of the forest will reward you. If you believe in sprites, they will guard you from all evil, for ever after. If you meet an elk in the forest and you don't harm him, you will live forever."

The young man heard what Fox whispered in his ear, but so enchanted was he, so caught up in the faeries' dance, that he didn't notice Pacific Fox slip off into the forest. She danced through the woods, singing to herself, "Let them find another fox like me. Just let them try to find another fox like me. A slinky, sexy, naughty fox like me. There is no fox in the forest as desirable as me."

The young man eventually met his client and closed the deal, and he took the long way home, avoiding the forest. Still, he never forgot Pacific Fox and once or twice a year, she came to him in dreams. Her voice whispered in his ear, "There are always kindred souls, kindred souls, a spark of recognition, if not the dopplegänger then the yin or yang, the other whole circle, the Divine Reflection, the inhalable energy, pheromones or not, a source of thrilling spark, a firestorm, another heartbeat felt and heard. There are always kindred souls, kindred souls."

And he wondered what she meant.

TWENTY-ONE

MS. VALKOINEN

ON THE LAST DAY of November, at the Ashland morgue, a tall, angular, blond woman stood beside the victim's unrecognizable cadaver and studied a distinctive gold ring that still encircled its right-hand ring finger. The woman reached out, hesitated, and sighed. "Can you put it in something?" she asked Claudia. Cutting the ring from the cold finger, Claudia washed it at the sink, dried it off, wrapped it in brown paper towels and placed it gingerly in the woman's gloved hand.

She was Anitta Valkoinen, a Finnish telephone executive who was attending an international communications conference in Seattle. "He was my husband, Johann Hintikka," she told Claudia quietly. "We are married ten years this December. He loved to go hiking. Everywhere we travel, Johann goes hiking."

AT TOLEAK LODGE, the newlyweds, trying their hands at domesticity, had just sat down to Richard's candlelit dinner of cracked King crab and ice-cold pilsner draft when the phone rang. Richard had a rule. No emergency, however dire, should interrupt the dinner hour. Richard always turned off his cell phone during meals. He held up a hand, but Venus took the call anyway. When she got off the phone, Richard said, "This was an illusion," and Venus, in her insensitive, sardonic manner, agreed.

"We aren't cut out for domesticity," she quipped, dead serious.

"Why not us? Millions of satisfied married couples share quiet, romantic dinners together, and they don't always answer the phone."

Her mind had already shifted to the path in the woods where the victim's mangled body was found. Her mind, but not her fingers.

The best way to eat King crab is over newsprint, with plenty of hot drawn butter and ice-cold pilsner to wash it down. It's a messy job, but someone has to do it. Absentmindedly, using her fingers, she cracked the crab's bumpy red foreclaw. The shell fissured, revealing plump, steaming, white flesh. With a tiny fork, she plucked out the firm flesh, dipped it in butter, and brought the rich morsel to her mouth. For an instant, her eyes shut, and Richard knew then that she appreciated his culinary efforts, no matter what ran through her mind.

"Tell me about elk," she said.

"Don't be disingenuous."

"I'm serious, Richard. I know the breed from a conservationist point of view. You hunted elk. Tell me from a hunter's point of view."

"I never hunted the Roosevelt."

"Tell me. Habits and such."

"A year in the life of an elk?"

She made a face.

He rolled cold pilsner around in his mouth, made love to her with his eyes. He said, "They like to play. Most of the time, they prance about and play games. Except in summer. In summer, they eat constantly."

"Then the rut."

"The rut's over by Halloween."

"Since when do elks celebrate Halloween?"

"All Saints' Day, then. They prance and leap and kick, and they splash around in ponds, squealing, bugling, calling each other. That's their raison d'être."

"What else?"

"The bulls travel in bands of ten or fifteen individuals. If you want to take the dominant bull, you've got to lure him away from the band. Some hunters have learned elk language, bugles and whistles, and they make noises like a cow in heat. Big Daddy comes running right into your sights. You plug it at the cleft just behind the shoulder blade, take home a five or six point rack. Seven points is the record. You probably learned all about firearms in poaching school, so you know that a .33 Winchester Magnum with a 200-grain Swift A-Frame or Nosler Partition bullet has been called the 'ultimate elk slayer.' A woman with a strong upper torso could handle that gun and load. Either load would punch a hole the size of a fifty-cent piece through the elk's hide, through the cartilage, even through a rib. Dead meat."

Venus said, "That was Claudia on the phone. Calling from Ashland. The victim was a Finnish tourist. Out hiking."

"Welcome to America."

Venus said, "His wife identified him. He had on a unique gold wedding band. I need to interview her tomorrow morning."

Richard said, "If an elk felt threatened, especially a bull, it could flail to death its perceived attacker. Elk don't usually attack with their antlers. They attack with their hooves. I've seen a couple coyotes and a bear cub pounded dead by elk."

They finished dinner in silence, listening to the screeching gulls and the occasional hiss of the candles sputtering wax. In the kitchen, he washed, she dried. When the dishes were done, he poured two glasses of Rémy Martin. They were snuggling by the fire when she reached up, touched his face. He looked down at her. She said, "I was wondering if you'd mind going to Los Angeles for a few days."

"With you?"

She shook her head. "Solo."

"Besides my parents, what's in Los Angeles?" He grimaced, remembering. "Don't tell me. You want me to sign on with Senator Lanai's crusade."

"Wexler's been looking for a volunteer. Someone outside the ranks."

"If I were crazy enough to agree, what would I have to do?"

She smiled a Venus smile, the look he couldn't resist. "Go to the Adonis Anti-Aging Spa. Get a few noninvasive treatments, maybe run through their massage menu. Richard-type stuff. Hang out, find out what you can. Very low-key, very LaLa."

He thought it over for about ten seconds. "First class?"

"You can charter a plane if you want."

He said, "I don't like the idea of leaving you up here alone."

"I'll be okay."

His eyes flickered. "By yourself?"

She touched his face gently. "You'd better trust me now that I'm Mrs. Winters, Mr. Winters."

He said, "The things I do to keep my baby happy."

"MOTHER, it's Venus."

Bella's chimes sounded even brighter than usual. "I hear you're having monsoons over there, darling. You really should be here on the mainland. Seattle is bright and clear and picture perfect." Bella's weather is always sunny and mild.

"Actually, we're coming home early."

"You mustn't ever cut short a honeymoon, Venus. It is bad luck. Not to mention rude."

"Richard has some business emergency or other." White lie number thirty thousand, four hundred fourteen. "We'll be in late tonight. What time are you going to bed?"

"Venus, I refuse to divulge my nocturnal habits and it is impertinent to inquire about them."

"I was just wondering—"

"Stop wondering. You wonder far too much. Now, why are you ringing me up again?"

"I was wondering...I mean, I wondered...that is, I was curious to know if Wexler came back to Seattle with you. He's not answering his D.C. number, and his office is closed for the night."

"What are you implying?"

"That you were in Washington, D.C. at Wexler's place when I phoned. That you came back, and maybe Wexler joined you."

Bella sniffed. "Curiosity is deadly. If you want to know Jerry's whereabouts, why don't you contact your office?"

"I did. Olson said Wexler never tells him anything. Olson suggested I phone you."

"I have no pertinent information."

"Mother, please...."

"Jerry's whereabouts are entirely his business, Venus."

"In this case, not true. He's running a government agency. He's supposed to be accessible to his underlings."

"I don't like that word."

"Accessible or underlings?"

"You know which."

"So where's Wexler, Mother?"

"If you must be so persistent, Jerry is currently in Los Angeles with Senator Lanai. They are cooking up some intrigue down there. Something to do with the senator's wife. That Lana is always making trouble for the poor senator. He should never have married an older woman."

"I thought age didn't matter to you."

"Venus, I have to ring off now. Pansy is almost out of the anesthesia and the vet says she can come home this afternoon. I have a thousand preparations to make for the poor dear."

"Pansy had surgery?"

"Nothing serious. Just a face lift."

"Your dog had a face lift?"

"Shar-peis are the best candidates for these operations. It was really just a matter of eyelids and jowls. Now, I am ringing off, Venus. Have a safe flight through the monsoons."

IN THE END, they stayed the night at Toleak, making love by the fire and sleeping till dawn. When the first light of day rimmed the Olympics, they were already driving through the misty rain forest. By sunrise, they'd reached the high prairies, then swung across the peninsula's northern end to Kingston, taking the Kingston ferry to Edmonds, arriving in Seattle before the morning pea soup had burnt off the Sound. Coming so close on the heels of waking hallucinations, the scenic drive forged a memory between them that would not be forgotten. When a cold sun illuminated Mount Rainier, and the city's glass heart sparkled against the Olympics and Puget Sound's rippling emerald cloak, they drove off the Klickitat onto land, their lips freshly recalling a saltwater-flavored kiss, and ferryboat coffee with butterhorns.

At the Olympic Four Seasons, a valet opened the passenger door and Venus stepped out. Dottie waited near the door. Lately Fish and Wildlife's least ambitious agent, no one understood what was scattering Dottie's mind these days like so much chaff in the wind. She came forward out of the shadows, gripping a black briefcase containing a laptop computer. She appeared disoriented, distracted. Venus waved, caught her flitting eye. Dottie nodded absentmindedly.

Richard remarked, "I wonder if the Finnish woman is staying in our Honeymoon Suite."

"Richard, for God's sake, her husband's just been killed."

"I'll call you when I get to L.A. You're sure you want me to do this?"

"You're the only one I can trust who's also health-spa friendly."

She watched him drive away, then went inside with Dottie to meet the Finnish widow, to take her statement, and offer condolences.

Anitta Valkoinen had already packed her suitcase. She wore a red woolen coat and sensible black pumps. She constantly daubed at the tears welling from her pale sapphire eyes, and constantly apologized for her lack of composure. When she gave her statement, she delivered her words in a flat, atonal voice, her English nearly perfect, and with only one or two pauses when the situation momentarily overwhelmed her.

Johann Hintikka was a junior member of Finnish parliament, just elected on the Green Party ticket. The couple lived in Helsinki, where Hintikka, an environmental engineer, designed ecologically friendly industrial systems. They had been married almost ten years. They had two children, a girl of six years and a boy, aged four.

Mr. Hintikka and Ms. Valkoinen had first come to Seattle five days ago at Johann's urging. The trip was meant as a holiday, but Anitta took advantage of the situation to attend an international communications congress in Seattle. Johann didn't seem to mind. He was a veteran hiker, having climbed Mount Kilimanjaro and also several peaks in the Swiss Alps, and he told Anitta he planned to go hiking. The day after they arrived in Seattle—last Wednesday—the congress opened, and Anitta was occupied with business concerns. On the Tuesday before American Thanksgiving Day, Johann drove a rented car to the Olympic Peninsula, saying he intended to climb a certain peak and that he would return on Thursday. Anitta thought the name of the peak was Mount Hoh. Johann had shown her on a map of Olympic National Park where he planned to hike. It was just a bump, really, compared to the mountaineering Johann had behind him. He wanted to experience the peninsula because he had heard so many stories about its grandeur. That's what he told her. When he didn't return to the hotel by Friday afternoon, Anitta went to the concierge desk and explained her concerns. The concierge consulted with the manager and, eventually, they called the Seattle police department. A bulletin was sent to the sheriffs' departments in Clallam, Jefferson, and Iron counties. The next afternoon, a report came back that a body had been found just two miles west of Bogachiel Peak, on the Bogachiel National Wildlife Preserve.

The body was flown to Oregon, Anitta Valkoinen understood, to be autopsied. She had flown down, identified her husband by the distinctive wedding ring—otherwise he was completely unrecognizable—and then had flown back to Seattle to gather her belongings.

Relatives in Helsinki had been notified. Ms. Valkoinen wanted permission to take her husband's remains home with her that afternoon. When it was explained to her that the remains could not be released until a thorough investigation was completed, Anitta sighed deeply and said that she understood. She could not think of any reason that her husband might have been the victim of such a horrible crime. In her mind, the only part that made sense was that Johann had been attacked by an elk. Things like that happened in Finland, in the north, with the reindeer herders. She remembered a story about a Lapp reindeer herder's child who had been stomped to death after spooking a mature bull during rutting season. She could easily accept that Johann had somehow startled a bull elk and it had attacked.

"But they aren't carnivores," she said. "And why did this elk ruin his face like that? That I do not understand. That makes me wonder about the whole thing."

Venus agreed that it did not fit a typical accidental encounter with an elk. She asked Anitta Valkoinen to sit down while she gently described the details of her husband's death. Anitta wore a deeply pained expression but did not openly weep, just dabbed at her glistening eyes. She wondered what good it would do to remain in the United States. Maybe it was better she went home today. If they needed her for anything, they could easily reach her in Helsinki.

"Was your husband a hunter?"

"Not since he was a teenager. When he was a teenager, Johann could identify all the different species of deer in our forests, and he hunted them with his father. But he hasn't hunted for many years. Johann didn't like to kill animals."

Venus said, "Can you think of any reason your husband would have wanted to visit the Olympic Peninsula? Besides hiking?"

Anitta's eyes darted, perusing the hotel room, as if the answer lay there in hiding. "No," she said finally, "no, I really can't."

After signing a transcript of her statement, Anitta Valkoinen was granted permission to return to Finland. She reached into her purse, extracted a thin leather wallet. From that, she removed a small photograph. She handed this to Venus, saying, "This is my husband. When you are finished, please return this photograph to me."

East Africa. Johann Hintikka stood leaning against a sign that said EQUATOR. He wore a khaki bushman's shirt, a red kerchief tied loosely around his neck, a bushman's safari hat pushed far back on his head. He had pale green eyes, white-blond hair, and a deep tan. His toothy smile dominated the shot. The grin of a proud and happy man.

VENUS WAS WALKING with Dottie up Sixth Avenue, headed for the Bumbershoot and the regional offices, when Dottie said, "I am so stupid." And smacked her head.

"What's wrong?"

"I forgot to put in a disk."

"So copy it off your hard drive when you get to the office."

"That's just it," Dottie moaned. "I already erased the hard drive."

When they arrived at the Bumbershoot, Venus pulled Dottie aside in the lobby.

"You want to tell me what's wrong, Dots?"

"What are you talking about?" Dottie acted surprised, confused.

Venus said, "You've been acting wacko for the last several months. Something must be on your mind. You weren't always like this. I know Olson has talked to you, and I know you haven't co-operated with him. We all care about you, Dots. We're worried."

Dottie averted her eyes. "I'm not ready to discuss it."

"You better be pretty soon, or else Olson's going to can you."

Dottie nodded. "I know that. I know that. I've got the picture." She nudged Venus aside. "Now, leave me alone. Just leave me the hell alone."

Venus watched Dottie enter an elevator, watched the door close. She went to the coffee stand, ordered a tall skinny double shooter with the lid on, went back to the elevators and waited for the next express.

TWENTY-TWO

BUFF. AS IF.

MOIRA WAS BUFFING her fingernails when she sensed a presence. Glancing up, she beheld the most radically gorgeous male she'd ever seen, or for that matter, even imagined. Men this sexy should be arrested just for how they look, just for their pheromone content. Caught off-guard, Moira stammered, couldn't coax real words out. All that came out was, "Uhhh, uhhhh, uhhhh…"

"I have an appointment for a massage," said the demiurge in a soothing, hypnotic voice. Moira was mesmerized. He might just as well have said, "I am your prince who has come to carry you off to Laguna Beach, where I will ravish and pamper you and buy you all the Chanel accessories and Manolo Blahnik shoes you desire." When he said, "My name's Richard Winters, and, as I said, I have an appointment," Moira blinked, came back, and flitted around, searching for the appointment book.

"Oh. Yes. Here it is. Uhmmmm…yes. Well. Uhmmmm…let's see. Velma, you're scheduled with Velma. Wait a sec. I think Bruce should take you." She picked up the phone. "Bruce? Honey, can you take a massage? One of Velma's, but he's too hunky for her. Oh, good." Moira hung up, kneaded her skirt, smiled saucily. "Won't you come with me, Mr.—Winters, is it?" As if.

While Bruce the masseuse massaged, soothing music floated in the background. Bruce had strong, muscular hands that plied flesh like bread dough. His chops and rolls made Richard's muscles sigh, his skin tingle. On the whole, Richard considered this an easy assignment. So far. When Bruce removed his paws, Richard sat up, said, "That was totally mythic." Richard had the vernacular down pat.

"That's what they all say." Bruce jabbed a finger. "Towels over there. Shower straight through that door. If you need me, press that button." He went away. Richard showered, toweled off, dressed. At the front desk, he said to Moira, "I was wondering if you carry a certain product line. Elixir of Youth?"

Moira regarded him warily. In spite of his killer bod, he might be another one of those pests. One of Senator Lanai's buddies. She shook her head. "We don't sell it."

"Really?" Surprise. "I thought someone told me you carried the product line."

"You can't buy that product line in any shop or store. You have to order it over the Internet."

Richard feigned confusion. "That's really strange. I was sure my friend said she bought hers at Adonis in Los Angeles."

"Who's your friend?"

Richard made a sheepish face. "I really shouldn't reveal her identity. She's a very famous movie star."

Moira arched an eyebrow. "Really? Well, we have an abundance of those crawling through our front door. So, this friend, this movie star, she claims to have purchased the product line at our spa?"

"Maybe I misunderstood..."

"Maybe you did. Unless, of course, your friend is a client—I mean, one of Dr. Kellogg's patients."

"As a matter fact, she did mention Dr. Kellogg. She said to tell Dr. Kellogg that I want the age-reversal elixir."

Moira studied Richard's physiognomy of innocence. He couldn't possibly work for Senator Lanai. Not this babe in the woods. He might be handsome, but he gave off a distinct naiveté that perceptive Moira recognized.

"You're new to Los Angeles, aren't you?"

"How'd you guess?"

Moira cocked her head coyly. "Something fresh about you. Like untainted fruit."

Richard said, "Thanks. I mean, I guess." As if.

Now Moira understood everything. "I imagine your friend is one of Dr. Kellogg's patients. In that case, Dr. Kellogg may have administered the product to her. Does she do the injections, or just take it orally?"

Richard thought it over. "I'm sure she said injections."

"That's Dr. Kellogg's client. I mean, patient."

Richard leaned across the reception counter, and for a split second Moira believed with all her heart that he was going to kiss her, but it was just her vivid imagination running wild, playing cruel games. Richard said, "Could I make an appointment with Dr. Kellogg?"

Moira pursed her lips. "Sure. But you don't need that stuff. You're perfect the way you are."

Richard smiled. "Just maintenance."

Moira nodded. "This stuff turns back the clock, that's for sure." Consulting the appointment screen, she said, Dr. Kellogg is booked solid through January. Would you like an appointment in February?"

Richard put a hand to his face. "You mean, wait that long? Oh, that's impossible."

Moira shrugged. "He's a busy man. But if you hold on a sec, I'll check with him, see if he can fit you in sooner." She slinked away. When she was out of sight, Richard swung around the reception desk, took Moira's seat at the computer. In less than a minute, he pulled up Adonis' inventory control list. He scrolled down the product lines. Age-Away, Cell-Renew, Divine Light Solutions, Elixir of Youth. Bingo. Company's local address: 828 Santa Rita Boulevard, Los Angeles. Another address, a post office box number in Copenhagen. Denmark? No phone number. Fax number? Yes. What's this?

Adonis had made copies of the Elixir Web site. Here was a "Mission Statement." Here was a complete description of its products and their applications, a blank order form, a blank invoice. Richard pressed "Print," then accessed Adonis's bookkeeping program. Scrolled up. Scrolled down. Where is it, where is it? Then it came up. Recent payments to the Elixir Foundation. Curious. The payments were made to the post office box number in Copenhagen. He printed out copies of this, but before the printer finished, he heard a swishing sound. Moira sweeping up the corridor. He had enough time to recall the screen Moira had up, then swing back around the desk. He was leafing through an old *GQ* when she reappeared. The damning documents lay in the printer basket.

Moira said, "I'm sorry, but Dr. Kellogg can't see you as a patient. He says he's got patient overload. He says you better just order directly from the Elixir company. I'll give you their Web site address if you'd like, but—uh, I heard it's frozen or something. You might have to write to them. I could give you the address."

Richard was wondering how to get the papers from the printer basket when Kellogg himself came clicking down the corridor.

"Oh, here's Dr. Kellogg now," chirped Moira brightly.

Richard shook Kellogg's slender hand. Firm, solid grip. Kellogg reminded Richard of his former roommate at Stanford, Eddie "Canoe" Evans, the same marvelous physique, the same pellucid complexion, bright and clear, and a mouth that smiled beyond the call of duty. Suave, smooth, the glint in his perfect eyes masked something dark but evident, something like desperation. Like the Canoe, who had landed in the gutter at twenty-five—oh-deed, oh-dead—Kellogg gave off a faux successful aura, the scent of a man in deep trouble. Men in trouble usually have financial problems. The Canoe did.

Kellogg studied Richard's face, said, "I've seen you before. Are you in films?"

"Not that I know of."

Kellogg insisted. "I'm sure I've seen you. I'd never forget a face like yours. Ah, I've got it." Kellogg jabbed a finger. "The newspapers. That's where I've seen you before. You married the daughter of Lady Bella Winsome-Diamond. Your wedding picture was in the *L.A. Times.*"

"Was it?" That amused Richard. Ticked off Moira.

Kellogg said, "You're a goddamn lucky son-of-a-bitch. Lady Bella has pots." He leered wickedly. "I hear your family's not too shabby, either."

"That's really none of your business."

Kellogg backed off. "Oops. Sorry. That was too rude."

Richard said, "I think my mother-in-law comes here for treatments."

Kellogg put a hand to his face. "Tsk. I'm sworn to secrecy." Coyly. "But I will tell you she has never had anything stronger than a mud bath in my spa. She has never taken advantage of our clinical procedures."

Richard smiled. "Perhaps one day she'll come around to that."

Kellogg shook his head. "I doubt that Lady Bella will ever need human growth hormone replacement therapy. She's one of those rare humans that we Dorian Grays of the world so envy." Kellogg smirked. "So you married into the genes. Cool." He tilted his head thoughtfully, dollar signs schooling in his clear eyes. He said, "Say, are you free for dinner this evening?"

Richard said, "I could be."

"Great. Do you know Perry's? Everybody knows Perry's. Meet me at Perry's at nine o'clock."

Moira was standing at the printer, waiting for something to spit out at her. Over her tiny shoulder, she purred, "Come back again, Mr. Winters," and smiled seductively. Married or not, there was no law against flirting, at least, not that Moira knew of.

TWENTY-THREE

PERRY'S

PERRY'S BARREL-CHESTED maître d' escorted Richard to an intimate corner table, where Brad Kellogg, dressed to kill, greeted him with the ersatz effervescence of a cocker spaniel on Prozac. Though Kellogg, being a health nut, probably didn't drop Prozac. Maybe only St. John's Wort. This ebullience was definitely superficial, a charade. How did Richard know this? He once had a wife who ate Prozac like jelly beans. That was before Venus.

The spaniel settled into his chair, ordered a round of drinks. When the waiter delivered Kellogg's oreganotini and Richard's single-malt, Kellogg said, "So, here's to new friends and prosperity. Heh heh." He sipped, adding casually, "By the way, what does your new wife do? Antiques? Travel?"

"She collects icons."

"Is that right?" Brad sounded impressed. "What a radical pastime. So, you must go to Russia often."

Richard shook his head. "She goes. I hang out in Paris, then she meets me."

Brad raised his eyebrows. "Perfecto."

"Sometimes I just hang out on the yacht at Monte Carlo."

Brad stared, his oreganotini poised midair. "You don't mean..."

"Lady Bella's yacht. We haven't got one yet."

"Oh, well." Brad dismissed this tiny detail. "Lady Bella can't live forever, after all."

They exchanged glances, both grinning devilishly.

Across the dining room, a pianist teased out the first strains of Schumann's *Kinderszenen*.

"Gawd," remarked Brad. " 'Scenes from Childhood.' How darkly poignant and inappropriate."

"Tugs your heartstrings."

Brad smacked his lips, set down his glass. "I'll have to speak to Perry."

The waiter brought another round of cocktails. Leaving behind indecorous melodies, they drank and verbally sparred, sizing each other up like a couple of wrestlers. Richard, the former timber executive, was a master of the lingua franca. His brain had substance, was more powerfully built than Kellogg's, stronger, and free of drugs, organic or otherwise, not counting minute traces of single-malt scotch. Kellogg was mentally lean and fit, cultivated, and he had muscle, but if Richard wanted to, he could drop Kellogg in the first round, before the bell stopped vibrating. He let Kellogg choose the subject matter: film, charitable causes and the attendant galas, up-to-the-minute celebrity gossip, anti-aging prattle. When Brad sucked into his third oreganotini, Richard said, "So tell me about this stuff that's going to make me young again."

Brad grinned roguishly. "You aren't a cop, are you? Or some sort of undercover agent?"

Richard raised his right hand, solemn.

Brad squinted, as if trying to remember something. "Tell me again, what do you do for a living?" That coyness again. He knew, but he just wanted to hear Richard say it again.

"I married a Winsome-Diamond."

Brad nodded. "Tha-a-a-at's right. Now I remember." Relaxing, he leaned back, summoned his inner guru, and revealed the truth, as Brad Kellogg saw it. "The natural aging process," he began, "triggers a sharp reduction of human growth hormone, which is secreted by the pituitary gland. These growth hormones are crucial to maintaining the body's general health and well-being. Are you with me so far?"

Richard nodded avidly.

Brad continued, "I've researched all these anti-aging therapies. It's an obsession with me. I want to live forever, and I truly believe we'll soon know how to prolong life indefinitely. Which is why I've invested in the very cutting-edge cryogenics market, but that's another story. Back to the anti-aging market. We know about exercise, and cardiovascular training and so forth. People who really care about their longevity avoid foods tainted with pesticides, and they take the vitamin and mineral supplements so crucial to maintaining optimal health. Then there are the herbal medicines, known as phytomedicines."

Richard cut in. "You mean, for example, instead of taking a synthetic drug like Prozac, a depressed patient might take St. John's Wort?"

"You've got the concept." In his best salesman's posture, Brad confided, "What I do at Adonis, Richard, is beyond your basic naturopathy, or herbal healing. Of course, we apply these practices where appropriate, but what I do, Richard, is truly a cutting-edge therapy. Am I boring you?"

"No way." Snore.

"Good." Brad sipped the 'tini, leaned across the table, lowered his voice. "The latest anti-aging rage is a substance called recombinant human growth hormone, or, rHGH. Recombinant, because it's a synthesized version of the real thing. Anti-aging research has proven that human growth hormone replacement therapy not only stops the clock, it can reverse the aging process by as much as ten to twenty years. The formula I administer promotes stronger bones, leaner muscle-to-fat ratio," he ticked these off on his fingers, "cell rejuvenation, increased energy, mental agility, heightened sexual performance and a generally youthful appearance. If, by chance, you and your new wife are looking for a firm investment, I'd be open to a partnership. Only because I know you're Lady Bella's heirs, of course. I wouldn't just partner with anybody."

Richard looked dubious. "Isn't this risky business? I mean, health-wise?"

"Used to be. Before rHGH was developed, scientists were extracting human growth hormone—HGH—from cadavers, and there was a high risk of acquiring disease from the cadaver material."

Richard said, "What about the FDA? Have they approved this rHGH product?"

"They've approved some formulas, but nothing nearly as potent as the formula we administer here." Brad waved a hand dismissively. "Oh, you'll see these little hormone clinics on every street corner in L.A. But their products aren't nearly as potent as mine. In fact, what we use here is by far the most controversial to hit the market, and thus, sold only under wraps, so to speak."

"Black market."

Brad stared at Richard. "Say, not to change the subject or anything, but you ought to be in movies. You've got the looks, the charisma. I could see you playing the next James Bond, for example. Hey—" Kellogg snapped his long fingers and it sounded like chalk breaking.

"I've got a faboo idea. I have this patient, she's a talent agent. I could introduce you to her. She'd go for you. How about it?"

Richard shrugged. "Let me think it over."

Brad smacked his forehead. "Jeez, what am I talking about? You want to be in movies, all you have to do is put a little bug in your mom-in-law's ear." Chummy now, he asked, "What's it like being married to her daughter? I hear the daughters and sons aren't nearly as sexy as La Belladonna."

Richard coaxed a smile from a sneer. Thankfully, dinner arrived.

Brad deftly carved his eggplant Provençal into neat squares that he speared precisely and brought to his mouth in one deft fillip. When he'd swallowed a couple of bites, he asked, "Have you told your wife?"

Richard said, "Told her what?"

Brad patted his mouth with a napkin. "That you want to start anti-aging therapy."

Richard said, "Uh, no. No, I haven't mentioned this to her. Should I have?"

Kellogg shrugged. "Depends. If you want her to join you in the longevity adventure, she should probably start injecting Elixir herself. Unless, of course, you plan to outlive her. Some of my patients intentionally withhold this information from their spouses. For personal reasons."

"Elixir. Is that what it's called?"

"That's the name of the company that manufactures it. Elixir of Youth. They're on the Internet. If you want to, you can order directly from them. But I have a special arrangement with the company. They supply me with a super-potent product. Better to obtain it from me."

Richard nodded, thinking this over. He was cutting into his prime rib, when Brad asked, "How much meat do you eat?"

"Probably more than I should. What about you?"

Brad laughed. "These days, you can't be in the health care industry and be a carnivore."

"Why not? Meat's a natural product." Richard glanced down at the medium-rare slab on his plate, with three baby carrots and a swish of hollandaise.

"Oh, hell," Kellogg confessed, "I eat red meat now and then, just not in public, where my vegan patients might see me. And what are they so all-holy about anyway? Since ancient history, natural medicine has used animal products. In fact, there's an ancient form of

Chinese medicine still practiced that involves rare products like monkey eyeballs and chicken feet and so forth. At Adonis, we go only as far as the bird's-nest-soup therapy, that's the closest we get to animal product. And that's just regurgitory junk, what sticks to the nest when a hen's feeding her chicks. The stuff is gathered and used in a broth, to relieve sinusitis and allergies. In our spa, we use all natural, all organic products. But in the clinic where we perform cosmetic surgery and administer the rHGH, we're a cutting-edge business. We rarely utilize the ancient therapies. It isn't lucrative anymore."

"Where do you find the bird nests?"

"Borneo. Oops, excuse me." Kellogg fished a cell phone out of his jacket. "Damned annoyance. Dr. Kellogg speaking."

Kellogg spoke to someone he alternately called "honey" and "gorgeous." Richard read his watch. Ten-thirty. Slowly, with relish, he finished the prime rib. A puddle of red blood remained on the plate. He sopped it up with a roll, and when the waiter glided past, ordered a Rémy Martin. Kellogg made a boring dinner companion.

Still on the phone, Kellogg's tone of voice turned urgent. Richard looked up, noticed a fine, beady sweat breaking across Kellogg's brow. Into the phone, Brad barked, "I don't think you mean that, honey. Anyway, you're blowing it all out of proportion. Now, I'm going up there day after tomorrow, and will bring the product back Sunday morning. Can you just give me until then? Until Sunday morning?"

Kellogg held the receiver away from his ear. Richard could hear a growling voice, some cursing, then the line went dead. He sipped his Rémy while Kellogg took a moment to compose himself.

"Sorry. That was a very impatient patient. Ha ha." Kellogg put the phone away, mined another pocket, and set something gingerly on the table.

"This is it," he said proudly.

The vial was three inches long, filled with a cloudy brown fluid. "Elixir of Youth. That's what you wanted, right?"

Richard nodded warily.

Kellogg pushed out his chair. "So, come on."

"Where?"

"To the men's room. I've got a syringe and needle. Let's go."

Richard hesitated. "I haven't paid you."

Brad waved a hand. "Don't worry. You can take care of that later. Let's go."

In the men's room, Kellogg drew the fluid from the vial into the syringe and said, "Best place is the flank. Give me a little cheek."

Richard said, "I don't even know what's in it. How do I know it's safe?"

"Hey, I'm a doc. I wouldn't do anything stupid. I know what I'm doing."

Stalling for time, Richard said, "I'm not crazy about needles."

Kellogg chortled. "You'll have to get used to them. Once a week for the rest of your life. I'll teach you how to inject it yourself. Hey, don't sweat it. It's just a little prick. Diabetics do it all the time. Hurry up, before someone comes in."

Technology may be the curse of some men, but often a curse is what's called for. Kellogg's cell phone rang. Setting the filled syringe down on a table, he fumbled for the phone. Richard ambled over to a sink, washed his hands, studied Kellogg in the mirror. He could see the back of Kellogg's head, the phone plastered to his ear. One swift movement captured the syringe, dropped it into Richard's pocket. Richard fished out his own phone, feigned a conversation, feigned dismay. Mouthed to Kellogg, "Emergency. So long." And, "Thank you for dinner." And got out of there fast. On Rodeo Drive, he hailed a taxi.

Eight twenty-eight Santa Rita Boulevard was a small building sandwiched between a sports bar and a McDonald's. Eight twenty-eight was a mail drop, private postal boxes. Closed for the night. By the time Richard returned to Adonis, the spa's lights were off, except for subtle night lighting in the foyer. He jiggled a credit card in the narrow crevice between the double entrance doors, and the lock clicked. He put his right hand against the right door. It opened inward, smoothly. No alarm sounded. Way too easy.

Inside, he locked the door, listened. He could hear the trickle of water running, lightly, like a decorative fountain. That was all he could hear. In the shadows, he moved like a cat over to the reception desk, then behind the desk. At the printer, he checked the basket. His printouts still lay in the basket by Moira's desk. Moira had attached a note to them.

"Mr. Handsome: Call me sometime." With her telephone numbers, including digital, home, answering service, and personal fax. Richard smiled at the note, seized the printouts, stashed them in his jacket pocket, and headed down the corridor toward Doc Kellogg's office. Moving along the corridor, he tried each door. The first two were locked. The third was unlocked. Cautiously, he entered.

A surgery. Here was the lunch-lift room, all spiffy and cool, full of equipment, waiting for the next victim of gravity. He needed more light, found the wall switch, flipped it up. Blazing, full spectrum surgery lights. In one corner of the surgery, was a strange type of chair with a cushioned headrest and straps to hold the patient in. In the center of the operating room stood an operating table, and on the operating table lay a body—he couldn't tell if it was alive or dead.

The man's milk-white skin verged on blue. Limp arms rested across his chest, a latter-day John of Arc, martyr to the Age of Youth Worship, plugged into an intravenous drip. Approaching the body, Richard hesitated—the sound of water again. Was somebody else inside the spa? His tentative hand reached out, his fingers on the eyelids. He drew them open. Blue orbs, pinpoint pupils. The man sighed. Richard backed off.

In Kellogg's office, he tried breaking into the computer files, but couldn't get past the doc's secret password. He rifled the desk. Nothing interesting, nothing compelling, unless you collect neckties. Brad Kellogg had dozens of neckties stuffed in all the desk drawers. The only other person Richard ever knew with a serious necktie fetish was Eddie "Canoe" Evans, who never actually wore the neckties. The Canoe used them to tie willing women to his bedposts. At least, he said they agreed to it.

Nothing here in this office. Richard put everything back in place, then returned to the operating room. The man on the table hadn't budged. Richard searched until he found the back room, the surgical instruments, the fridge. Voil. He groped through the anti-aging cornucopia, retrieved a few selected samples. In the surgery, he located some plastic bags, shoved his loot into a trash bag. The cat burglar in the House of Youth. He was moving down the corridor when he heard Brad's voice. Richard ducked back into the surgery.

Brad's voice came from the direction of the reception area. He was speaking to someone, apparently on the telephone. Brad said, "That's right. This might be my ticket to freedom from Lana. If they invest, I can cut Lana loose. I won't need her money. And if she goes to the Senator with stories, I can just deny everything. It's her word against mine. Hey, I'm a physician, right? She's a frigging politician's wife. So, things are looking brighter, pal."

When he heard Brad clicking along the marble corridor, whistling cheerfully, Richard located a convenient hiding place, a closet filled with Kellogg's scrubs. Kellogg's footsteps passed the surgery, continued toward his office. In a few minutes, Richard heard him coming back. Footsteps along the corridor, and this time, approaching the operating room. Then Brad was inside. Richard heard him approach the body on the table. Silence, then Brad exclaimed out loud, "Oh dear, Mr. Pearson, I completely forgot about you."

Brad went over to the sink, scrubbed. Went to the closet. Reached in, his fingers walking across Richard's chest, located scrubs. Brad put them on, went back to the sink, scrubbed some more. From the closet, Richard watched through the partly open door. Brad, hands high, approached the operating table.

"All right, Mr. Pearson," said Doc Kellogg, "let's suck out that sagging jowl, shall we?"

SHE ANSWERED on the third ring. Playing hard to get. Richard said, "I have presents for you."

"Where are you?" Breathlessly.

"Sea-Tac."

"Hurry," she said.

"How fast does the Alfa go?"

"You're driving my car?"

Richard said, "What, I should sprout wings, maybe?"

"I'm desperate for you," she said. "Topsy-turvy. Hurry."

TWENTY-FOUR

THE UNKNOWN

LUCKY THING Bob Brightman worked nights at the county transportation garage, otherwise Carolee and Winn would have had to sneak around in daylight. True, sometimes Bob knocked off early, when the work was slow, but that happened once in a blue moon, so most nights they could get away with sleeping over at their nest in the Pine Fresh Motel. The old couple who owned the Pine Fresh were discreet and half-blind anyway, so Carolee didn't worry over the clandestine affair. And Theresa, being so drugged-out with sleeping pills, probably never even noticed Winn wasn't in their bed. Anyway, all Carolee was doing, come right down to it, was keeping Winn halfway sane. Men need nooky to maintain their sanity, where women can go for months on pure emotional strength. Some women, anyway. Not Carolee.

Winn had come to rely on Carolee's companionship. She had to admit she resented their only meeting under the cover of the Pine Fresh Motel, and yet she understood how Winn had to be discreet for the time being, especially since the law was always watching him in case he might slip up and do something stupid that would prove he killed his own child. Everywhere she went in Iron County, Carolee heard people talking about Winn, and how Winn had left his own son out for the beast to tear apart. Sheriff Tobin had told Bob and Bob had told Carolee that Agent Diamond had her eyes on Winn; the classic alcoholic father abusing his child in a drunken blind, leaving him out to be snatched by animals so no one would discover how Winn had beaten the baby. Hearsay, but Bob wouldn't twist Tobin's words. Then Carolee heard from Irene Polk that Theresa had sold her baby to a Satanic cult that sent Satan himself to claim Paris Nighteagle. For all Carolee knew, Theresa might be a witch herself. Not like white witches, but some kind of evil shaman. Nothing would surprise Carolee.

On this December night, when Winn showed up with Carolee at the casino, the regulars on blackjack didn't even blink. Everyone knew Winn Nighteagle had taken up with Carolee Brightman, except maybe Bob Brightman—or maybe he knew and didn't care. Carolee came from bad seed, the worst kind of seed. You come from Hell, you're born in Hell, you die in Hell kind of seed. Just as you can't go back in time, you can't change who your ancestors were. So it didn't surprise anyone when Carolee Brightman slunk into the casino at Whaler's Landing, hanging on Winn's arm, wearing pancake makeup and exhibiting her charms for all to leer over. Even Daniel Dean wanted to puke. And there was poor Theresa Nighteagle back up in the forest, deserted by her husband, one baby sick with fever, her other baby lost to the Unknown. No wonder she's afflicted by madness. God help the world.

"Raise you fifty."

Dean glanced up from his hand and saw Sheriff Tobin swagger into the casino, and now here came that blond frail, the Fish and Wildlife chick. Tobin and the blond hung by the bar sucking spring water, keeping their eyes on the poker boys. Dean raked in the pot. When Winn untangled himself from Carolee and sat down, the dealer threw out a new hand.

"Bet a hundred."

Dean raised him, and raised him again. Winn folded, watched Dean rake in another pot. Winn bet again, but even the fresh hand folded. This went on for a solid hour before Winn started thinking maybe Carolee was bringing him bad luck. He sent her to the bar to get some fresh drinks and as soon as she was gone, he won his first hand of the evening. You could hear the hoots and hollers; even Tobin and the blond heard all the racket. When Carolee returned with the booze, wanting to know what had happened while she was gone, Winn said, "Go on home."

"Winn," she whined.

"I said, go on."

Carolee pouted. "I'm not leaving."

Winn jumped to his feet, grabbed Carolee by the shoulders, shoved her backwards against a triple-deal slot machine. "I said get out of here. And this time, take your own damn car." Winn returned to the card table. Carolee, fuming, grabbed her purse and skulked out.

The road between the casino and Forks curved and wound around thick forest that hung like black curtains on each side of the pavement.

A thin, peek-a-boo moon teased the center line. Carolee put her headlights on high and tried tuning in the one station that was receivable on a car radio, but got nothing but flat static. A few raindrops splattered the Fairlane's windshield and the wind picked up and bent cedar branches into the road. Carolee kicked on the heater and defroster and when she glanced at the road again, she saw the beast.

She tried braking gradually so as not to hit it broadside, but the huge creature turned and flashed its red neon eyes, instantly mesmerizing her, as she later recalled, so that she couldn't remember what happened next.

What happened was, the great beast attacked Carolee's Ford Fairlane, its seven-point antlers and its hooves crashing against the hood, against the windshield, as Carolee screamed and screamed inside. Finally, battered and bruised, bloodied and exhausted, the creature sprang back into the forest, into the darkness, into hiding. Carolee fainted.

AT TOLEAK LODGE, Richard sat by the roaring fire, his laptop up and running, his concentration fully aimed at the screen. Venus knelt behind him, watching over his shoulder. Richard said, "SpaVida's Web site is still frozen, the Life Eternal Institute's Web site is still frozen, and Elixir's still frozen. This is going to be harder than I thought."

She said, "No one surfs better than you. Must be your Southern Cal roots."

"Hush." He typed in the words, "anti-aging products." The laptop made grinding sounds. He said, "I need a new laptop."

She caressed his shoulder. "If you solve this puzzle, I'll buy you one."

When the groaning stopped, Richard studied the screen, scrolled up and down, performed some keyboard magic and said, "We've hit pay dirt."

They printed out the document, an obscure academic paper about synthetic human growth hormone therapy. Twelve pages. When they finished reading, she said, "I don't know what I'd do without you."

He shut off the printer. "I'll be up all night with this stuff," he said. "Why don't we take a little break?" He pulled her close, kissed her.

"Richard, we have work to do." Mild protest.

"Hey, I have to go back to L.A. in the morning. Don't I deserve a little recreation?"

"Sure, but couldn't we just do this first..."

"Shhh. You talk too much."

THE ONLY THING Carolee clearly remembered was coming to consciousness on the side of the highway, the Fairlane parked on the road's narrow shoulder, her torso draped over the steering wheel. It took a full twenty minutes to stop shaking and get up the nerve to restart the car and drive home where Becca was waiting up for her with some bad news.

"Mom," she said, "you look awful. Are you sick or something?"

Carolee couldn't find words to speak. Her tongue didn't work. She sat down on the couch and shivered and trembled until Becca decided against delivering the bad news and instead brought her some warm blankets and wrapped her up. Then finally the words came, and Becca heard a distant plaintive voice crying, "The Unknown attacked me. He raped me, Becca. He raped me with his eyes."

Becca shook her head. "Mom, you are so melodramatic." She padded off in the direction of her bedroom, muttering disgust at adults in general.

Outside, Carolee's Ford Fairlane sat in the driveway, its hood and fenders crushed, the windshield smashed.

BOB BRIGHTMAN wiped axle grease off his meaty hands. Eight a.m. Quitting time. The tools of his trade lay strewn across the garage's concrete floor and the big Mercedes truck he was giving a new transmission to sat high on jacks. Bob felt tired after a long night's work but, being a meticulous man, he gathered up his tools and placed them neatly in his toolbox. As he steered his big Pontiac out of the garage lot, the sun was just peeking over the Olympics, pinking their snowy caps. Driving down Highway 101, Brightman noticed Winn Nighteagle's pickup parked in front of the Pine Fresh Motel. He put on his blinker, turned into the Pine Fresh. Winn's pickup was parked in front of cabin Eight. Bob pounded on the door. No answer. Bob pounded harder. Pretty soon he heard noises inside and in a few minutes, Winn opened the door.

Bob said, "Tell Carolee I want to talk to her."

Winn rubbed his eyes. "Carolee? Why, Bob, she's not here."

"The hell she's not." Bob pushed past Winn, went inside. He couldn't find Carolee anywhere. He checked all the rooms and closets, everywhere. No sign of Carolee. Bob felt a flush on his neck.

"You satisfied?" said Winn, hitching up his pants.

Bob didn't reply, just got back into the Pontiac and drove away.

Half an hour later, pulling into Cedar Grove Trailer Park, Bob saw something that made his stomach churn. He blinked and looked again, just to be sure he wasn't having a nightmare. Sure enough, it was there: a big real estate sign that said SOLD nailed to the Cedar Grove Trailer Park sign. What did that mean?

Becca met her father at the front door. Though it was early, she was fully dressed, drinking a Diet Pepsi. Bob jerked his thumb back toward the sign. "What's that all about?"

Becca said, "You won't like it, Dad."

"Like what? Speak up."

Becca followed Bob into the kitchen. "Winn Nighteagle bought the trailer park, Dad. He's our landlord now."

Brightman froze. "Nobody's my landlord. I own this trailer free and clear."

"But Winn owns the land we're parked on. It's his land now. And yesterday evening, he handed out these notices." She plucked a sheet of paper off the kitchen table, handed it to Bob. Bob read it, shock and disbelief chilling his blood, turning his face pale white.

"He can't do this. This is a goddamn eviction notice."

"Thirty days," confirmed Becca. "Where will we go, Dad?"

"Where's your mother?"

Becca pointed to her parents' bedroom. "Asleep. She had a bad night."

"Has she seen this?"

Becca shook her head. "She came home last night all upset. I didn't show it to her."

"What happened to her car?"

Becca smirked. "She said the Unknown attacked it."

Bob didn't believe that for one minute. He crumpled the paper in his meaty hand and said, "I'll kill the SOB."

"Oh, come on, Dad."

"Why's he doing this anyway?"

"Winn's going to build a big house here, Dad. For him and Theresa and Milan. A big mansion, right here on this land. He had the architect over here yesterday. I saw them sketching out plans. He's a millionaire now, Dad, he can do anything he wants.''

"No, he cannot," shouted Bob. "And Winn Nighteagle is no millionaire. After all he's squandered and lost at the casino, hell, I probably have more money than he does now."

"Don't exaggerate. Anyway, he's rich." Becca poured some Honeycombs into a bowl, got milk from the fridge, poured it over the cereal. "I just wish we had all that money. Think what we could do."

Bob didn't hear the last part. He was already out the door, marching across the park to the Nighteagle trailer. He pounded on the door. Theresa opened it. Bob shoved the paper at her. "What's the meaning of this?" he demanded.

Tiredly, Theresa said, "I'm sorry, Bob. Everybody's asking me. It's Winn. He's gone crazy."

Bob heard a noise behind him. He turned and saw Daniel Dean standing there, holding a similar paper. Dean snarled, "Goddamn Indian."

TWENTY-FIVE

PENDER

BECCA DRESSED Ocean Boy in a thick snowsuit, mittens, heavy woolen socks, boots, and a woolen knit cap pulled down over his ears. When he was bundled up against the weather, Becca picked him up and stepped outdoors, locking the door behind her. She walked around to the side of the building, made sure no one was lurking nearby, and headed into the forest. A seagull soared overhead. In her arms, Ocean Boy gurgled, "Bud," and grinned.

"Shush now, Paris," Becca said urgently. "Shhh. We're not supposed to be outdoors, so be very quiet." Becca turned off onto an old logging trail, its floor carpeted with pine needles and dappled by stark autumn sunlight. The footpath led downhill to the highway where it abruptly ended. Before stepping onto the highway, Becca looked both ways. No vehicles. No one in sight, except for that big elk standing on the road's shoulder about a hundred yards up the highway, his cloudy breath glistening in the sun. Holding tight to Ocean Boy, she streaked across the highway and disappeared among the fine, tall cedars. In a few minutes, she emerged on the other side of the trees, on the beach side where the ocean roared onto a narrow strip of rocky beach and high tides came all the way up to the tree trunks. She carried the boy across the driftwood logs, across the rocky beach, down to the tideline, where she set him gently upon a smooth boulder.

Ocean Boy blinked once or twice at the brightness of the light reflecting on the water. His eyes, grown accustomed to the dim recesses of the room that had been his home for one tenth of his life, strained to adjust to the brightness of beach light. Once he could focus clearly, Ocean Boy shrieked in delight at the sight of the great roiling body of water, the waves clawing the shore. He said, "Wah-ee."

"Water. Say wa-ter."

"Wa-er."

"Wa-ter." Becca emphasized the "t."

A brief pause, then, "Wa-der."

Becca smiled. "Very good, Paris." Just then, another seagull swooped down in front of them and landed in the breakers. "Oh, look, what's that?" She pointed at the gull.

"Bud."

"Yes, yes, Paris. Very good. You're a very smart little boy."

They played together at the tideline, fashioning an intricate castle from the tacky sand, cementing it together with saltwater baths. When at last the tide rolled in and smashed their castle all to bits, Becca looked up and saw that the cold pink sun hung straight overhead.

"Omigosh." Becca scrambled to her feet. "We have to get back, Paris."

Gathering Ocean Boy in her arms, she ran across the beach, through the tall cedars, across Highway 101, into the forest, up over a rise, where she crossed the bridge over the Little Hoh River, then ran downhill to where the Little Hoh branched, the main body going northward, a little brook singing off southward. Becca followed the little stream downhill until she reached the building. Making sure no one saw her, she sneaked in through the back door, and once inside the room, she tore off the boy's outer clothing and placed him in his playpen, as if he had never been outdoors at all. She was just opening Clint Kellogg's book of fables when the door flew open and the visitor entered.

Ocean Boy opened his little mouth and announced, "Wa-ter." Clear as day. The visitor didn't stay long, only long enough to check the boy's pulse, take his temperature, and walk around inspecting things. When finally the visitor had gone, Becca said, "Paris, you mustn't tell on us. The beach is our secret. You mustn't tell."

Ocean Boy smiled at Becca. "Wa-ter bud."

"Now, Paris, this is a very special story. It's about a silly man who was afraid to grow old." Becca began to read from Clint Kellogg's book of fables.

Once not so long ago, a boy named Anton and his sister, whose name was Elektra, became lost in the forest. The sun was high and the forest sounds were friendly, and they could hear the swishing of the ocean not far away. But as they searched for the way out of the forest through fragrant cedar groves, over two crystalline brooks, up a steep slope and down the other side, the children lost all sense of direction. They walked and walked through the darkening forest and soon night fell and the forest filled with mist and turned to blackness, lit only by a thin slice of moon. The children grew cold and rain began falling. Anton took his sister's soggy hand and led her through the dense woods. Plodding and tripping through brambles and mud slides, Elektra slipped and almost fell but Anton pulled her up, and when she shivered he took his jacket off and put it around her shoulders. Anton did not tell his sister, but he had seen a pair of eyes watching them from behind a tree.

It might come after us, he thought, and to Elektra he said, "Hurry, let's walk faster."

But Elektra was exhausted and her feet could hardly move. "I have to stop and rest," she pleaded.

Just then, Anton noticed a small cabin. "Look, Elektra. Someone's house. And there's a light in the window. I think we're safe now." He grabbed Elektra's hand and ran to the little cabin's front door. Finding no doorbell, he knocked. In a few minutes, the door swung slowly open and a very old man—stooped over and barely able to raise his head—appeared. "What do you want?" the old man demanded.

"We are lost," Anton explained, "and something is chasing us. Can we come inside?"

The old man made a grunting sound that reminded Elektra more of a pig than a human. "All right, then, come inside if you must. But don't hold me responsible for anything that happens in here."

Without paying any attention to the old man's warning, the children rushed inside the cabin. "Whew, that was a close call," said Elektra. But just then, Anton put a hand on Elektra's shoulder and said, "Be careful, Elektra. That thing over in the corner might bite."

Elektra looked in the corner of the cabin and saw a wretched beast. Part human, part something else, the beast had a human face but legs like a deer with cloven hooves. "Just what are you supposed to be?" asked Elektra.

The beast snarled but did not answer her question. The old man came hobbling over and said, "He can't answer you. Back before he ate the elk's hooves, he spoke English. Good, proper English. Now he can't speak anything but pig latin, and even that is fading rapidly.''

Anton made a disgusted face. "Why would anyone want to eat elk's hooves?''

The old man tittered and eased back into an overstuffed armchair. "Come sit by the fire, my children," he said. "Let me tell you about death and the forest.''

"Oh no, that's far too scary a subject," protested Elektra, but Anton made her go over and sit by the fire.

"Tell us about death and the forest, old man," said Anton.

The fire crackled and warmed the children as the old man told the strange tale of the beast in the corner. "He came to me as a middle-aged man, a nice-looking if slightly jowly gentleman. The only thing he owned was an exquisite gold ring which he wore all the time. He wanted to work for me here in the forest, so I gave him an ax and a saw and put him to work chopping wood. I let him sleep in my guest room, and every morning and evening, I fed him a square meal. Before long, the man, whose name was Pender, had earned enough money—I paid him handsomely for his work—to build a cabin of his own. But do you suppose he would build it? No sirree, not this Pender. Instead, Pender went to the young woman in the village who claimed to have the secret of eternal youth. Pender paid her all his scrimped and saved wages for the secret.''

"What was the secret?" asked Elektra. "Hurry up and get to the point.''

The old man raised a gnarly hand. "Patience, girl, patience. Time is on your side. So anyway, Pender came home, and by the time he reached my cabin, he had lost twenty years off his age and recovered every aspect of his youth. Vitality, energy, fresh good looks, a brilliant memory, every facet of youthfulness. He was so fine-looking a young man that soon every unattached girl in the village came calling for Pender. My cabin was overrun with smitten creatures. I often had to flee up into my attic and hide from them, so irksome were they. Finally, Pender told all the girls that they would have to compete for his affections, and the winner would become Pender's bride.''

"What sort of competition?" asked Elektra.

"You see, when Pender was on his way home from the village, growing younger all the time, his fingers became so slim that the gold ring fell off somewhere in the forest. So, as I was saying, Pender set up a competition. The girls were told to go into the forest, and the one who could bring back Pender's gold ring would win the competition and Pender would marry her."

Anton could hear the beast in the corner grunting and groaning and trying to speak. Anton said, "I think Pender wants to finish the tale."

The old man said, "Never mind Pender. Unless you want to hear this tale in pig latin."

Anton held up a hand. "Oh no, no, please. My sister speaks it all the time and it drives me crazy. You go on, sir, with your story."

The old man continued. "After six days and nights, not a single girl had turned up the gold ring. Several of the girls tried bringing fake golden rings to Pender, but he always saw through their trickery and chased them off. Then, on the tenth day of the competition, a lovely young lady appeared at my front door, right out here, mind you, and in her hand, she held Pender's gold ring. Pender leaped up and grabbed the ring from the girl's hand, slipped the ring on his finger, and danced outdoors and into the woods, singing in an obstreperous voice:

Pender's got his golden ring
Pender's got his youth and fairness
Pender doesn't need a thing
Certainly not a miss or missus

"And so, Pender ran off to be a bachelor, breaking his promise to all the fair young ladies of the village. But what Pender did not know was that the fairest young lady of them all, the one who found his gold ring, was Wapiti in disguise."

"Who's Wapiti?" asked Elektra.

"Wapiti, the Great Elk, is prince of the forest," said the old man. "Wapiti's hooves had been cut off to make the elixir of eternal youth. Pender had benefited from Wapiti's suffering, and Wapiti had come back to test Pender's honesty. As you already know, Pender failed that test miserably. When Pender broke his promise to the girls of the village, Wapiti punished

him by turning him into an ugly, wart-covered, sagging, wrinkled old beast. And because Pender took such terrible advantage of all the young ladies of the village, Wapiti made his
curse eternal.''

Anton glanced over at Pender cowering in the corner, grunting and groaning. "So there's no hope for Pender, then?''

"How sad,'' sighed Elektra.

The old man smiled a toothless smile. "There's always
hope, my children, always hope. Where truth exists, so does
hope. Wapiti gave Pender one last chance to return to normal.''

"You mean young-normal or old-normal?'' said Elektra,
ever finicky.

"I mean normal, just like he was when he came to me,''
said the old man. "Wapiti told Pender that if he would go
around the forest scaring away all the hunters, all the invaders
who came to kill and maim the creatures of the woodlands,
that Pender would win back his normal self.''

Anton said, "But he wouldn't do it?''

The old man sighed. "Pender doesn't have the courage.
Every day he sits in that corner and grunts and groans and
tries to gather the courage to go out and run off the invaders,
but so far, he hasn't found it. You see, Pender's a moral weak-
ling. All his character was derived from his physical appearance. When he lost his good looks, his courage went too.''

Elektra said, "But then, it's all quite simple, don't you see?''
She reached out a hand. "Come here, you ugly beast,'' she
commanded.

Pender heard Elektra and padded over to her side. Elektra
placed her hand on Pender's warty head. It felt like diseased
crocodile skin. She leaned down and faced Pender eye to eye.
"Now, you listen here, Pender,'' said the little girl in her firmest tone of voice, "I know what's wrong with you. You have
lost your courage underneath all that ugliness. Instead of being
proud of what Nature gave you, you were afraid of aging,
ashamed of the changes in your body, so you sought out the
Fountain of Youth. You sold your soul and all your integrity
to gain back your youth. Well, Pender, just look at you now.
What an ugly creature you are.''

Pender grunted miserably.

Elektra went on. "You brought on all these changes yourself, by your behavior, by your carelessness and insensitivity. Do you understand me, Pender?''

Pender moaned and tears dripped from his rheumy eyes.

Elektra said, ''Respect yourself, no matter what you look like, and don't be afraid to grow old. Then you will find your courage. I promise you, Pender, if you can just learn to love who you are, you'll be a happy man once again. Middle-aged, mind you, and growing older, but truly happy.''

Elektra leaned over and caressed the beast. Pender turned his rheumy eyes upward and gazed into Elektra's twinkling orbs. At that moment, Pender felt proud of who he was and, instantly regained his courage. He scampered out of the house and into the forest.

After Anton and Elektra left the woods, Pender saved so many creatures from invaders that Wapiti turned Pender back to his normal self. Pender devoted the rest of his life to saving the creatures of the forest. Wapiti became his guardian spirit, and Pender grew younger at heart and more wizenly handsome with every day that passed.

TWENTY-SIX

AGE MATTERS

MEL ROSE WAS hysterical. No one in show business had ever pulled such a nasty trick. In all his years as a performer—no, as a serious actor—disappointment had never touched him so deeply as this news just presented him from the honeyed lips of Lana Lanai. Outrageous, that's what Mel called it. Lana agreed, in her own way. "What can you do?" she remarked. "Producers have the right to change their minds. Anyway," she added nonchalantly, "there was a technical glitch in the contract."

Mel Rose was a middle-aged character actor—until today, the most sought-after villain in the business. "Technical glitch? *Technical glitch?* What do you mean by technical glitch? They signed the contract, and they made me the star of this film. Don't talk to me about technical glitches."

"There was a teensy clause, darling, about not altering your appearance. Your appearance changed, so they canceled the contract." Lana shrugged. "My guess is, they'll bring on Henry Chow."

"What's Henry Chow got that I don't, huh? What's he got?" Mel screamed.

"Youth, darling. Youth," Lana replied cruelly.

Mel's jaw dropped open, and Lana thought he looked like a ventriloquist's doll. He said, "Don't tease me, Lana. I'm warning you, don't tease me."

Lana smirked. "If you want my candid opinion, Mel, dear, you're getting a bit mature for these enigmatic villain roles. You should probably consider downsizing your ambitions at this point. That, or do something radical about your appearance. Maybe you should go see Doc Kellogg."

Mel waved a hand. "That hormone man?"

Lana pursed her lips, nodded.

Mel said, "He's a damn quack."

"He can help you, sweetheart. Take Lana's word. You want your youth back? Go see Doc Kellogg. Otherwise, you might start thinking about a career change."

Mel shouted at Lana. "I'm not going to that charlatan for any damn snake oil or anything else. No, sirree. I'll report this to the Actors' Guild."

Lana shuffled video disks, searching for the next starlet. To Mel, she said, "Do that, Mel, dear. And phone me next week. I might have something for you by then."

Mel Rose had reached the threshold when he remembered an important point. "I'll bet," he shouted across Lana's great divide, "it's because Henry Chow is Asian."

Lana popped a disk into the VCR. Her bony fingers, limp beneath the weight of elaborate rings, adjusted the contrast. She glanced up at Mel. Half of her mouth curved ironically. The other half remained thoughtfully pursed. "I don't think so," she murmured. "We don't have reverse racism anymore. In the film industry, I mean."

Nubile blond star material blazed across Lana's screen, grabbing her attention. Mel fled, honestly fearing what destructive thing he might do if he stuck around. When he'd gone, Lana picked up the phone and called the nubile blond star material. She was just introducing herself when Lance called on the other line, demanding to speak to her immediately. No, he wouldn't wait through the next Miss Baywatch recruitment ploy, he had something to tell Lana right now. Sighing, Lana hung up on the hot prospect and turned her attention to Lance.

Lance said, "When is your next appointment at Adonis?"

"Tomorrow morning. Why?" Lana studied the image of the cute blond.

"I want you to cancel it, Lana. Cancel all your appointments at Adonis. And do it today, in fact do it right now."

"What in the world has gotten into you, Lance? Are you crazy or what?"

"Lana, it's very important that you completely disassociate yourself from that business. In fact, if anyone ever connects you to Brad Kellogg, that might cost me my senate seat."

Lana could sound sweet if need be. "Lance, you are so cute, really you are. I love it when you get so worked up over your causes. It's really quite seductive."

Lance was on his digital phone, a more secure device, he'd been assured, than his old cell phone. Lance and Wexler were holed up in a corner of Perry's, where they had just finished lunch. Lance had beef tenderloin. Wexler had the mahimahi. Wexler was sated. Lance had indigestion. Lance belched and said, "Listen, angel, I know I'm sounding macho-pushy-interfering-husbandy, but you've just got to cooperate with me now. Just cancel your appointments at Adonis. I'll explain everything tonight."

"You'll be home tonight?"

"I'm already in town. I'll meet you at home in an hour."

Lana studied her wristwatch, more intrigued with the diamond encirclement than the clock face, the clock hands. "All right, Lance. But if this is one of your silly pranks, already it's not funny."

"Cancel those appointments right now, angel. Lancey loves you, babe."

Lana set the phone into its cradle, then said out loud, "Lancey loves Lancey, that's who Lancey loves."

A SLIM MAN in dark sunglasses, pink polo shirt, and white Bermuda shorts invaded Moira's private territory. Situated on the high stool, Moira straightened her spine, all the better to peer steeply down at him. "You are...?"

The man said, "Mr. Jones. Calvin Jones. I have an appointment with Dr. Kellogg." He seemed embarrassed. "I've never been here before. When I called, they told me I could park in the private drive."

Moira consulted the books. "Oh, yes, I see you here, Mr....well, Jones. But first, you're scheduled with Gordon, for a colonic and mud. Dr. Kellogg always requires a patient to do the colonic and mud before his therapy sessions."

Moira felt under the desk for the entrance gate release button, pressed it. The man in the sunglasses and white Bermudas went outside, slid behind the wheel of a pearl Lexus, and smoothly navigated the spa's private drive. The gates closed behind the car just as Moira reached for the phone. The man was heading toward the door. Moira buzzed Gordon. "Your next client is here," she told Gordon. "It's Mel Rose, that aging character actor. Only, he's incognito. Should I call the *National Enquirer*, or do you want to?"

LANA LANAI had hair-trigger syndrome. When Lana got ticked, the whole world shivered. When somebody promised Lana something and didn't deliver, Lana went ballistic. When Lana's ego butted up against deception, rejection and/or desertion, great temblors shook the City of Los Angeles.

All fresh and dressed to break hearts, Lana swept into Adonis. Moira checked the appointment book, but Lana's name wasn't there, and this wasn't her usual day. Moira opened her mouth to say something, but Lana had faster lips.

Lana said, "I need to see Brad."

Moira blinked. Ms. Lanai seemed awfully terse today. The senator must be on one of his famous rampages. Moira had read about Senator Lanai's flaming temper in the gossip columns. Moira said, "Dr. Kellogg's just finishing up surgery, Mrs. Lanai. Would you care to wait a few minutes?"

"No, I wouldn't."

Moira nodded warily and picked up the phone.

LANA HAD JUST EXITED, and Doc Kellogg was wiping the sweat bullets from his forehead when Richard entered his sanctum sanctorum. "How'd you get back here?" Kellogg asked, surprised. "Moira's usually worse than Immigration."

Richard smiled. "She got distracted by something, so I just slipped past her."

Kellogg watched him warily. "So what happened to you the other night?"

Richard sighed. "Emergency. Sorry I had to rush off like that. I came by today to pay you for the product. And learn how to inject it."

Kellogg consulted his desk calendar. "I've got a patient scheduled, but I'll be free for a few minutes after that." He gestured outside. "Why don't you just make yourself at home around here, and I'll find you when I'm finished."

Richard said, "Sure. That would be just fine."

Kellogg thought of something. He paused at the door, said, "You haven't tried to inject it yourself?"

Richard's face adopted a sheepish expression.

Doc Kellogg shook his head. "That's dangerous, man. Don't ever try that again. You're lucky you didn't kill yourself."

RICHARD WAS LOUNGING in the sauna when Mel Rose walked in, naked as a jaybird, and sat down across from him on a cedar bench.

Even naked, the famous character actor was immediately recognizable. Richard's voice of discretion ventured, "So you're on the program, too, eh, buddy?"

Like he didn't recognize Mel Rose.

Rose nodded sheepishly. "Goddamn quack's robbing me blind," he grumbled.

Richard nodded sympathetically. "You on the injections, too?"

Rose nodded curtly.

Richard said, "Say, aren't you—?"

"Calvin Jones," Rose lied.

"Ah, yes. Mr. Jones. For a minute there," said Richard, "I had you confused with that famous character actor."

"You mean Mel Rose?"

Richard nodded enthusiastically.

Rose shook his head. "He's a much younger man than me. Much younger."

Richard nodded. "Sure," he said. "That's it. Younger." And added, "Cool."

VENUS WAS snooping around Toleak Lodge when Bill Dravus came up behind her and said, "Looking for something?"

"Just sightseeing."

Dravus grinned smugly. "Sightseeing brings you up here to the second floor along the back hall where no one but the manager is ever allowed to go?"

She shrugged. "I took a wrong turn."

Dravus nodded. "Sure. Well, this is private quarters back here. So if you don't mind..."

Dravus guided her along the hall, down the stairs to the lobby. In the lobby, Clint Kellogg stood near the door to the restaurant. When he saw Venus, he said, "I was looking for you. How about lunch?"

They went into the restaurant, found a table with an ocean view, ordered lunch, and made small talk until the meal arrived. The food was hot and fresh and they ate in silence. Dravus stood over by the cash register, watching them. Venus wondered what Kellogg was thinking, and she wondered what Dravus was hiding up in his private quarters. He might just be a privacy fanatic, like herself, and resent uninvited incursions into his personal space. Or, he might be hiding something up there on the second floor along that back hallway. She couldn't decide. And she wondered why Clint Kellogg had sought her out this afternoon, when he would finally speak up, say what was on his mind. She didn't have to wait very long, because when dessert and coffee arrived, Clint leaned back in his chair and said, "It's time I leveled with you."

Venus nodded, sipped café au lait, and waited for Clint to elaborate.

Clint said, "I went over to your headquarters this morning and gave my revised statement. Agent Yamada took it. I'm sure that when you read it, you'll have some questions, so I thought I'd just save both of us a lot of time."

She said, "What changed in your statement?"

"I lied the first time." He looked straight at her, his eyes piercing and direct. "I wasn't at home watching the football game the afternoon Paris disappeared."

She nodded. Waited.

His fingers played with his coffee cup, with the creamer, with the sugar bowl. When he realized she wasn't going to prod him, he said, "The truth is, I was up on the preserve. Harvesting a crop of mushrooms. I know that's illegal. I'm aware that I was breaking the law. But that's where I was. And I was alone, so there's no one to corroborate my story. And Daniel Dean was at my place. Marilyn finally told me that Dean came to visit her while I was out."

He watched her, tried reading her reaction, but her facial expression revealed nothing. Coolly, she said, "Go on."

"I guess you've heard tales about the existence of an old Quinault sweat lodge?"

She nodded.

Clint said, "I've been searching for that place for years. Back when I was up here for my college field studies, I heard the stories, and I spent one whole summer trying to locate that lodge. Never did. But because I was here, that summer changed my life."

She held up a hand. "Let me guess," she said. "You fell in love with Theresa Creed, now Theresa Nighteagle."

Clint sighed. "Right. We were both young. She was only sixteen. I was nineteen. We had a very intense relationship. Theresa got pregnant. It wasn't so much to protect her reputation, but because my family was so damned judgmental, and racially prejudiced that we decided to keep the pregnancy a secret. I would have been disowned by my family. So when Theresa started showing, we took off to Seattle. Theresa's mother, Frances Creed? She made up a story to tell the neighbors, saying Theresa had gone away to a special school in Seattle, to study Native American craftmaking. I took that semester off school and Theresa and I got a little apartment in Seattle. But the baby died. It was stillborn. Theresa and I split up right after that.''

''Why'd you split up?''

Clint grimaced. ''Brad. My bigoted brother. He's a flaming racist. He put enormous pressure on me to end the relationship with Theresa. Basically, Brad was putting me through school, paying my tuition and expenses. He threatened to cut off his support if I didn't break up with Theresa. I was stupid enough to listen to him. I've regretted it ever since.''

Venus said, ''Is that why you came back up here?''

Clint shrugged. ''Partly. I guess I hoped that somehow Theresa and I would get back together. But a lot of years passed between our breakup and when I returned to live up here. Both our lives had changed. Theresa had married Winn Nighteagle. I had finished school, had written a best-seller, and launched my career as a writer. Our worlds were a universe apart. Even though we live within thirty miles of each other, Theresa and I are culturally worlds apart.''

''Not to mention economically.''

Clint nodded. ''I've offered to help her financially. Before Winn hit that jackpot, when they were really struggling to get by, I offered Theresa money, but she refused. We've remained close friends, but Theresa has always made it clear that her loyalty is to Winn.''

''What about her feelings?''

Clint said, ''She tells me she's in love with Winn. Even with all this heartache he's put her through, she still loves him. I'll be honest with you. I begged her to come back to me. She refused. I can offer her the world, all the security and love she'd ever hoped for, but she refused. She loves Winn, and I guess she always will.''

Venus said, ''Why are you telling me this?''

Clint shrugged. ''I think because we've all become desperate about Paris, and we're all looking for any small thing that might lead to answers. I want you to have all the facts at your disposal. I'm hoping that by telling you about my relationship with Theresa, you'll somehow fit this piece of the puzzle into the larger picture, and maybe it will alter the picture enough to help. I don't know. I should have been more forthright in the first place.''

She said, "While you're in this forthright mood, what can you tell me about your brother's business?"

Clint stared out the window. She sipped café au lait, waited for him to speak. The dining room had emptied out; theirs was the only table left occupied. At the cash register, Dravus was tallying up the lunch tabs. Finally, Clint pushed back his chair, picked up the check, stood, and said, "Brad took care of me, gave me love and support. I owe him everything. That's all I care to say about my brother."

She watched him pay the bill and hand the waiter a generous tip. When he had left the restaurant, Dravus turned to her and called across the dining room, "Guess that leaves the two of us, eh?" and smirked.

She got up to leave. Dravus came over, stared out the window. "You know what I think?" he said.

"What do you think?"

"I think that little Becca Brightman is behind all these rumors about the Unknown."

TWENTY-SEVEN

HIT ME

WINN PUSHED OPEN the door of Grays Harbor National Bank and stepped into the winter sunshine. It blinded him at first, so he paused a minute on the sidewalk, blinking. He didn't see Carolee Brightman come up alongside him and when she touched his arm, Winn jumped to the moon.

"Hey, Winn." Carolee had a distinctive voice, and he recognized her grip on his arm. He jerked it away.

"Jeez, you scared me, Carolee."

Now Winn could see, and he noticed Carolee wasn't alone. A dude Winn recognized but couldn't place stood beside Carolee. Winn couldn't tell for sure if he was Indian or white.

Carolee said, "This is Mr. Dravus, Winn. My new mentor."

Winn shook Dravus's clammy hand. It felt like slime. He grunted. Dravus grunted back. Carolee patted Dravus's arm.

"Mr. Dravus reads goat entrails, Winn. Isn't that just cool? Mr. Dravus is going to teach me the process. He learned how to read goat guts up at Leavenworth when he was serving time for spousal abuse. But he's a widower now."

Winn grunted again. Carolee talked out of school. Winn didn't like that in a person. People shouldn't violate other people's privacy. Before she could say anything else, Winn broke away and hurried around the corner to the bank's parking lot. His truck was parked there. In the cabin, Theresa sat in the passenger seat, holding Milan on her lap. Milan's fever had flared up again and she was fussing and had the hiccups.

Winn slid into the driver's seat. Theresa didn't acknowledge his presence, except to turn her face away from him. She hoisted the bawling Milan back into her safety seat, buckled her up. Winn started the ignition, turned on the heater, backed up, swung around, and headed out of the lot. They drove through town in silence, except for the tinny sounds of country-fm leaking from the bad radio in Winn's truck. People stopped to stare as they drove past in the truck. Millionaires don't drive beat-up Chevy Workmans. That's what everyone said about Winn behind his back. That he was a no-good drunk who won money when he should have been out looking for the beast that killed his son. Or, that he was a baby-killer. Winn knew they were gossiping. They were saying that in the one short month since his son disappeared, Winn Nighteagle had changed—that since he'd won all that money, he'd started drinking and gambling and carousing again. But he hadn't changed at all. He was the same as before. When he looked in the mirror, he saw the same Winn Nighteagle. They were wrong about him, the gossips.

At Aberdeen, Winn turned into the shopping-mall parking lot, found a place near the Fred Meyer's store, parked. Theresa unbuckled Milan and Winn held the door open as she stepped down with the baby in her arms. Theresa and Winn walked side by side into the store. People pretended not to stare, but they did, furtively.

It's those Nighteagles.

In the Menswear department, Theresa asked a clerk to fit Winn into a black suit, white shirt, and black bolo tie. Black oxfords, or wing tips, whichever matched the suit. The clerk found a cheap polyester/wool blend suit that fit Winn, and a pure cotton white dress shirt. Theresa insisted it be pure cotton. The clerk found a pair of size-thirteen oxfords that fit Winn's feet. Winn paid cash for everything. In Ladies' Dresses, a clerk found Theresa a black polyester skirt and jacket. Theresa asked if the clerk had a black woolen dress, but he couldn't find a pure black dress, so Theresa settled for the polyester suit with a tailored white blouse. Theresa bought a pair of stockings and some low-heeled black pumps. Winn paid for it all in cash. In the Infants' department, Theresa picked out a little white woolen frock with smocking across the chest. Held it up to Milan, who kicked and fussed. Winn paid cash for the frock, for a pair of white socks with lace trim, and for white baby shoes.

On the way home, Theresa spoke to Winn for the first time all day. It was when he turned the truck onto Highway 101, and pointed it north toward Cedar Grove Trailer Park. Theresa said, "I'll go to this memorial service. I'll grieve along with everyone. I'll pretend, just so's not to embarrass you. But he's not dead, Winn. He's somewhere in those woods."

Winn said, "How many times do I have to tell you? This is not a memorial service. It is a prayer service. Can't you get that straight in your head?"

Father Brendan's service was brief and tactful. Frances took charge of things, and a few of the trailer-park neighbors came to pray along with the family. The Polks came, and the Brightmans, including Becca. Becca cried something awful. Standing beside his daughter, Bob Brightman removed his glasses, wiped something from his eyes. Maybe tears. Carolee kept her dry eyes focused on Theresa, a compassionate expression softening her hard features. Theresa knew the compassion play was phony, put on so that she'd think Carolee really had a heart. She did. A black stone.

Frances showed no expression at all. She had arranged the prayer service because she wanted closure, but Frances didn't say that out loud. Father Brendan's appropriate ceremony brought closure. After they prayed for Paris, Father Brendan baptized Milan, giving her "Antonia" for her saint's name. After Saint Anthony, the patron saint of lost articles.

Dear Saint Anthony, please come round
Paris is lost and cannot be found.

THAT NIGHT, Winn came home after a quick rendezvous with Carolee and was fitting his key into the lock when he heard the sound. A baby's cry? Was that possible? A small, insistent cry. Weak. Winn stood still, listened. Nothing. Must have been his active imagination. He forgot about it right away when he saw Theresa sitting on the couch with Father Brendan. They'd been waiting for him. Theresa in her house robe and big woolen socks. Father Brendan in a navy parka with fox-fur collar. Winn stared at them.

Father Brendan said, "Sit down, Winn. Theresa has something to tell you."

Winn sat down, folded his hands between his spread legs. Theresa looked straight at him but Winn was too ashamed to meet her glance. He watched his big hands. Theresa said, "Milan is sick, Winn. She's at the clinic. Mom is staying with her."

Winn dropped his head into his hands. "Oh, God. Oh, good Jesus."

Father Brendan said, "She might be contagious. Dr. Fish has placed her in isolation. They think it's meningitis."

Winn began weeping. From the couch, Theresa watched her husband and secretly thought he deserved to be miserable. If he wanted sympathy right now, he could go back to Carolee. Theresa thought this, but she didn't say it out loud. But Winn didn't want sympathy. He wanted a drink.

When Winn came crawling back at 6:00 a.m., he found Theresa asleep in bed, the amethyst rosary glistening on her pillow. The rosary had twisted in the night, winding its beaded way around Theresa's loose cascading hair. Winn stared at the amethyst beads, the silver cross that lately possessed his wife. He started to reach out, to touch Theresa's hair, but drew back when a shaft of dawn light from the window connected with the beads and nearly blinded him. He could almost hear God's voice. "Don't touch her, Winn. She's mine."

Winn listened to Theresa's soft breathing. She's not dead, for crying out loud. She's not Yours yet, goddamnit.

The rosary beads winked and dazzled. A lock of Theresa's glorious hair had wrapped itself around the cross and Winn couldn't see where it started or where it ended, it was so damn tangled. She'd have to cut it off with scissors. Or, Winn might undo the mess. Might even do it without waking her. His fingers crossed the threshold, breaching the radiant gap where amethyst glass refracted points of dawn light. Gently, he touched the tangled lock, the cross. He worked slowly, his nimble fingers shaking slightly from the alcohol hangover. Theresa sighed and Winn pulled his hands away from her hair. She mumbled, "Winn, honey, look over there in the flour bin."

Winn wasn't sure he heard her right. He whispered, "What for, Tee?" She didn't answer, but now Winn was bothered. He got up and walked softly across the trailer to the kitchen. What flour bin? There's no damn flour bin in this trailer. Then he remembered the special place Tee had once called her flour bin. It was a deep drawer beside the fridge. Winn went over and opened the drawer. It was empty. Just a dark bare hole. From the bedroom came Theresa's screams. Winn ran back. She was sitting straight up in bed, screaming at the top of her lungs. He shouted, "Wake up. Wake up, you're dreaming."

Theresa woke up and stopped screaming. By then, the whole trailer park had been roused by her nightmare.

THE FOLLOWING AFTERNOON, Winn wanted to take a nap, but sleep wouldn't come. He lay across the bed, thinking of the debauchery of his life, how in a few short weeks, he'd sunk to the depths of depravity. Carousing in bars. Gambling his fortune away. Pretty soon, he'd be broke, unless he quit playing cards up at the casino. Sleeping with his next-door-neighbor's wife. What else could he do to prove he was a no-good bastard? Oh, here's an idea. He could leave Milan outside in the woods to get eaten by bears. Hell, she'll die anyway, from the meningitis. Winn wanted to die, too—or, he guessed, instead of—Milan. Just get it over with. The gossips were right about Winn—he had turned into a no-good louse.

Outside the bedroom window, a breeze caught Theresa's laundry hanging on the line. He saw his favorite shirt, inflated, performing a macabre dance. Behind the laundry, the forest loomed dark and haunting. The forest that had swallowed up his son, the heart of his heart, the light of his life. The forest he had once loved and respected. How could he have respected a place where evil spirits dwelt?

Winn thought he saw something move through the woods. He blinked. It came out of the forest, came straight toward the trailer, toward the window, toward Winn. He watched it come, and even as he realized what it was, his heart leaped. It came to the window glass, stood very still, staring in at Winn.

"Come out here, Winn," said Elk.

Winn sat up. Should he go out there? Elk's gaze mesmerized him, and soon he stood and walked out of the trailer. Elk led him into the forest, Winn following at a respectful distance. When they had gone as far as Elk Pond, Elk stopped.

"Take a drink of that water, Winn," commanded Elk.

Winn bent down over Elk Pond, cupped his hand, brought pond water to his mouth and drank. Just then, Winn saw his own reflection in the pond's surface.

Elk said, "Look deeper, Winn. Look beyond your own reflection."

Winn looked deeper into the pond and saw the souls of his dead ancestors, the souls of all the great chiefs of the Hoh and Quillayute, of the Quinault and Queets and Muckleshoots, all the souls of the bravest warriors who lived from all eternity in this territory. Winn saw the souls and he began to cry.

"Don't show him to me," he pleaded of Elk. "Don't show me my son's spirit."

Elk said, "Paris Nighteagle's spirit isn't down there, Winn. These are the spirits of all who had Elk's guardian spirit in them. Your son has not yet received his guardian spirit."

Winn turned to Elk. "But is my son dead or alive?"

Elk said, "Paris Nighteagle is not my concern. I am your guardian spirit, Winn. You are my concern. I have come to offer you another chance at a happy life."

"How can I be happy without my son?" cried Winn.

"Give me your daughter, Milan Nighteagle. Then I will return your son and you can live a happy life once again."

Winn said, "I'll never give up my baby girl."

Elk said, "It's one or the other, Winn. You choose."

Winn stared into the pond. This time, all he saw was his own reflection. Then he saw Milan's reflection beside his own, and on his other side, he saw Paris reflected in the pond. Elk said, "Choose, Winn."

Winn sprang up and dove into the pond. With crashing strokes, he swam across the pond yelling, "Never. I'll never give up my babies."

When he reached the other side, Elk was waiting for him.

"Why are you following me?" cried Winn.

Elk said, "I am your guardian spirit. Now I see that you are more interested in your children than in your own happiness. There might still be hope for you, Winn Nighteagle. Go to the sweat lodge."

"There isn't any sweat lodge anymore. The Hoh sweat lodge burned down last winter."

Elk said, "Not that sweat lodge. Go to the ancient Quinault warriors' sweat lodge, where in ages past, your ancestors received their guardian spirits."

"But where is that sweat lodge?" cried Winn.

"Follow me." Elk turned and sprang into the forest. Winn hesitated at first, then followed, feeling scared as hell but believing.

THE CLINIC'S waiting room overflowed with patients. Flu season. A harried nurse held forth at reception. "Dr. Fish is swamped," she said. "Why don't you take a seat like everyone else?"

Venus sat between an elderly man with dermatitis and a young mother holding a screaming child. She counted ten patients ahead of her. Fifteen minutes later, with seven patients ahead of her, she went back over to the desk. "Can I leave a message for Dr. Fish?"

The nurse scowled. "Only if you write it down for me. I don't have time."

The nurse slid a prescription pad in front of her. Venus wrote. "Where did you say you did your residency?" She handed the note to the nurse who handed it off to another nurse who went off somewhere. A minute later, the second nurse returned and said, "If you can see blood without fainting, he says you can go back."

Fish was stitching up a hand wound on a kid who'd lost a knife fight. She waited until he'd finished the fine whip stitch and was cleaning up at the sink before she said, "Children's Orthopedic?"

"Right." Fish, over his shoulder.

"Pediatrics?"

Fish came over, stood directly in front of her, so close she could step on his toes if she really wanted to hurt him. She didn't. Fish said, "Yeah. Pediatrics."

She thought this over for about ten seconds, then said, "The certificate on your wall in your office says you did a surgery residency."

"Pediatric surgery. You didn't read it carefully."

"Oh." She backed off about three feet and said, "Mrs. Nighteagle tells me Paris's twin sister has meningitis."

"She's been a very sick little girl. She's going to be fine, though."

She stood by the door, leaning against the threshold. Fish came over, peered past her into the corridor. The usual charity-clinic chaos and cacophony ruled the halls. From his demeanor, she knew he was overworked, exhausted, wishing the suffering patients would go away, come back tomorrow, give him just a few hours rest. Stop assuming he was God, take pity on his feet of clay. Physicians need sleep, too, just like every other creature. Without proper rest, a physician might make a horrible, irreversible error in judgment. Or, the scalpel might slip. In the precise world of medicine, there's no room for recklessness. She said, "Why don't you knock off, go home and catch some z's? The nurses can handle the reception room crowd."

Fish rubbed his eyes. "So, like, you'd have me just desert these suffering individuals? Maybe because they're all poor folk, because they don't really count in the great big picture? So I should just tell them to take their stupid cancer and their stupid broken bones and flake off, and then walk out on them, just like that?"

"I was merely articulating what I read in your body language."

"Well, who asked you to read it anyway?" Fish sighed, sat down wearily on a stool, sank his face into the palms of his hands. She stood in the doorway, silent, allowing him a few seconds of peace. After a while, when she began to think he might have dozed off, he suddenly looked up from his hands and said, "Maybe I'm just paranoid, but I have this terrible sense of impending doom."

She noticed his fingers trembled. She said, "When was the last time you ate something?"

"God, I can't remember. I think it was last evening. Yes, it was dinner. I had a salad over at Rick's, then came back here and spent the night tending to the Nighteagle girl. Her fever finally broke about three o'clock this morning." He sighed. "We need another doc up here. But, hey, fat chance."

In the corridor, a nurse crashed through the chaos, a white spurt of energy shooting from misery's black hole. "Dr. Fish," she called out. "Dr. Fish, Room Six is buzzing. Code Blue."

Fish jumped to his feet. "That's the isolation room. I have to go."

They were running along the corridor toward Room Six when she said, "Maybe it's depression."

"I doubt it. Code Blue means a life-threatening situation."

"I didn't mean Room Six. I was referring to you. Depression can be life-threatening."

He paused, mouth open as if to reply, but instead he shook his head and went into Room Six, shutting the door behind him.

IN A SMALL ROOM off the corridor, Venus found Frances Creed seated in a straight-back chair beside Milan's hospital bed. Milan was sleeping soundly and Frances was reading a TV Guide. Venus said, "How's she doing?"

When Frances looked up, her brilliant eyes reflected sixty-eight years of hardscrabble misery. She glanced over at Milan and said, "She misses Paris. That's what's the matter with her. That's what makes her sick. Her heart is broken. She misses her twin."

The girl stirred, cried out. Frances reached over, placed a hand across Milan's chest and patted gently. Milan relaxed, went back to sleep. Venus was almost out the door when Frances Creed declared, "I won't leave this baby's side."

"That's good, Mrs. Creed."

Frances Creed said, "You go see Simon."

"Simon?" asked Venus.

TWENTY-EIGHT

THUNDERCLOUD

SIMON THUNDERCLOUD lived on the Hoh reservation, two cabins west of his daughter, Frances Creed. The cabin was built of wood shingles, its roof tarpapered. A single galvanized-steel chimney set to one side of the house coughed smoke into the pale morning sky. When Venus pulled into his gravel drive, old Simon came outside, stood on his stoop. Simon had on a bulky sweater and canvas pants. He wore black horn-rimmed glasses, like Buddy Holly. He was older than Buddy Holly, his hair white as the head of a bald eagle. Simon Thundercloud said, "Where's Frances?"

"At the hospital."

"What about the girl?"

Venus walked up the drive toward him. "The girl's much better. The doctor says maybe she can go home tomorrow or the next day."

Old Simon nodded, motioned her up onto the porch. "You stay right here."

She waited while he went inside. The air felt crisp and fresh. In the woods surrounding the cabin, scattered patches of snow lingered after the storm. She saw a blue jay flit across the forest floor, up into the branches of an old hemlock. Simon came back outside. "This is for you," he said, handing her a folded piece of paper. "Maybe you can use it."

It was a crude map, hand-drawn with sepia ink on paper so worn and wrinkled that the markings were nearly illegible. She strained her eyes to make sense of it. A pond. Forest. A creek. Another creek with a bridge. A cabin. She looked up at old Simon.

Simon said, "You go there."

"Where is this?"

Simon pointed toward the southeast. "Over on Bogachiel, on the preserve. That map was made by my father, Ray Thundercloud, just before he passed away."

"What's there?" She indicated the cabin.

Simon said, "My father always said that's where the first sweat lodge was."

"Have you ever been there?" She felt her pulse quicken.

Simon shook his head. "Not since my naming day. Too long ago. I can't find it now."

She studied the old man's eyes, which were failing with age, yet seemed so full of wisdom and experience. "Why should I go there, Mr. Thundercloud?"

"May be the only place left," he said. "Maybe that's where you'll find the boy."

He was right, of course. Every possible hiding place had to be ferreted out, searched. She said, "How are you at walking, Mr. Thundercloud?"

He shook his head again. "No good. You go there. Find that old sweat lodge. Or what's left of it. Start from Elk Pond." He turned and went indoors and shut the door quietly behind him. Driving off the reservation, she watched the sky clear; watched sunshine pour into the forest and spill across the highway. On the hairpin curve, she looked up and saw the Hoh cemetery. It wouldn't be too long before Simon Thundercloud moved up there.

ELK POND LAY smooth as glass across the densely wooded glade, its black surface dimpling at the edges where gnats and mosquitoes plagued the vacant lily pads. No toad came out in this crisp air. At noon, the autumn sunlight beat horizontally across the glade: Flat, angular light ricocheting off cedar and hemlock trunks illuminated the forest floor the way footlights play the stage. The deep pond couldn't speak but it sent up shivering ghosts that told stories of eons past, and standing on its banks, she absorbed the mysterious message. So much had happened on these shores since the first people discovered the freshwater pond made of glacial melt. If she had a boat—a canoe—she'd paddle across to the opposite shore. As it was, she would have to travel afoot, through the spruce groves, in the scattering afternoon light. She'd gone halfway around the pond's northern edge when her telephone rang.

Anitta Valkoinen was calling from Helsinki, from her husband's physician's office. "I don't know if this is relevant," she said. "I have just spoken with Johann's physician. He tells me that over two years ago, Johann was diagnosed as HIV-positive. The doctor says Johann didn't want me to know about his illness. I had noticed some changes in Johann, but attributed them to stress. The physician says Johann was ordering some medicine over the Internet, something to treat the wasting symptoms that afflict AIDS victims.''

"But he didn't have AIDS?"

"According to the doctor, no, but being HIV-positive, Johann was hoping to prevent any breakdown of his system. This medicine, or whatever it was he ordered over the Internet, was supposed to prevent the wasting of muscles and tissue. Those needle marks you mentioned that were found on his hips? Those were apparently from injecting the medication he ordered on the Internet. The physician said Johann injected it into himself once a week. And the doctor said the medication really did help prevent wasting, and he said it made Johann feel stronger, gave him more energy.''

"Anitta, where did Johann get the medicine?"

"I think it came from Denmark. I think that's what Johann's doctor said.''

"Did he mention a return address?"

"No. And I never saw the packages. I can check, if you want. I'll ask the doctor. If he doesn't know, I'll go straight home, and see if I can find the address in Johann's papers.''

"Anitta, have you thought of any other reason your husband might have wanted to visit the Olympic Peninsula? Maybe to look up a friend? Any reason at all?''

She thought about it and finally said, "No. I know of no reason he would visit that area, except, of course, to hike.''

"He was registered at a local lodge. The records show he stayed Tuesday night in a place called Toleak Lodge. According to our coroner's timetable, it was Wednesday night that he was murdered.''

Anitta said, "I knew nothing about that. It's very strange. He would tell me if he went to visit a friend.''

"I'm sorry, Anitta. I'm sure this is very painful.''

"Yes. Yes, it is. I'll phone you back in about an hour.''

When Venus reached the eastern shore of Elk Pond, she took out Simon Thundercloud's father's map. If the body of water on the map truly was Elk Pond, the mule trail on the map must begin at the midpoint of the eastern shore. She walked to that point, surveyed the ground, the woods. At first, nothing seemed to indicate a trail had ever been blazed through this thickly wooded area. She inspected the ground for signs of wildlife, hunters, or poachers. Once, when inspecting some bear tracks on Bogachiel, she had found a stone arrow.

She had a feeling this wasn't one of those lucky days when small, exotic treasures pop right out at you, just begging to be plucked up and possessed. Artifacts found on federal land must be turned over to the government for cataloging. Possession is illegal. She'd forked over the beautiful stone arrow, but she still possessed the thrilling memory of its discovery.

No signs of an old trail. She walked further south along the pond's banks, where an ancient cedar stood regally apart from the spruce, its soft, green fronds overhanging the pond. She reached up, felt its thick, red bark, and rubbed gently until a small piece of the bark fell away, exposing another, deeper layer. She repeated this twice more, cutting down to the trunk with her penknife, before finding what she sought: a faint trailblazer's sign chipped into the cedar bone.

She turned, faced the east and the woods that led into the rain forest. She walked in a straight line from the tree to the woods, pausing at each old-growth tree to check for trailblazer's signs. Out of ten old-growth trees leading into the rain forest, she found four more blazes. The trail seemed to match the one drawn on Ray Thundercloud's map. When she reached the entrance to the rain forest, where the moss-draped tree canopy shut out all but a few low sunbeams, she stopped, listened.

She heard a stream trickling, murmuring, wending down from Mount Hoh, down through the rain forest, on its way to the Pacific Ocean. A branch of the Little Hoh River. Once a sacred salmon run, the branch was now in the possession of the Interior Department, which was trying to rescue its inhabitants from the overharvesting that had almost decimated the chum population.

She heard the trill of songbirds, a cacophony of birdsong coming from inside the tree canopy. She could pick them out by their songs. "Tuck...three bears!"—the olive-sided flycatcher, a little behind the migratory timetable. The gray jay, the Clark's nutcracker. Their robust warbles filled the cool afternoon air.

When she had listened to every sound, she moved forward, entering the rain forest, consulting the map, occasionally looking over her shoulder to be sure Elk Pond stayed in her sights. Later on, with a search party, she could return and hike the rest of the way, up into the rain forest, to the next river or creek or brook shown on the map. Right now, all she wanted was to confirm that this was the old mule trail drawn by Ray Thundercloud's hand so many years ago.

When she tripped and fell, she had been checking over her shoulder for the view of the pond. She fell forward, across the object that had tripped her. She lay across the solid thing and in the fading light, she thought at first she had stumbled over a rotting cedar log. But as she struggled to her feet, she touched the thing with one hand, felt fur against skin, and knew at once it was no cedar log, but a body, cold, stiff, dead. A rotting elk carcass. A young buck—its hooves sawed off, the stumpy wounds matted with flies and maggots. Dizzy, she leaned up against a tree and nearly jumped out of her skin when her phone rang.

"This is Anitta Valkoinen. I have the name and address of the company Johann ordered his medicine from. It's a post office box in Copenhagen. The company's name is Elixir of Youth."

SHORTLY BEFORE MIDNIGHT, Claudia finished the elk autopsy. When the phone rang, Venus was sitting by the fire, nursing the memory of the maggots crawling over the dead buck, and a Rémy. Song sat on the couch, pulling on a Pyramid draft. After Venus hung up the phone, Song said, "When's hubby coming home?"

"Shut up."

"Seriously. You need Richard at a time like this."

She looked at Song. She couldn't tell if he was mocking or sincere. She said, "He can't leave L.A. until Kellogg makes his move. He has to keep an eye on Kellogg."

"What did Claudia say?"

"He'd been dead only a few hours. Poacher used a hacksaw."

Song said, "Something's afoot, that's for sure."

"You have a sick mind, Louie."

Song nodded thoughtfully. Maybe he agreed with her. The fire spit and crackled. She tossed another log in. Blue flames rose to brilliant heights and firecrackers sparkled, sputtered, fell.

She said, "What did you find up there?"

"Darkness."

She sighed.

"Sorry. Just trying jocularity on for size."

She said, "Lately, it doesn't fit you."

Song went into the kitchen, brought back another beer, and the bottle of Rémy. He poured more cognac into her glass. He sat down on the couch, pulled on the fresh Pyramid. "We recovered the elk carcass, and by then, it was pitch-dark. I had the hounds out for a couple hours. We didn't find anything. Just the dead buck."

She said, "All right. What's your hit on this?"

"You know exactly what I think."

She said, "Tell me."

He said, "The elk poaching is probably just a bunch of local yokels having sadistic fun. That's my bet. The missing kid? I say the Gecko got him. Has to be. He's a psychopath, and he's loose out there on the preserve. He got the tourist, too."

"We don't know for certain—"

Song cut her off. "He's a psycho, probably gets his kicks watching little kids in pain. He was seen entering the preserve. We've been watching the perimeter, and he hasn't come out. What more proof do you need?"

She pulled the blanket closer around her shoulders, but couldn't manage to get warm. She said, "I was going to say that we don't know for certain that Hintikka was murdered on the preserve."

"He was attacked by an elk. Stomped to death." Said emphatically. Song added, "Gecko-man trained the elk to attack these victims. I know this for a fact."

Half an hour later, they stood on the tideline and watched as, in a still wind and fine mist, the chopper set down on Toleak Beach. Venus and Song climbed up into passenger seats. At the controls, Sweetwater throttled back up into the star-studded sky, leveled off, and aimed the chopper southward.

An hour later, in Seattle, a security guard at the Bumbershoot let Venus into the offices. She went to her small cubicle, the place she rarely visited but called her office, sat down, placed a phone call. When he answered, she said, "I really need you. I know you can't come home now. But I just wanted to hear your voice."

He said, "I'm coming right now."

"No," she protested, "don't do that. I'm okay. You need to stay there, keep an eye on the medicine man."

"He's in my sights as we speak."

"Where are you, Richard?"

"At LAX. Kellogg's boarding a flight to Seattle. Funny thing. We'll be flying first class together. I'll pretend to leave him at SEA-TAC, but I'll trail him up to Grays Harbor, or wherever he goes, unless you think I should come for you first...."

"No, I'm fine, really."

Four hours later, Olson found her in his office, supine on the couch, a vision of loveliness or a pain in the keister, depending on your point of view.

TWENTY-NINE

RAY BANS

"ELIXIR OF YOUTH," began Claudia, "contains a liquefied keratin derived from elk hooves. Besides the elk keratin, the product contains extracts of *Oplopanax horridum*, commonly known as devil's club, *Prunella vulgaris*, commonly known as self-heal, *Valeriana sitchensis*, or Sitka valerian, peppermint oil, minute traces of *Castilleja livisecta*, the endangered Golden Paintbrush, and last but not least, natural human growth hormone."

"The genuine article?" Olson, fascinated, not quite convinced.

"It's the real thing, all right," said Claudia. "This material was definitely removed from human pituitary glands."

Al Yamada said, "From Johann Hintikka?"

"This material wasn't taken from Hintikka. It doesn't match his DNA. We'd be able to match the DNA, but right now, we don't have anything to match with."

Crowded into Olson's office were nine stymied team players and one cocksure individual with sexy, smoky eyes hiding behind Ray Ban wraps. From the westward-facing windows, pale silver daylight streamed into the room, casting shadows across their figures so that some faces were harder to read than others. Venus could see Olson's silhouette, backlit, and enough of his profile to know he sipped Evian water; she heard the drum of his fingers against the plastic bottle. Claudia sat on the couch beside Wexler. Marla Mason and Dottie stood near the door. Al Yamada sat near them on Olson's antique Bentwood. Song, Sweetwater, Sparks, and Venus stood against a wall, watching Claudia's articulate lips move, hearing her soft consonants. She'd flown in from Ashland this morning, bringing along a little show-and-tell platinum Halliburton suitcase. The Halliburton sat on the coffee table in front of Claudia and Wexler. Now she leaned over, unlatched it, opened it wide.

"These are medical instruments," she explained." She held up a long, slender tube with a tiny light and tweezerlike pincers at one end. "This is a surgical instrument for a procedure called endoscopy. The surgeon makes a small opening in the patient's upper gums, runs this up through the patient's nasal passage, through the sinus, back to the base of the brain. The pituitary gland is attached to the base of the brain. It's grape-sized, shaped a little like a tulip bulb. With these snippers," she indicated the pincers, "the surgeon snips off the gland, or maybe just a portion of the gland, depending on the reason for the procedure." She held up another small device. "This is a sort of basket that retrieves the gland once it's been severed from the brain stem. It's a delicate procedure, but with a little training, any surgically adept physician could master it."

Sparks said, "Why would anyone besides a sadist want to remove a pituitary gland?"

"Tumor. The pituitary gland might be tumescent, or there might be a tumor nearby. This is one way of removing tumors of the head without going through the skull. It's only used in certain cases, depending on a number of factors, including the location of the tumor. In this case, in the case of Johann Hintikka, the surgeon has removed not a tumor, but the entire pituitary gland."

Al Yamada said, "But why was his pituitary gland removed?"

"You better let Venus answer that. She's the theorist."

Venus said, "To extract human growth hormone. From the data that Richard's gathered, we've learned that the latest Fountain of Youth fad is human-growth-hormone therapy. A number of clinics throughout the world, particularly in major cities like Los Angeles, are treating people who want to extend their life spans with a synthetic form of human growth hormone, or recombinant human growth hormone, known by the simple abbreviated term *rHGH*. rHGH actually reverses some aspects of aging, and apparently also helps prevent the terrible wasting of muscle mass that often occurs in AIDS victims. It's a pricey product, selling for an average of five to seven hundred dollars per injection, with at least one injection per week required. Add that up over a lifetime, and you're spending a small fortune. It's a lucrative industry. It's not always illegal, but many of the anti-aging gurus who are hawking hormone therapies on the Internet are charlatans whose rHGH formulas haven't been approved by the Food and Drug Administration. Most of these so-called age-reversal formulas are pure snake oil, but the sources are almost impossible to track down. The company we're concerned with here sells only on the Internet, calling itself Elixir of Youth. As Claudia has pointed out, they're using the genuine article."

Marla Mason blurted out, "Venus, are you trying to tell us that this Finnish man's pituitary gland was removed and then concocted into some kind of anti-aging medicine?"

"Actually, as Claudia said, we know for certain the pituitary material in the vials Richard took from Adonis didn't match the victim's DNA, although I suspect that someone did remove his pituitary hoping to harvest HGH."

Claudia added, "Though the material removed from Mr. Hintikka would have been diseased."

Olson said, "So what happens to the patient after his pituitary gland is extracted?"

Claudia said, "It depends. He might live for a while, especially if a certain portion of the pituitary was allowed to remain intact. But if the entire pituitary is extracted, as was the case with our cadaver, the individual's body goes haywire, its hormonal and metabolic systems crash, and unless endocrine replacement therapy was begun immediately, the individual would eventually die. Not overnight necessarily, but not long after the excision. Our victim was lucky. He died while unconscious, from anesthesia poisoning."

When he leaned back and folded his arms across his chest, Olson's chair usually creaked. Now he leaned back, but no creak. He'd lost weight, and Venus noticed he no longer had a beer belly to rest his arms on. He looked healthy, she thought to herself; his personal training was finally paying off. Wexler, on the other hand, looked sallow and bleary-eyed this morning, no doubt a result of late-night cavorting with a certain vivacious party animal known to some as La Belladonna, to others simply as Mother. No one could match Bella's energy level and verve.

Song, Sweetwater, and Claudia all oozed physical fitness, and their usual self-confidence. So here were America's fit and not-so-fit generations, come together to track down the Fountain of Youth. Maybe Ponce de Len could find a cure for her drug-resistant malaria, and a few other things, for instance, Song's recently exhibited overconfidence.

Olson said, "Wouldn't you need an operating room to perform this surgery?"

"At least a facsimile," agreed Claudia. "Just a basic facility, but most important, you'd need the proper equipment. This surgery isn't performed on an operating table, though. The patient is usually placed in a special chair used by ear, nose, and throat specialists. The chair's head tilts way back so the surgeon can see up the patient's nasal passage, through the sinus. In most cases nowadays, the endoscopic instruments are connected to a computer monitor and there's a tiny camera device that feeds down the nasal passage. The surgeon guides the instruments by watching what he or she is doing on the monitor. But you don't absolutely need the monitor, especially if you've performed this procedure many times.''

Venus read her Swatch. Time had worked against them so far. They couldn't afford to squander another minute. She said, "This is where we stand. The Nighteagle baby has now been missing for thirty-two days. No signs of him, or his abductor, except for the notorious hoofprints thus far ascribed to a bull elk. Most of Bogachiel preserve has been scoured, although there are some areas of the preserve, sections of the rain forest, for example, that are nearly impossible to reach on foot. Those sections have all been surveyed from the air using heat sensors. So far, nothing. The APBs, the national and international missing-child postings—nothing has produced a single lead.

"Meanwhile, the boy's parents have been closely watched. In fact, I've taken that duty upon myself." She glanced at Wexler, hoped he picked up the sarcasm in her voice. A waste of time watching the Nighteagles. She continued, "One week following the baby's disappearance, a remnant of human tissue was found on the preserve. Lab tests proved it was a piece of a human heart, probably from an infant, but DNA tests showed that the tissue did not belong to Paris Nighteagle, the missing child. And no, that DNA didn't match what we took from the Elixir vials.''

Claudia's quiet voice said, "I can speak about the human tissue. I just finally got the lab report on that specimen. The analyses indicate the tissue came from an embalmed body.''

"Oh, great," groaned Sweetwater. "Now we'll have grave-robbing-alien rumors.''

Wexler rubbed his eyes, making them redder. "Let's stop here," he said, "and take a ten-minute coffee break. We're going to be in here all morning.''

Song placed a well-built arm around Venus's shoulders. "How are you feeling, best buddy?''

She said, "Faboo. Why?''

Song felt her forehead. "You look a little pale. Can I buy you a cup of tea?"

"Thanks, no. I need to call Richard."

Song feigned surprise. "Need to? *Need to?* Need to, or want to?"

She looked up and saw her own face reflected in Song's Ray Bans. She said, "Want to. I want to call Richard."

She rode the Bumbershoot's elevator down thirty-seven floors. Sardines from thirty-eight to the mezzanine level. At the mezzanine, they swam out, and she drifted with the flow. At the SBC stand, she bought a hot pastry and double latte, found a table by the window. She turned to face the view of Puget Sound and took out her phone, called Richard's phone.

He'd been waiting for her call. He said, "Kellogg has a Seattle pad. Little place on Alki Point, where he keeps his Porsche Boxster. He went there last night. I slept in the Alfa Romeo all night, and now I need another massage."

She said, "We can take care of that. Where are you now?"

"On Kellogg's tail. He left Alki Point early this morning. We're in Olympia. He stopped at a motel and checked in. A few minutes after he checked in, a taxicab drove up, and a woman got out and went into his room."

"Can you describe her?"

"She wore a long raincoat and a scarf wrapped around her head, Jackie O, style. Also dark glasses. She had nice lips, though."

"I'm glad to hear that. What else?"

"She was carrying a tapestry garment bag and a thing that looked like a makeup case. But I can't positively identify her."

Venus said, "What about your friend Moira?"

"Definitely not Moira."

"How can you be sure?"

"The lips. Moira's lips are a lot fuller, a lot more sensual. And Moira wears a sexier shade of lipstick."

"I'm impressed with your attention to detail."

He said, "Can't take a little ribbing?"

"Are you okay?" Avoiding the issue.

He said, "A little punchy from lack of sleep. Otherwise, fine. How about you?"

"Other than insanely jealous, super."

He said, "I have a cure for what ails you. I could come right now." His voice was hoarse—and, she thought, sexier than ever.

She said, "Hmmm. You better stay with Kellogg. And Hot Lips. Maybe they'll spend the night in Olympia, and you can get a good night's sleep."

Richard said, "I checked out Kellogg's medical degree. He's a bonafide physician. UCSD at La Jolla. He started a residency, also at La Jolla, but got kicked out after a few months. Then right after that, he started his anti-aging spa. He told me himself that he never dug conventional medicine."

"What field? I mean his residency."

"Plastic surgery." While she was thinking that over, he rehearsed in his mind what he had to say next, then blurted too cheerily, too offhandedly, "After this is all over, I have a special request."

"What's that?" She sipped her latte.

He said, "I want you to quit your job."

Across the cafeteria, a group of business executives laughed raucously, presumably sharing some amusing anecdote. Probably at someone else's expense. Their laughs had that kind of vicious tinge. Her ears balked at processing crude dins. Outside the window, a seagull swooped onto the terrace, landed with a Brian Boitano loop, and scooped up a remnant from the Ivar's Fish and Chips Bar. Seagulls might reach a point where they prefer their catch deep-fried in grease and salted. They'd have to set up fish and chip stands out at sea, floating, like oil rigs, just to meet the demand. Commercial wizards were up to the task. Where there's a market, there's an enterprising go-getter. Just look at the Fountain of Youth industry.

"Mrs. Winters?"

She blinked. She said, "Can we discuss this later?"

"Sure. But think it over."

She said, "I better get back to this meeting."

He reported a few more details about Kellogg's background, then said, "You be careful, wife."

"What a funny word," she mused aloud, "'wife.'"

THIRTY

THE DEER TRAILER

OLSON RECONVENED the meeting with an announcement of grand proportions. "If anyone wants a piece of fruit, help yourself." He'd placed a large bowl of Satsumas and Boscos on his desk. To break the ice, he plucked up a Bosco and bit into it. No one else wanted fruit. This wasn't a fruity crowd. Song wanted the Gecko. Wexler wanted Bella. No one knew what Dottie wanted. The rest wanted answers.

"One thing I want to know," said Al Yamada, "is why Hintikka's body was found on Bogachiel, and so close to that lake."

"Elk Pond." Song, correcting Yamada.

Venus said, "Obviously the manufacturer of Elixir of Youth is located near Bogachiel. At least, the facts point in that direction."

"What facts?" Song, dubiously.

She said, "The company's Internet site shows an image of Bogachiel's rain forest, a place called the Hall of Mosses. I'd recognize it anywhere. And, Hintikka had connections to the company, through a post office box in Copenhagen, to which he mailed his payments for the Elixir of Youth products."

"Might be coincidental." Song, being helpful. She wished he'd shut up.

Marla Mason said, "Please, we're veering off course. Let's save that for later."

Venus continued, "Eight days after the Nighteagle baby's disappearance on the preserve, a fugitive wanted for questioning in an alleged child-molestation case was apprehended near the southern edge of the preserve. I briefly interrogated him, found no evidence connecting him to Paris Nighteagle's disappearance. He was held, pending transfer on the molestation charge, in the Grays Harbor County jail, from which he escaped a few days ago. He was last seen entering the woods at the southernmost end of Bogachiel preserve."

Song said, "Three days before Hintikka's body turned up on Bogachiel, to be exact."

Venus said, "Thanks to Song, the Gecko—actually his name is Branson—has a bad leg wound, and he can't have gone far on foot. He hijacked a UPS truck and abandoned it on the southern edge of the preserve. He may have gone back into the preserve, or he may have stolen another vehicle, but we have no reports of stolen vehicles in the area. He's still at large. Three days after Branson escaped, as Song just said, on Thanksgiving Day, Johann Hintikka's body was found on Bogachiel preserve. When found, the body was covered with elk hoofprints, and elk tracks were found on the ground beside the body. No scat, just tracks. I tracked the prints, and I can tell you right now, that was no bull elk that made those hoofprints."

"Then what made them?" Song, holding his mouth against a smirk.

"I don't know."

Song wisecracked, "Here we are, back to the alien Satan."

Ignoring Song's impertinence, she said, "I assume all of you have studied Claudia's autopsy report. Indications are that Hintikka was either captured or went of his own free will to a place where the surgical procedure, the removal of his pituitary gland, could be performed, and he expired while under anesthesia. The victim's body was then dumped on Bogachiel preserve, either by the killer or an accomplice. Whether or not the body was later the victim of an elk— I realize this sounds absurd—of an elk attack—"

Olson cut in. "Elk don't attack corpses. Human or otherwise."

"And they sure don't operate on pituitary glands," Dottie added, laughing inappropriately. Everyone looked at her. The laughing impulse intensified until it overwhelmed her, and she fled the room, covering her mouth. Claudia exchanged a glance with Venus.

Venus said, "No other ungulates inhabit the preserve, unless you count the bighorns, but their hooves are much smaller. Now, have you all read the documents from Senator Lanai's investigation?"

Nods and twitches.

Venus said, "Here's what we do know. The victim, Johann Hintikka, was injecting Elixir of Youth human-growth hormones, which he received through a mail drop in Copenhagen. Recently, Hintikka contracted Creutzfeldt-Jacob disease, which is consistent with having injected some infected pituitary material, probably derived from a cadaver. We also know that Dr. Kellogg is a licensed physician with some surgical training, who specializes in human-growth-hormone therapies, and who performs routine plastic surgery, so-called lunch lifts.''

Yamada massaged his jowl thoughtfully. He didn't say anything, just massaged the loose skin around his chin and neck. Dottie, her laughing fit under control, came back and stood beside Marla at the door. Venus continued.

"Kellogg did a plastic surgery residency at U.C. La Jolla, but according to Richard's inquiries, he failed the residency. Richard spoke to one of his professors who told him that Kellogg was a particularly difficult resident; arrogant, self-righteous, and self-promoting. He had a side business in mini-lifts and anti-aging therapies even while still in his surgery residency. They kicked him out within six months of his arrival. That means he isn't a board-certified surgeon, even though a plaque on his office wall claims he's a member of the American College of Plastic Surgeons.''

"Charlatan.'' Song.

Venus said, "Aside from the malpractice aspect, which is not our venue, we know that Dr. Kellogg is buying and using Elixir of Youth anti-aging serum on his patients. We also know that the Elixir company manufactures many products using illegally harvested forest products, endangered plant species, and ground keratin derived from elk hooves.''

She paused, allowed this data to sink in, then went on. "We now have enough of the product line and enough of a paper trail to nail Dr. Kellogg for violating the Endangered Species Act and trafficking in protected animal parts. We have evidence to nail his brother, the writer, Clint Kellogg, for trespassing on a federally protected wildlife preserve, and we have his own admission that he's illegally harvesting. We can also formally charge one or two other wildcrafters who've been harvesting on the preserve and selling ingredients to Kellogg's spa, and to several organic health products manufacturers.''

Song piped up. "It's a big jump from wildcrafting for herbs and roots to sawing off elk hooves and murdering. I hope you're not implying that a wildcrafter did that.''

"I'm not implying anything. Just let me finish.''

Song's eyes flickered behind the Ray Bans.

Venus said, "Now, here's the bad news.''

Dottie whined, "I hate it when people keep the bad news till last.''

Venus said, "The bad news, in chronological order, is, we haven't found the poacher who's mutilating these Roosevelts. We haven't found the Nighteagle baby, nor uncovered any hard evidence explaining what happened to him. We have no proof who killed Hintikka, though we can speculate on why, and we still haven't identified who's behind the Elixir of Youth products. We've got a police officer in Copenhagen watching the post office box there. We've staked out the company's postal box in Los Angeles. Since discovering the Bogachiel-Elixir of Youth connection, we've watched the Toleak post office like hawks. We've tried ordering the Elixir from the Internet, but the Web site is frozen—I suspect because Senator Lanai's investigation has gotten too close lately, making deliveries dicey. Oh, and, too, the Gecko is still at large. And, if we don't find that Nighteagle boy soon, we may have to conclude that he is dead."

Olson said, "What's a nine-month-old baby's pituitary worth?"

Claudia said, "Probably quite a lot. The baby is in a rapid growth period, so his growth hormones are very active at this stage."

Olson said, "And Hintikka's pituitary? What's that worth?"

Claudia raised a gentle hand. "As I said a while ago, Mr. Hintikka had apparently received a tainted dosage of human growth hormone from which he contracted Creutzfeldt-Jakob disease, and also had contracted HIV. Any material harvested from this victim's glands would certainly be diseased. Anyone receiving an injection of HGH taken from him would stand a good chance of contracting CJD, if not also HIV. But to answer your question about worth, I can't place a monetary value on harvested human organs."

Olson said, "Did your autopsy reveal the HIV condition?"

Claudia shook her head.

Olson said, "Why not?"

"The lab has been very slow lately. And mistakes are being made. Maybe they're shorthanded, I don't know. We only learned about the HIV condition yesterday, from the victim's widow. Since then, I have verified it with new lab tests."

In the ensuing silence, Venus heard Olson's stomach rumble. She watched him pick up another bottle of Evian, guzzle. Anything to fill the void. Olson swallowed and said, "Show them the map."

Venus switched off the lights, turned on a laptop projector. An image of Simon Thundercloud's father's map filled the wall screen. She explained how it came into her hands. With a laser pointer, she emphasized salient details. "This is an old mule trail running through Bogachiel's rain forest. I've marked the trail with a bold line to distinguish it from all other trails on the map. This is Elk Pond, a pristine freshwater pond on the perimeter of the rain forest. And somewhere, near the end of this trail, is an old sweat lodge, if it's still standing.''

Song moved in closer to the screen. ''You're sure this is on Bogachiel?''

''If, as Simon Thundercloud says, the pond on the map is truly Elk Pond, then we're talking about Bogachiel. Theoretically, the sweat lodge would be located not far from where I found the buck carcass. By not far, I mean maybe a mile, a mile and a half.''

Yamada said, ''So what's holding us up? Let's go take a look.''

Venus pointed to a small squiggly line on Ray Thundercloud's map. ''This is a small branch of the Little Hoh River. According to the map, the trail should lead to this little brook, then across a bridge. But I can't locate the brook. Yesterday, Eric went up in the chopper, scoured the topography. Even this late in the season, it's impossible to see through that heavy canopy.''

Sweetwater spoke up. ''I even commandeered a crane from the canopy research project. I couldn't locate that little creek. It's not on any of our current maps.''

Al Yamada said, ''So what's next?''

Venus switched the lights back on, said, ''Richard has learned that today or possibly tomorrow, Dr. Kellogg and a woman who's accompanying him plan to visit Kellogg's brother over at Grays Harbor. I want to know the source of Kellogg's contraband. Richard's tailing them now, but we'll need part of the team to help. Sooner or later, Kellogg is bound to lead us to the Elixir source. Meanwhile, it's imperative that we move into the rain forest immediately, locate that old sweat lodge.''

''Because...?'' Song, being flip.

''Because if it's still there, it hasn't been searched.''

Yamada said, ''Let's take this one thing at a time. We have several crimes here, not even counting wildcrafters harvesting on a federal preserve. We have elk poachings on the preserve, with hooves being sawed off. We have the Nighteagle baby's disappearance, though that might have been a cougar or bear for all we know. We have an apparently related but separate killing, the man with HIV. And then there's the Gecko. So, what, if anything, ties them all together?''

Venus said, ''The elk poachings and the murdered man both provide ingredients for Elixir of Youth's injection formula. Other ingredients in the recipe, some of the plant species, can be traced to the preserve. In the case of the baby and the murdered man, the crimes both took place on the preserve. And there're the hoofprints. As for the Gecko, I don't think he's a part of this."

Song laughed out loud.

Venus ignored him; said, "Let's focus on the immediate problem. We need to find that creek or river shown on the map. The old sweat lodge is not far from its bank. When we've located the sweat lodge, we need to move in on foot, with the chopper standing by. We want to use surprise, so Sweetwater lays back in the chopper until we give him a signal to move in, and we only use him if absolutely necessary. Under that tree canopy, it won't be easy tracking from the chopper."

Song said, "He can't flee. He's got my bullet in his thigh."

Olson said, "Why are you so cocksure the Gecko is our target?"

Heartbreak Louie had been waiting all morning for this moment in the spotlight. When he unwrapped the Ray Bans, and everyone could see his smoky, sexy eyes, he said, "Branson's on that preserve. He was stalking the preserve during the same time period the Nighteagle boy was snatched. We apprehended him, and nothing happened for a while. Then he escaped, and what happens? We get Hintikka's body."

Marla said, "I seriously doubt that the Gecko's qualified to perform brain surgery."

Song was ready for the challenge. "I didn't say he did. Branson's a pedophile and a psychopath. I'm convinced he abducted the Nighteagle baby, and he probably killed him."

Olson said, "Motive?"

"No motive. Psychopaths don't need a motive. Same with the Finn, with Hintikka. Branson encountered Hintikka, and who knows why, he wanted to kill him. It's a clean and simple explanation. Most criminal investigations are simple, once you get past all the crap created to confuse you."

Claudia said, "What about the autopsy?"

Song said, "I think it's flawed. I think the body, especially the skull, was too mutilated to make judgments about a pituitary gland being missing. Hintikka died from an attack by a bull elk."

Outside, the sun slipped behind a gray haze. The room darkened and the shadows melted. No one spoke until the silence grew painful, then Claudia said, "The autopsy clearly demonstrates the cause of death was anesthesia poisoning. The elk hoof attack came later, after death."

Song said, "Don't you need lab analyses to conclude that?"

Claudia flushed crimson. "Yes. Yes, we do."

"I thought so. And lately, your lab folks haven't proved very reliable. So I disagree with their finding." Then Song delivered his bombshell, catching everyone by surprise. "Branson's a Vietnam vet. Special Forces. He worked with Vietnamese Special Forces on the front lines. This information is all in his Army records. In Vietnam, Branson developed a peculiar talent, taught to him by Vietnamese soldiers."

Olson said, "What talent is that?"

"The Vietnamese taught Branson how to train deer to attack on command, to stomp the enemy to death, to kill the enemy."

Song rotated his head, stretching the neck muscles, his eyes shut, waiting for anyone to challenge him. Somebody wanted to, and it was Eric Sweetwater. Sweetwater said, "A Roosevelt does not necessarily have the same temperament as an Asian species."

Song grinned, said, "I rest my case." Convinced that, inevitably, simplicity reigned over complex plots and machinations.

Yamada spoke up. "Can we just get back to the pressing issue, which, as I see it, is locating this sweat lodge?"

Song opened his eyes and said, "That's not the pressing issue, Al. The pressing issue is apprehending a murderer before he strikes again. That's Branson. The Gecko. We take him into custody and our case is closed. The Gecko snatched the baby and killed him. He molested that girl—"

Yamada almost yelled, "I know, I know. And his trained elk stomped Hintikka to death on command."

Song's eyes flickered and his voice held a sharp edge. "I am merely raising the potential scenario we face going in there. I agree about the old sweat lodge. It's apparently in an area we haven't yet searched. So let's go, let's go in there. If that lodge still exists, my bet is we'll find Branson there."

"And his pet elk?" Sweetwater, tongue-in-cheek.

Dottie piped up then. "I'm with Louie. This Branson creature sounds like our man."

Olson said, "Maybe there's some merit to the Branson theory. This ability to train a deer. Are you sure about this, Song?"

Song nodded. "I've heard about this technique all my life. It's a well-established war tactic in many parts of Asia."

Olson shrugged. "Branson's apparently hiding out on the preserve.

It does seem to fit. That is, if we set aside the autopsy results. They could be flawed. Could be the lab made mistakes. Or someone." He avoided Claudia's hard stare.

Yamada caved next. "Might be. Song might be right."

Marla spoke up. "I agree. I think the Gecko got the baby, killed him. And the Finnish man. I think our biggest mistake would be to depend on that autopsy report. It just doesn't cut it for me. Coroners aren't infallible."

The Acting Secretary of the Interior rose from the dead, raised an authoritative hand and declared, "I've heard enough. In fact, I've heard too much. Let's go have a look."

"You're going along?" Song, sounding impressed.

Wexler said, "I've never seen a sweat lodge before. I'm going along on this one."

Venus looked at Claudia. Claudia was studying the palms of her hands, her lips silently moving. Maybe cursing, maybe a prayer.

Wexler read his watch; said to Olson, "Do I have time to make a phone call before we take off?"

Olson nodded. To Venus, he said, "You and Al leave immediately, by car. We'll meet you in Grays Harbor in, say, four hours."

"Make it snappy," she said, and walked out, Yamada in tow.

THIRTY-ONE

DEADLY HOOVES

AT THE FORKS ANNEX Al Yamada took Theresa Nighteagle's call.

"My husband hasn't come home since the day before yesterday," she said, sounding frantic. "I'm worried."

Yamada turned to Venus. "You better talk to her."

"I've tried everywhere," Theresa told Venus. "I thought he might go to the clinic, check on Milan, but he's not there, and neither is my mother. I need him at home."

"Where's your mother, Theresa?"

"The doctor sent her home. He said she was getting in the way. They made her leave. I called her, but she hasn't seen Winn either. I tried the Pine Fresh Motel. They say they haven't seen him since day before yesterday. His truck is parked right out front here. I even asked Carolee. She swears she hasn't seen him for two days, and I believe her. I need my husband to come home right now."

"I'll be right over, Mrs. Nighteagle. Meanwhile, keep your doors locked."

"I'm not afraid of anything. Just find Winn and tell him to come home."

"Have you got a weapon over there?"

Theresa began crying. "I have Winn's hunting rifle. It's sitting in the other room, by the front door. And it's loaded."

"I'll see you in a few minutes."

"I'm all right," Theresa insisted. "Leave me alone. I just need Winn. I don't want anyone else coming over here." She hung up.

To Yamada, Venus said, "Is the team here yet?"

Yamada shook his head. "Sweetwater called from Olympia. Weather. They can't take off for at least three or four more hours."

"Great." She loaded her pistol.

Yamada said, "Where do you think you're going?"

"To Bogachiel Clinic, then to Cedar Grove Trailer Park."

Yamada jumped up. "The hell you are. You don't go anywhere until the team arrives."

Ignoring his protest, she put on her jacket, opened the door. "Stay right here. I'll check in every half hour." She grabbed the keys to the Land Rover, went out into the misty morning, slid behind the Rover's wheel. Although it was only 11:00 a.m., the sky hung dark and gloomy, and she flicked the headlights on high beam along Highway 101.

At Bogachiel Clinic, the head nurse said Fish wasn't available. She said, "He's with that baby."

"What baby?"

The harried nurse was already halfway down the corridor. She pointed at a closed door, said, "The Nighteagle baby. The one that wasn't snatched by the Unknown."

The nurse stood at the end of the corridor, near the reception desk. The reception room was full and frantic, as usual. Behind the desk, a brand-new bank of computers sparkled and gleamed, technological hope in the midst of dingy despair.

To the nurse, Venus said, "I see you finally got your computers."

The nurse grinned. "And the CAT scan. And the laser. Yes ma'am, we hit the jackpot." She shimmied away.

Becca Brightman appeared from nowhere, it seemed, a ghostly, pale figure lurking at the end of the corridor, holding a book. When she saw Venus coming toward her, Becca held out the book.

"You better read this."

Venus accepted the book Becca offered, read the title, the author's name. "This was written by Clint Kellogg?"

Becca nodded. In a husky voice, she said, "He gave it to me a few weeks ago. The day after Paris got snatched by the Unknown." Venus leafed through the pages. Fables. Becca added, "You better read it."

Venus looked at the girl. "Why, Becca? Why should I read it?"

Becca trembled and her eyes grew wide and pooled tears. "It's scary stuff," she stammered, "but I, well, I think these are true stories. You better read it."

She turned then and ran down the corridor, disappearing around a corner.

THE TRAILER PARK echoed like a ghost town, though she knew people were lurking in their homes, peeking out from behind curtains, watching her. The rusted pink trailer stood still and silent. No answer to her hard knocking. In the eerie silence, she yelled, but no one came to the door. She drew her gun, aimed, blasted off the door lock, kicked in the door.

Theresa Nighteagle wasn't home. The rifle Theresa had said was near the front door was not there. The television was on, some soap-opera weeping noise. She moved from one room to the next, taking each corner with caution. In the master bedroom, she found a window wide open, the latch forced. In the kitchen, on the table, a coffee mug, half full, kissed a scuzzy ashtray filled with cigarette butts and ashes, still warm to the touch. The refrigerator door hung open, its contents tossed on the floor. Empty milk carton. Empty cans of chili beans. Empty bread bag. Somebody had been hungry. She moved along the corridor to the twins' bedroom, the last room left to search. The door was closed, locked. She raised her foot, kicked it in. She found the Gecko on the nursery floor, shot once through the heart.

Bending over him, she felt a weak pulse. She dialed 911, then turned the Gecko over onto his back. His clothing was tattered, and one of his shoes was missing a lace that matched the one she'd sent to the lab. His glassy stare found her and his lips came halfway to life. "He took the baby," the Gecko rasped. He coughed up some crimson blood and a chill seized him. She grabbed a blanket, placed it over him, wadded up another and placed it under his head. He didn't have much longer.

She said, "Where's Paris?"

The Gecko worked his parched lips, trying to speak. She took his hand, felt the pulse at his wrist growing weaker. She bent her head, the better to hear his wheezy breath. His throat choked with blood, he whispered, "Elk-man," and inhaled, sounding a death rattle.

IN THE RAIN FOREST, beneath the foliage canopy, the dry ground escaped a relentless falling rain. Venus moved swiftly. Had to. No time left. Time had run out—she'd figured things out too late. Maybe too late for Paris, maybe too late for everyone. Maybe this was destiny. Like any other creature, a human life is both rare and insignificant; a body possesses valuable organs, lucrative parts. In a murderer's mind, some humans count more than others. Paris Nighteagle might already be a victim, no longer a baby, just body parts, product. Now time was everything. Now another baby was about to be sacrificed. Unless she could stop it. She broke into a run.

What was this evil oozing from the forest? What species of beast or man had cast its baneful spell upon this once fecund and tranquil place? Where once upon a time every creature and bird and crawling insect and every fish in every stream had dwelt harmoniously, and where death had existed—but a rational death, death by Nature— beneath this mythic forest canopy, now fear reigned, all because this one, living, evil thing had cast its spell upon the land. God help the forest—God save it from this awful curse, this dark satanic entity, this Unknown.

But how had evil come to transform this enchanted forest—this so-called protected preserve, where all wildlife should be safe from predators—into a realm of stark, unbounded fear? Nothing here was safe now. Maybe the forest should be chopped down, tree by tree, until Paris Nighteagle was avenged, until the poachers and madmen were finally burned out of their hiding places, until every inch of soil lay bare, fire-scorched, and every creature ceased to breathe the gift of life.

In a dense copse, she saw Winn, saw him pour the gasoline, but before she could reach him, the stack of kindling he'd built beneath the trees burst into flame. Winn's face turned gold in the firelight. He stood back as a yellow tongue rose, licking at the draping canopy. She dove at the leaping flames, but Winn grabbed her, wrestled her away. She fought back. He pinned her to the ground, shouted, "Let it burn." She jerked one swift leg, sent Winn flying backward. Scrambling to her feet, she ran to the blaze, covered it with her jacket, beat the flames, stomped on them, kicked dirt over them until the fire gasped and died. She turned to Winn, who stood watching, frozen to the ground.

Winn wailed, "I just want to die, man."

She tossed more earth over the embers, checked the cedar boughs for sparks, and said, "Where've you been, Winn?"

Winn passed a hand across his brow, made incoherent sounds.

She grabbed hold of him, shook him. "Talk to me. There isn't much time left."

"Searching," he said. "Two goddamn days and nights, without sleep, without food, man. I know he's in here somewhere. I got to find him."

She showed Winn old Ray Thundercloud's map. He held it close to his eyes, squinted. "Oh my God," he said. "That's where it is. That's where the old sweat lodge is."

"Where it was," she corrected him. "It must have been destroyed long ago. They rebuilt over it."

Winn said, "You think he's there?"

She said, "Maybe. It's the only place we haven't searched."

Winn grabbed her arm. "Let's go."

She led the way up deeper into the forest, up and over a steep rise where at the crest, planks of wood formed a rickety bridge over the Little Hoh River. They crossed gingerly. On the other side, they followed a zigzag line of old-growth cedars higher, higher into the moss-covered terrain. She told Winn that she was glad for his company, glad that he hadn't totally despaired, relieved that he still carried a glimmer of hope in his heart. As she did. But Winn had no weapon. Where was his rifle?

"I left it at home," he told her. "By the front door."

When they came to the second stream, a small brooking glacial flow, she stopped, turned to Winn. "It's close now." They began a steep downhill climb, and soon heard the breakers crashing against the beach at Bogachiel.

Not Toleak. Bogachiel.

When they had walked a little farther, she took out her .38 Smith and Wesson, and warned Winn to be quiet, cautious. They crept softly, she adept at vigilance, he clumsily breaking twigs underfoot. When she saw the building's roof, she nodded to Winn, and he looked and saw it, too. She took out her phone, made one crucial call, and hoped the fog had lifted over Olympia, hoped the chopper had taken off.

IN GRAYS HARBOR, Dr. Bradford Kellogg stood in line at the cash register in Bartell's Drug Store, waiting to pay for a supply of diabetic's syringes with needles. Kellogg's green eyes darted around anxiously. He wore shabby jeans, a logger's plaid shirt and boots, and he hadn't shaved. If Winn Nighteagle had been there to notice him, Winn would have thought of a praying mantis he once saw in the woods behind the trailer park where he lived. Brad Kellogg looked nothing like a physician, more like an urban yuppie grunger come over to the peninsula to slum, or maybe to fish. When Kellogg finished paying for the package of needles and syringes, he went out to the parking lot and slid behind the wheel of a black Porsche Boxster. A woman sat in the passenger seat, waiting. She wore dark glasses and a scarf tied Jackie O-style around her hair. When Kellogg slid into the driver's seat, she turned and said something to him. He nodded and started the car. He turned on the headlights because even though it was just 11:00 a.m., a dark sky loomed menacingly, a light mist fell, and dense fog drifted down to the highway's yellow line. You had to drive cautiously in this hellish weather, even in a Porsche.

Kellogg and the woman with him didn't see the red Alfa Romeo cruising at a safe distance behind the Boxster. Two sweet vehicles crawling against character along this godforsaken road in America's wringing-wet hinterland. Behind the wheel of Venus's Alfa, Richard felt confident, in control. He reached down to the console, popped it open. The pistol he'd borrowed from Venus's lingerie drawer was loaded, the safety on. He tucked it in his jacket pocket because Richard had no such fancy accouterment as shoulder or leg holsters: He wasn't a cop, after all—he was a conservationist. He wasn't even licensed to pack a weapon. The only reason he was shadowing this snake-oil salesman was because as soon as he caught the doc in the act of purchasing illegal animal—or human—product, he'd be one step closer to enjoying a genuine honeymoon. Maybe this time in Maui. We'll see.

NORTH OF Grays Harbor, the Boxster veered left off the highway onto a narrow gravel road and disappeared behind the line of weathered beach pines that hid the beach from the highway. Richard swung the Alfa onto the road's shoulder, parked, got out, pulled his jacket tighter around his neck to fend off the damp chill, and walked down the gravel road. Rounding a bend, he saw the cabin on the beach, situated just above the driftwood line. Thick fog obscured the ocean, but he could hear the crashing breakers and the seagulls shrieking. He saw Clint Kellogg's Jeep parked in front of the cabin, and he saw the Boxster pulled up beside it. He saw Doc Kellogg step out of the Boxster, retrieve a suitcase, the woman's tapestry garment bag, and the Bartell's bag from the trunk, and go inside the cabin. He saw the woman get out and follow Kellogg inside. He ducked into the woods, pulled out his cell phone, and made a call.

IN OLYMPIA, Eric Sweetwater was arguing with the air traffic controller when Song took Richard's call. Into the phone, Song said, "They won't let us go up in this storm. We're socked in. You'll have to keep an eye on them for a while longer." He added, "Don't do anything dangerous, Winters. I wouldn't want you getting hurt." Sarcastically.

Richard retorted, "Well, let's put it this way, Song. If anything happens to me, she might settle for you, but she's not used to cut-rate merchandise." And signed off.

Sweetwater came over, frowning. "Change of plans," he said. "We're taking off, against air traffic control's advice, but we're taking off now."

Song said, "Something go wrong?"

Sweetwater nodded. "Venus just called. We've run out of time. Maybe everything's wrong now."

The chopper shimmied and swayed across the southern shore of Puget Sound, hugged the eastern slopes of the Olympics, buffered by the range from the winds off the ocean. When it crossed over to the windward side, Sweetwater struggled to keep the chopper upright. At Grays Harbor, he tried to land at the municipal landing pad on the beach, but was refused permission. The air traffic controller, an old man in a hut beside the landing pad with nothing but a paper chart and a set of binoculars, said, "You go back. You can't land in this storm. Go back to Olympia."

Sweetwater shouted, "Can we land at Toleak Beach?"

"Hell no," came back the traffic controller's voice. "That's even worse up there. Hell no."

Song shouted into his mouthpiece, "We're landing this crate on your pad, buster. Here we come now." Sweetwater glanced up. Over the howling wind and the rains, Song shouted, "Take her down."

The perilous landing made chaos of the arms and ammunition stowed in the hatch. The bloodhounds bayed sickly, and their howling rode the winds. Yamada held onto Sparks for dear life. Marla Mason clung to her seat and Dottie cried, "God, Marla, we're all going to die."

Marla, desperate for a diversion said, "So then, tell me your secret, Dots. Why've you been such a pain in the arse lately?"

"All right, all right," Dottie cried. "I'm in love with Louie Song and he's in love with Venus and I just can't take it anymore. I can't...I can't." She buried her face in her hands, wept. Marla patted Dottie comfortingly. The chopper lurched and shimmied.

Olson kept rubbing his mouth, Wexler made a phone call to someone special. Claudia and Sparks remained cool, composed, watching every move Sweetwater made. He brought her down in a sharp arc onto the lunatic beach, where the wind and the unleashed tides battered the shore. Sweetwater sat motionless until his heart stopped pounding, then joined the exodus onto the beach. On the way out of the chopper, Song offered Dottie his hand.

"I heard what you told Marla," Song grinned.

Dottie moaned, "Oh, God."

Song pulled her close, kissed her. When he paused for air, Song held Dottie's face in his hands and quipped, "You're asking for trouble, Dorothy."

"Don't call me Dorothy."

Marla shouted, "Will you guys get moving?"

RICHARD HAD FOUND a hiding place among the trees that allowed him to fade into the fog and mist and still see inside the cabin's windows. He saw Brad inside, moving around. In a few minutes, smoke poured from the chimney, and Clint Kellogg came to the door, opened it, looked up into the sky, then ducked back inside and shut the door. The storm moved up the coast. In the thickets, Richard grew cold, his feet went numb, and his clothing got soaked by a wind-whipped rain. Nothing happened for half an hour, then the door opened, and Brad and Clint Kellogg stepped outside, walked toward the driveway. Richard heard them arguing.

"I just can't believe you'd be so stupid." Clint, to Brad.

Brad said, "Lana was going to turn over everything to her husband. What else was I supposed to do?"

The two men stood between the two vehicles and continued the heated exchange.

"I want nothing to do with this, Brad. I can't help you with this one. Not this. It's loathsome and repulsive, and I can't believe someone in my family would do what you've done."

Brad pleaded now. "Clint, listen to me. Nobody was hurt. He told me they were all dead before he touched them. They all died of natural causes, Clint. Nobody killed over this."

Clint said, "Until Lana demanded fresh product. Hormones from people on their deathbeds wasn't good enough for Lana. She had to have guaranteed fresh, healthy product. How many people did you kill for Lana Lanai? So Lana could be young forever? It's an atrocity, Brad. I won't tolerate it. You better turn yourself in, or else I will."

Brad grabbed Clint's arm in a crushing entreaty. "We only killed one of them, Brad, a worthless human being. He didn't need to live.

The others were already corpses, I swear. Clint, this is my entire practice at stake. If I'm caught, it'll be the end of me.'' Clint tried to shake him off, but Brad wrestled with him.

Clint shouted above the wind, "I'm going to turn you in, Brad. For your own damn good.''

Brad broke away from Clint, ran down to the beach and across the driftwood into surf that mauled the shore. Knee deep, he ploughed north a few yards, then turned suddenly, tricking Clint, and raced through the trees until he reached the Boxster's passenger side. He opened the door, got in. Clint, who had gone down on the beach looking for him, now saw how he'd been tricked and came running back.

Richard made a dash for the Boxster, his gun drawn. Too late. He saw the barrel of Brad's gun at the driver's window and he saw it fire, saw the blue blaze. It fired once, twice, barely missing Richard both times. The Boxster wheeled around and headed straight at him. Richard fired at the car's tires, crippling the getaway vehicle. Brad jumped out of the Boxster leading with his gun, firing, and beat it into the woods. Clint and Richard chased behind.

Somewhere in the fog and mist, Brad disappeared. When the team came racing up the beach, they fanned out along the highway, hoping to trap Kellogg on the beach, to prevent him from crossing into the preserve where it would be harder to capture him. Song ran the hounds to the Boxster, let them sniff around, then turned them loose on the beach. Richard and Claudia jumped into the Alfa Romeo and screamed up the highway, hoping to reach Venus in time. Time's swift passage preyed on them, and Richard floored the gas.

WHEN THEY HAD ALL disappeared from sight, Lana stepped out of the cabin, and stole across the grass to Clint's Jeep. The keys were in the ignition. Lana started up the Jeep, slammed it into reverse, swung the vehicle around and peeled out onto Highway 101. Lana wasn't comfortable with a standard shift, and this one had more positions than she could fathom. With that hassle and with all the fog on the road, she had difficulty navigating. She turned the headlights on high, and the two beams reflected back off the fog into her eyes. She couldn't see worth a damn but she drove anyway, just to get out of there. Squinting through the thick fog, Lana cursed her dilemma.

The human growth hormone she had been promised hadn't been delivered. Now Lana had gone over two weeks without her injections and already she believed she could feel her body degenerating, aging. All because Brad Kellogg couldn't get his stupid act together. She should have shopped around for another source of hormone therapy. She should have seen Brad's incompetence long ago. Why had she invested her life's savings in this dumbo's business when he couldn't even figure out how to harvest fresh product without getting caught? Some people just aren't too bright. She should never have changed her mind and agreed to come back up here. For all she knew, Brad might have intended to murder her. And now Brad was a fugitive. If they caught him, would he turn her in? Would he implicate her? Knowing Brad, he'd blame her for everything. Well, Lana wouldn't be chased down and captured like a common criminal, no, not Lana Lapidus Lanai. She could drive this Jeep right over the Canadian border, and that was what she was planning to do when she rounded a hairpin curve and saw the elk.

She saw the eyes first, then the antlers. If she could have counted at that moment, Lana would have counted seven points on the antlers. An enormous beast, with glaring red eyes, its huge nostrils quivering, its mouth dripping foam. It blocked her path. Lana screamed and hit the brakes. The Jeep skidded, spun out, slammed over a low stone wall, took flight. The airborne Jeep with screaming Lana inside sailed off the highway and crashed headlong into a cedar trunk. Lana's lunch lift hit the windshield, splattered, and her skull cracked open. When they carved her body out of the wreck a few hours later, the sheriff's deputies found her crumpled corpse slung over the steering wheel, a suspicious-looking, sooty-colored fluid leaking from her skull. When asked, the deputy who first saw the dead Lana said the stuff leaking from her head looked like "gray matter," but he allowed for his own wild imagination.

THIRTY-TWO

BLOOD LIBERAL

THE RACKET IN the clinic's reception room was so loud that no one heard the gun go off. Dr. Fish stood behind the drapes of his office window. The window was open a crack. He aimed his gun into the woods behind the clinic, and shot a second time. This bullet sang off a cedar trunk, in the exact key of the gurgling brook. In the silence that followed, Fish realized that his number was up, his name had been called, his secret revealed. He'd seen her in there—he'd spotted Agent Diamond, and he'd seen Winn Nighteagle with her. Coming after him. Coming to strip him of all secrets and dignity.

Fish wore green surgical scrubs, a hair net, and a scrub cap over that. His feet wore green rubber clogs, and his hands wore tissue-thin latex gloves. If anyone were to see him now, they would say, "Dr. Fish is going into surgery," and think nothing of it. Except for the gun in his hand.

The hardest part had been getting rid of Frances Creed. She stuck to Milan like superglue. When he finally got rid of the grandmother, and the nurses were handling the crowds of misery, Fish saw his chance.

He'd strapped baby Milan to the surgical chair, placing towels around her tiny head so that it would fit into the big headrest. He'd started the IV drip. When Milan had gone under the anesthesia, he double-checked that the surgery door was locked, read his watch, checked his surgical equipment, picked up a scalpel and approached the baby girl. Surgery on a nine-month-old child has its pros and cons. The incision would take less time to heal, but because of the small size of the sinus cavity, the operation would prove more delicate than others. This was the surgery Fish had performed on so many freshly dead corpses, the surgery he'd hoped to perform on Paris Nighteagle.

The deal between Doc Kellogg and Doc Fish began with an unpleasant exchange; at one of Clint's faboo parties, Brad had caught

Lawrence in the act of ingesting narcotics he'd appropriated from the clinic for indigents. Kellogg made Fish a proposition. Fish would supply Doc Kellogg with human growth hormone from cadavers. In exchange, Doc Kellogg would pay Fish a handsome sum of money and keep silent about Fish's chronic drug abuse and narcotics theft. Fish was caught in a quandary, 100 percent at Kellogg's mercy.

For two years, Fish had harvested the pituitary material from freshly dead corpses. Then one of Kellogg's patients got finicky about receiving material from cadavers, and Doc Kellogg demanded fresh HGH from a living person. The idea was to remove a portion of the person's pituitary gland, from which to extract hormones, while leaving the rest intact. Kellogg suggested Fish harvest the material from one of his hospital patients, but Fish balked at taking chances with ill patients. Kellogg then suggested the Nighteagle twins. Kellogg had observed the twins with their parents. They were "trailer-park trash," and kidnapping a child, a baby, from a trailer park on the edge of a forest should prove fairly simple.

After the boy healed from his surgery, he would then be "found" in the forest, and returned to his parents. That was the idea at first, before things went all wrong.

Fish had almost abandoned the plan to kidnap Paris and take his pituitary, but the clinic needed a new computer system, and it needed a CAT scanner. Fish rationalized that the desperate condition of the clinic justified taking this one living sample. But when Paris was brought to him, straight from his bassinet, Fish realized the boy's arrhythmia had worsened and he didn't want to risk surgery just yet.

Johann Hintikka then proved an opportune victim. When Elixir of Youth's Web site had frozen suddenly, Hintikka had panicked. No longer could he obtain in Finland the medication he so desperately needed. But Johann was a bright, resourceful man. From the picture of Bogachiel preserve on Elixir's Web site, Johann identified the elk species that appeared in the Web site's image. A unique species, found only on the Olympic Peninsula in the Northwestern United States. From this Website scene, Hintikka guessed that the company was located in the Pacific Northwest. He had come to the United States, driven up to the peninsula, asked around. Nobody knew what the Finnish man was talking about. Then someone at the county transportation garage suggested that Hintikka try Bogachiel clinic. It was the only place within miles where there was a real medical doctor.

Hintikka had driven to the clinic, where he had encountered Fish and Kellogg outside the building. When he told them what he was looking for, Kellogg had immediately realized the danger of allowing Hintikka to keep asking around. The two docs arranged for Hintikka to see them that evening, the night before Thanksgiving. Kellogg called for Hintikka at Toleak Lodge, and brought him to the clinic, where he and Fish removed the man's pituitary gland. They didn't know Hintikka was HIV-positive. Kellogg had personally pumped the anesthesia overdose into Hintikka.

Disposing of the body had presented endless frustration, untold anxiety. Fortunately, Fish had a willing collaborator, though he never fully trusted the man. No wonder Fish felt so stressed all the time.

When later Kellogg discovered the pituitary material was diseased, he discarded it. Lana went ballistic on him, so he frantically looked around for another source. What a dilemma for Fish. When your charity clinic's chief source of income is derived from illegal means, you can't just blow off your best client. Fish had to supply Doc Kellogg with product, or else face indictment for narcotics theft. He'd lose his medical license. Go to prison. His life would be ruined.

Then Fish realized that the other Nighteagle twin was in the clinic, being treated for a mild fever. Fish made up a story about the baby having meningitis as an excuse to keep her hospitalized. He made preparations to perform his surgical procedure—a baby can't talk. He wouldn't kill her, would only remove a portion of the pituitary, so that she might recover and develop normally. He'd do the same with Paris, too, when the boy outgrew his arrhythmia.

When he'd started cooperating with Doc Kellogg's mail order "Elixir of Youth" business, Fish never really meant to kill anyone, not in the beginning. All he meant to do was keep Kellogg from turning him in for stealing narcotics. Then, too, there was the benevolent aspect. Kellogg paid Fish handsomely for the product. To assuage his guilt, and because he was a nice guy at heart, Fish used the payments from Kellogg to keep the clinic functioning, to buy new computers and medical equipment and supplies for the clinic, to make decent treatment available to all of his impoverished patients. At heart, Fish was a blood liberal. An overworked, fatigued blood liberal.

Venus had been right about his depression. She'd recognized it even before Fish saw it in himself. Fish had run out of energy, and when his blackmailer demanded fresh HGH, he was too addled, too stressed out to resist Kellogg's demands.

If anyone were to see Dr. Fish now, dressed in his scrubs, the gun in his hand, they would say, "I thought Doctor was going into surgery, but it appears I was wrong. Doctor is going to shoot himself."

HE HAD BEEN holding the scalpel above Milan's head when a nurse had come, pounded on the door.

"Dr. Fish," she called through the door, "Agent Diamond is on the telephone."

Fish couldn't open the door, couldn't let the nurse see what he was doing. He called back through the door, "What does she want?"

The nurse said, "She says to stop what you're doing and come out with your hands up. What do you suppose she means by that?"

NOW DR. LAWRENCE FISH faced the lovely woodland view. The singing brook, the little curved bridge, the tall, ancient cedars. She was in there somewhere, and she had figured it out. She was coming to get him, to arrest him and tell the world what an evil monster he was. Damn his good intentions, his almost pure motive. Malpractice is never justified. Neither is murder. He'd figured that out too late.

IN THE FOREST, Becca and Ocean Boy were heading back from the beach when the man met them on the Little Hoh bridge.

"Give Paris to me," he said to Becca. "The father is at the clinic, looking for his son. Give me Paris, so I can hide him."

Trusting him, Becca handed Paris to the man, who carried the boy into the forest and disappeared. Becca continued on her way.

THE HAND with the gun rose slowly to Fish's head. He stood framed in evergreen splendor. One year, one hundred and sixteen days to go in service to the indigent patients of Bogachiel clinic. But time was never on his side. His time had run out. He felt for the trigger.

"Put it down, Lawrence," Venus said gently.

He froze, except for his heart. His heart leapt gladly. He didn't want to die. Her voice had stopped him. An angel couldn't have sounded better. He lowered his arm, placed the gun on his desk.

"Now turn around."

Fish turned around. His face was ashen, his eyes buried in their sockets. A single tear bled from the dark pools, and then another, and another, until streams of crystalline remorse flowed, releasing rage, loneliness, depression. When she cuffed him, Fish whispered, "Thanks."

Winn had gone straight to the surgery, straight to Milan, detached the IV, unstrapped her from the awful chair. He held the limp, unconscious child in his arms, so tight against him that she might have smothered if a nurse hadn't come in suddenly and admonished him.

Venus said, "Where's Paris?"

Fish nodded toward the corridor. "Room Six."

"Where you had a Code Blue the other day?"

Fish said, "It wasn't really a Code Blue. I have the room rigged. Not even the nurses knew about it. That alarm goes off at the reception desk, and all they know is one of my isolated patients is in trouble. The girl was inside, and she sounded the alarm. All it meant was, the baby was hungry."

She ran down the corridor, Winn following. The door to Room Six was locked. A nurse ran to Fish, got the keys. When they unlocked the door, Venus went in first. The examining room had been transformed into a nursery, with a playpen, a crib, a training pot, and toys everywhere.

But no Paris.

Lawrence Fish came walking down the corridor, handcuffed and weeping. "Oh dear," he lamented. "She must have taken him out again. I've told her not to take him out."

And then Becca appeared, ambling down the corridor, grinning ear to ear, her arms empty, her expression victorious. "You'll never hurt Paris again," she spat at Winn. "Paris is safe from you now."

Venus grabbed Becca. "Where is he?"

Becca cried, "Let go of me."

"Where is he?" Venus yelled. "Hurry up, Becca. He's going to kill Paris."

Becca pointed to the woods. "Up there," she squeaked, "back up on that ridge."

Venus ran across the arcing bridge over the singing brook, through that peaceful scene, uphill through the dense woods, up onto the ridge. From the top of the ridge, she could see the man with the baby heading down the other side, heading toward Elk Pond. He wasn't in a hurry now, was ambling slowly, taking his time, carrying Paris in his arms, a macabre Saint Christopher bearing the Infant. Only this was no saint carrying a baby through the forest to safety. This was a ruthless, violent man who meant to kill the infant in his arms. She moved quickly, agilely, quietly. He never saw her, never once turned to see if someone followed him. She came up behind the anti-Christopher and said, "Put him down, slowly."

He stopped, froze in his tracks. Again she said, "Put him down slowly, and turn around."

He turned around, saw the barrel of her gun. Instead of putting the baby down, he held Paris up as his shield.

"You'd kill him," he shouted. "You won't kill me."

Ocean Boy said, "Water."

Venus said, "Put him down."

The man holding the baby suddenly cried for mercy, and his mouth hung wide open when a bullet whizzed out of the thickets, struck him in the brain, instantly killing him. He crumpled, fell to the tender earth, blood coursing from his mouth, and Ocean Boy fell, too, as if in slow motion, landing in a heap on top of the fallen man, on top of the corpse.

He would never again repair a county vehicle, or search cheesy motels trying to catch his wife with another man, or wildcraft, or for that matter, make death by anesthesia poisoning appear to be death at the hooves of an elk. He would never again profit from elk poaching and from covering up the murderous deeds of others. Beside Bob Brightman's body lay a walking stick, and each end of the stick had an elk's hoof nailed to it. Bull elk. Seven-inch-wide hooves.

Theresa emerged from behind a cedar bough, put down the rifle, gathered her son into her arms, and whispered, "Paris. Oh, my Paris."

THROUGH THE DENSE MIST, Brad, the fugitive, raced along the rocky beach, heading north toward the sea cliffs. Brad didn't know about the cliffs, all he knew was that on his trail was a team of federal agents with bloodhounds and guns. Desperate men take extraordinary measures, and so when Brad encountered the first tall cliff shooting straight up out of the ocean, making a dead end of the beach, he had no choice but to climb the cliff's craggy wall, to inch his way up off the pounding surf and along the cliff face, grasping onto any little protuberance, any little branch or ledge, and some of those were slime-coated, causing him to slip. Slowly, excruciatingly, Brad scaled the cliff, moving up inch by tortuous inch. Once as he paused for breath, he felt the airline ticket to Copenhagen slide out of his pocket, and saw his boarding pass take flight and twirl down, down, toward the ocean a hundred feet below. He watched it disappear, then scrambled higher up the cliffside, his hands bloodied, his clothing ripping as he slid and regained position. Then his gun slipped out of his pocket and fell away. Finally, his hands reached up and felt the soft earth.

Pulling himself up and over the ledge, Brad lay panting on the ground, thanking his lucky stars that he hadn't fallen backward into the raging sea. His breath came hard and fast and when he heard a whinnying sound, he thought it came from his own mouth, but then he looked up and through the dense mist, he saw the horses and the riders. Unless his eyes were fooling him, Brad saw a band of Indians on horseback standing at the cliff's edge, standing over him, and one of them was pointing a gun at his head.

Frances Creed, on the pinto, her rifle aimed at Brad, said, "Get up."

Brad struggled to his feet, exhausted, bleeding, his hands held high over his head, an urban rave dancer lost in the wild. "I'm not armed," he said unnecessarily.

Gordon Toolong, on the horse beside Frances's pony, said to Brad, "You tell us. How many of our people did you kill?"

Sweat poured down Brad's forehead into his eyes. Brad blinked, but the scene before him didn't change, didn't dissolve. He said, "I never killed your people. I never killed, I swear it. I never killed."

Frances Creed pressed the rifle's barrel against Brad's temple. "I saw you watching my grandchildren. I saw you in Grays Harbor, and I saw you at Bogachiel Clinic. You're behind all this heartache."

Brad's heart pounded and his knees wobbled. The band of Indians had formed a semicircle around the edge of the cliff. Now his only hope for escape was back down the cliff wall. But how? Then one of the horses sneezed, distracting Frances, and Brad moved fast, grabbing the rifle from her hands, turning it on her. Backing toward the cliff, he shouted, "Don't any of you move or I'll shoot her."

The Hoh riders sat still, not daring to move, not daring to chance Frances Creed's life. Brad inched his way back over the cliff's edge, found some footing on a narrow ledge, and dropped down out of sight, taking Frances's rifle along with him. Moving further along the sheer cliff, he glanced down once and in the dizzying distance, saw the roaring ocean below, and almost lost his foothold. Inching along, his feet found another tiny ledge and he balanced himself and the rifle. The ledge felt secure, solid, and Brad paused to rest, and that was when his hand went down into the bald eagle's nest, disturbing her young, enraging her. She flapped up into Brad's face—one claw swiped his eyeball, drawing blood, and then her beak plucked his other eyeball and the pain caused Brad to rear back and fall. He landed somewhere in the churning ocean swell and was never seen again.

THIRTY-THREE

EXHUMATION

SNOW FELL in the night, laying a fresh blanket across the land, softly curving the rugged earth, frosting the evergreen boughs, delivering sacred silence over the whole territory watched over by Great Elk. On the hilltop, Hoh men on horseback formed a full circle around thirty-four graves in the Hoh cemetery, as the gravediggers dug each one up, raised each coffin and set it upon the frozen ground. One after another, the graves were unearthed, and the bodies removed. The macabre activity lasted two days, and the men on horseback stayed through the entire operation, always watching, witnessing the extraction, from the graves, of parents, spouses, children. When Gordon Toolong's boy was brought up in his coffin, a tear appeared at the corner of Gordon's eye, but he did not resist this disturbance of his son's remains. No survivor resisted the terrible but necessary deed. When, finally, each of the thirty-four graves had been disinterred, each of the thirty-four bodies autopsied, and the remains returned to the fecund, forgiving earth, the men on horseback returned to their homes on the reservation.

On the day after Christmas, Venus delivered the autopsy reports to the tribal council. The council and many who lived on the reservation gathered in the community center to hear her report. Thirty-four deaths since Dr. Lawrence Fish had come to work at Bogachiel Clinic. Of those thirty-four, twenty-six had had their pituitary glands removed immediately after death. The number included the Toolong boy, and it included every patient who had died at the clinic under Fish's care.

In the packed community center, Venus explained every detail, patiently answered every question put to her by tribal members. Richard stood in the back of the hall, watching her.

Brightman had kidnapped the Nighteagle boy. Fish and Bob Brightman told Becca that they were keeping Paris safe from an abusive father. Becca could keep a secret, and she could baby-sit.

She spent many afternoons and some evenings at the clinic, providing Paris with tender care. Fish took over the night shift, virtually living in the clinic, to keep an eye on Paris.

When Venus came for Fish, Bob Brightman was in the woods near the beach, watching Becca and Paris play. He had seen Winn and Venus heading for the clinic. Brightman took Paris from Becca and headed up into the preserve, intending to kill the boy, leave no trace of him for the law to find. Except hoofprints. Hoofprints always caused a diversion. And if Becca tried to talk, he'd find ways to deal with her.

Song was right about Branson being a psychopath, and maybe about his talent for training deer to kill. And Song had been right about the shoelace. It was the Gecko's. But that's all Song had been right about. The Gecko had been set up by his former girlfriend, and was only hiding out on the preserve, hiding from the law and the trumped-up charge against him. Fish knew the Gecko had been set up by the girl and her mother. He went along with the trumped-up charge against the Gecko, exploited it. Suspicion of the Gecko had provided the doctor with another smoke screen. Lurking on the preserve, the Gecko may have witnessed much of Brightman's activities.

When the Gecko broke into the Nighteagle trailer, he was apparently hungry, for he ate every item of food in the fridge before Theresa woke up from a nap and caught him. She'd already shot the Gecko when she called Fish and Wildlife headquarters, frantically seeking Winn. Maybe he'd meant to harm a child, maybe he just wanted to inhale the scent of a nursery. Whatever his reason for being there, Theresa shot Branson when she caught him prowling in the twins' bedroom.

When the meeting ended, the people filed out of the community hall and returned to their humble homes, their simple, hardscrabble existence. Richard took Venus's hand, and together they walked to the Land Rover, got in, drove off the reservation. They rode in silence until they passed Cedar Grove Trailer Park. Richard said, "Look."

Venus looked and saw the sold sign had come down. Winn had decided against building, had allowed his neighbors to remain in the park. Maybe things had returned to normal, or as close to normal as it gets in a squalid, poverty-stricken trailer park on the sodden edge of nowhere. Except, the Nighteagles no longer lived there. The Nighteagles had moved their rusting pink trailer onto the reservation, where Winn planned to build a sweet cabin in the woods behind

Simon Thundercloud's house, far enough from Bogachiel preserve to keep the memories at bay.

Over time, Winn Nighteagle got back his guardian spirit and got back his forthright character. Now he understood the delicate balance between a human and his guardian spirit, how both must work in harmony, how the spirit sometimes tests the human's strength and courage. Winn might have failed time and again, but Great Elk remained faithful and in the end, Winn got his courage back. When he went to Theresa to beg forgiveness, she told him, "Winn, when we lost Paris, we both lost our minds. If you forgive me, then I forgive you. Let's go on with our life now. Let's raise Paris and Milan to be strong and courageous, and respectful of others. Let's never fear again, but always believe in ourselves."

Right then, Winn vowed to devote his life to his family and his community, the community that had suffered so much at the hands of outsiders. Winn used the remainder of his casino winnings to build a new sweat lodge on the reservation. And he never touched another drop of alcohol.

Every day, Theresa walked Milan and Ocean Boy down to the beach, to the tideline, and talked to them about the great spirits, Whale and Raven, Thunderbird and Eagle, and Elk. Milan would listen, enraptured by her mother's sweet voice. Ocean Boy would hoot and holler at the seagulls, and run off into the surf, because he couldn't wait to grow up and learn to swim.

On New Year's Day, Winn, Theresa, Paris, and Milan were riding in Winn's pickup along Highway 101 when suddenly a huge elk sprang from the forest right into their path. Winn slammed on the brakes. The big bull elk froze in its tracks. A standoff. Winn rolled down the window and shouted at the elk.

"Thanks, man."

The elk snorted, then sprang back into the forest and disappeared, and Winn never saw him again.

A WARM January breeze swept across Lahaina Beach, rattling the newspaper in Venus's hands. She folded *The Honolulu Times* into thirds, and that was when she saw the glowing review of Clint Kellogg's latest book of fables. Handing it to Richard, she said, "All right. But just a leave of absence. I'm not a quitter."

One of Richard's gentle hands caressed her face. "Fair enough, fair enough."

She leaned over to kiss him. He said, "By the way, whatever happened to that hacksaw you bought?"

"I gave it to Dravus. He's expanding his private quarters. I felt we owed him something."

Richard snorted. "Lodge Man never did us any favors."

She hadn't heard him. She was studying her face in a pocket mirror. She said, "Do you think I need a lunch lift?"

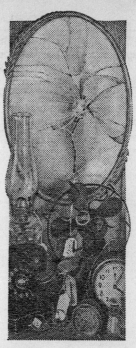

Denise Dietz

**AN ELLIE BERNSTEIN/
LIEUTENANT
PETER MILLER
MYSTERY**

Throw Darts at a Cheesecake

Fat Free Murder

At the weekly meeting of Weight Winners, losing
is everything. Group leader Ellie Bernstein herself
has shed fifty-five pounds, along with a cheating
husband and an unfulfilling life. But she quickly
discovers losing weight is not only murder,
it's downright lethal.

One by one, the group's Big Losers are being
murdered. Is some jealous member of the Friday
meeting a secret killer? Motive aside, Ellie's got
to watch her back as well as her calories before
she finds herself on the most permanent
diet of all...death.

Available December 1999 at your favorite retail outlet.

WORLDWIDE LIBRARY®

Visit us at www.worldwidemystery.com   WDD334